ORBITSVILLE JUDGEMENT

Orbitsville Judgement

BOB SHAW

LONDON
VICTOR GOLLANCZ LTD
1990

First published in Great Britain 1990
by Victor Gollancz Ltd,
14 Henrietta Street, London WC2E 8QJ

British Library Cataloguing in Publication Data
Shaw, Bob, *1931–*
    Orbitsville judgement.
    I. Title
    823'.914 [F]

    ISBN 0-575-04551-5

Typeset at The Spartan Press Ltd,
Lymington, Hants
Printed in Great Britain by
St Edmundsbury Press Ltd, Bury St Edmunds, Suffolk

. . . could thou and I with Fate conspire,
To grasp this sorry Scheme of Things entire,
Would we not scatter it to bits – and then
Re-mould it nearer to the Heart's Desire!

Omar Khayyam

PART ONE: THE HAMMER RISES

CHAPTER 1

The ancient constellations – star groups which had presided over mankind's entire history – vanished in one quiet instant, and were immediately replaced by new stars arrayed in unfamiliar patterns.

It was the most astounding event in the annals of astronomy, but it was witnessed by relatively few people. Only those who happened to be working near portals and looking outwards at the crucial moment saw the cosmos being transfigured. The news of it spread to the far interior of Orbitsville, of course, but the process took time and had little impact on the complacent market town of Orangefield. Most of Orangefield's inhabitants had never made the journey to a portal – and therefore had never even *seen* a star – and happenings in the outside universe tended to be of secondary importance to them.

Distant suns might have changed their positions; remote galaxies might have done a strange shuffle – but crops still had to be gathered in the apron of cultivated land surrounding the town. The wheels of commerce and local industry still had to turn; no man or woman had been excused any chores; and infants still had to be fed, bathed and powdered before being tucked into bed for the night. During the hours of darkness the Orbitsville sky, which had never known stars, continued to exhibit its watered-silk striations, hundreds of delicate arches of blue and darker blue spanning the horizons – and life gave every indication of proceeding very much as usual . . .

Jim Nicklin's home, lending library and workshop were combined in a single timber-framed building which occupied a pleasant site on the north edge of the town. It was constructed of fortwood, a local timber which, even when left unpainted, had a satisfying appearance and the durability of stone. Considered simply as a building, it was somewhat lacking in architectural merit – having been added to in a haphazard manner at various times in the previous fifty years – but it suited Nicklin's needs and life style very well. It was easy to clean and maintain, and yet provided ample space for all his activities. It was within easy reach of the town's amenities, and yet for the most part looked out on farmlands and distant savannahs.

There was a good fused-earth road a little more than a hundred paces from Nicklin's front porch, but his property was separated from it by a broad stream. The clear water contained several varieties of fish which had been imported from Earth more than a century earlier, and now were as well established as if they had been there for geological eras. In addition to providing Nicklin with sport and occasional fare for the table, the stream gave him a comforting sense of being partitioned from the outside world.

To reach his premises, personal visitors and customers were obliged to make use of a small wooden bridge, at the far end of which was a gate which he could lock when he was in the mood for solitude. The fact that the stream could easily be waded, and also was well provided with stepping stones, was immaterial. When would-be callers saw that Nicklin's gate was closed they understood they had chosen an unsuitable time, and – unless their business had a fair degree of urgency – would turn away. Respect for a person's wish to be alone was basic to society in most regions of Orbitsville.

Although Nicklin had the reputation of being a moody and changeable individual, his unsociable spells usually manifested themselves only when nightfall was drawing near. That's what he gets for being a bachelor, was the view of most of Orangefield county's women and quite a few of the men. It isn't right for a normal, healthy young man to be living on his own and going to a lonely bed at night. However, in spite of their reservations concerning Nicklin's bachelorhood, very few of the eligible females had ever seriously thought of trying to attract him into the socially acceptable state of marriage.

He had not yet turned thirty, was tall, fair-haired, reasonably handsome and had only the faintest trace of a bulge above the belt buckle – but his boyish face, with its small nose and blue eyes, was slightly *too* boyish. It often bore a philosophic and mildly puzzled expression, as though he had just worked out how many angels could stand on the head of a pin and was dissatisfied with the answer. His eyes sometimes seemed amused when the folk about him were engaged in serious debate; or they could mirror a deep concern when there was nothing but laughter all around. In spite of his acknowledged genius for the repair of domestic appliances and light machinery, he gave the impression of somehow being impractical. He struck people as being soft, a dreamer who was ill-equipped to deal with the hard knocks which rural life could deal out on a plentiful basis. The women of Orangefield township and county were conditioned to respect tough, pragmatic men who had the potential to be tireless workers and good providers – so when choosing husbands they tended to overlook Jim Nicklin.

That arrangement suited Nicklin quite well. Orangefield was a low-tech community which was modelled on the ideal of a small town in the American mid-west, circa 1910, with some elements borrowed from equally idealised English villages of the same period. The quality of life was good – enhanced by the fact that high-tech resources could be called upon from outside when emergencies occurred – but Nicklin had observed that married men always had to work harder than bachelors, and led lives which on occasion were marred by domestic troubles. Not being greatly enamoured of toil, he was quite satisfied with his mode of existence, especially as there were more than enough times when he got himself into ample trouble with no assistance from a marriage partner.

He had an uneasy suspicion that one of those times was near at hand as he watched the heavy-shouldered figure of Cort Brannigan cross the bridge and come striding towards the workshop entrance. It was early on a fine spring morning, the sort of morning which might have been designed to uplift the human spirit, but there was something about Brannigan's gait and out-thrust jaw which suggested that, if anything, his spirit was in a meaner and more joyless condition than usual.

He was a sixty-year-old farmer, who had a mixed-produce spread eight kilometres north of the town, and in spite of being obese he was renowned as a brawler. His great belly, which could absorb strong men's best punches, surged as he walked, glowing intermittently as it moved in and out of the cylinder of shadow created by his wide-brimmed hat. Several of the cinnamon sticks he habitually chewed to obliterate the smell of alcohol projected from his shirt pocket. He had no time for Nicklin as a person, and only dealt with him because there was no other competent repair service in the county.

Some ten days earlier he had brought in his wife's sewing-machine, which needed to have a bracket welded or brazed, and had demanded priority service. Nicklin was afraid of the big man, although he did his best to conceal the fact, and had promised the repair would be taken care of within a couple of days. He had intended to pass it over without delay to Maxy Millom, his part-time employee, but Maxy had not been around that afternoon. There had been a flurry of urgent work the following morning, and somehow the sewing-machine had been forgotten. When Brannigan had telephoned to enquire about it Nicklin had put him off with a hastily concocted excuse, and then – incredibly, it seemed in retrospect – had forgotten the machine all over again.

At that very moment it was being worked upon by Maxy in the shed he used for welding operations. The job would take only a few minutes, so Brannigan would not have to leave empty-handed, but the machine was bound to reek of hot metal when finally produced, and the big man would realise at once just how much priority his esteemed order had been given . . .

"Good morning, Cort," Nicklin said, mustering a smile as Brannigan came into the shop and approached the low counter. "Great morning, isn't it?"

"Hadn't noticed." Brannigan glanced over the shelves behind Nicklin. "Where is it?"

"It? Oh, the sewing-machine! Maxy will be bringing it through in a minute."

"Isn't it ready?"

"It's been ready for ages, Cort . . . sitting right here and ready to go . . . " Nicklin forced his brain into higher gear. "I just noticed a rough spot on the welding – just a minute ago – so I told Maxy to take it back and smooth it out. We don't want your good lady scratching her hand, do we?"

Brannigan studied Nicklin as though he were some unpleasant primitive life form. "I bumped into young Maxy in the bar of the

Victoria Hotel last night. Got to talking to him for a while." Brannigan increased the intensity of his stare, as though he had just said something very significant.

"Really?" Nicklin toyed nervously with his empty coffee cup as he divined what was coming next. "That was nice."

"When I asked him about my machine he said he didn't even know I'd brought it in. What have you to say to that?"

Nicklin mentally cursed his assistant for not having either the loyalty or the savvy to cover up for him. "You can't trust a word Maxy says when he's had a couple. Poor kid gets confused. I think his memory goes."

"It had gone last night, that's for sure," Brannigan growled, his gaze probing Nicklin's soul. "He couldn't even remember *having* any relatives over in Poynting – let alone a favourite uncle who had just died, and whose funeral he had just attended."

"My problem is that I trust people too much." Nicklin put on a disappointed expression, at the same time wondering what insane impulse had prompted him to blurt out that particular lie. To make matters worse, he had completely forgotten having done it, otherwise he might have been able to bribe Maxy into collusion.

"I let Maxy put just about anything over on me when he wants some extra time off," he went on. "You know what? I'm going to go over to the welding shop right now and fetch your machine, and while I'm there I'm going to give that kid the worst . . . "

Nicklin's voice faltered as he glanced out through the nearest window and saw the pear-shaped figure of Maxy approaching with the sewing-machine tucked under his arm. Maxy's bottle shoulders and wide, slabby hips made him look older than his nineteen years when he was seen at a distance. Like many slightly misshapen men, he had great physical strength, and was walking so energetically that he appeared to spring clear of the ground with every step. He had not bothered to put on his hat for the short walk between the two buildings, and his scalp – shaven to forestall premature baldness – shone in the sunlight with the whiteness of lard.

Nicklin, who had been hoping to keep Maxy and Brannigan apart, almost groaned aloud at the sight. *Please, O Gaseous Vertebrate*, he prayed inwardly, *please allow Maxy to have developed some common sense, diplomacy, loyalty or compassion during the night.*

13

Make him keep his mouth shut about the dead uncle business. That's not too much to ask . . .

Maxy burst into the shop with unnecessary force, glaring at Nicklin with hostile eyes. "What for," he demanded, "did you tell Mr Brannigan I had an uncle in Poynting who died?"

Terrible sentence construction, Maxy, Nicklin thought, his mind trying to escape into irrelevances as he realised he was well and truly boxed in. His brow prickled with cool sweat.

"Yeah, that's what I'd like to know." Beneath its frosting of silver stubble, Brannigan's face was that of a man who was prepared to commit murder.

Confronted by his accusers, Nicklin was suddenly amazed by how *angry* they were. They were behaving as though he had committed some terrible crime against them . . . as though he had betrayed their trust in a matter of the utmost gravity . . . and, when it came down to it, who *were* they? Nobodies! He had no need of them. In fact, they were the ones who needed him! It was, now that he thought of it, rather like the trial scene at the end of *Alice in Wonderland*, where Alice is coming to her senses and realises that all the entities who are crowding and harassing her are nothing more than playing cards. There was absolutely nothing to prevent him from, as Alice had done, rising up and venting his irritation with one great shout of, *Who cares for you? You're nothing but a pack of cards!*

"What are you grinning at?" Brannigan shot Maxy a can-you-believe-this? glance and leaned across the counter, coming so close that Nicklin received a warm gust of cinnamon from his breath. "I don't see anything funny."

Nicklin, who had not been aware of showing amusement, did his utmost to emit that single devastating shout which would scatter his oppressors as though they were leaves caught up in a tornado. His mouth opened, but no matter how he strained no sound was issued, and he realised amid an upwelling of despair that the simple act – natural to anyone who had any backbone to speak of – was beyond his capabilities. He was hemmed in, trapped, about to be humiliated, and could envisage no possible means of escape.

"There must be some misunderstanding here, gentlemen," he said, mind racing with the futility of an engine which has just snapped its load shaft. "I don't think I ever actually said anything about . . . "

He broke off, becoming aware of a new element in the scene, something which with a modicum of luck could terminate the current unpleasantness. Beyond the wide shady eaves of the building, the agile figure of Zindee White – aged thirteen and a bit – could be seen sprinting across the stretch of grass which separated her family's home from Nicklin's property. She was wearing a bright red T-shirt and orange shorts, and was moving so fast that a visible cloud of dust and pollen swirled in her wake. She was the most regular customer for Nicklin's library service, and – in spite of the age difference – possibly his best friend. It was obvious that she had some important news to impart to him. From past experience he knew that "important" could embrace anything from the acquisition of a desired toy to the discovery of a jewel-bug with exceptional markings. Whatever it was on this occasion, Nicklin vowed, he was going to find some way to make it his ticket to freedom.

Thank you, O Gaseous Vertebrate, he thought while giving a theatrical start of surprise. "Here's young Zindee!" he exclaimed. "And just look at that *speed*. I hope there isn't anything wrong at home."

Before Brannigan and Maxy could reply, Zindee stormed in through the shop's open door, her sneakers slapping the floor with the force of her deceleration. "*Jim*! Have you heard the –?"

Realising that Nicklin was not alone, she stopped speaking, folded her hands behind her back and came around the counter to stand at his side. He saw it as a little gesture of solidarity, and was gratified. Zindee was breathing heavily after the run, and Nicklin detected from her the buttery smell of clean perspiration.

"What d'you want, kid?" Maxy said irritably.

Zindee gazed coldly at an old adversary. "Nothing to do with you, baldy."

A look of outrage appeared on Maxy's face, and Nicklin wished he had the child's casual facility with insults. It was a matter of ingrained principle with him that he would never make offensive remarks about any feature which had been foisted on a person by the lottery of birth. If people had unpleasant personality traits, something for which they could be held responsible, then on that score they were fair game – the only snag being that, even so, he found it almost impossible to inflict verbal wounds.

"That brat needs a lesson in manners," Brannigan said.

Zindee studied him for a moment, decided it could be imprudent to cross swords, and moved a little closer to Nicklin. "Have you heard the news, Jim?" she whispered.

Maxy cupped a hand to his ear, intruding. "What news? Speak up a bit, kid."

Zindee hesitated, but Nicklin – determined to develop the situation – gave her a nod of encouragement. "Go ahead, Zindee – what is it?"

"It's just been on our television – the world has moved!"

Nicklin half-smiled as he looked down at Zindee. Her face was round and freckled, with a chin which was tiny and yet determined, and with wide-set eyes which beaconed intelligence and integrity. Her features were perfect, those of an archetypal little girl as envisaged by generations of artists, and over the years Nicklin had learned how to read that face. His smile faded as he saw the anxiety there.

"What do you mean, Zindee?" he said. "How could the world move?"

"Somebody's been on the job," Maxy put in with a guffaw and switched to a falsetto voice. "Did the world move for you, darling?"

"It's just been on television," Zindee insisted. "All the stars are different, Jim. All the ships that were docked outside the portals have disappeared. There was a woman who had just arrived from Earth . . . Silvia London, I think she was called . . . and she was crying a lot . . . and she said her ship had vanished . . ."

"The Council should never have allowed television to come into Orangefield," Brannigan said, shaking his huge head – in spite of his violent streak and weakness for alcohol, he was quite puritanical and righteous in most other aspects of his life. "It rots people's minds, that's all it does, with them trashy three-dees. That kid's a perfect example – she don't know what's real and what isn't."

Nicklin did not even subscribe to the sound service which was cabled in from Weston Bridge, but within the last few days he had heard talk of an odd phenomenon which was supposed to be affecting Orbitsville's great shell. It had been said that luminous green lines were moving across both surfaces of the sphere. There had been no way for him to verify the report in person, because the soil and rock strata were more than a thousand metres deep in the Orangefield region. In any case, he had a subconscious desire to forget that he lived in the interior of a shell of ylem which was 320 million kilometres in diameter and only eight centimetres thick.

A product of two centuries of migration, during which virtually the entire population of Earth had moved to Orbitsville, Nicklin thought of his environment simply as "the world" and lived his life exactly as he would have done on a normal planet. But the shining green lines had been something entirely new, and some of the townsfolk had mooted the idea that they were an omen, a prelude to some great event . . .

"Come on, Zindee!" Nicklin took the child's hand in his and walked with her towards the door of the shop, feeling more relief over his fortuitous escape than concern about any putative threat to his pleasantly humdrum existence. "Let's go over to your place and get ourselves a better idea of what this thing is all about."

"I was talking to you," Brannigan said, scowling.

Nicklin flicked Maxy's shoulder as he passed him. "See to Mr Brannigan for me – and don't forget to give him his bill."

CHAPTER 2

Cham and Nora White – Zindee's parents – had a veterinary practice which they operated from their home on the plot next to Nicklin's land. The fact that they dealt solely with small animals made the couple appear almost as idiosyncratic as Nicklin in the eyes of a sizeable section of the community. The farmers of the area adjudged maintaining the health of livestock to be a worthy occupation, but devoting one's energies to the care of sickly cats, hamsters and the like was regarded as – to say the least of it – a mildly eccentric form of behaviour.

Being classed as oddities had created something of a bond between Nicklin and the adult Whites, but that was almost as far as the relationship went. They were remarkably similar in appearance for a couple with no blood ties – medium build with a tendency to chubbiness, sharp noses, florid complexions and a general red-gold-brown coloration. Nicklin quite liked the Whites' squirrelly appearance, but their unfailing industriousness and lack of humour had deterred him from trying to build up a close friendship.

Unexpectedly, in view of their Calvinistic outlook, they were among the few people in Orangefield who subscribed to the television service which could be piped in at some expense from Weston Bridge. Nicklin knew that Cham and Nora atoned for the self-indulgence by restricting their viewing to the evening hours, and therefore he was surprised on entering the house to find them seated near the set in the main room. It was an indication that Zindee's obvious concern was justified, that something really serious was taking place.

"Morning, Jim!" Cham called out, gesturing for him to sit down. "What do you think of this caper?"

Nickin nodded a greeting in response to Nora White's tense smile. "I don't know what to think yet. Zindee gave me the bare details."

"It was Zindee who alerted us – that's why we're in here at this time of the day," Cham said, defending himself against any possible charge of sinful sloth. "Can you credit this? They're saying that Orbitsville has moved!"

Nicklin released Zindee's hand and lowered himself into a plumply cushioned armchair. "How do they know?"

"Apparently it's either the universe or us. Look!"

Nicklin directed his attention to the televiewer stage which occupied one corner of the room. The scale control had been set for roughly half-size projection, with the result that the stage appeared to be populated by groups of perfectly formed midgets, male and female, some of whom were obviously distraught. The grassy surface on which they were standing was littered with discarded space suits, some of them resembling corpses. It was obvious that there had been little or no development of the area – the background, apart from a scattering of single-storey prefabs, was the featureless green of Orbitsville's ubiquitous savannahs.

"Where is that?" Nicklin said.

"Portal 36. There's nothing there but an agricultural research station." Cham paused as a series of ripples swept through the scene, momentarily distorting the human figures and reminding the viewers that those seemingly real and solid human figures were only bi-laser projections, holomorphs. "We were warned the image quality could be pretty poor. Apparently all the permanent outside antennae and reflector satellites have disappeared. The TV engineers are working with lash-ups."

"This is a kind of amateur broadcast, anyway," Nora White added as Zindee went to sit on her knee. "The network is showing it because those people were in the middle of disembarking when their ship vanished. They actually saw it happen."

Cham flapped one hand in an appeal for silence. "Listen to this guy – he was on before."

"We are about to have another word with Rick Renard, the owner of the *Hawkshead*, the cargo ship which was attempting to dock at Portal 36 when – literally – it vanished into nothingness," an invisible commentator said. The televiewer scene changed, flowing outwards around Renard until he occupied the centre of the stage. He was a curly-haired young man with the sort of buoyant and healthy plumpness which is underpinned by well-developed muscle.

"As has already been mentioned," he said in a high-income drawl, "my ship had *attempted* to dock in the normal manner, but Captain Lessen was unable to complete his manoeuvre. There appeared to be some kind of repulsive force acting on the ship and preventing it from getting to within thirty metres of the Orbitsville shell.

"The shell itself was in a highly unusual condition – it was shining with a greenish light which was pulsing on and off several times a second. It is possible that the radiation had something to do with repelling the ship. Perhaps it hadn't – I don't really know. It was all so . . . I mean . . . "

Renard smiled unhappily and Nicklin saw that his lips had begun to quiver. The man looked as though he would have the sleek arrogance of the very wealthy in normal circumstances, but it was obvious that he was now in a state of shock. He shook his head, bringing the interview to a premature end, and turned to a black-haired woman of striking appearance who was standing just behind him, looking equally distraught. He put his arms around her and she slowly inclined her head on to his shoulder.

"I've seen that woman before," Cham White announced triumphantly, as though claiming a prize. "She's connected with some so-called scientific organisation which says it has proof of life after death. Her name is Silvia . . . Silvia . . . "

"London," Zindee supplied.

"That's right. Of the . . . um . . . Anima Mundi Foundation. I wonder what she was doing on that ship."

"If you find her so fascinating, why don't you just take yourself off to Portal 36 and ask her?" Nora said tartly.

"There's no call for you to be jealous," Cham replied, looking gratified over what he saw as a compliment. "Besides, from what we've heard so far, it'll be quite some time before *anybody* will be able to travel between portals."

"Why is that?" Nicklin said.

"No ships! You're not paying attention, Jim. Everything, but *everything*, that was outside the shell has disappeared – and that includes all the interportal ships."

"I wasn't thinking," Nicklin mumbled, shrugging slightly in response to a sympathetic glance from Zindee. It came to him that he had not really accepted the sensational news as being true. The portals, those kilometre-wide circular holes in the Orbitsville shell, were almost five million kilometres apart. Taking a direct interior route from one portal to another, even if Mach 2 aircraft were available, would entail ninety days of non-stop flying – the kind of odyssey which was ruled out by logistics and economics.

"I keep expecting somebody to discover that it's all been a hoax, or a mistake," Nicklin explained. "Two or three hundred years ago, back on Earth, somebody made a radio broadcast of a play about invaders from some nearby planet and it panicked a lot of people."

"H. G. Wells," Cham said knowledgeably. "It was H. G. Wells who made that broadcast."

"Whoever it was, he scared a lot of people and there was no need for it."

"This is different, Jim," Nora White said. "I wish they would skip all this human interest stuff and take us back to the scientists in Beachhead. At least they had some idea of what they were talking about."

As if responding to her wish, the scene on the platform faded and, after some sparkling swirls of colour, was replaced by a holomorphic group of men and women seated at a circular table. A female voice announced the return to the main OTTV studios in Beachhead City for further expert comment, then went on to name all the members of the panel and list their qualifications. The first speaker, named Carpenter, was a youthful professor of observational astronomy from the Garamond University.

"The events of the past few hours are unique in the history of Optima Thule," he began. "Incredible though it may seem . . ."

"You can easily tell that guy's a scientist," Cham said loudly. "Nobody else would be pompous enough to refer to the Big O as Optima Thule."

"Be quiet," Nora chided. "The rest of us want to hear what he's saying."

". . . understand that when we say everything outside the shell has disappeared, we mean *everything*! At close range, all interstellar and interportal ships which were in dock have vanished, plus several of the latter which were *en route* between portals. And not only ships – docking cradles, cargo handling gear, passenger transfer tubes, even radio and TV antennae. Anything which was projecting beyond the boundary line of Optima Thule has been sheared off – with a perfect mirror finish on the metal sections, incidentally – and has vanished from our awareness."

Professor Carpenter paused to take a sip of water. "At what we might style as intermediate range, the outer planet of our own local system – Napier – has vanished. All this is trivial, however, compared to the fact that – on the cosmic scale – every *star* known to us can no longer be observed, every *galaxy* known to us can no longer be observed.

"To my mind, there is only one possible interpretation of those facts, incredible though it may seem – and that is that Optima Thule has been repositioned."

"I can't believe this," a grey-haired woman said, shaking her head with an air of sadness. "You claim to be a qualified scientist, and yet you sit there and try to make us believe that our world – Orbitsville – has been moved!"

"I *am* a qualified scientist," Carpenter replied, in the measured tones of one who was determined not to be provoked. "And I did not say that Orbitsville had been moved. The word I used was 'repositioned'. It is obvious that no movement in the conventional sense of the word was involved – the repositioning was achieved instantaneously."

His words were followed by a babel of voices as all the holomorphs tried to make points at the same time. Nicklin gave up trying to follow the various threads of argument and lapsed into a reverie until the televiewer scene changed. The group at the table dissolved, to be replaced by an outdoors shot – a view of Portal 1 at the centre of Beachhead City. It was recognisable because of the statue of Vance Garamond, the discoverer of Orbitsville, at the edge of what appeared to the casual eye as a circular black lake.

The camera advanced until it was poised at the edge of the aperture then rotated forwards, simulating a leisurely dive into space. When it steadied the corner of the Whites' living room was filled with an intense blackness which was stippled with hundreds of glowing specks. Professor Carpenter could be heard in voice-over, commenting on the complete absence of familiar star patterns and the presence of totally alien constellations.

As always, Nicklin found the view of the outside universe to be something of a disappointment. Orangefield was less than a thousand kilometres from Beachhead – an easy enough journey by air – but he had never taken the trouble to go there, and hence had never seen the stars in actuality. For him, those remote flecks of light had very little relevance to the problems, pressures and pleasures of everyday life. His family had been on Orbitsville for six generations, and the course of their lives had not been affected in any way by stars or patterns of stars . . .

"And what about Earth?" another man was heard to say.

"We no longer know where Earth is. We don't know how to get there." Carpenter sounded as though he was deriving a perverse satisfaction from the negatives. "Therefore all contact with Earth has been lost, probably for ever. That also goes for Terranova, of course."

Who cares about Earth or Terranova? Nicklin thought. *Museum pieces!* Staring into the near-featureless blackness was beginning to make him feel drowsy. He decided to give it just another five minutes, time enough to be sure that Cort Brannigan had vacated his premises, then he would take his leave of the Whites and get back to important business. It was the task of the astronomers to find out why the universe looked different – in the meantime he had a juice extractor and a bicycle wheel to repair, jobs which had been promised for that very afternoon.

Nicklin allowed his eyelids to close, creating an exquisite feeling of relaxation in his eyes. The sensation was so pleasant that he was immediately aware of the risk of lapsing into sleep, something which would be embarrassing in front of the tireless Whites . . .

"Just look at old man Jim," Cham White said loudly, his voice reaching Nicklin across murmurous summer meadows of contentment. "Working for ten minutes has worn him out."

Nicklin roused himself with a start. "Sorry, sorry – I got very little sleep last night." The lie came unbidden to his lips.

"What was the matter?" Nora said, showing a neighbourly concern. "Tummy troubles?"

"Yes." Nicklin seized on the suggestion with gratitude and

23

began to elaborate on it. "I ate a chunk of apple pie just before bed, and I made the mistake of putting a slice of cheese on it."

"Apple pie, eh? Have you started taking cookery lessons?"

"No – it was a little gift from May McVickar." Nicklin listened to his own words with growing dismay. Why did he get himself into this kind of situation? And what had possessed him to appoint May McVickar as his fictional benefactor? She lived only a couple of kilometres away, and was quite friendly with the Whites, and the two women could easily meet and begin chatting and comparing notes within the next day or two. In fact, with his luck, the silly old bitch could arrive on the Whites' doorstep at any minute . . .

Nicklin was casting around in sudden alarm for a way to get off the subject of apple pie when he became aware of an unusual sound from outside the house, one which was beginning to conflict with the voices of the televiewer. It was growing in volume, and was so incongruous in the rural quietness of the area that several seconds went by before he was able to resolve it into separate components. There was brassy marching music overlaid with an amplified male voice which, although the words could not yet be distinguished, sounded like that of a politician or an evangelist.

"Seems like we've got visitors," Nicklin said, rising to his feet and making for the door. "This I must see."

He gave the Whites a perfunctory wave and escaped from the house into the vertical rays of the Orbitsville sun. Its warmth seeped through his hair and spread like hot oil on the crown of his head, making him wish he had brought a hat. He shaded his eyes and peered through curtains of midge-clouded brilliance. On the road beyond the stream was a slow-moving procession of about ten vehicles, a mix of campers and trucks, all of them painted powder blue. On the side of each, pulsing in photoactive orange dyes, was the message: *COREY MONTANE is leading you home.*

"Oh no," Nicklin whispered, "not another bible thumper! Please, O Gaseous Vertebrate, not another holy roller!"

Denial of his prayer came in the form of a crashingly distorted announcement, the gist of which was that evangelist Corey Montane would be visiting Orangefield for three days. His intention was to bring salvation to any of the locals who had the good sense to heed his preachings. All the others would, naturally enough, be doomed.

The speaker's words faded and became even less decipherable as the cavalcade began to pass out of sight behind a stand of whistle trees. But before intelligibility was lost altogether Nicklin picked out a fragment – "Orbitsville is a tool of the Devil."

That's just great, he thought bitterly as he began walking towards his own property. It looked as though for the next three days he would be under the threat of having his privacy invaded by earnest heliumheads. And worse, the therapeutic calm of the village green, where he liked to stroll in the evenings, was likely to be shattered by noisy sermons, appalling music and collectors of cash. There was one feature that all religious missions, all purveyors of spiritual peace, all renouncers of worldly gain had in common – somebody had to collect the cash.

All thought of what was going on in the outside universe had been displaced from Nicklin's mind. Frowning and looking disconsolate, as befitted one who had found genuine cause for concern, he made his way home through the lush green grass.

CHAPTER 3

Helping to erect the marquee had left Corey Montane feeling tired and slightly shaky, and now he was sitting on a canvas chair outside his camper, refreshing himself with a pot of his favourite tea. As he sipped the fragrant brew he allowed his gaze to drift around the shops, inns and occasional private dwellings which ringed Orangefield's central green. The scene – with its imported oaks and chestnut trees – was one of idyllic, nostalgic tranquillity.

Throughout history different sections of humanity had formed their own visions of the perfect setting for the jewel of life, ranging from the sentimental New York of Frank Capra to the serene Antarctic demesnes of the twenty-first-century poet, Richard Caine. But for an astonishing number of people the ideal would always closely approximate what Montane was seeing now. In the charmed age which the surroundings lovingly recreated, cigarettes did not cause cancer, it was no sin to eat butter and cream, nuclear weapons were unthought-of, and work brought fulfilment and not hypertension. Hefty, bearded cricketers might be on their way by steam train to contend with the local team; a distant mechanical murmur might be the Wright brothers tinkering with some impractical machine in their corrugated-iron workshop.

At times like this it was easy for Montane to understand why so many inhabitants of Orbitsville opted to live in low-tech communities. It pained him, therefore, to remember that his natural human response to all he saw was part of the terrible danger which Orbitsville held in store for all of God's children. It was the bait in the Orbitsville trap . . .

"You all right, Corey?" The speaker was Nibs Affleck, who had approached from the direction of the marquee, where the adjustment of turnbuckles was still going on. He was a serious-eyed young man whose florid complexion was the legacy of a long spell of alcoholism. He had joined the crusade a year earlier and had found in it enough inspiration to enable him to fight free of his habit. As a result, he was fiercely loyal to Montane and showed his gratitude by being solicitous – embarrassingly so at times – about his mentor's health.

"I'm fine, Nibs," Montane said, glancing up from under the flat cone of his sun-hat. "Just a little tired, that's all."

"You should leave jobs like putting up the tent to the rest of us."

"You may be interested to learn that being sixty years old does *not* qualify one for a wheelchair." Montane smiled to show that he was not offended. "Besides, you know our rules. Nobody is so high and mighty that he is excused his share of work – and that includes me."

Affleck shuffled his feet and looked miserable. "I didn't mean you were . . ."

"It's all right, Nibs – you were just being thoughtful and I thank you for that. Now, will you do me a favour?"

"You bet, Corey!" Affleck said eagerly, his round face brightening. "Just name it!"

"This town actually has a daily newspaper – a real Mark Twain job, by all accounts – and I might consider advertising in it. I'd appreciate it if you would go and get me a copy."

"You bet, Corey!" His eyes glowing with simple happiness, Affleck turned and bounded away across the green.

Montane watched his progress with troubled eyes. Affleck was a good-hearted, industrious man, but he was an innocent – not the kind of disciple the crusade was desperately short of. What Montane really needed was a team of smart fast-talkers with the talent for raising large sums of money, the sort of men and women who – with a mesmeric combination of business acumen and evangelistic fervour – could induce rich men to part with fortunes. It was quite difficult to find millionaires on Orbitsville, because the acquisition of great wealth involved the manipulation and control of others, and it was no easy matter to do that to individuals whose birthright it was to trek off into the interior, at any time the mood took them, and claim the equivalent of a county, or a country, or even a continent. And such wealthy people as could be lured out of their strongholds were disinclined to hand large sums of money over to what they saw as ingenuous Jesus freaks.

There had been a time when Montane had believed that *he* would be able to attract the sort of funding necessary for the success of the crusade, that God would speak through him and touch the hearts of men – but that had been six years ago. He almost groaned aloud when he thought of how much time had gone by since his awakening, and of how little had been achieved . . .

For the first fifty years of his life Corey Montane had been a conventional and unremarkable inhabitant of Pewterspear 97. The numerical suffix given to any place-name referred to the nearest portal, and that was as close as Orbitsville had come to devising a zip code system. The fact that Pewterspear had a number close to 100 meant that the city was almost as far from Beachhead as it was possible to get, but that had not troubled Montane. He had liked being well away from the great urban centres of commerce and industry. He had owned and run a small home bakery, which yielded a modest but comfortable income from the sale of a variety of spicy meat pies and elaborate Danish pastries. His wife, Milly, and grown-up daughter, Tara, had helped in the business in a relationship that was nearly always harmonious. He enjoyed a range of outdoor pursuits – principally flying light aircraft – and was well liked in the town.

The chances were that Montane would have lived out his allotted ninety years in the same pleasant and undemanding manner, but everything had changed for him in the space of a few seconds . . .

It was a wet morning in the early part of the year – but Montane was not in a mood to find the rain depressing. It was coming down in the form of very large, clean, tumbling drops, each of which created a spiky crystal crown in miniature as it impacted with the pavement. His vision seemed preternaturally clear – the way it could be in the prelude to a migraine – and he saw the crowns in diamond-sharp detail, just as he had done in childhood. He wondered if that could be what had inspired his present feelings of boyhood optimism, in which for him the bad weather was recreating the ambience of Christmas Eve. The section of the street he could see was crowded with shoppers, complete with umbrellas and turned-up collars, who were determined to obtain last-minute Christmas gifts in spite of the rain, and the lighted windows of the other stores were cheerily reflected on the wet ground, adding to the Yuletide atmosphere.

Montane smiled as he noted yet another similarity to the festive season – business had been exceptionally brisk that morning, so good that it was already necessary for him to replenish his window display. He decided to begin at once – while there was a break in the flow of customers – by slicing up a large veal-ham-and-egg pie, and perhaps a couple of the battenbergs, which sold well under the folksy name of marzipan windows.

"Milly," he called out, taking a brick-shaped pie out of the refrigerator, "What did you do with the knives?"

"They're here – in the steriliser." His wife was in the kitchen at the rear of the shop.

"Would you like to bring them out here?"

Milly gave a barely audible tut of impatience and he remembered that she was about to go over to the Canterbury to have morning coffee with a few friends. A moment later she came hurrying into the front of the shop with the knives on a tray. And somehow – it was surmised afterwards that wetness tramped in from the street had been responsible – she managed to slip and fall forwards.

Montane expected anything but tragedy on that nostalgic grey morning, but the sound that Milly emitted as she hit the floor told him at once that something terrible, something totally unreasonable and unfair had happened. It was an appalling sound – part grunt, part sigh – expressive of pain, surprise and fear.

"Milly!" Montane ran to the end of the counter, looked down and saw his wife lying face downwards on the floor. The tray was beneath her. Face contorting with shock, he dropped to his knees and rolled her over. A knife, which must have turned its point up to meet her descending body, was protruding from just below the left breast.

She died in his arms, staring up at him with a bemused expression, while the knife-handle – stirred by her heart's last contractions – playfully wiggled and circled amid the growing stain on her tangerine blouse.

Montane tilted his head back and howled with grief.

The hours and days that followed were almost as nightmarish as the initial cataclysmic event. After the police had made some preliminary enquiries and the ambulance had departed with the body, he turned to his daughter in the depths of his despair, needing support and consolation. To

*his astonishment, she reacted to him with silent, glacial fury, almost
as though he had engineered her mother's death. He was unable to
penetrate the barrier she had erected between them, and as soon as the
funeral was over she packed a bag and walked out, refusing to give
any hint as to where she was going . . .*

Thinking back to those traumatic days of six years ago, Montane
found cause for philosophical wonderment in the fact that his
awakening had been prompted, not by the loss of his wife and
daughter, but by a geological peculiarity of the Pewterspear
area.

The town was situated in a broad dish-shaped depression
which, on the old survey maps, was designated as McIntosh's
Bottom. Montane had always been aware of the name, but to
him it had been little more than an inspiration for vulgar
schoolboy jokes. He had also been aware, though with little
interest, that the rocky soil on which the town was built was as
little as two metres thick in many places. It was common practice in the local construction industry to support the more massive buildings on short piles which penetrated down to the
Orbitsville shell, but that too had been of minimal concern to
Montane – until his first visit to his wife's grave.

He had been kneeling by the still-fresh plot, striving to wrest
some degree of reconciliation from the notion that she would
become one with the earth. Death was part of a natural
cycle . . . springing from the soil, returning to the soil . . .

Then had come the shocking realisation that Milly's body, her
sacred body, was suspended only a hand's breadth above the
featureless grey sheet of ylem which formed Orbitsville's vast
shell. And beyond that, only centimetres away, was the harsh
emptiness of interstellar space! There could never be any peace
for her, for either of them, in those supremely unnatural circumstances; there could be no gentle absorption into the ancest-
ral unity of a God-given world; there was no *rightness* to Milly's
shallow interment . . .

Montane had remained kneeling by the grave for more than
an hour – his mind poised like a hovering kestrel half-way between divine inspiration and insanity – and when finally he had
stood up on aching legs he had been a different man.

People with medical knowledge had later told him that his transformation had been a consequence of delayed shock, rather than a profound religious experience, but Montane had known better. Much better. Infinitely better.

Even while sitting, as he now was, sipping tea on Orangefield's sun-dappled common, the principal element of his thoughts was bafflement over the fact that virtually nobody else was aware of having fallen into a devilish trap. What kind of mass insanity, what form of collective blindness, had suddenly afflicted humanity upon the discovery of Orbitsville?

The people of two centuries ago were products of a civilisation which had always been forced to fight tooth-and-nail simply to remain in existence. They were hard, cynical and suspicious; they *knew* the cosmos provided no free lunches – and yet when Orbitsville had been found they had swarmed to it like wasps to the honeypot.

Nobody had said: *Wait a minute! Let's think this thing over before we do anything hasty. What we have here is a huge sphere made of some material which defies analysis, but which has artificial gravity. It also has force lines around its sun in the form of a cage which has been beautifully engineered to provide night and day, and a progression of seasons. The thing is obviously an artefact! It seduces us by promising to meet all our needs, to fulfil all our dreams. It is too good to be true – therefore it has to be a TRAP!*

Montane had no idea who had created Orbitsville, but he knew in his heart and soul that the makers – those who had schemed to pervert the course of human destiny – were no friends of God. Orbitsville had remained quiescent for what men regarded as a long time, two whole centuries, but that was a brief span in the context of the history of the universe. A carnivorous flower always remained motionless until its victim was far back in its throat, beyond any possibility of escape.

There had been reports recently of glowing green lines moving across the surface of the great sphere, and to Montane they were the equivalent of the first hungry quiverings of a Venus fly-trap's jaws, just before the trap was sprung . . .

His thoughts returned to more mundane matters as he again caught sight of Nibs Affleck in the distance. A fleck of white showed that he had obtained the newspaper, and a rapid change of position indicated that he was still running. Montane half-smiled as he tried to recall the times when he too had been blessed with so much physical energy that he could afford to burn some of it off in needless exertion. At sixty, he still looked vigorous – with his glossy dark hair, unlined face and straight back – but recently his capacity for manual work had been greatly diminished. He did not suspect any furtively gnawing illness; it was just that his mental burden seemed to weigh him down more with each passing year. Mettle fatigue, he had dubbed it. The spirit could become poisoned with the toxins of weariness in the same way as an overworked body.

Affleck slid to a halt beside him, his complexion rendered even more hectic through running in the heat. "Here's your paper, Corey. I got you one."

"I can see you did." Montane set his cup on the ground. "How much did it cost?"

"I wouldn't take any money from you, Corey," Affleck said, looking offended. "It was nothing anyhows – only a quarter."

"Thank you, Nibs." Montane considered pressing the money on Affleck, then realised the youngster would get the maximum value out of it in the form of the giving pleasure. He raised a hand to acknowledge Affleck's departure in the direction of the marquee, then turned his attention to the newspaper. It was large and unwieldy, like those in historic videos, but it had been laser-printed in a modern open typeface – the publishers had not gone overboard in their devotion to the past and its ways. Montane, having no wish to strain his eyes, nodded in approval.

The front page lead – headlined MAIN STREET TO STAY IN THE DARK – was a long piece about a wrangle in the town council caused by some local businessmen applying for permission to erect illuminated signs on the façades of their stores. The other reports dealt with such issues as an unfamiliar type of tough ground-hugging weed being found on a farm, and the mayor's wife putting on an exhibition of her own water-colours.

Montane scanned the columns with indulgent interest, and was about to go to the next page when he noticed a very brief story right at the bottom of the sheet. It was the mention of astronomers in the sub-heading which caught his eye – he had long been sensitised to anything dealing with Orbitsville's relationship to the natural galaxy. The piece read:

32

EMBARRASSED ASTRONOMERS

If anybody notices a pink glow on the horizon tonight, in the general direction of Beachhead, it will not be caused by that city's surfeit of stoplights. Instead, it will be emanating from the red faces of our overpaid stargazers who today were forced to admit that they have lost visual contact with our known universe!

Professor Carpenter of the Garamond University tried to explain away this minor act of carelessness – after all, *anybody* could mislay a few billion galaxies – by claiming that Orbitsville has moved to a new position in space!

Take heart anybody who noticed a peculiar lurching sensation during the night. It was not the foundations of your houses shifting – just the foundations of science!

Montane's heart had begun a powerful thudding as he lowered the newspaper to his lap and stared blindly into the distance. He was neither deceived nor reassured by the anti-science, debunking tone of the report. He would have to verify the story, of course, but it was evident to him that some astounding cosmic event had occurred. The all-important questions now were: *Had the Orbitsville trap been fully sprung, or was this some preliminary stage? Were all of Orbitsville's inhabitants doomed, or could there yet be time for a few of them to escape by starship to a natural and God-given planet? Was he, by virtue of not having done enough during his six years of awareness, responsible for the ultimate demise of the human race?*

Racked by guilt and dread, he rose to his feet and walked quickly towards the marquee, where his followers were laughing as their day's labours came to an end.

CHAPTER 4

In preparation for leaving the library, Nicklin checked over his list of deliveries and found there were three that he could conveniently drop off at customers' houses on his way into town. They were softbacks – a Western by Jack Schaefer; a slim volume on the design and making of different shapes of paper gliders; and a cheerfully illustrated treatise on the railways of Victorian England. The books were slightly bulkier than they would have been when first printed, because of the permatome coating which made the pages virtually indestructible, but otherwise it was hard to tell from their condition that they were well over two centuries old.

It occurred to Nicklin that the library trade might be adversely affected if the astronomers took any length of time to sort themselves and their equipment out and re-establish contact with Earth. Like most other library operators, he dealt mainly with the past. Orbitsville had produced practically no literature of distinction, or even works of passing interest – a consequence, the experts claimed, of all social pressures and constraints having been removed. Competition and conflict had always been the mainsprings of great art, and on Orbitsville – with free land equivalent to five billion Earths available – there was little reason for people to compete for anything, and even less for going to war. As an inevitable result, the experts went on, the few individuals who bothered to put pen to paper, or finger to keyboard, were unable to produce anything that was not passionless, shallow and trivial.

Nicklin doubted if his customers in low-tech Orangefield had bothered to analyse their tastes in reading matter to that extent, but he knew they showed a solid preference for books which had been published on pre-migration Earth. They seemed to be motivated by nostalgia, not for the Old World itself but for the *feel* of a period characterised by cosy security and comfortable certitudes. The market was too diffuse to interest publishers on Orbitsville, so the small commercial vacuum had been filled by LOG – the Library Owners' Guild – which imported containers of miscellaneous books scavenged from the abandoned towns and cities of Earth.

Turning his attention to more immediate concerns, Nicklin set out the notepad which would enable late callers to help themselves to books and record the details for him. He gave the counter a final wipe with a duster and, without locking the door, went outside to wait for Zindee.

She must have been watching from her window because she appeared at once, bounding across the intervening grass with her usual display of energy. With her parents' permission, Nicklin was taking Zindee into town for a sundae, and she had acknowledged the specialness of the occasion by putting on her best sunhat, the pink one with the pictures of Toby the Tortoise speeding around the rim in a manner which no real life chelonian could emulate. Nicklin put on his own hat – a flat cone of reflective gold – as soon as he moved out from under the broad eaves of his shop, and was grateful for the protection it provided. Orbitsville's sun was always directly overhead, night coming only when it was eclipsed by the next bar of the solar cage, and as a result the heat from it built up steadily throughout the day. To venture out at any time of the day without donning suitable headgear was to invite a severe case of sunstroke, but the period still referred to as "evening" was the riskiest.

"Hi, Jim!" Zindee arrived at his side in a perceptible swirl of air currents. "Know something? I could eat the biggest sundae in the whole world."

"You'll have to graft for it," Nicklin said, putting on a tough voice as he handed over his three books. "I'm going to trust you to deliver those, and each time you drop one you'll forfeit a scoop of ice cream. Is that clear?"

"Yes, boss." Zindee gave him a kind of cringing salute and they set off in the direction of the town centre. They crossed the bridge and were walking in the shade of the tall whistle trees which lined the road when Nicklin noticed that the child seemed slightly subdued. Praying that it was nothing to do with Orbitsville's supposed change of location, he asked what was on her mind.

"I keep thinking about all those weird things they said on TV this morning," she replied.

He snorted with amusement. "I wouldn't worry about it."

"But it's *scary*, Jim. Doesn't it bother you?"

"About the world having moved?" He gave another snort. "I'm a light sleeper, Zindee – I think I would have noticed something if the world had moved during the night."

"But what about the stars? They're all different."

"How do we *know* that?" Nicklin, who had never seen a star and whose knowledge of astronomy was sketchy, began to invent new theories of cosmic physics. "I read that astronomers sometimes discover a cluster of a dozen or so really distant galaxies. Then they look a bit harder and find that the so-called cluster is actually just *one* galaxy. The light coming from it gets bent this way and bent that way as it is travelling towards the wise men. So they run around squawking, getting themselves into a state over discovering eleven galaxies that don't even *exist!*"

Zindee frowned. "What has that got to do with . . . ?"

"It shows that when it comes to stars and the like you just can't trust your eyes. Light rays can bend. It could be that space . . . that space . . ." Nicklin felt a surge of the old heady, guilty elation which often gripped him when he found that what had started off as a rubble of words was cementing itself into a lofty edifice. ". . . is not homogenous, not the same everywhere. There could be inclusions, anomalous regions where light gets *really* twisted up, where what you see is all scrambled. If Orbitsville has drifted into one of those regions the outside universe is *bound* to look different. It's only natural."

"Jim," Zindee looked up at him with the absurdly solemn face of a thirteen-year-old professor of logic, "to me that sounds like a load of male ox."

"It explains the facts better than all that stuff about Orbitsville having moved millions of light years during the night."

"Yeah? And what about all the ships and docks that have disappeared?"

"The anomaly doesn't confine itself to affecting light," Nicklin went on, still on a creative high. "It's a kind of a storm, a spatial tornado which whips interstellar dust particles up to near the speed of light. That increases their mass, you see . . . builds up their energy . . . Particles in that state could scour Orbitsville clean in a few seconds, like a giant sandblaster."

"And what about . . . ?" Zindee closed her eyes for a moment and shook her head. "I wonder if Mr Chickley has got in a fresh supply of chopped walnuts. He didn't have them last time – remember? – and you can't make a sundae that's worth a doodle without chopped walnuts."

"Very smooth change of subject," Nicklin said. "Almost imperceptible."

"I got bored talking about . . . all that stuff."

"I told you at the start that it was pretty dull." Nicklin nudged Zindee with his elbow, putting her off her stride, and she came back at him by shoving hard with her shoulder. They continued walking towards the town centre, their progress slowed by sporadic horseplay and the three small detours needed for the book deliveries. The district was quite typical of Orangefield, with its hushed avenues and masses of ornamental vegetation screening low houses which were roofed with red or green tiles. The scene, Nicklin decided, could have been some privileged part of Earth, except that at this time of the day the sun would have been low in the sky, sinking to the western horizon. He tried to imagine living in an environment in which the sun wandered right across the dome of the heavens during the course of the day, but he only succeeded in conjuring up a queasy sensation, a feeling of balancing on a slowly tilting platform.

"I hear something," Zindee said. "What do I hear?"

They were still a few minutes' walk from the town common, but when Nicklin concentrated he became aware of a grumbly, low-frequency agitation of the air, a disturbance which was alien to Orangefield's sleepy suburbs. "It's the holy rollers. They didn't waste much time getting started on the spiel, but they're not getting any money out of me, and I'll tell you that for nothing."

"What's a spiel?"

"It's when some character sets out to persuade you that things would be much better if you transferred all the money in your pocket into his pocket."

To Nicklin's surprise, Zindee looked up at him in sudden eagerness. "Let's go and hear what they're saying."

"What about your ice cream?"

"It won't melt." She moved slightly ahead of him, tugging his arm. "Come *on*, Jim!"

Nicklin shrugged and compliantly quickened his pace. The sound of amplified speech grew louder as they neared the common, and when the open space came into view he saw that a large tent had been erected at the centre. It seemed to have been intended only for use in rainy weather, because in front of it there was some low staging supporting a platform. On the platform was a tall dark-haired man who was addressing an audience of perhaps four hundred, most of whom were seated on stacking chairs. The remainder were straggled in a rough circle, having chosen to stand although quite a few of the seats had not been taken. *Hedging their bets*, Nicklin thought approvingly. *That way they can hear what's going on and still make a quick getaway before the collectors try to nab them.*

When Zindee and he reached the perimeter of the crowd she made as if to squeeze through and claim a seat, but he held her back. She scowled up at him for a moment, but with a good-natured quirk to her lips, then took up a position where the human barricade was thin enough to let her get a good view of the speaker. Nicklin stood behind her, and it was only then that he was able to tune his senses into what the man on the platform was saying.

". . . this evening's edition of the *Orangefield Recorder*. The piece I am referring to was very witty. It was well written, in a sarcastic style. Perhaps its author is here with us tonight? No? It doesn't really matter too much if he or she is here or not, because I have no bones to pick with the anonymous scribe. That journalist was simply doing a job, stating the newspaper's point of view on what no doubt appeared to be yet another classic case of the learned scientist revealing that he hasn't enough sense to come in out of the rain.

"We have a saying back in Pewterspear – that being educated doesn't stop you being stupid – so I have some sympathy with the popular vision of the scientist who splits his pants as often as he splits atoms."

The speaker paused to allow gratified laughter from the audience to subside – then his mood changed. His stance was unaltered, even his expression remained the same, but everyone who was there knew at once that the jokes were over, that it was time to get down to the serious business of the meeting. In spite of himself, Nicklin was impressed. Assuming that the speaker was Corey Montane, Nicklin took note of the fact that he was dressed in very ordinary clothes – a plain grey coolie hat, blue short-sleeved shirt, grey slacks – not the robe or ultra-respectable business suit usually associated with hawkers of faith. Montane also spoke in normal tones, his speech completely devoid of showy mannerisms. He appeared to rely on the direct, unvarnished communication of thoughts. Nicklin liked that and, against his expectations, found himself waiting with genuine interest for the main content of Montane's message.

"But on this occasion, my friends, I have to tell you something you have no wish to hear." Montane's voice, picked up by out-facing loudspeakers, could be heard rolling away into the distance through the immaculate gardens and around the redundant chimneys of Orangefield. "On this occasion, my friends, I have to tell you that not only were the astronomers in Beachhead City perfectly justified in sounding a warning – they have failed, *completely*, to appreciate the terrible dangers facing every man, woman and child on this huge bubble that they so naïvely think of as 'the world'.

"How do I know this? I'll tell you how I know. I know because I have been *expecting* an event like this for the past six years. I have been expecting it ever since I came to the realisation that Orbitsville is the Devil's trap. It was carefully laid out by the Devil, it was oh so carefully baited by the Devil – and now it is in the process of being *sprung* by the Devil!"

A murmur passed through the audience, a shifting sound equally expressive of surprise, concern and derision. The glowing expanse of sun-hats, variously coloured ellipses which appeared narrower the farther they were away from Nicklin, became briefly agitated.

Montane raised his hands and waited for the disturbance to subside. "I am not omniscient. I have no direct line to God, on which He tells me what the future holds in store for His children. I do not know what the Devil's exact plans are – all I know is that, through God's divine mercy, we have been granted a breathing space. He could have ignored our predicament, and we would have deserved that, because it was through our own wilfulness that we left the world which He specially created for us. We turned our backs on the Eden He provided, and in our arrogance and blind stupidity we flocked to this metallic bubble. We allowed ourselves to be enticed into the trap.

"*But*, as I have already said, there is still a little time left. God willing, there may be enough time for some of us to escape from the Devil's snare, and to do that we have to build starships. We have to quit Orbitsville. Earth may be denied to us for ever – a fitting punishment for our transgressions – but we can still fly to another God-given world, a new Eden, and make a new beginning for the human race."

There was a fresh disturbance in the audience, a subdued commotion which took longer to die away, and in the midst of it could be heard voices of protest reinforced by sceptical laughter. *It costs a lot of money to build starships*, Nicklin thought, *and you don't need to be the Gaseous Vertebrate to work out where the money is supposed to come from.* He glanced about him warily, wondering how long it would be before the collectors got to work.

"I am not asking you to accept anything on blind faith," Montane went on, raising his voice to quell the sounds of protest. "I know only too well that faith is a very scarce commodity these days – so all I am asking you to do is to weigh up the evidence. The cold, hard, *indisputable* evidence. Consider, for example, the curious fact that Orbitsville's environment is so *exactly* suited to . . ."

The realisation that ·Corey Montane had to be certifiable, regardless of his rational manner, immediately caused Nicklin to lose all interest in what was being said. He shook his head, feeling oddly saddened, and was about to tap Zindee on the shoulder when she turned to him. She crooked a finger, signalling for him to bring his head down to her level.

"Jim," she whispered, "this is another load of male ox. I think we should head over to Mr Chickley's."

"Good idea!" Nicklin pressed his forefinger to his lips and began to do a cartoon-style sneaking-away-in-silence walk, circling each foot in the air twice before placing it on the ground. Zindee chortled into her cupped hand and fell in at his side, doing her own version of the walk. They had taken only a few grotesque paces when Nicklin noticed they were being observed at close range by a young woman. She was holding a wicker dish, which identified her as a member of Montane's collecting team, and her expression was one of mingled amusement and gentle reproof.

"Leaving us so soon?" she said in a low and pleasantly accented voice. "Have you not been touched by *anything* that Corey has said?"

Nicklin heard his mouth go into action at once. "It was all fascinating, truly fascinating, but we have some family business to attend to at the other side of town. My uncle is building himself a rock garden, you see, and he needs me to help him lift the . . . "

Embellishments to the basic lie – including a partial biography of the imaginary uncle – crowded into his mind, and he was selecting the most promising when, belatedly, his gaze focused on the woman.

He was totally unprepared for what happened next.

The astonishing reality of the woman flowed into him by way of his eyes, and in that instant – quite simply – he became a different person.

A major component of the starshell of emotion that burst inside him was straightforward physical lust. He wanted to go to bed with her, there and then. He craved to perform with her every act of passion that men and women had ever known and treasured as the means of giving and receiving pleasure. But there was much more to it than that. He also wanted to sleep with the woman, to experience the asexual delight of wakening beside her in the night, slipping his arm around her and nesting with her like spoons as he waited for sleep to return. He wanted to go shopping with her, to fend off doorstep salesmen together, to dab dust motes from each other's eyes, to find out what she thought of contemporary music and of the farming of trout, to discover how far she could run, what childhood ailments she had suffered, how good she was at crosswords . . .

This is serious, Nicklin thought strickenly. *I'm supposed to be immune to this kind of irrationality.*

He tried to decide what it was about her that had had such a devastating effect on him. She was about thirty, somewhere close to his own age, and he decided at once that she was not at all beautiful. Her face was squarish and unremarkable, with eyelids that seemed heavy and druggy; her mouth was wide, with an upper

41

lip that was much fuller than the lower, almost as if it had been swollen by a blow. She was tall and black-haired, and her body – beneath the black sylkon blouse and taut black trousers – was slim and athletic, looking as though it had been pared down by exercise rather than dieting. She wore a flat black stetson instead of the standard coolie-style sun-hat, a flourish which indicated that the ensemble had been consciously chosen to create a certain effect. Nicklin was not sure what the effect was meant to be in terms of fashion, but he knew that for him it worked – the thought of unbuttoning the blouse actually made him feel weak at the knees.

"You must go and help your uncle, of course," the woman said, "but perhaps you'll come back and listen to Corey when you're not so pressed for time. He really has something of great importance to say."

"I'll certainly give it serious thought."

"That's wonderful. By the way, my name is Danea."

"Mine's Jim," Nicklin said, deeply thrilled by the realisation that there had been no need for the woman to give him her name. "Jim Nicklin, and I've just been thinking . . . "

He glanced at the people sitting and standing nearby, who were beginning to look around at him with curiosity or resentment because the conversation was an unwelcome distraction. He pointed at his ear and then at an area of trampled grass which was at a remove from the audience but still inside the ring of pole-mounted speakers which were relaying Montane's words to the outside world. Danea nodded and moved in the indicated direction on black, spike-heeled sandals. Nicklin grabbed at Zindee's hand and followed.

"That's better – there were too many decibels to compete against back there," he said when they stopped walking. "Look, I've been thinking things over. It'll soon be getting dark and there probably isn't enough time to get any useful work in on the rock garden. I think I'll just stay on here for a while and – " He paused, becoming aware that Zindee had gripped his wrist with both hands and was trying to drag him away.

"Jim," she whispered fiercely. "*Jim!*"

Danea looked down at her in a friendly manner. "Is this your daughter?"

"*No!*" Nicklin realised he had put too much emphasis into the denial. "No, I'm not married. This is my friend Zindee. We were going to have us a sundae – on the way to my uncle's place, that is."

"Hello, Zindee," Danea said. "Don't worry about getting that sundae. We all know how important sundaes are, and I'm sure Jim didn't mean that terrible thing he said about staying on here." She raised her gaze and her eyes locked with Nicklin's. "After all, he can come back here at any time."

"Yes." Nicklin nodded vigorously as, annoyingly, Zindee redoubled her efforts to pull him off his feet. "I'll do that. I'll certainly do that."

"Well, we'll see you then." Danea smiled at him, and he saw that her teeth were perfect, and that when she smiled the heaviness left her eyes, making them lively, star-centred and bold. The tremulous feeling returned to his knee joints. He raised his free hand in a farewell gesture and allowed Zindee to haul him away in the direction of Mr Chickley's ice-cream parlour.

"Why didn't you answer Danea when she said hello to you?" he demanded as soon as they had walked far enough to gain some privacy.

"You were doing enough talking for both of us," Zindee replied, the set of her tiny chin showing that she was furious with him. "And what was all that bullshit about an uncle and a rock garden?" The fact that she had not used her customary euphemism – male ox droppings – confirmed to Nicklin that he was really in trouble with her.

"You wouldn't understand," he said lamely.

"What I don't understand is why you tell lies all the time. What makes you *do* it, Jim?"

That's what I'd like to know, Nicklin thought, his cheeks beginning to grow hot with embarrassment. "You still haven't said why you were rude to Danea."

"She talked to me like I was a kid. Sundaes are important. Huh!"

Nicklin remained silent until they had reached the edge of the common, crossed Coach-and-Four Lane and taken up good window seats in Chickley's. The place was quite narrow, but it extended a long way back from the street and had a glittering chrome-and-glass counter right across the inner end. Fat Mr Chickley was proud of having designed the period décor himself, even though there was some uncertainty about which period he had been aiming at. Clumps of coloured neon strips broke out here and there among the pseudo-Victorian gaslights on the walls. There were only a few customers in the twin rows of booths, presumably because of the rival attraction of Montane's meeting.

While Zindee was up at the counter placing her complex order he took stock of himself and was not surprised to find that his hands were slightly unsteady. What had happened to him out there on the common? By inviting the woman to move to a quieter place he had, by his standards of behaviour, been making a pass at her – and he had never before behaved that way with a stranger. The unsettling thing, however, was that she had *known* he was making the pass and had continued to give him positive signals. No local woman would have responded to an advance from him in that way.

He was well aware that, as well as having the reputation of being ineffectual and eccentric, he was suspected of homosexuality by most people in Orangefield. He could have earned the esteem of many men, and probably of quite a few women, by being seen visiting certain homes in the town where the lady of the house had fallen back, so to speak, on an ancient means of earning a living. The main reason he had not given those houses any business was that he was an intensely private person, and did not like the idea of the town gossips knowing the exact dates on which he had found it necessary to relieve biological pressures. He therefore restricted himself to those occasions when he was over in Weston Bridge buying books or machine parts.

It was quite some coincidence, he decided, that the only woman ever to blitz him in such a way was also just about the first ever to respond encouragingly to his show of interest. As a result, there was nothing else in the world that he wanted more than to be with Danea. That was why he had lied about the rock garden in front of Zindee – she had ceased to register on his senses, she had effectively ceased to exist. And, right now, the thought that but for her intrusive presence he could still have been talking to Danea was inspiring him with resentment towards the child.

"Here we go," Zindee said, arriving at the table with two imposing confections in tall glasses balanced on a tray. "Just *look* at them! Feast your eyes, Jim! How's that for a vision of paradise?"

"Not bad."

"Not *bad*!" As she sat down it was apparent from Zindee's expression and manner that she had been restored to good humour. "Peasant! Philistine! Have you no appreciation for genuine works of art?"

"Perhaps not," Nicklin said, taking his spoon and tentatively probing a pale green area of his sundae.

"Who's being rude now?"

"Sorry." He was dully surprised to find that he was not at all sorry. *Why don't you take yourself for a long walk and leave me in peace for a while?*

"I know what's the matter with you." Zindee gave him a knowing smirk, the downy hair on her upper lip already blobbed with white. "I know what's eating our Jim."

"Do you?"

"He's in love! The poor guy's got the throbs for the Lady in Black."

"Eat your ice cream, Zindee," Nicklin said, eyeing her with growing dislike. "You're talking rubbish."

"Oh, no I'm not! I was watching you." Zindee popped a cherry into her mouth and chewed contemplatively. "She's got a good pair of headlights."

Nicklin felt he ought to tell Zindee off for using language unbecoming to a well-brought-up child, but her comment had rekindled his furnace. Now that he thought about it, Danea's breasts *had* been quite full in comparison to the slimness of her body, creating horizontal wrinkles in her sylkon blouse. And there was her smile! He was inclined to smile as little as possible, because when he did so his mouth curved too far up at the corners, giving him what he regarded as a goofy hayseed appearance. Danea's smile, however, was straight, and perhaps her mouth even turned down a little at the corners – a feature which Nicklin had always envied and regarded as a hallmark of mature and worldly sophistication. What was her surname? And was the heaviness of her eyes and possible bruising of the upper lip a sign that she had spent most of the previous night in strenuous sexual activity? With Montane? Nicklin had read that it was quite commonplace for leaders of quirky religious groups to bed the most attractive of their acolytes. Perhaps this particular group went in for sex in a big way, in rituals and so forth. Perhaps Danea had been doing it with *everybody*! If that were the case, he wanted his share of her – even if it meant joining her nutty religion . . .

A mental picture of Danea coupling promiscuously with all the men with whom she travelled filled Nicklin with a pang of desire, jealousy and outrage so powerful that it caused him to squirm in his seat. He should be with her at that very moment, instead of playing nursemaid to a precocious brat who insisted on clinging to him like a leech. Looking out above the half-length net curtain which gave Mr Chickley's window seats some privacy, Nicklin tried to see Danea, but the trees and shifting groups of townsfolk made it impossible.

"Jim, I've got an idea," Zindee said. "You don't really want your sundae, do you?"

"I guess not. I guess I'm not in the mood for an ice."

"That's the understatement of the century. Look, hows about you giving your sundae to me? I'll be able to eat the two of them –no problem – but it's bound to take me quite a while." Zindee spoke with the grave tones of a general laying out a major campaign. "That would give you time to nip back across the street and see if you can fix yourself a date with the Lady in Black. What do you say?"

"I . . . " Nicklin gazed at her with an upwelling of affection so strong that it was little short of adoration. "Are you sure you would be all right? Sitting here by yourself?"

Zindee shrugged. "What could happen to a girl in an ice-cream joint?"

He stood up, drummed a message of thanks with his fingers on the crown of her sun-hat, and hurried out into the street. As he crossed to the common he realised that, without actual sight of Danea to goad him to recklessness, his cursed timidity had returned in force. He had no idea of what to say to her and, perversely, he now wished he had remained with Zindee. A glance at the sky showed that the eastern edge of the sun was being clipped by the next advancing force bar. Night would arrive quite soon, and he felt he might recapture his surprising boldness under cover of darkness, but he would have been obliged to rejoin Zindee by then.

Breasting waves of sound from the loudspeakers, he walked towards the meeting. Montane was still delivering his dire warnings, but the message was no longer penetrating to Nicklin's brain. He circled around the listening crowd, the white marquee and all the associated vehicles three times, but was unable to see any sign of Danea.

Steeped in black, bitter disappointment – but at the same time feeling oddly relieved – he headed back towards Mr Chickley's. From the edge of the green he saw the small and indomitable figure of Zindee outlined by the peach-coloured lights which had just been switched on in the shop. She was busily working on the sundaes.

He smiled as he thought of how pleasant it was going to be, walking home with her and savouring her safe, undemanding companionship.

CHAPTER 5

"By our old standards," Corey Montane said, "we did quite well today."

His audience – some forty strong and composed solely of his own workers – made sounds of gratification, but in a subdued and tentative manner. It was highly unusual for Montane to call a general meeting so late in the day, and each of them knew that something serious was afoot. They were sitting in a tight group in a corner of the marquee. All the door flaps had been drawn shut and tied, and the only illumination came from a single overhead globe which served to emphasise the darkness in the shadowy reaches of the huge tent. The conspiratorial atmosphere was enhanced by the fact that Montane had positioned himself in the midst of his team and was speaking in a low voice, obviously determined that any strangers who might be lurking outside would not hear what he was saying.

"We took in almost six hundred orbs today," Montane went on. "And six hundred orbs is quite a creditable sum–*by our old standards*. The trouble is that our old standards no longer apply. They have lost all relevance. They are totally without meaning for us."

Montane paused, surveying his audience with sombre eyes. They were a mixed bag of men and women, and he loved them all. Some – like the electricians Petra Davies and old Jock Craig – had joined him in the knowledge that they had useful skills to offer; others had come along with no special aptitudes, but prepared to do or learn to do anything that was asked of them. What they had in common was their belief in his message, their loyalty and their trust.

And now it was required of him, in this grim hour, that he should put all those qualities to the test.

"You already know, from today's news, that the world has been moved to some alien part of the continuum, to a new location so remote that the astronomers cannot even find the Local Group – the twenty or more galaxies that made up our cosmic neighbour-hood. The event is a vindication of all that I have told people in the last six years, but sadly, *incredibly*, they still do not believe. The blindness continues.

"But *we* are not blind. *We* know that the iron jaws of the Devil's trap have quivered and have now begun to snap shut!

"I have to admit that, all along, I have been much too complacent. It is now almost two centuries since the migrations to Orbitsville began. By human standards that is a long time, but to God it is the mere blink of an eye, and to the Devil it is the mere blink of an eye.

"I was lulled by those two centuries into thinking that the time scale was much more leisurely than it has proved to be. I began my mission with grand plans to raise the funding to build a fleet of starships. The money came in much more slowly than I had expected in those days of my naïvety, but I was able to adapt to that. If the worst comes to the worst, I reassured myself, it will be enough for me to set up a foundation. I will be able to die content in the knowledge that a fleet will some day set sail towards the new Eden, even if I am not there to embark with it."

Montane gave his listeners a sad, rueful smile. "But today's news has changed all that, and it must change *us*. I am now prepared to settle for just one starship, one ark which will preserve the seeds of a new branch of humanity. It must be built with all possible speed. There may not even be enough time in which to complete the ship, but we must try. It is our only hope of salvation and therefore we must make the utmost effort.

"Until this day we have been content to gather money in small amounts, but now we have to change our ways. We have to put aside our morals, to stifle the voice of our consciences. In short, we have to do everything in our power to bring in that money, even if it means descending to methods which – in other circumstances – we would find repugnant.

"I hate to use words which are associated with some of the darkest episodes in human history – but, in this unique case, the end justifies the means."

There was a taut silence then Mace Winnick, a skeletal, shrunken-faced man who had done time in a correction clinic, cleared his throat. "Corey, are you talking about stealing?"

Montane shook his head. "No stealing. I rule it out, not on moral grounds, but because of the high probability of being caught."

There was another silence while his audience stared at Montane with speculative eyes, trying to assess the stranger that their leader had become. Dee Smethurst, the head cook – plump, pink and matronly, looking exactly as a cook should – raised her hand.

"You almost . . . " There was a pained look on her face. "You almost sound as if you would condone prostitution."

Montane carefully avoided looking anywhere near the women in the group – Danea Farthing, Christine McGivern and Audrey Lightfoot among them – who were physically equipped to earn good money by hustling. "I will condone prostitution, male or female, if it builds us that ship."

"Corey *Montane!*" Dee shot an outraged glance at those seated next to her and tightened her lips in a way which indicated that she would have a lot more to say at a later time.

It came to Montane that he was likely to lose some of his team as a result of the new rules of conduct, but that simply had to be accepted. His mission had been run too much on the lines of a mobile retreat for society's gentle drop-outs. The time had come to stop playing games, and anybody who was not prepared to commit every personal resource to the cause would have to be treated as dead wood.

"I should qualify my last remark," he added. "I am quite prepared to condone ordinary casual prostitution, but bringing in fifty or a hundred orbs a day – I am not conversant with the going rates – would only be a tiny step in the right direction. I would, however, *applaud* strategic prostitution, in which the client was induced to join or support our movement to the extent of selling up his or her possessions and donating the proceeds to our fund.

"It gives me no pleasure to speak to you in these terms – but our immortal souls are at stake. *Nothing less than the future of the human race is at stake!*"

Montane invited his listeners to join with him in open discussion, and he stayed with them for more than an hour while the tides of emotional debate raged back and forth. Finally, when he had become too tired to continue, he took his leave of them and walked back to his camper in the darkness. When he was inside the roomy vehicle he switched on no lights except for the small reading lamp at his desk. The warm glow from its toffee-coloured glass shade enabled him to prepare the pot of tea which he always drank before going to bed. His mind was racing, trying to assimilate all that had happened during the momentous day, but a sense of deep weariness told him he would have no trouble getting to sleep.

When he had finished the tea he undressed and brushed his teeth. He switched off the reading lamp and, on the way to bed, paused by the silver coffin which occupied the centre of the vehicle's living space.

Placing both hands on the cool metal, he closed his eyes and in a low voice said, "I'm sorry about the way things are working out, Milly – but some day we'll both be at peace."

CHAPTER 6

Nicklin stood behind the counter of his repair shop and gazed around him with a kind of sad astonishment. The morning was just like that of the previous day – sunny, clear, warm and invigorating. There had been a succession of such mornings recently, and he had luxuriated in every one of them, but today there was something dismally wrong. Not with the familiar surroundings and appurtenances of his life, but with his reaction to them.

Was it simply that he had had a poor night's sleep? He had lain awake for long periods, reliving his meeting with the Lady in Black, inventing different outcomes for the too-brief encounter. At times he had congratulated himself, with forced sincerity, on having escaped any entanglement with her; but for the most part he had become lost in vivid scenarios which ended with the two of them in bed together. During those episodes he had found himself with a raging, rock-hard erection which kept grinding itself into the mattress, seemingly of its own volition, while he cursed the criminal waste of his youth represented by his spending all the long nights alone.

He had had restless nights in the past, but had always welcomed the morning and the return of the bright, trustworthy realities of existence. On this morning, however, life was flat and boring. Not ordinarily flat and boring, but *unbearably* so. The things which used to interest him, no longer interested him. The cheerful environs of his repair shop and library now had all the appeal of a morgue, and the mere idea of having to retune even one more magnetic pulse motor was almost enough to make him sit down and weep.

What am I going to do, O Gaseous Vertebrate? he thought. *I can't see how I'm going to get through a single day like this – let alone the next sixty years . . .*

With an effort of will, he picked up the order book and checked on what work was pending. The first two items, logged in Maxy Millom's scrupulously legible writing, were a circular saw and a lawn-mower. Beside each was the legend 'MT', which meant that according to Maxy's initial diagnosis their motors needed to be retuned. It was work which Maxy could not even begin to learn because he had an almost superstitious fear of the way a faulty motor could release bursts of gyromagnetic energy, causing tools to leap off the bench like startled animals.

Nicklin had always regarded adjusting the semi-sentient para-mag blocks of a motor, persuading them to deliver their energy pulses at precisely the right instant, as the most boring job ever invented – and that was when he was in a good mood. Today the prospect seemed dire. Wishing that the diffuseness of Orbits-ville's population and the lack of universal engineering standards had not made repair-by-replacement unfeasible, he slammed the order book down.

At that moment the bleached-out stillness of the world beyond the window was disturbed by a moving flurry of dust near the bridge. It was Maxy Millom, late as usual, arriving for work on his old Bronco scooter. As he neared the shop, Maxy stood up on the machine's footrests and gave Nicklin a military-style salute. Maintaining the pose like a rider in a parade, he passed the window, slowing down all the while, and – as he had done perhaps a dozen times in the past – went straight into the tip of a rock about the size of a football projecting from the sun-baked clay. The scooter bucked and fell sideways, bearing Maxy to the ground with it. He jumped up swearing, kicked the scooter a couple of times to punish it for having obeyed the law of gravity, and retrieved his bright green sun-hat. Leaving the Bronco where it lay, he came towards the shop, walking grotesquely as he tried with both hands to extricate the seat of his pants from the cleft of his slabby behind.

Nicklin glowered at him with purest malevolence, wondering how *anybody* could be dim enough to stage the identical accident so often without learning to avoid it. *Just think of it*, he told himself, appalled, *unless I do something really drastic Maxy and I could grow old together – with him gradually wearing that rock down to a frigging pebble.*

"Good morrow, Jim," Maxy bellowed, grinning hugely, as he came into the shop. "Did you see that one? I nearly deballed myself."

I wish you had, Nicklin thought. "You're late again."

"Yeah." Maxy was totally unabashed. "Didn't get to bed till all hours last night. A couple of the boys and me went over to the travellin' show, just to see what sort of things was going on, then we went down to the White Spot for a few beers. Seen you at the show."

"I didn't see you."

"Naw, but I seen *you*, all right," Maxy said triumphantly. "You seemed to be doing okay for yourself. I was nearly going to butt in and tell snake-hips how she was wasting her time on you, and she oughta come along for a few beers with me and the boys, but my generations of good breeding stopped me."

It has just told me it thinks I'm a homosexual – to my face! – and I go on meekly standing here. "I'm sure Danea will be deeply disappointed when she hears what she missed," Nicklin said. "I'll break the news to her tonight – as gently as I can, of course. We mustn't have the poor woman bursting into tears."

"Are you saying you'll be seeing her tonight?"

"No, we've arranged to communicate by carrier pigeon! What do you *think* I'm saying? Of *course* I'm seeing her tonight."

Maxy hopped from one foot to the other, grinning in gleeful disbelief. "Is that a fact, Jim? You've got yourself a hot date? Me and the boys'll watch out for you – maybe pick up a few tips."

Knowing that Maxy, who had remarkably little to do in his spare time, was quite capable of maintaining surveillance on him for an entire evening, Nicklin shrugged and turned away. How was he going to get out of this one? Was he going to have to plead illness and stay home? Brooding on this new annoyance, he went to the square metre of work surface which was referred to as the kitchen, and began to brew coffee. Starting the job while Maxy was present would be interpreted as an invitation for him to share. That was not what he wanted, but it was much preferable to letting Maxy prepare the drinks. He had an unfortunate habit of handling the cups by putting two fingers deep inside them, even when they were full – fingers which if examined under a microscope, Nicklin was sure, would register as a seething mass of bacteria.

"Just what I need," Maxy said, following him. "Hey! Know who else I saw at the rent-a-freak last night?"

"No, but perhaps you'll be good enough to tell me."

Impervious to sarcasm, Maxy nodded vigorously. "A black man! 'Strewth, Jim – they've got a black geezer working for them! He's as black as . . . as . . . "

As your fingernails, Nicklin supplied mentally.

" . . . as your boot," Maxy concluded.

Although Nicklin did not want to encourage Maxy by showing any degree of interest, he was quite intrigued. He had seen only one black person in his entire life, and that had been when he was a child. Now he found it quite difficult to visualise a human being who had black skin.

The old Orbitsville syndrome again, he thought. *So much for all that ancient stuff about the universal brotherhood of man! With living space equal to five billion Earths available, like had gone off into the wild green yonder with like. Nobody was going to hang around to be persecuted, discriminated against, tolerated or even cultivated by liberals merely because of having the wrong shade of epidermis or politics, speaking the wrong language or having wrong ideas about religion, having been born to the wrong parents or in one of the vast selection of wrong places. Regardless of all teachings and preachings, the ordinary Joe had decided it was best to be with his own . . .*

"Anyway," Maxy said. "I've decided I don't like black people."

"That was quick." Nicklin took two plastic cups from the dispenser. "May I ask why?"

"They're too short-tempered, too touchy. Me and the boys was just standing there – friendly, like – looking at this guy, and all of a sudden, for no reason at all, he tells us to bog off." An indignant expression appeared on Maxy's tallowy face as he relived the incident in his mind. "I mean, if you can't just stand and *look* at somebody!"

"What's the world coming to? That's what I always say." Nicklin poured coffee into the two cups, picked up his own and moved to the front end of the shop. It was a vantage point which gave him a good view of the stream, the small bridge and the road. Beyond the building's wide eaves the sunlight was a silent, vertical torrent of platinum-coloured rays, hammering down on the bleached-out scene with almost tangible force. The world was embedded – preserved and hermetically sealed – in the clear rigid plastic of that light. Dayton, Ohio, where it was forever 1910. Nothing was ever going to happen in Orangefield, and he was going to be right there, through all of it. The thought was enough to make him want to sit down and weep. Dismayed to feel his lower lip give a preliminary tremble, he took a sip of his coffee and winced as the near-scalding fluid coursed down his throat.

Lost in his melancholia, Nicklin had been gazing at the approaching blue Unimot convertible for several seconds before he realised it was slowing down to stop at his place. It was lost to view behind the stand of whistle trees, reappeared and turned right, coming to a halt when its driver was confronted by the footbridge. A moment later the driver got out and Nicklin's heart gave a giddy lurch as he saw the woman. *The* woman.

She was no longer the Lady in Black, but was wearing a similar outfit – glistening blouse, slimfit pants, high-heel boots and flat stetson – in which the predominant colour was primrose. Glancing about her with evident interest, she came towards the shop. She was walking almost like a ballet dancer on stage, with one foot going down directly in front of the other in a way which emphasised the economical curvatures of thighs, calves and ankles.

Nicklin felt a cool prickling on his brow as he analysed the possibilities. The chances that she was coming to borrow a book or to have an eggbeater mended were just about zero – which meant that the visit was personal. Could it be – could it really *be* – that she wanted to take up where they had left off last night? *But nothing actually happened between us last night,* Nicklin reminded himself. *It was all a product of my fevered imagination. This sort of thing only happens to me in the opening phases of an erotic dream.*

He set his cup down, found the presence of mind to wink at Maxy, and went out of the shop without taking time to pick up his sun-hat. When the woman saw him advancing to meet her she gave him a smile which was so fleeting that it would have been possible to miss it, then her expression became severe.

"What happened to you last night?" she said abruptly.

"I . . . " Nicklin was lost for words. "What do you mean?"

"Jim, you know very well what I mean."

Her use of his first name excited and encouraged him. "I assure you, Danea, I don't know what you're talking about."

"At least you remember my name," she said, beginning to look mollified. "I suppose that's something, but don't think it lets you off the hook, Jim Nicklin. Why didn't you come back to see me last night, the way we arranged?"

Nicklin felt a gusher of pure joy shaking his intellectual landscape. It had not yet spumed up through him, but it was getting itself ready. This *was* the first part of an erotic dream, but it was a dream that was coming true – and all he needed to do was make the final check which would remove even the slightest possibility of his suffering a crushing humiliation or disappointment.

"Montane must have a dash of tax collector's blood in him if he lets you go drive all the way out of town for a couple of orbs," he said, forcing a grin. "Where's your collecting plate?"

"That isn't funny, Jim." Danea gazed at him seriously from under heavy eyelids. "This sort of thing has never happened to me before, and you're not making it any easier. You may be used to this, but I'm not."

"I'm *not* used to . . . Danea, there was nothing actually said last night."

"Do you think I don't know that?" she replied, her eyes holding steady on his, imploring. "Do you think I'm not quivering like a jelly over all the embarrassment I'll have to go through if I'm wrong?"

"You're not wrong," he said, entranced, taking one of her hands in his. The gusher was exploding up through the ground now, blasting all that remained of the old Jim Nicklin into the high blue.

"Thank God!" She smiled and moved her hand in such a way that his knuckles were pressed into her left breast. "I didn't sleep much last night, Jim – why didn't you come back to me?"

"I *did* go back. I left Zindee with her ice cream for a few minutes and went back to look for you."

"I was hiding in the marquee trying to calm myself down a little bit." Her breast, beneath the sylkon blouse, felt like bare flesh against the back of his hand. "Anyway, a couple of minutes wouldn't have been much use to us. I'm really hurting for you, Jim. I want you *in* me. Does that sound awful?"

"It sounds wonderful." The former Jim Nicklin would have been reduced to incoherence by the question, but the new version remained more or less in control of himself, doing his best to act like the cool roué Danea believed him to be. "I have an apartment above the library – let's go there."

"No!" Danea looked over his shoulder, in the direction of the workshop. "That horrible person – the one who was hanging around the meeting last night – is watching us. I'd never be able to relax if I knew he was near us . . . listening . . . Does he work for you?"

"In a manner of speaking." Nicklin glanced back at the window in which the open-mouthed figure of Maxy was posed like a statue. "Only the Gaseous Vertebrate knows why I keep him on. I could send him home."

Danea shook her head. "That would be too obvious."

"Do you want to wait till tonight?" Nicklin said, his joy beginning to cloud with anxiety. He knew with absolute certainty, because it was in the nature of such things, that if he let this opportunity slip away it would never return. Tonight was an aeon away in the future, and by the time it came Danea would have recovered her sanity, or started menstruating, or been called away to tend a sick aunt. Or he would have tripped over something and broken both his legs, or – worst of all – the Mr Hyde potion would have worn off and he would be in such a state of yellow-bellied funk that he would be unable to set foot outside the house.

"Let's go for a walk," Danea said, nodding in the direction of the low crest behind his premises. "What's on the other side of that hill?"

Thank you, thank you, O Gaseous Vertebrate, Nicklin chanted in his mind. "There's nothing over there," he said, keeping his voice calm. "No people, anyway. Just little hills and lots more little hills. It's just right for walking."

Danea gave him a conspiratorial smile. "Do you want to go in and fetch your hat?"

"No, the sun never bothers me much," he lied, unwilling to risk leaving her side for even a few seconds.

Conscious of still being gaped at by Maxy, he linked arms with Danea and walked with her towards the grassy crest. There was silence between them as they moved up the slope. Nicklin wondered if he should try to maintain a flow of sophisticated and tension-easing conversation, but perhaps there was no real need for words. In a lower corner of his vision he could see the buoyant cones of Danea's bosom – *you were right, Zindee, good headlamps* – and the easy, languorous, alternating movement of her slim thighs. And each time he reminded himself it was all really happening, and not part of a dream, his feet seemed to lose all contact with the ground. *I'm walking on air, just as the cliché says. I want this to go on for ever. Love took its time in finding me, but when it finally got here it did the job in the classic across-a-crowded-room style, and I want this to go on for ever and ever . . .*

As soon as they were over the ridge and out of sight of Nicklin's place and the few other buildings dotted along Cork Road, Danea turned to him and they kissed. The smell and the taste and the feel of her swamped his senses.

"Not here," she whispered gently. "It's too near to your place – that *person* might follow us."

Belatedly aware of having tried to sink with Danea to the ground, he said, "You're quite right – I wouldn't put it past him. There's a better spot over here."

He guided her around an egg-shaped hummock to its north side, from where endless green billows stretched to the up-curved horizon. Fringing the hill were clusters of bandannas which were just coming into full flower. The trailing red-and-orange blossoms which gave the shrub its name made a colourful outpost on the edge of the ocean of grass. One of the largest clumps had grown in a U-shape which was a good size to screen a recumbent couple and even provided some degree of protection against the sun. Nicklin had noticed the leafy boudoir on previous walks, and in his imagination – inspired by constant loneliness – had peopled it with lovers, never supposing that he would be one of them.

"How's this?" he said.

For an answer, Danea began to undress, her solemn brown eyes never leaving his. Nicklin stripped off in unison with her, throwing his clothes into the nook to form a makeshift blanket. As soon as both were naked they kissed once more – breast to breast, belly to belly, thigh to thigh.

Then they lay down together . . .

It might have been an hour – he had no means of judging the time – before Nicklin slowly spiralled back down into the mundane world. He was lying over Danea, but taking most of his weight on his elbows and knees, and was looking into her eyes. They were so close to his own that he was unable to focus on them. They registered as lambent brown-and-white blurs, lacking in detail, but in a little while he became aware that she was crying. He promptly rolled to the ground on his left side, disturbed by a lover's fears, and touched the cool transparent ribbons on her cheek.

"What's wrong, Danea?" he whispered. "You're not sorry, are you?"

She pressed her teeth down on her lower lip to stop its trembling. "I *am* sorry, but not about us. Not about this."

"What then?"

"Corey . . . The mission will be leaving Orangefield the day after tomorrow. I have to go with it, and that means . . . " She gave a sob and pressed her face into his shoulder. "I don't want to leave you, Jim. I don't want this to end."

"Does it have to?" Nicklin's consciousness, which had been totally absorbed with the present, suddenly reached out to the future and encountered – only hours ahead – a barrier of black jet, a dark wall where happiness ended and the old despairing solitude and futility began. "Do you *have* to leave? Couldn't you stay here with me?"

Danea shook her head and he felt her tears smearing on his skin. "I'm committed to the mission," she said in a muffled voice. "It's what I believe in, Jim. I can't forget all the vows I . . . Besides, I don't think I could stand living in a place like Orangefield."

"I've got news for you, Danea." Bolts of white lightning cleaved the landscape of Nicklin's mind. "I can't stand living in Orangefield either."

He felt her body go rigid. She raised her head and gave him several light kisses, dabbing his face with her tears.

"That's very sweet of you," she murmured. "I feel so very honoured that you would even consider leaving your home and everything you know and going out on the road with me. *Is* that what you meant, or am I . . . ?"

"That's what I meant, and you know it."

She gave him a tremulous smile and gently nuzzled her pubis against his hip. "You're a lovely man, Jim, but there are things you don't know about."

"What sort of things?"

"Corey doesn't permit people to come along for the ride. We'd be swamped with fellow-travellers – in both senses – if he allowed that. Everyone who joins us has to be totally committed, and that means . . . " She tried to lower her head again, but he placed his hand on her brow, forcing her to continue looking at him.

"Go on," he said.

"It means selling everything you own . . . your home, your business, your insurance . . . *everything* . . . and donating all the proceeds to the mission."

"Is *that* all you're worried about?" Nicklin laughed with genuine relief. "Consider it done, little girl! Consider it *done!*"

All the heaviness disappeared from Danea's eyes. "Do you mean it, Jim? Do you really mean it? We could have a little camper all to ourselves – and you don't even have to marry me if you don't want to."

"I want to."

"We've got all the time in the world to talk about that," she said, raising herself to a sitting position, looking radiantly excited. She remained that way for a few seconds, then her expression became pensive.

Nicklin was more confident now, and no alarm bells rang for him. "What is it this time?"

"I've just thought of something." Her eyes were speculative and oddly watchful as they searched his face. "I don't know what the others, especially Corey, will think of me if I go back as bold as brass and tell them I'm moving in with a man I met only last night. That probably sounds silly to you, Jim. You're probably used to a procession of women going in and out of your bed – and you don't have to care one hoot what people say about it – but things are a bit different for me at the mission. It's all a bit straight-laced. It's all very old-fashioned, but I really value the respect of the people I work with there . . . "

Danea paused, looking self-conscious. "What a big speech! And I don't even know if what I said makes any kind of sense to you."

"I understand." Nicklin felt some disappointment, but he was already possessive towards Danea and the disappointment was more than offset by his learning that Montane's followers were not proponents of communal or even casual sex. "You're saying we can't start living together right off. I can handle that."

"Thank you, Jim, thank you!" She hugged him, pressing in hard with her breasts. "We'll only have to wait a little while after Corey accepts you. And we won't be apart *all* the time, my lovely horny darling – every now and then we'll be able to take ourselves for a little walk."

The inflection Danea put on the last word, the assignment to it of a special secret meaning, made Nicklin's throat close up painfully with sheer happiness. In future, when they were in the company of others, he or she would only have to suggest going for a "walk", and nobody else present would know what was meant, but he and Danea would know, and it would be more of the kind of ecstatic love-making they had just experienced. The world was a wonderful place in which to live – and how could he ever have thought that Danea was not beautiful?

While they were dressing he found a damp patch near the bottom edge of his shirt which made him wince as he crammed it under his belt. Danea laughed and told him he had only himself to blame for being so virile. After they were clothed again they remained in the lee of the bandanna for a minute while he tried to explain, with some guesswork here and there, how he would go about disposing of all his assets in a very short time. Danea looked embarrassed and asked him not to talk about such things until he was with Corey Montane. Nicklin loved her all the more because she so obviously wanted to keep their personal relationship uncontaminated by financial matters.

As they were walking back to his place, his arm around her shoulder and hers around his waist, a new thought occurred to him "If we're going to be married," he said lightly, "I suppose it would be only proper if I got to know your second name."

"You mean you took me into your love nest and you didn't even know my . . . !" She pushed him away from her with a scandalised laugh. "Farthing! My name is Farthing – I told you that last night."

"You didn't! I swear to you by the Gaseous Vertebrate that you didn't." He tilted his head thoughtfully. "At least, I don't think you did."

"You see! You're not even sure!" Danea came back to him and put her arms around his neck. "Tell me the truth, Jim – just how many women *have* you taken for a walk up here?"

"You're the only one," Nicklin protested, but was unable to resist allowing the claim to sound unconvincing. He was more flattered than he cared to admit by her repeated suggestions that he was a sexual conquistador. And if she happened to be impressed by men of wide experience there was no point in his going all out to change her opinion of him. Life was suddenly opening up in a big way. Now that he had been with Danea he could admit that the women of Orangefield, with their dismissive and condescending manner, had always given him a sense of sexual inadequacy. But the fault had been with them all along! They were small-towners, hidebound and limited by their Hicksville upbringing, whereas he was a natural cosmopolitan who could only be appreciated by other cosmopolitans.

As he walked in the sunlight with Danea's hip gently nudging his, he thought for a moment about the fact that he was on the point of selling up everything he owned, for no other reason than his desire to be with her. But he felt no doubts, no qualms, no apprehensions. He was going to rid himself of his shackles and become free to begin his *real* life.

"Tell me something," Danea said. "What is this Gaseous Vertebrate you keep mentioning? What do you mean?"

Nicklin was surprised. "I didn't realise that I . . . It's a name that somebody – one of the old German philosophers, I think – invented for God."

"*God*? It sounds strange. Not very respectful."

"It's meant to be the opposite of respectful. It's meant to express disbelief. The Bible claims that God made man in His own image. So, if we look like Him, He must look like us, and that means He has a backbone. But if He's a spirit – by definition a creature who has no weight – why does He need a backbone to support His weight?"

"Please do me a favour," Danea said, a barely noticeable wrinkle appearing between her eyebrows. "Don't refer to God in that way when you're with Corey – I'm sure it would hurt his feelings."

Nicklin gave her a compliant nod, and – for no reason which could be isolated from the clamorous background of his thoughts – it came to him that there was something important, something *very* important, which he should have discussed with the woman he loved.

CHAPTER 7

An hour spent with the manager of the Orangefield branch of the Portal One Bank had left Nicklin emotionally exhausted. He was not sure why an interview with Dixon Figg should have that kind of an effect on him, but it always had, and he was glad to leave the hushed dove-grey offices of the bank and go for a restorative walk in Mumford Park.

Except in large cities, the profession of realtor had all but ceased to exist in the two centuries that man had been on Orbitsville. It was ironic, Nicklin often thought, that it was a surfeit of the very commodity they traded in which had practically forced real estate dealers out of existence. With entire continents available for nothing, clients willing to pay more than peanuts per hectare had become elusive.

The banks, ever ready to fill a commercial vacuum, had absorbed land management into their activities, and as a consequence Figg had a comprehensive knowledge of Nicklin's affairs. The thing which annoyed Nicklin was that Figg always treated him with barely hidden disapproval, even contempt, in spite of his sensible business practices, avoidance of debt, and an accumulation of some 40,000 orbs in his personal savings account. Figg was only reflecting the town's prejudices, Nicklin surmised, but surely it was incumbent upon the manager of a bank to be more civilised than the local stubblejaws.

On being told that Nicklin wanted to liquidate every one of his assets in preparation for leaving town in a couple of days, Dixon Figg's expression had gone from shock to outrage to deep suspicion in as many seconds. The display had cowed Nicklin so thoroughly that he had not dared to give the real reason for his drastic proposal. Instead he had launched into a series of lies about a cousin in

65

Beachhead City who had presented him with a once-in-a-lifetime opportunity to buy into the family's ventilation engineering business. Under Figg's astute probing the structure of lies had become more complicated and increasingly shaky, until in the end – his intelligence roundly insulted – the banker had withdrawn into the hostile iciness with which he concluded the interview.

Now, walking amidst the greenery of the park, Nicklin was reproaching himself for not having been tough and cold with Figg. Tough, cold and – if necessary – brutal. When the questioning started he should have silenced Figg with the verbal equivalent of a broadsword. Perhaps he would do just that in the morning when he went to collect his underwritten draft for 82,000 orbs, but it was much more likely that he would be as ineffectual as ever. It was only when he was with Danea that the bold and positive side of his personality seemed to emerge, enhanced by the power of her feelings for him.

The realisation that he would soon be quitting oppressive Orangefield for ever, and going off into the unknown with her, gave his spirits a powerful boost, enabling him to drive the crabbed Mr Figg out of his thoughts. He strolled around the little park twice, breathing deeply and consciously relaxing, until it was almost time for his 11.00 a.m. appointment with Corey Montane. Leaving by the east gate, he walked the length of Telegraph Row, making good progress because there were few shoppers around at that drowsy time of day, the tail-end of the mid-morning lull. He emerged on Buckboard Lane, one of the boundaries of the common, which was comparatively free of vehicles and easy to get across.

The mission's marquee glowed like a snowdrift beyond the screen of trees. As he approached it he saw that the site, with its rectangular group of cars, campers and trailers, was almost deserted. Several men and women were sitting on the steps of the platform, talking earnestly among themselves, but he knew not to look for Danea among them. For reasons he had not fully understood, she had thought it best to remain out of sight until after his talk with Montane. The most convenient person to ask guidance from was a man who was leaning against a nearby tree, his head concealed beneath an enormous droop-rimmed straw sun-hat. His back was to Nicklin and he appeared to be eating a banapple.

"Hi, there!" Nicklin said. "Can you tell me where I might find Corey Montane?"

The man turned, smiling, and Nicklin saw that he was the black of whom Maxy had spoken. "No might about it! I can tell you where you will *definitely* find Corey."

"That's even better," Nicklin replied, smiling in return, and doing his best not to stare at the deeply pigmented skin of the man's face and hands.

"Over there. The silver job with no writing on the side."

"Thank you." Nicklin nodded and went in the indicated direction. He was pleased because the black man had treated him with amiable courtesy, as few locals would have done, and it reinforced his feeling that he was throwing his lot in with soulmates – travellers, cosmopolitans, people who had seen a thing or two.

As he neared the silver trailer, Corey Montane appeared in the open doorway and came on to the step to meet him. The first thing Nicklin noticed was that the impression of *ordinariness* he had projected from the stage was no longer present. It was his face that made the difference when Montane was seen at close range. The features were conventionally handsome and as clearly defined as those of a cartoon character. Nicklin, in spite of having no art training, felt he could have produced a recognisable lightning sketch of Montane. The regular features – ruler-straight nose and square chin, glossy dark hair coming to a widow's peak – would have taken just a few strokes of the charcoal. Only the eyes would have been difficult, impossible, even for a master portraitist. They were grey, deep-set and full of lively interest, but at the same time they seemed to be focused on some point very far beyond Nicklin. It was as if the mind behind them had weighed him up and found him to be of only transient interest. While Nicklin was there in the flesh that interest would be as complete and sympathetic as Montane could make it, but his true concern was with matters infinite and eternal.

Nicklin liked him immediately, and – against his expectations – felt considerable respect for him. "I'm Jim Nicklin," he said, extending his hand.

"Hello, Jim." Montane's handshake was firm and dry. "Danea has been telling me all about you. Would you like to come inside and have a cup of tea? We can talk better in the old bus and it's a lot cooler inside – at least it would be if the air conditioning was working properly."

"I can put it right for you," Nicklin said as he followed Montane into the vehicle. "It's probably just a matter of – " He broke off on seeing the long silvery box occupying the centre of the floor space.

Montane gave him an appraising, slightly amused glance. "Yes, it's just what it appears to be – a coffin. Temporary resting place for my wife. Didn't Danea tell you about my unusual domestic arrangement?"

"Ah . . . no."

"She probably didn't want you to think I was crazy." Montane nodded towards a cushioned bench, inviting Nicklin to be seated. "We run the mission on strictly democratic lines, you know. One of our principal rules is that accommodation has to be shared out equally, but although there's enough room in my vehicle for a few more people nobody ever suggests moving in. They pretend it's out of respect for me, but who would want to share with a casket? Especially one that was occupied . . . "

Nicklin tried to smile. "Not too many, I suppose."

"It's understandable, but my circumstances are far from being normal."

That has to be the understatement of the decade, Nicklin thought, an ambivalence creeping into his opinion of Montane. The initial instinctive respect was still there, but what man in his right mind toted his wife's dead body around everywhere he went? Or even *any*where he went? It was bound to be against some statute or other, and had it ever been possible to introduce effective law enforcement on the Big O – in place of the prevalent system of restrained anarchy – Montane would have been in trouble. Something else the man had said was causing tremors of unease far back in Nicklin's consciousness, but he had no time to identify it.

"This is a very big step you're contemplating," Montane commented as he began to prepare the tea. "You fully understand, I take it, that the money you transfer to the mission will be in the form of a donation?"

"What else could it be?"

"My point is that you won't be buying a holding in some kind of commercial enterprise – a starship construction company, let's say – a holding which you could dispose of at some future date should you wish to do so."

"You're saying I won't be able to get my money back."

"I'm saying precisely that." Montane set out two antique-looking china cups and saucers. "And the amount involved is bound to be quite large."

"Oh, well – in for an orb, in for a crescent," Nicklin said, immediately regretting his attempt at flippancy as he noted the seriousness of Montane's expression.

"There's a lot more than mere orbs and 'cents at stake here," Montane replied. "I'm very happy for Danea and you, of course, and I wish you every happiness together, but – "

"My feelings about her aren't going to change, and even if they did – which they *aren't* – I don't see that it would have any bearing on any financial agreement between you and me." Nicklin was surprised to hear himself speaking with a degree of forcefulness which he had rarely achieved before – especially with a stranger – and he tentatively identified the Danea effect again.

Montane halted in the act of opening a jar of milk capsules. "I apologise, Jim. I intended no slur on Danea or you. I accept that you love each other, although it was all rather sudden by my personal timetable, but will you give me a direct answer to a direct question?"

"Of course."

Montane set the jar down and turned to face Nicklin. "Are you a believer, Jim? Do you truly believe in God and in the message I bring to mankind on His behalf?"

"I . . . " Nicklin looked into the calmness of the grey eyes and for once in his life understood the futility of lying. He turned his head from side to side, slowly, once.

Unexpectedly, Montane gave him a broad smile. "If you had tried to fool me on that one, I'd have booted you out of here, Jim – regardless of how much money it cost the mission. I can only work with people I respect, and who respect me. Milk?"

"One," Nicklin said as Montane picked up the small jar. "I'm glad we cleared the air, but I'm a bit surprised."

"At my taking on a non-believer? These are very special times, Jim. Naturally, I would prefer it if everybody I came in contact with was a disciple of the Lord, but this is an imperfect world and I have to use any instrument that He sends in my direction. The mission will benefit in two ways from your joining us – firstly, from your generous donation to our funds; secondly, from your practical skills. Danea tells me you are an excellent engineer."

"Technician might be a better word, and only in a small way." Nicklin accepted a cup of tea, and as he sipped it the feeling that something was amiss returned to him. Was it that Danea had warned him about speaking of his atheism to Montane? She had indicated that Montane would be deeply displeased, but in the event the man had proved to be quite indifferent. She had also said that no "paying guests" were permitted to come along for the ride, and that too was incorrect. It appeared she was not as familiar with her leader's views as one might have expected . . .

"Well, I'm pleased to accept you into my team, and I'm sure you'll be a useful member regardless of whether we style you engineer or technician," Montane said. "And now we ought to sort out some necessary details – does it embarrass you to talk about money?"

"It's one of my favourite subjects."

"Good! Money is very important to us." Montane came to sit on an old adjustable chair opposite Nicklin, a move which brought him close to the metal coffin. He placed his cup and saucer on it while he angled the seat to a more comfortable position. As an avowed materialist, Nicklin tried not to show any reaction, but using a loved one's coffin as an occasional table struck him as being vaguely distasteful. Unfortunately for him, he also saw the little domestic absurdity as being very funny – especially for a religious leader – and he was not at all certain of being able to control his amusement.

"Milly would have liked being helpful around the place," Montane explained, apparently prompted by some kind of near-telepathy as he retrieved his tea. "This way we're still man and wife – if you see what I mean – until she is properly laid to rest."

"I quite understand," Nicklin muttered, staring fixedly into his cup and fighting the urge to laugh. *Why, O Gaseous Vertebrate, does life never serve anything up to us absolutely straight? Why does every drama have to contain its element of the ludicrous? Why does every leader have to have a squeaky voice or a boil on his bum? Is it your way of hinting to us that everything might be part of a big joke?*

"You're looking a bit pensive, son," Montane said. "Is there anything on your mind?"

"Nothing too weighty," Nicklin assured the older man. "Just odd thoughts about this and that. It isn't every day that a man begins a brand-new life, you know."

Although he had put just about everything he owned into the hands of the Portal One Bank, it took Nicklin longer than he had expected to vacate his premises. He kept finding last-minute jobs to do, personal minutiae to preserve or destroy, all kinds of trivial items which somehow could not be abandoned without leaving notes for future users. When he had arranged for Danea to pick him up at midday it had seemed that he was allowing ample time in which to pull out, but now a distinct undertone of panic was creeping into everything.

The weather had changed during the night. Opaque grey clouds had come sifting in from the west, and the breeze which had sprung up was strong enough to activate the whistle trees on the far bank of the stream. They had curled their leaves and were emitting a mournful, ruminative keening which reminded Nicklin of the sound effects in a bad melodrama. There had been no rain as yet, but the air felt cool, moist and heavy.

Luckily, this was one of the days on which Maxy Millom was not due to put in an appearance, so Nicklin was spared the interrogation which would have been inevitable. He had the pleasure of penning Maxy a note which informed him that he was no longer in employment, then he concentrated on the series of less rewarding chores.

Everywhere he went he was conscious of being observed by Zindee. She had been in bed and asleep the previous night when he had paid the Whites a courtesy call to let them know he was pulling out. He had told Cham and Nora practically nothing about his true motivations, but on the instant of hearing the news from her parents Zindee would have understood that it was all to do with Danea Farthing. She was out there somewhere as he worked, near by, covertly watching him while she weighed up the changes that were going to be wrought in her life. He very much wanted them to part as good friends, but there was little point in his going to the Whites' house and trying to speak to her – if everything was going to be all right Zindee would come to him.

Fifteen minutes before midday, magically, all the necessary chores had been completed. He made one last tour of his apartment, the library and the workshop, then locked the place up. He put the keys and all documents required by Mr Figg into a pocket, carried his single suitcase across the footbridge and set it on the ground to await Danea's arrival. Zindee was bound to realise that he was on the point of leaving, but she remained out of sight. The first of the rain began to fall, huge tumbling drops which popped audibly into the dust, and he took shelter under a tree.

A moment later a blue car appeared in the distance. Nicklin picked up his case, but dropped it immediately as he saw Zindee running towards him from the direction of a clump of tangle-weed. He knelt and took the impact of her body full on the chest as she threw her arms around his neck.

"Thanks, Zindee," he whispered. "Thanks for coming."

"You're going to miss my birthday party." Her voice was reproachful. "It's the day after tomorrow."

"I have to miss this one – and I'm sorry about that – but there'll be lots of other birthday parties."

"They're too far off."

"I promise I'll come back and see you." Hearing the car approaching, Nicklin reached into his pocket and brought out a memento he had found in a drawer a little earlier – a bronze Roman coin – and pressed it into Zindee's hand. "Don't spend it all in one shop."

She gave a reluctant little snort of amusement, rubbed a moist cheek against his own and backed out of his embrace.

Nicklin stood up, brushing dust from his knees. "Wait and say goodbye to Danea," he urged.

Zindee set her tiny chin and gave the blue car a venomous glance, then turned and ran towards home. Rain was dappling the back of her light orange T-shirt with tangerine. Nicklin stared thoughtfully at the swiftly departing figure until the car had rolled to a halt beside him. When he looked around Danea had slid the

Unimot's roof into place and was smiling at him from the vehicle's shaded interior.

"Don't stand there in the rain," she called out. "Otherwise you'll take root."

Nicklin's new home was a camper whose interior was almost completely filled by eight bunk beds. His initial glimpse of the layout, which he found rather reminiscent of a submarine, had produced a pang of depression which he had fought off by thinking hard about Danea. He had told himself he could put up with any kind of discomfort for the sake of what lay ahead, but had known that his prospects of sleep on that first night were not good. He was too keyed up and had too many thoughts clamouring inside his skull. It had come as a pleasant surprise, therefore, when he had been asked to drive the camper and to take what was referred to as the dead dog shift – four hours starting at midnight. For some ill-defined reason he had expected to be left to his own devices for the first day or two, and he welcomed the opportunity to do something which was guaranteed to tire him out.

Now, sitting on his own at the camper's wheel, he was in the kind of bemused philosophical mood in which ideas can be examined without being analysed. Processions of them rolled through his uncritical mind, reflecting the events of the last three days, to mental commentaries no more penetrating than *Isn't life weird?* or *You never know what to expect, do you?* or *I wish I was back in old Orangefield right now – just to see their faces* or *Here's one for the books!*

Physically, he was surrounded by the Orbitsville nightland – hundreds of indigo and sapphire ribbons arching across the heavens, narrowing and merging into a prismatic glow above the polar horizon, while the world beneath was an ocean of purest blackness. The vehicles ahead of Nicklin were the only things visible in the darkness. Their lights gave them the semblance of ships, and their wakes were the random whorls and feathers which patterned the fused-earth road.

The spectacle soothed and uplifted Nicklin, but at the same time it reminded him that his happiness was only complete when Danea was at his side. The night would have been perfect had she been with him right there in the driving cabin, but he had seen surprisingly little of her during the day and now she was asleep in the camper she shared with six other women. She was reluctant to make too great a display of her feelings for him, he guessed. He could understand that kind of reticence, which had always been part of his own make-up, especially as it rendered all the more precious the secret things that had passed between them.

When he had got into the car beside Danea that morning she had leaned across to kiss him, and in doing so had placed her hand squarely on his crotch. The little act of familiarity, unseen by the rest of the universe, had spoken volumes to Nicklin, and he was totally secure in their mutual love. Ahead of him lay a future which was mysterious and unpredictable in many respects, but he was sure of the fulfilment that Danea and he would bring to each other. All that was required of him was some patience until they had their own private mobile home, and then . . .

He frowned as a quirk of memory brought into sharp focus something which had cropped up during the conversation with Montane that morning, and which had been a burr in Nicklin's subconscious ever since. One of the mission's principal rules, Montane had said, was that accommodation had to be shared out equally. There had been no mention of special exceptions, and – now that Nicklin thought of it – he had not noticed any vehicles which appeared to be given over to couples, or even groups of couples. Did that mean that he and Danea were to be the *first* to live as man and wife?

"Why not?" He spoke the question aloud as he reminded himself that this was a time of upheaval for Corey Montane and his followers. Big changes were supposed to have taken place in the cosmos and they were being mirrored by radical new policies within the itinerant community. He had those selfsame changes to thank for his being allowed to join the caravan and take up the life of a . . . vagabond. Having dredged up the old word, he savoured its archaic and romantic flavour.

Now that he thought of it, a large proportion of Orbitsville's population consisted of vagabonds. The people he was accustomed to meeting in everyday life had stopped travelling, but nobody knew how many others had kept on moving, spreading from the triple ring of portals into the green immensities of the Big O. They could have travelled a long way in two centuries – splitting up into more and more divergent tribes, each claiming its autonomy and moving onwards for reasons that seemed less and less important to outsiders.

Nicklin had seen the powerful divisive force at work even within his own limited compass. It was, for example, practically impossible to find in the Orangefield area families which did not have Anglo-Saxon surnames. Given a telescope of limitless light-gathering power and resolution, it would have been possible to aim the instrument at any of the dark bands of the night sky and pick out the city lights, the village lights – or even the campfires – of those who had found new reasons to draw apart from their neighbours. He had little doubt that somewhere up there were communities which had chosen to separate from the rest of mankind over disagreements about how to prepare food, or the number of letters in their alphabet, or whether their deities should be portrayed with or without navels.

And the distant glimmers would betoken not only the presence of humans. Alien races had discovered Orbitsville long before Vance Garamond's fugitive ship had come probing through the interstellar void. One of those vanished races had actually mustered the resources and sheer arrogance to try taking control of Orbitsville by sealing all but one of the 548 portals with diaphragms of steel. It had been an awesome attempt to monopolise the vastness of the Big O, and those who made it had flourished perhaps for millennia. But others had challenged their supremacy, unimaginable battles had been fought both inside and outside the great shell, and in the end there had been nobody left to claim victory.

What had happened, Nicklin wondered, to the descendants of those ancient, alien warriors? A few dozen extraterrestrial species – none related to any of the others – had been found in regions close to portals. The only traits they had in common were passivity and lack of curiosity, a willingness to go on for ever re-inventing the steam engine, and Nicklin sometimes suspected that the same destiny was in store for humanity. The Orbitsville syndrome! The big question was: should he laugh or cry? Was it a matter for despair or rejoicing that the future promised to be an eternal Sunday afternoon?

The mood of gentle melancholia which had crept over him was suddenly dispersed by an unexpected event.

There were six vehicles ahead of the camper, and all the time he had been at the wheel they had maintained a fairly steady formation, the configuration of their lights changing only where the road dipped or turned. Now, however, brake warnings were staining the night with crimson and the line was compacting into an irregular group. Nicklin used his heel on the camper's single control pedal and brought the vehicle to a halt. Less than three hours of his shift had passed, so it was too soon for changeover, and as he descended from the cabin he surmised that somebody up front was having mechanical trouble.

The guess was proved wrong even before he had joined the knot of drivers who were standing by the lead vehicle. They were looking down at what seemed to be a luminous green tape which lay across the road and stretched off into the darkly mysterious grasslands on either side. As Nicklin approached the group he realised that the glowing strip was insubstantial. The surface of the road was giving off the green light, in a band about eight centimetres wide, but there was no evidence of any special pigment having been applied. It was as if the molecules of the rock-hard material had been agitated.

"That can't be a traffic marking." The speaker was a man whose name Nicklin had not yet memorised. "Not away out here, at the ass-end of nowhere."

"Specially as it goes all that way off the road," a tall woman said. The others in the group turned their heads from side to side, their eyes following the glowing strip until it faded into the distance.

"Perhaps it's a boundary . . . some kind of county line," put in Nibs Affleck. He had not been on a driving stint, but was among several people who had been resting and were now joining the company, holding coats around themselves to ward off the cold. Nicklin found himself scanning the dimly seen figures in search of Danea.

"That's not too likely, Nibs," the first speaker said. "Boundaries went out with the ark."

"Whatever it is, it has killed off the grass." The tall woman had switched on a flashlamp and was aiming it at the ground where the green strip angled away from the road. All vegetation rooted within the edges of the strip had turned white or pale gold, and was very obviously dead.

Nicklin conjured up an absurd picture of a little man pushing a sportsfield marker – one that was filled with powerful weed-killer instead of white paint – all the way around the interior of Orbitsville. A kind of Johnny Appleseed in reverse. Interested in having a closer look at the phenomenon, he stepped across the line and was startled to feel himself passing through a plane of spongy resistance. The effect was mild, rather like a momentary conflict of small magnets, but it produced an odd and slightly queasy sensation as it slid through his body. He moved back and forth several times, confirming that the intimate disturbance was real, and that it was limited to a plane which rose vertically from the glowing strip. Others noticed what he was doing and began similar experiments, some of them murmuring with surprise.

"Hey, Jim!" The tall woman with the flashlight – he had seen her with Danea and now remembered her name as Christine McGivern – was standing near him. She was beckoning for him to draw even closer, and as he did so he was aware that she was straddling the green line and slowly moving her hips from side to side.

"This is *fun*," she whispered. "You can feel it touching you up."

"It's an ill wind," Nicklin muttered, trying to match Christine's disconcerting smile. He looked away from her and was relieved to see Corey Montane approaching the group. Montane had wrapped himself in a striped raincloak and his black hair was tousled, but *neatly* so, like that of an actor portraying a man freshly roused from his bed. Several men moved towards him to explain what had been found, and Nicklin hastily joined them.

"Would someone kindly fetch a spade?" Montane said, after examining the green strip. A short-handled emergency spade was handed to him almost immediately. He took it and made to lift some earth which was crossed by the luminosity, but red-nosed Nibs Affleck took the implement from him, with gentle insistence, and began to dig at a furious rate. Spectators shuffled back as their feet were bombarded with flying dirt, and within seconds Affleck had created a sizable hole.

"Thank you, Nibs," Montane said. "I think that's enough."

Affleck, who apparently had been prepared to dig until he collapsed, reluctantly moved away from the excavation. Nicklin, still trying to recover his equilibrium after the little encounter with

Christine, was able to see into the hole and at once understood why Montane had wanted it dug.

The lime-green strip had not been broken by the digging. It now followed the precise contours of the excavation, glowing on the surface of the raw earth as though projected by a powerful optical device. *It's a cross-section through that weird rubbery field*, Nicklin thought. *An effect that shows at the ground-air interface. I wonder if the field goes right down to the Orbitsville shell.*

"This thing . . . this *manifestation* . . . must extend all the way down to the shell," Montane proclaimed without hesitation or signs of doubt, raising his voice for the benefit of individuals who were belatedly emerging from their campers to join the group. "My friends, this is a portent! We have been given yet another sign that Orbitsville is entering its final hour. The Devil's trap is closing!"

"Lord save us!" somebody cried out among the exclamations of alarm which arose from the assembly.

Montane seized on the emotional flux of the moment. "It is still within His power to do exactly that. Although the hour is perilously late, although we stand on the very brink of the abyss, God's mercy is infinite – and we may yet be saved. Let us bow our heads and pray to Him." Montane raised his hands, palms facing downwards, and those around him lowered their heads.

Nimble footwork, Corey, Nicklin thought, marvelling at the speed with which the preacher had reacted to and made use of the situation. *Any old portent in a storm!* While Montane was leading his followers in the improvised prayers, Nicklin renewed his search for Danea and was disappointed not to see her. The thought of Danea reminded him of her friend Christine, who was now standing chastely with the rest of the group. Suddenly he understood why he had been so taken aback by her conversational gambit, which had been somewhat indelicate to say the least of it. The conspiratorial whisper and the use of his first name had linked them together as a pair of freewheelers surrounded by prudes – but what had led her to that presumption about him, a man she had hardly even seen before?

The only explanation he could come up with was that Danea had been talking freely to Christine about matters which he regarded as private. Indeed, the word private came nowhere near to expressing his feelings – sacred would have been more appropriate. The notion of Danea and her friend giggling over confidences, especially if graphic sexual details were involved, brought a warm tingling to Nicklin's face.

Was it possible? *Was it possible?*

Standing there – in the complex patterns of light and darkness created by the enigmatic green-glowing strip, the ribbed Orbitsville sky, and the splashes of brilliance from vehicle headlamps – Nicklin felt totally alone, isolated from the group of strangers he had planned to espouse.

He turned away, walked slowly to his camper and climbed into the driving cabin. Sitting hunched over the wheel, he told himself he was thinking like a hypersensitive adolescent. It was all too easy for an introspective dreamer such as he to build fantasies based on nothing more than a misinterpreted word. All he needed was a little time alone with Danea. One smile from her, one sympathetic glance from those heavy-lidded eyes was all it would take to put everything in his universe to rights. But why had he seen so little of her since joining the mission? Why had she become so damned elusive?

A short time later the caravan was on the move again, and as Nicklin's vehicle crossed the lime-green strip he felt its magnetic pulse motor falter for just an instant. The power loss was so slight and so fleeting that only one attuned to such things by many years of experience would have noticed it.

Nicklin flicked his gaze over the dashboard instruments, frowning, then allowed his thoughts to drift back to problems which seemed infinitely more serious.

CHAPTER 8

Corey Montane was shivering with the cold by the time he got back to his own vehicle. When going out into the night he had put a raincape on over his pyjamas, expecting to be away from his bed for only a few minutes while the details of some mechanical problem were explained to him. He had not anticipated being shown new proof that the Devil was actively going about his evil work. The subsequent prayers for salvation had taken a considerable time, and during them the chill of the clear night air had seeped a long way into Montane's body. He felt as if his internal organs had grown cold and had slowed down in their various activities.

"Good night," he said to Gerl Kingsley, the hulking ex-farmer who was driving dead dog for him. "I'll see you when four o'clock comes round."

"Corey, why not let me handle the next shift as well?" Kingsley said, opening the camper's mid-section door for Montane. "You look real done out."

"Nice of you to say so!"

"I didn't mean to – " Kingsley slapped himself lightly on the forehead for lacking diplomacy. "What I meant to say was you're bound to be tired, and I'm as chirpy as a barrel of budgies. I could *easy* go on till eight or even tomorrow noon."

Montane smiled. "We all take our due turn."

"Yeah, but I won't sleep anyway. I got more energy than I know what to do with."

Looking up at the hugely indomitable man, Montane could easily accept the statement. It was one of his precepts that he did his share of all tasks, including the most menial, and it brought an ample reward in the form of devotion – such as Kingsley was showing at that moment – but he *was* tired and he had much to think about.

"Perhaps I could stand in for you sometime," he conceded reluctantly and in seconds Kingsley had bundled him, with a kind of respectful roughness, into the camper's warm interior. He locked the door, slipped out of his cape and steadied himself against the silver coffin as the vehicle began to move.

"I'm sorry about all this, Milly," he said, addressing his wife. "Satan never sleeps – so he's bound to disturb us during the night every now and then."

He tilted his head, waiting to see if Milly would reply, but there was no response from within the coffin and he went to his bed. Switching off the light, he made himself comfortable beneath the covers and turned his thoughts to the phenomenon of the glowing green line. His instinctive awareness of the Devil and all his moves told him the line was an evil manifestation, but it was hard to guess its exact purpose. It *had* to be an indication that the Orbitsville trap was closing, but what could be the function of a weak, spongy force field which produced green luminosity where earth and air met?

Montane craved to know how far the line extended around the shell. Were there others? Were they straight or curved, and did they form patterns? He could get some of the answers when the caravan reached the next town, now that new antennae were being run out into space to permit the re-establishment of radio and television communication between the portals. But having to wait a day was an annoyance, especially as the Evil One had chosen to increase the tempo of events.

Not for the first time, Montane found himself wishing he could understand why the transmission of signals on radio frequencies had always been impossible within the vast hollow sphere that was Orbitsville. The early explorers had noticed the effect within minutes of their arrival, but two centuries of subsequent research had failed to explain why the lower part of the electromagnetic spectrum was completely blanked out. Montane knew in his heart that it was more of the Evil One's scheming – perhaps intended to prevent Orbitsville's diverse inhabitants from forming a global society – but *why*? How, precisely, did the Devil benefit?

The question had troubled Montane for years, and it was the lack of any plausible answer which had discouraged him from bringing the subject into his preaching. It was not the only hidden card in the Devil's hand, and no doubt it would be played when the time was exactly right.

Besides, there were more immediate problems to be dealt with – including that of Jim Nicklin. Montane shifted uneasily in the bed, goaded by his conscience. Nicklin was a decent young man – intelligent yet naïve, complicated yet unworldly – and what was being done to him was an undoubted sin. Danea Farthing had hooked and landed him like a skilled angler bringing in a salmon, but the sin was not really hers. She was only Montane's agent, and he in turn was acting on behalf of God. These were dire times, and no individual sacrifice was too great if it helped bring about the salvation of the human race.

Montane's problem was that, after all the philosophical arguments had been advanced and all the profound words spoken, an innocent man had – pursuing the angling metaphor – to be gutted like a fish.

And he, Corey Montane, was the one who would ultimately have to face up to those puzzled blue eyes. What would he say to Nicklin? What justification could he give? The Lord has made me a fisher of men? I was only obeying orders?

Montane twisted again beneath the covers, searching for the elusive position of comfort which might enable him to slip away into impartial sleep. He could only hope that the essential softness he had identified in Nicklin would lead to the forthcoming ordeal being a brief one. Nicklin was not the type of man to become violent, even on realising that he had just been fleeced of everything he owned. In all probability he would, after a short confrontation, wander off back to Orangefield as a sadder and wiser man, and endeavour to pick up the threads of his old life. Montane punched his pillow, trying to beat it into submission.

"Why are you torturing yourself over this thing?" Milly's voice, reaching him from the interior of the coffin, was compassionate, brimming with sympathy. "You know very well that you had no choice in the matter."

Montane gazed in the direction of the oblong casket, the dull sheen of which was discernible even in the near-darkness. "Yes, but will Jim Nicklin see it like that?"

"Darling, you did what you had to do."

"It's just that I feel so *guilty*," Montane replied, taking a deep, quavering breath. "And what makes it far worse is knowing in advance that young Nicklin will be so easy to deal with and get rid of. I'd feel better if I had to face some hard case who'd raise hell and start throwing things around."

"If Jim Nicklin was a hard case his money would still be in his own bank – not yours."

"I know that, I know that!" Montane realised he was beginning to sound irritable. "I'm sorry, Milly – it's just that things are . . . We're going to have to move to Beachhead and stay there, you know. Life's been too much of a holiday for us – cruising around the countryside – and there just isn't enough money in that. Neither of us likes living in a big city. In fact, we *hate* it. Things won't be easy for us."

"God didn't say things would be easy." His wife's voice now contained a hint of admonition, of the corrective forcefulness he so badly needed. "You've never had the future of mankind riding on your shoulders before."

"I . . . I suppose you're right, Milly – as always. Thank you." Montane closed his eyes, and within a very short time had drifted away into peaceful estuaries of sleep.

CHAPTER 9

When Nicklin squeezed into his bunk, shortly after the changeover at four, he did so with no expectations of sleep. Even had he been in the right frame of mind the conditions in the camper would not have been conducive to proper rest. All his life he had been accustomed to a spacious and comfortable bed in a room all to himself. He had surrendered those prerequisites of civilised existence for the privilege of lying down with Danea, the two of them nested like spoons, and holding her in his arms the whole night through. The contrast between that deferred bliss and what he had to put up with in the meantime was almost too great to contemplate.

Henty, the man due to take over the driving, had done a lot of resentful mumbling while getting ready, as though Nicklin had been in charge of the rota and had marked him down for the worst shift out of personal spite. The six other men had been disturbed to varying degrees by Henty's griping, and were making restless sounds and movements as the vehicle got back on the road. Seen in the patchy dimness, the twinned rows of double-decker bunks more than ever resembled the interior of a submarine, and Nicklin began to feel claustrophobic. To make matters worse, Henty – isolated in the separate driving cabin up front – seemed to be working off his bad temper by steering with unnecessary roughness.

All things considered, Nicklin's prospects of sleep were very poor, but in a remarkably short time he had entered the world of the dream.

The setting was in sunlit open air, and featured a small rounded hill whose slopes had been fashioned into a beautiful alpine garden. It was obvious that a great deal of loving and painstaking work had been poured into the construction of the garden. The rocky banks, underpinning for shoals of blossoms, contrived to look natural while at the same time their symmetry betrayed the handiwork of a master architect. Paths of meticulously fitted stone wound their way around the hill, beneath small archways and past numerous sculpted benches.

Apart from Nicklin himself, there were two characters in the dream. One was his mother, who in reality had died when he was seven; the other was the terrifying figure of a fox who walked upright on his hind legs and was as tall as a man. The fox wore antique clothing – a shabby frocked coat, a winged collar and a greasy cravat secured by a horseshoe pin – and for some reason Mrs Nicklin was blind to the fact that he was not another human being.

She was laughing with him, treating him like a close member of the family. Nicklin was a small boy cowering behind his mother's skirts, appalled by her inability to notice the fox's pointed yellow teeth, his Disney-animal nose – like a shiny black olive standing upright on the end of his snout, and his red-brown coloration, the essence of all that was fox.

For his part, the fox was playing up to Mrs Nicklin. He was grinning, nudging, telling little jokes, and every now and again his red-veined eyes glanced appreciatively and knowingly at little Jim. *Isn't this the best laugh ever?* the eyes seemed to gloat. *Your mother doesn't know I'm a fox. And – best of all – she doesn't know I'm going to eat you up!*

Little Jim's fear increased as he heard the fox proposing that it should take him for a walk through the alpine garden. There were many secluded corners in the garden, places where a fox could kill and devour a small boy without being disturbed in its work. And his fear became pure terror when he heard his mother welcoming the suggestion because she needed time to go shopping.

"It's not a man – it's a *fox*," he screamed, clinging to her thighs. "Can't you see it's a *fox*?"

His mother and the fox laughed together at the childish absurdity. Saliva dripped from the beast's yellow teeth.

"Don't be such a silly boy," his mother said, thrusting him forward with an adult's irresistible force. "Go along with your nice uncle and have a lovely time."

Betrayed, weeping, doomed – Jim was propelled into the fox's grasp. Its hand was hard and strong, covered with hairs which looked and felt like strands from a brown doormat. Jim's mother was already turning away, uncaring, as the fox dragged him towards the hill. In just a few seconds the fox and he were alone in one of the quiet places, where stone walls hid them from the rest of the world.

The fox wasted no time. It turned on him, its mouth yawning widely enough to engulf his head, so widely that he could see the pink uvula doing a funny little dance at the entrance to its throat.

That was what gave the game away – one Disney touch too many!

Jim had seen the fox before, or creatures rather like it, in dozens of half-remembered cartoons, and he knew it was only a drawing on a sheet of transparent plastic. He knew it had no ability to hurt him – and with that abrupt realisation the dream became a lucid one, giving him control over the course of events. Suddenly he was safe, and had power, enormous power which he could *enjoy* – just like Alice in the last chapter of the Wonderland book.

Taking a deep breath he bellowed, "Who cares for you? You're nothing but a cartoon!"

The force of the shout sent the fox reeling backwards, his face comically aghast and his hair blown into receding red-brown points. Giggling with glee, little Jim turned and sprinted away along the stone path. He had taken only a few bounding steps when the solid-seeming pavement opened up in front of him, forming a gaping black pit. As Jim went helplessly over the edge and began the downward plunge he realised that the beautiful little hill, so plentifully encrusted with stone, was hollow.

And the things waiting for him inside it had no place in children's cartoons . . .

Nicklin opened his eyes wide and stared at the underside of the bunk above. His first thought was: *What the hell was all that about?* The dream had not exactly been a nightmare – it had been too preposterous to ram the icy dagger of terror all the way through his guts – but it had been a disturbing one nevertheless. He had little or no time for historic Freudian theory, yet he had an uncomfortable feeling that the odd dream had been laden with symbolism. And it was quite remarkable how, after more than three centuries, the

Disney style – his particular brand of anthropomorphism, which hinted at an underlying fear of all wild creatures – could still exercise such a powerful influence over the unconscious minds of children and adults alike.

It suddenly came to Nicklin that he was seeing the base of the bunk above in the meagre daylight which seeped through a tiny circular window. Furthermore, the camper had stopped moving and there were sounds of activity from outside. He put an eye to the window and saw that the caravan had come to a halt in what appeared to be a sports field. There was little in the way of facilities – just some forsaken goalposts, a scoreboard and a small pavilion. The roofs of a few dwellings could be seen above the somewhat scrawny hedge which marked the field's perimeter. In the distance the tops of several tall buildings projected up from layers of morning mist, slim pastel streaks against the sky. A star-like point of light glowed on one of them, trembling in the moist air, evidence that a photocast station was in operation.

Millennium City, Nicklin thought, sinking back on to his pillow as he identified the location. Where he came from the town was the butt of many jokes because of the discrepancy between its grand name and the red-grimed wasteland of open-cast bauxite mines, purification plants and railroad sidings. He was in no hurry to leave his bed for the privilege of seeing more of Millennium City or its inhabitants. Gentle snores from other bunks suggested to Nicklin that his new companions were of a like frame of mind.

He expected that they would all soon be rousted out to begin erecting the big marquee, but for the present he had the symbolism of the strange dream to think about. Why had a *fox* been part of the cast? Was it merely because of the menacing fox character in the half-remembered Disney version of *Pinocchio*? And what was the significance of that most implausible geographical feature – the hollow hill? Could it have represented the womb? Had it had something to do with his mother's presence? Nicklin had not dreamed of her in a long time, and it was strange that his unconscious mind had chosen to portray her as one who was prepared to hand him over to a monster. Monster . . . mons . . . mons veneris . . . *Montane*! Had Nicklin, in the dream, been handed over to and swallowed up by a small mountain – Montane? Had his mother, his *betraying* mother, represented Danea Farthing, whom he had only last night begun to suspect of . . . ?

The whirlwind of confusing questions and simplistic, amateurish associations abruptly collapsed in Nicklin's mind, deprived of its motive power by the aridity of the real world. It was an objective fact that Danea had been avoiding him ever since he had joined the mission; and there was no doubt at all that she had been talking too freely to the tall one with the flashlight – what was her name? – Christine. Why had he not sought Danea out yesterday and forced the issue? Why, in the name of the Gaseous Vertebrate, had he delayed so long before deciding to confront Danea and get everything straight between them?

Feeling cold and sick, impelled by an urge to learn and verify the worst, Nicklin got out of his bunk. Ignoring the sonic shower cubicle, he pulled on the clothes he had worn the previous day and went out into the morning sunlight. The first thing he noticed was the marquee spread out over a large area of grass, but no work was actually being done to erect it. A number of people were gathered near the expanse of lazily rippling material, some of them arguing with each other.

As Nicklin was stepping down from the camper, two men and two women detached themselves from the larger group and strode towards the sports field's entrance. They were carrying suitcases and had some extra items of clothing slung over shoulders or arms. The leader was Dee Smethurst, the plump archetypal cook, whose face bore an expression of outrage.

"It's *you* I feel sorry for, mister," she said to Nicklin as she passed by. "I don't hold anything against *you*."

Her companions nodded, their sun-hats bobbing, and they went on their determined way before Nicklin could ask what the cook had meant. The driver of a taxi which was waiting beyond the field's single gate got out of his vehicle to greet them. Nicklin heard one of the four say something about a railroad station, confirming that he had just witnessed a small desertion among Montane's followers.

Puzzled, he took his own sun-hat out of his pocket, spread it into a circle and jammed it on to his head before walking towards the larger group. He now felt keyed up, yet cool and balanced, ready for anything – the epitome of the new urbane Jim Nicklin who had been too big for Orangefield to hold. The state of mind lasted until he saw Danea Farthing, and not one second longer.

She was dressed in black again, but with a circular skirt instead of pants, and the sight of the lean-hipped figure in among all the ordinary faceless people did peculiar things to Nicklin's pulse. The sensation of all resolve draining out of him was almost a physical one, evocative of childhood dismay on finding hot urine running down his legs. *The Danea effect in reverse*, he thought. *What am I going to say to her?*

He began to force a cold smile as he drew close to Danea, but felt his mouth curve up at the corners – giving him his old happy hayseed expression – and he settled for a look of calm seriousness. For one craven instant he hoped she would evade him, but her eyes met his without hesitation.

"*There* you are, Jim," she said smiling warmly. "Where have you been hiding yourself?"

He responded with a nod, less confident than ever, wondering if he was about to make a fool of himself because of an attack of lover's paranoia. "Can we talk?"

The men and women standing within earshot did not actually nudge each other, but an unmistakable *frisson* went through them, and their reaction saddened Nicklin. It was all the confirmation he needed.

"What do you want to talk about?" Danea enquired, with more brightness than was strictly necessary.

"Not here." He glanced around the others, taking in their frozen grins and casually averted eyes.

"I'm supposed to be helping here, but . . . " Danea shrugged and fell in beside him as he began walking towards the goalposts in an empty quarter of the field. "Well, how did you sleep last night? I heard we stopped for something out in the middle of nowhere, but I slept right through it, myself. Did you get up?"

"Didn't Christine tell you I was there?"

"What do you . . . ? Why should she?"

The blue ribs of the Orbitsville sky pulsed at the edges of Nicklin's vision. "You and Christine tell each other everything, don't you?"

Danea wheeled on him immediately, all trace of heaviness gone from her eyes. "What the fuck is this all about?"

"Nothing," he said quietly. "I guess it's about nothing."

"Look, I'm sorry." Danea pressed the back of a hand to her forehead, slightly altering the tilt of her black stetson. "I don't usually talk like that – it's just that I've been so worried. I feel guilty about you, Jim. What happened between us . . . it was all a mistake."

Nicklin's throat closed up painfully, preventing him from speaking.

"I've no idea what could have happened to me," Danea went on. "I don't know what kind of impression I gave you."

Nicklin's memory stirred into action, restoring his power of speech. "You gave me the impression that we could live together in our own camper – but Montane told me that was never on the cards."

"Do you wear a recorder everywhere you go? Do you record every casual remark then pick it apart afterwards?"

"*What?*"

"Well let me tell you something for nothing, Mata Hari – I don't like being spied on by anybody, especially *you!*"

The sheer irrationality of the attack confounded Nicklin. "I think Mata Hari was a woman," he said automatically, and on the instant of speaking saw the verbal cudgel he had put into Danea's hands. *Will she use it? Please, O Gaseous Vertebrate, don't let her sink that low.* Time seemed to slow to a crawl, and he watched in fascination as surprise, gratification and triumph flitted across her features.

"Do you think," she said, savouring every word, "I didn't know that?"

And there we have it, he thought. *Danea, of all people, has no reason to doubt my sexuality – and yet something told her what to say. Something about me tells all of them what to say. When they want to put me down, or when the opposite is the case and they want to . . .* Nicklin blinked as his thoughts led him unerringly to the solution of another little mystery, one which had been quietly but persistently tugging at an obscure corner of his mind.

On the morning Danea had driven out to his place, the morning he had ceased being an ugly duckling and had become a swan, she had referred time and time again to his prowess with women. It had been a keynote of her conversation. *Tell me the truth, Jim – just how many women* have *you taken for a walk up here?* Words spoken in tones of rueful admiration. Words spoken by a woman acknowledging her helplessness while under the spell of a charming roué. Words that throughout his adult life he had craved to hear!

Danea had known *exactly* what to say, because something about him always gave the game away. On the evening of that first meeting on Orangefield common she had looked at him, and had done a perfect cold reading on him, and known at once how to go about robbing him of everything he owned. Not only that – she had known how to make him *enjoy* being plucked and trussed and handed over to Montane. In the space of only a few hours he had gone from duckling to swan to oven-ready turkey, and had loved every moment of it!

"You're good, Danea," he said simply. "You're very good at what you do."

As he was turning away he thought he saw, perhaps for one fraction of a second, a stricken look in Danea's eyes, but if he had learned one lesson it was not to trust his judgement in such matters. That look had probably been manufactured just for his benefit – showing a master's painstaking attention to the very last and finest detail. Danea had made it clear what she really thought of him – and it had turned out to be much the same as what all other women thought of him – and the only important thing now was deciding what to do with the rest of his life.

He could never again face up to all the good burghers of Orangefield, even though it would have been so nice to be in Zindee's wise-beyond-her-years company once more; and he had no intention of staying on in Millennium City. The best plan might be to head for the anonymity of Beachhead, but he had no more than ten orbs in his pocket, not even enough for the rail fare. A murmur of voices reached Nicklin from the group by the marquee and his face began to burn as he guessed Danea had rejoined her friends, possibly to regale them with new details of how she had handled the simpleton from Orangefield.

He had to get away from the scene of his mortification as quickly as he possibly could. For that he needed some money, and the only source he could think of was Corey Montane. It was hard to think of a greater humiliation than going cap in hand to the sanctimonious Fagin who had cleaned him out, but if Montane wanted to go on with his man-of-God impersonation he might be willing to part with a hundred or two. Especially if he were threatened with trouble!

Nicklin tried to imagine himself bursting into Montane's camper with an iron bar in his hand, and his misery intensified as he realised how preposterous the notion was. Violence simply was not in his nature, no matter how much he might be provoked, and he could not even envisage going to the police or the local news media. Montane had been very careful to establish that there was no connection between Nicklin's personal relationship with Danea Farthing and his donation to the mission's funds. The most Nicklin could hope to achieve by kicking up a public rumpus would be to multiply the number of people who saw him as a prize ass.

As he was walking towards Montane's vehicle it occurred to him that, considering all that had happened to him, he was reacting more like an automaton than a human being. He was being a bit too civilised and passive, even for Jim Nicklin, but there was a *strangeness* somewhere deep inside him – an ineffable psychic tremor which hinted at emotional earthquakes to come. It was advisable for him to make what practical arrangements he could while the blessed numbness persisted.

Finding the middle door of Montane's camper open, he went up the steps and into the vehicle without preamble. Montane was sitting on the side bench, cup of tea in hand, watching a small television set which he had placed on his wife's coffin. Even though it could not have been more than five or six kilometres to the local photocast station, the image of a newsman was poor, thanks to mist in the intervening air. The sound quality was reasonable, however, and Montane seemed totally absorbed by what was being said.

He raised his free hand in a mute hello to Nicklin, then pointed at a chair, inviting him to sit down. Feeling that he had already been placed at a tactical disadvantage, Nicklin reluctantly lowered himself into the seat. His knees were almost touching the coffin, and as he gazed at the silvery surface he found himself speculating about its contents. Had the body of Milly Montane been specially treated to prevent decomposition? Or was he sitting right up against a box full of . . . ? He aborted the thought with all possible speed and turned his attention to the newscast in which Montane was so engrossed.

". . . stressed that they could only make an educated guess at this stage, because radio links between all portals have not yet been fully re-established," the announcer was saying. "It does appear, however, that the mysterious green lines are a global phenomenon. They have been reported in the vicinity of more than twenty portal cities, and experts who have been extrapolating the figures think that the lines are roughly 950 kilometres apart, all the way around the Orbitsville equator.

"The mind boggles, doesn't it? Mine certainly does, but a good boggle has never done anybody any harm – that's what I always say.

"We'll bring you more on that story later, but now we are returning to our panel discussion on the economic effects of what some scientists are already referring to as the Big Jump. With the portal communities now effectively cut off from each other, many manufacturing centres are denied access to their markets. If the present situation continues, the greatest growth industry of all time is likely to be the construction of interportal spaceships.

"With us to talk about the problem is Rick Renard, who has scarcely been off the air in the last few days, because – as you are no doubt aware – he is the owner of the *Hawkshead*, the starship which vanished while disembarking at Portal 36. Mr Renard is already forming a consortium for the design and building of . . . " Image and voice faded together as Montane reached out and switched off the television.

"Good morning, Jim," he said. "Tea?"

Nicklin continued staring into the lifeless grey screen, hardly aware that the other man had spoken. Something uncanny had happened to him while he was listening to the photocast, something outside all his previous experience. At the mention of Renard's name there had been a *heaving* – that was the only word he could apply to the sensation – in the deepest levels of his consciousness . . . a leviathan had stirred briefly in some black prehistoric swamp of his mind . . .

Renard! The name threw off expanding circular echoes of itself. *Reynard! That means fox. But this fox doesn't want to eat small boys – he wants to build spaceships. The fox and the spaceship! It sounds like one of those cute pubs, and what has that got to do with . . . ?*

"Are you with me, Jim?" Montane said, giving him a quizzical look. "I'm offering you a cup of my best tea."

Nicklin made his eyes focus on Montane's face. "No tea for me, thanks – I need to talk to you."

"I'm always ready to listen." Montane went on very quickly, not giving Nicklin the chance to continue. "I was right about that green line we found last night. Remember I said it probably went all the way down to the shell? Well, according to the local news there are *hundreds* of the damned things – and they *do* go right down to the shell. I don't like it, Jim. This is the Devil's work. What did you want to talk about?"

Nicklin, still recovering his mental equilibrium, was not quite ready for the question. "I . . . I suppose I ought to congratulate you."

"Congratulate me?" Montane looked puzzled but very much at his ease. "On what?"

"On the neat and highly professional way you and one of your prostitutes stripped me of everything I owned." Nicklin was surprised to see the preacher's bright, penetrating eyes become cloudy and vague. He had not expected that much of a reaction from a professional.

"You're talking in riddles, son."

"I'm talking about the excellent job done on me by you and your prostitute."

Montane glanced uneasily at his wife's coffin. "We don't like that kind of talk in here."

"Oh, I'm *sorry!*" Nicklin said, unable to resist the kind of sarcasm he normally disdained. "Pardon me for not measuring up to your high standards of behaviour."

"I gather," Montane said stonily, "that something has gone wrong between you and Danea."

"You gather correctly."

Montane sighed and shook his head, the picture of a man saddened by news he had expected but had hoped against the odds not to hear. "I'm really sorry about that, Jim – and, naturally, I'll give you what counsel I can – but you must understand that my workers' interpersonal relationships have nothing to do with me. And I made it clear to you, right at the outset, that any donation you chose to – "

94

"There's no need for you to worry yourself about that side of things," Nicklin cut in. "I fully accept the consequences of my own stupidity, and all I want to do now is get far away from here as fast as I can. I presume you won't mind letting me have a couple of hundred, just to get me started."

Montane frowned. "I can't do that, Jim."

Nicklin's jaw tried to sag. "All I'm asking is the rail fare to Beachhead City, and a bit more for a room!"

"I'm sorry," Montane replied, "I just don't have that kind of money."

"I *know* you don't have that kind of money." Nicklin was hardly able to believe what was happening. "My 82,000 orbs – *that's* the kind of money you have."

Montane gave him a patient little smile. "You don't seem to understand, Jim. It is *God* who owns that money now. You gave it to *Him* – and I could no more think of taking some of it back than I could of taking a life."

"Beautiful," Nicklin said bitterly. "That's really beautiful, Corey. You and Danea make a great team."

Montane appeared not to notice the insult. "What I *could* do – in fact, I'd be neglecting my Christian duty if I didn't do it – is let you have something out of my own pocket. Out of the housekeeping. I only have about thirty orbs, but you're welcome to all of it."

Too fucking kind, Nicklin thought, watching in disbelief as Montane stood up, set his cup aside and took a reproduction lacquered tea caddy down from the shelf over his cooking area. He opened the box, brought out three ten-orb bills and – with the air of a monarch conferring a knighthood – handed them to Nicklin.

"I'll always remember you for this," Nicklin said as he stood up and shoved the photo-pulsing rectangles into his hip pocket. Abruptly turning his back on Montane, he ducked out through the camper's door and stepped down on to the trampled grass. The group by the marquee had grown quite a bit larger, and it seemed to him that every face in it was turned in his direction. They were all set to gawp at him while he went to retrieve his few belongings from his locker, and no doubt when he reappeared with them everybody in the mission would be assembled to watch his departure.

He hesitated, his face throbbing hotly in tune with his heartbeat, and for a moment he actually considered walking straight on out of the field and away from the whole sorry mess. It might be worth abandoning his meagre possessions if doing so spared him any extra embarrassment. The pounding in his chest intensified, causing him to feel a little nauseated and light in the head, and there came a real fear that for the first time in his life he could be about to faint. He fought to regulate his breathing, to use the yoga technique for inducing serenity, and it was while he was standing there in the intrusive light of the morning sun that he became aware of something strange.

Behind him – in the shaded solitude of the camper – Corey Montane was speaking to someone.

"I'm sorry, my dear," Montane was saying. "As you heard, that young man had got himself worked up into quite an emotional state. The only way I could get rid of him was to give him some of your housekeeping money, but I'll see to it that you don't go short. I promise you he won't disturb us again, so let's finish our tea in peace, and then perhaps we'll pray together for a few minutes. You'd like that, wouldn't you?"

Nicklin inhaled deeply, blinked at his surroundings as though seeing them for the first time, and began to smile.

A wearisome psychogenic burden was being lifted from his shoulders. He could feel mental fetters dissolving, chains falling away, prison doors opening . . . Metaphors abounded. The air he had drawn into his lungs retained all the pastel colours of dawn, and those colours were diffusing through his system, creating a nacreous glow, sparkling in his mind.

It's all a joke, he told himself. *Thank you, O Gaseous Vertebrate, for reminding me that everything is just one big joke. Conceits such as embarrassment and humiliation are no longer valid as far as I am concerned. I repudiate them! Montane has my money, and there's nothing much I can do about it, but he can no longer simply face me down. Nobody can do that any more – especially not some silly old coot who lugs his better half around in a tin box and chats to her over his corn flakes; especially not a bunch of heliumheads who believe the world is going to end next Tuesday . . .*

Remembering he had an attentive audience in the group who were supposed to be erecting the marquee, Nicklin raised one hand

and gave them a cheerful wave. His smile grew wider as he noted the uncertainty with which several of them returned the salute. He spun on the ball of his foot and went back into the camper. Montane, who had resumed his seat, looked up in some surprise – teacup in hand – and a look of priestly displeasure appeared on his face.

"Jim, I've been as generous to you as I possibly could," he said. "Is there any point in spinning this thing out?"

"I've been thinking the whole business over," Nicklin replied. "I've been thinking about what you said yesterday. You know – about how the mission could make good use of all my technical skills and that kind of stuff. What I've been thinking is that it's my Christian duty to stay on here with you . . . and Danea . . . and the rest of the gang."

Nicklin took the three ten-orb notes out of his pocket and, with a meaningful wink, placed them on top of the silver coffin.

"After all," he added, maintaining his cheerful smile, "I still have so much to give . . ."

CHAPTER 10

As soon as possible after the transit entered Beachhead City's central area Nicklin got out on to the crowded footpath. He knew by the route diagram that he was still three stages short of his actual destination – which was Garamond Park – but this was his first visit to Beachhead and he wanted to get the feel of the place, something which could best be done on foot. He fanned his sun-hat into a circle, placed it squarely on his head and began to walk.

The first thing he noticed, apart from the seemingly endless throng, was that the environment was much cleaner than he had expected. The shops and small offices on each side of the street looked fresh and well maintained, and the pavement was remarkably free of litter considering the number of people at large. Nicklin allowed himself a wry smile. As a dweller in a small town he had shared the common belief that all big cities were filthy, garbage-strewn places. Another Orangefield illusion which did not travel well!

After walking for only a few minutes he was also struck by the degree of specialisation that was possible for various retail outlets. There were stores which sold nothing but garden tools, or picture frames, or equipment for a single sport such as archery or subaquatics. That fact alone gave Nicklin the sense of being in a metropolis where the consumer population ran into millions. Another exotic note, to him, was the way in which prices were prefixed by the letter M, standing for monits or monetary units. Metagov had long ago decreed that a global economy – one which embraced every one of the cities strung out along Orbitsville's billion-kilometre equatorial band – could only operate on the basis of a universal currency which had a fixed value at all portals. The monit was therefore the city dwellers' exchange medium, while rural communities used the more homely orb, whose value fluctuated in accordance with local conditions. Notices displayed in the windows of some of the shops he passed informed Nicklin that Portal One hinterland orbs were worth 83.23 per cent of a monit, but as he had only a few bills in his pocket the pecuniary disadvantage meant little to him.

Attracted by the aromatic coolness wafting out of a bar, he went inside to quench his growing thirst with a glass of beer. The dim interior was devoid of clientele at that time of the morning. He went to the counter, behind which a young man and a woman were engrossed in a game of stacks, a simplified form of 3D chess. The man's gaze flicked towards Nicklin for an instant, but otherwise the pair did not acknowledge his presence.

It was a situation in which the old Jim Nicklin would have waited timidly for many minutes, scarcely daring to clear his throat in a bid for attention, but the new liberated Jim Nicklin was not so easily put off.

"Take a good look at me," he said in a loud voice. "I am what's known as a customer. You two are what's known as barkeeps, and – this may come as a great surprise to you – your function in this establishment is to serve customers with any drink they ask for, which in my case happens to be a beer."

The young man looked up from the game, dull-eyed, still digesting what Nicklin had said. "A beer?"

Nicklin nodded. "Yes, you must have heard of beer – it's that yellow frothy stuff that comes out of those pumps. Or perhaps you missed the relevant lecture at Barkeep Academy."

The man's brow wrinkled and he turned for enlightenment to his companion, who appeared to be the older and brighter of the pair. Lips compressed with resentment, she drew a beer and clumped it down in front of Nicklin. The head rocked and some of it slopped over the rim of the glass.

"Eighty cents," she said in a cold voice.

As Nicklin was setting a one-orb note on the counter he remembered with malicious satisfaction that it was worth only three cents above the price of the drink. "Keep the change," he said grandly. "Buy yourself something extra nice."

Feeling well pleased with himself, he carried his glass to the most distant corner of the room and sat at a table. It had taken the mission ten days to reach Beachhead, with stops at two intervening towns, and he had been pleasantly surprised when Montane had announced a short break. The arrival of the caravan at a small town usually generated enough interest to guarantee an audience, but it had scarcely been noticed by the incurious citizens of Beachhead, and Montane needed some time in which to advertise his presence.

Grateful for the chance to be his own master for a while, Nicklin had grabbed his twenty-orb allowance – quaintly described by Montane as a stipend – and had bolted into the city. Visiting the famous Portal One to view the stars for the first time was at the top of his list of priorities, but he also had to have a period of quiet contemplation. The cool, deserted bar was ideal for that purpose, and as he sipped his beer – freed of the continuous pressure of other personalities – he could feel himself beginning to relax. So much had happened in such a short time that he felt rather like a curio collector who had acquired many pieces on a single buying trip and now desperately wanted a lull in which to study and catalogue them.

There was Danea Farthing, for instance – one of the most curious curios of the lot . . .

Nicklin's mouth quirked into its U-shaped smile as in his mind he went over the first encounter with her after his road-to-Damascus brainstorm outside Montane's camper.

He strolled towards the group by the marquee, enjoying being the focus of their attention, and Danea – as though sensing some vital change in him – drew closer to her tall friend, Christine McGivern. He gave Christine an amiable and salacious wink, then addressed himself to Danea.

"I'm sorry about getting a bit prickly a while ago," he said. "You see, I never paid so much to get laid before, and I was sort of expecting – for that kind of money – to get a few repeat peformances."

Christine gave a delighted gasp, but the colour drained from Danea's face.

"I see now that it wouldn't be good business for you to issue season tickets – not when you're humping for the Lord," Nicklin went on. "But I would like some more. Nothing too fancy, you understand – just straight stuff. How much would you charge a regular customer?"

Danea's mouth opened silently several times, then she pushed her way through the circle of listeners and ran off in the direction of her camper.

"Would a hundred orbs a shot be all right?" Nicklin called after her. "I don't mind saving up my stipend." Putting on a look of honest puzzlement, he faced his audience, most of whom were gazing at him with shock or growing resentment. "Is Danea upset about something? I wonder what could have upset her. I hope it wasn't something I said."

"You shouldn't ought've talked to Danea like that," Nibs Affleck muttered. His blue-red dipso's nose was gleaming with sweat, and he appeared to be full of righteous anger, the most dangerous kind.

"Really?" Nicklin enquired mildly. "What's so awful about having a little business discussion?"

Affleck moved towards him, his breastbone thrusting forward like the prow of a boat, but those next to him grabbed his arms and pulled him back. With a reproachful glance at Nicklin, he shrugged off his restraints, walked to the flat expanse of the marquee and began tugging on the guy ropes. The rest of the erection crew eagerly joined in the work, and in a few seconds Nicklin found himself alone with Christine.

"Well, hello," she said warmly, with a look that was both amused and speculative.

He met her gaze directly. "Are you doing anything special tonight?"

"I don't know – how special can you make it?"

"We'll get away from here for an hour or two and have a few drinks," he said. "Then I'll show you my prospectus."

The incident had been a definite high point in his brand-new life, Nicklin decided, marred only by the odd way in which Danea had caved in so easily. Corey Montane had spoken to him about it afterwards, trying to make the point that the mission observed certain standards of propriety, but in spite of much frowning and piercing with the eyes he had appeared ineffectual. That was because his position was basically untenable – like that of someone who was trying to run a genteel brothel and had no contingency plans for dealing with the unpleasant customers who were bound to show up now and again. What he should have done was to employ a couple of his largest disciples to work Nicklin over with iron bars and dump him in a convenient alley. But Montane, having branched out into a line of business for which he had no vocation, was caught in a trap of his own making.

Now that Nicklin was considering the matter, he could see that Montane had not even been much shakes in his former role as a simple roving evangelist. Lacking the personal flair for attracting large sums of money, he had compounded his problem by surrounding himself with a bunch of society's drop-outs, most of whom were liabilities rather than assets. About the only thing they had in common was the belief that Orbitsville was the Devil's lobster pot, and that Montane was going to get them out of it and lead them to a new Eden.

Nicklin smiled again as he toyed with the notion. It was his ingrained scepticism which had created a barrier between him and the other members of the mission in the first place. Quite a few of them, Christine being a good example, were only vaguely religious in their outlook, but their unshakable faith in Montane's word tended to distance them from unbelievers. The barrier had rapidly solidified itself into a rampart after Nicklin had adopted his new persona – or had it adopted him? – but he had no complaints on that score. He had never been accepted by society in general; now the non-acceptance was under his own terms, and that was a much better arrangement.

Suddenly impatient to get on with the business of the day, he finished his beer and walked towards the door. "I'm leaving you now," he called out to the couple behind the bar, giving them a genial wave. The venomous look it drew from the woman gladdened his heart as he went out to join the crowds in the street.

Although he was seeing Garamond Park in person for the first time, the place had an air of familiarity to Nicklin. The wandering groups of sightseers, the vivid botanical displays, the trees which partially screened the lustrous city buildings – television had turned all of these into visual clichés. Nevertheless, Nicklin felt a pang of excitement as he came in view of the portal itself.

It registered on the eye as a circular black lake, about a kilometre in diameter, which was surrounded by sloping lime-green lawns. Clustered on its nearer edge were low mounds of masonry which were all that remained of fortifications built by the enigmatic Primers, who had dominated Orbitsville many thousands of years before mankind's arrival. At the far side of the aperture were the passenger buildings and warehouses of the space terminal. In the distance they still looked fully functional, even though the great starship docking cradles – which should have projected into the void beneath them – had been conjured out of existence.

The single new element in the scene was a group of mobile laboratories at the eastern side of the portal, close to the old Metagov observation post. They had been cordoned off from the public and the immediate area was a profusion of cables, crates, trolleys and gantries. Metal frameworks were clamped on the rim of the aperture, their lower halves extending down into the black, making it easy for spacesuited technicians to force their way in and out through the diaphragm field which retained Orbitsville's air.

Something really has *happened on the Outside*, Nicklin thought, *otherwise there wouldn't be all this fuss.*

The realisation was accompanied by the special feeling of wonderment which comes when a concept which has been held in intellectual probation is finally accepted. Now totally beguiled by the prospect of actually *seeing* the stars, the alien stars which were the subject of so much controversy, he walked towards the night-black portal. Picking his way among family groups who were having picnic snacks on the grass, he reached the place where the path skirting the portal broadened into a small semicircular plaza.

At its focus, standing on the very rim of space, was the famous Garamond statue. Although it was the most over-publicised object in the globe, he paused before the heroic bronze which depicted a man clad in a vacuum suit of a design which had been in service two centuries earlier. The spaceman, helmet in one hand, was shading his eyes from the sun's vertical rays with his free hand while he scanned the horizon. On the statue's granite base was a plaque inscribed with three words:

VANCE GARAMOND, EXPLORER

Nicklin flinched as a wash of coloured light flooded into his eyes. It was accompanied by the sound of a gentle sexless voice, and he realised that a multi-lingual information beam projected from the statue's plinth had centred itself on his face. Scarcely without delay, a computer had – by interpreting his optical response to subliminal signals – deduced that English was his first language.

. . . *of a large fleet of exploration ships owned and operated by Starflight Incorporated, the historic company which at that time had a monopoly of space travel*, the voice murmured with the disturbing intimacy of precisely beamed sound. *The* Bissendorf *was under the command of Captain* . . .

Images of a triple-hulled starship, as seen from space, had begun to fill Nicklin's vision, but he moved away from the statue and broke the beam contact. He had no need of a potted refresher course in Orbitsville's early history, especially at this particular moment, when he had only to take a few paces to see the universe spread out at his feet. Aware of feeling like a child about to unwrap a long-awaited gift, he moved away from the plaza and the immobilised tourists with their rapt expressions and blindly gazing eyes. Others in brightly coloured holiday clothing were leaning on the low balustrade which rimmed the portal, strung out like birds on a line. He walked past them to reach an uncrowded section, then placed his elbows on the rail and looked down at the stars.

His initial impression was that something had gone wrong. The blackness below him seemed quite unrelieved at first, and it was only when his eyes began to adjust that he was able to discern a sprinkling of faint-glowing specks. Disappointed, feeling that he had somehow been cheated, he glanced at the other spectators. They were staring into the portal with every appearance of being fascinated. Some were pointing out items of special interest to companions or children. *Perhaps it's all in the way you focus your eyes*, he thought. *After all, some people can't adjust to the old stereo viewers, and others can never see fine rain.*

He looked down again, blinking, trying to perform unwonted tricks with his optical ·muscles, but no luminous splendours emerged from the blackness. The universe continued to register on his vision as nothing more than a meagre scattering of dim points of light. He raised his eyes a little and tried looking further afield, but towards the centre of the portal the timid stars were completely invisible, hidden by the mirages which shimmered on the surface of the diaphragm field.

He turned away from the rail and walked slowly along the perimeter path, feeling slightly depressed and lost for something to do. At intervals along the path there were observation booths with hoods which curved down into the portal. He guessed that inside one of them, shielded from the brilliance of the sun, it would be possible to get a much better view of the cosmic environment, but there were long lines of would-be spectators waiting at all the booths. In any case, all he could expect to see was brighter specks of light and more of them. It hardly seemed worth the trouble.

I must admit that you really had me going for a while, O Gaseous Vertebrate, he thought ruefully. *But now that I've peeped at the universe I do believe that it, too, is all part of the Big Joke. And what next? Why, I think the most sensible thing to do right now would be to bugger off somewhere and have another beer . . .*

By late afternoon Nicklin was beginning to tire of exploring Beachhead City on foot. The beneficial effect of the eight or so glasses of beer he had consumed during his wanderings was wearing off, giving way to a drowsy apathy. He had never expected to develop any attachment for his cramped new sleeping quarters, but now he yearned to squeeze himself into the bunk bed and simply lose consciousness.

Drawing on his sketchy knowledge of the city centre, he headed in a direction he believed would let him intercept the transit to Cinnamon Brow, where the mission was stationed. He was walking past a window display of 3D television sets when the row of solid images abruptly changed. In place of graphs showing some kind of production figures there appeared the head and shoulders of a pink-faced, well-padded man who was giving the world a confident smile. A slight prominence of his teeth seemed to add aggressiveness to his expression.

I know that face, Nicklin thought, his memory stirring. *The spaceship man . . . Rick Renard . . . Renard . . . Reynard!*

Nicklin's stride faltered as into his mind there flashed the likeness of the Fox from Disney's *Pinocchio* – toothy, slavering, menacing, nose like a shiny black olive perched on the end of his snout. The dream! That damned dream with the fox in man's clothing and the garden which covered a hollow hill. What had it to do with spaceships? Nicklin experienced a coolness along his spine as the leviathan heaved once more in the black swamps of his subconscious. For one pounding instant he seemed on the verge of understanding the whole bizarre scenario, then there came the maddening sensation which accompanies the escape of elusive memories, the sense of a door slamming in the mind just as the grinning quarry slips through to the other side.

Irritated by the incident and hoping he was not going to become obsessive about it, Nicklin went on his way, growing more tired with every step.

Darkness had slid across the world by the time he got back to the mission, and although he was still weary he now wanted something to eat before bed. He had gone all day without food, mainly because his miserly allowance would not have covered the cost of a decent meal.

The site was a vacant section in the kind of area where low-cost housing struggled for territorial control against light engineering units and anonymous storage buildings. How Montane selected such places and got authorisation to use them was something Nicklin had yet to learn, and he cursed the general lack of amenities as he stumbled across the rutted ground with little more than the luminosity from the ribbed sky to guide him. Why had Montane never learned that it paid to think big? Or that money attracts money? The mission should have taken over the biggest and most prestigious stadium in the city, and made a show of installing its workers in the best hotels. That way – quite apart from matters of high finance – Nicklin could have had a first-class meal before retiring to bed, instead of the uninspiring stodge served up by Carlos Kempson, the so-called cook who had replaced Dee Smethurst.

When he reached the marquee and its retinue of vehicles he discovered that Kempson's trailer – which had been dubbed the chuck-up wagon – was locked. Mildly annoyed, he glanced about him and became aware that someone was speaking inside the marquee, although its interior lighting was not switched on. He walked to the entrance, looked inside and discovered that Montane was quietly addressing a group of his followers. They were sitting in the front two rows of one section, illuminated only by a single portable lamp. Montane had not gone up on the stage, but was standing on the flattened grass just in front of his audience. To Nicklin the scene looked oddly furtive, reminiscent of a meeting of early Christians in pagan Rome.

". . . much more serious than I thought it was," Montane was saying. He paused as Nicklin entered the marquee, and some of his listeners looked around to see what had caused the interruption. A few made noises which indicated that they regarded Nicklin's presence as an intrusion, but Montane silenced them with a damping movement of his hands.

"Come and join us, Jim," he said. "This is a ways-and-means session, and God knows we need all the fresh ideas we can get, regardless of the source."

Choosing not to be offended by the last words of the sentence, Nicklin – his curiosity aroused – advanced along the left aisle. As he neared the group he saw that Danea Farthing was sitting in the second row. He sidled into the third row, sat down directly behind her and blew gently on the back of her neck.

"Hello, darling," he whispered. "I got back from town as soon as I could – I hope you didn't miss me too much."

Her only response was to hunch her shoulders and lean forward to distance herself from him. Smiling with malicious satisfaction, Nicklin made himself at ease and directed his gaze towards Montane.

"For the benefit of anyone who has come in late," Montane went on, a certain dryness in his voice showing that he wanted Nicklin's full attention, "we are discussing an extremely serious new setback in our plans for the future.

"As you all know, eleven or twelve days ago – when this globe we inhabit made what people have begun to refer to as the Big Jump – Orbitsville lost contact with *everything* that had previously existed outside the shell. That included all the interstellar ships which were either approaching Orbitsville or were already docked outside all the portals.

"At the time, I saw no reason to be concerned over the disappearance, because it had never been my intention to buy a fully operative vessel. Even a ship nearing the end of its certification would have cost something in the region of two million monits – a price which was far outside our limited resources. I should say at this point that none of you is to blame for our not having built up the necessary funds. You have all worked hard, and the fault lies entirely in the way I directed your efforts."

Corey, old son, them is the truest words you ever spoke, Nicklin thought, but a murmur of disagreement arose from the audience. Montane – a homely figure in his short-sleeved tan shirt and off-the-peg slacks – swallowed visibly and nodded in gratification. Nicklin, realising the man was under a considerable degree of stress, began to sense that what he was hearing was no ordinary pep talk.

"Some time ago I chose what seemed a reasonable alternative, under the circumstances," Montane continued. "I contacted a leading repair yard, right here in Beachhead, and took an option on an obsolescent Type 93 passenger ship. Apparently its owners had put it into land-dock for a major overhaul, but had gone out of business before the work was completed.

"It was not the ideal ship for our needs, but the asking price was only three-quarters of a million, plus approximately another 200,000 for completing the refurbishment. We haven't got all the money yet, but I had hopes of reaching the target before next winter."

All you needed was a few more heliumheads like me. Nicklin shifted impatiently in his chair. *So what happened next?*

"But I have to report to you that today when I contacted the brokers concerned – Mather and Czubek – I was informed that my contract had been cancelled. It seems that I was a few days late with one of my interim payments, and that was all the excuse they needed. In normal circumstances a slight delay with an instalment would have been neither here nor there, but ever since the Big Jump circumstances have been very far from normal.

"It turns out that a huge consortium has been formed with the object of re-establishing interportal trade in the shortest possible time. The members of this consortium are buying up all available spacecraft – interstellar ships included – and, as far as I can determine, money is no object with them. We are in a sellers' market, I was told today, and the laws of supply and demand have pushed the price of *our* ship up to more than three million monits.

"There you have it, my friends." Montane's voice, which up to that point had been well under his control, hoarsened into something like a sob. "I . . . I don't know what to do next. The Devil is laughing at us tonight . . . and I simply don't know what to do next."

A man in the front row spoke up. "You can't blame yourself, Corey – for three million they'd have found *some* way to break the contract."

"Yes, but on top of everything else I've lost the deposit I put down."

"How much was it?"

Montane gave a wan smile. "The deposit was a hundred big ones."

Nicklin noticed the atypical use of slang, albeit ancient slang, and knew that Montane was trying to be casual, as a way of dealing with a desperate sense of guilt. There was a general gasp of dismay at the news of the loss, but Nicklin had turned his thoughts to the central issue – was Montane about to abandon his pathetic attempt to become a new Saviour?

Unexpectedly, he found little to savour in the idea. He expected to quit the mission some time in the nearish future and find a job with decent pay and prospects, but he still despised Montane and Danea, and craved a chance to revenge himself on them. What had just happened to Montane was clearly a major disaster, but it had not been personally and visibly inflicted by Nicklin. Therefore it did not count for much in the revenge stakes.

As for Danea – he had devised a special super-duper all-singing, all-dancing scheme of vengeance for her, one which would bring him complete satisfaction in every sense of the word. The plan was to amass a good sum of money – the how of it was not clear to him yet – but he wanted so much cash that neither she nor her bumbling Svengali would in all conscience (great word!) be able to refuse it on behalf of the Lord. She would be obliged to prostitute herself for him again, and when that happened he would make use of that splendid body as it had never been made use of before. If she was going to play the role of temple prostitute, priestess-whore, he was going to be the most ardent worshipper in the land. It was a consummation devoutly to be wished, and when the happy day came he was going to fuck her and humiliate her and fuck her again and make her sorry she had ever . . .

Hold on! he told himself in near-panic as fury geysered through him. *You've got to play it cool. Icy cold, in fact. They won't hate you properly unless you are seen to be chilly and emotionless, inhuman and implacable . . .*

In the front row the electrician Petra Davies raised her hand to ask a question. "Corey, could we not appeal directly to the boss men in this consortium? When they hear that we are a religious organisation – "

"That's right," a man cut in. "Or maybe we could just rent the ship from them for a while. After all, we only want to make one trip in it – then they could have it back."

Montane shook his head. "It's a good idea, but I very much doubt that these people would be in sympathy with our objectives. In fact, I'm *sure* they wouldn't. The head of the consortium is a man called Rick Renard . . ."

The remainder of the sentence was lost to Nicklin. He was already in a mental turmoil when the mention of Renard caused a veritable explosion in the depths of his subconscious, a psychic detonation which hurled a shrapnel of tumbling memory fragments up into the forefront of his mind. Renard . . . Reynard! He had had an uncle by the name of Reynard. Not an uncle – Reynard had been his mother's uncle. A great-uncle. As a small child he had been deeply afraid of his great-uncle Reynard, because his mother had a habit of referring to him as a wily old fox, and little Jimmy Nicklin had been convinced that Reynard really had the ability to turn himself into a fox when nobody else was around. Jimmy knew in his heart that if he were ever left on his own with great-uncle Reynard the dreadful transformation would take place, and that Reynard the Fox would eat him all up. Luckily, great-uncle Reynard was a rare visitor to the Nicklin home, because his job as a land surveyor took him to distant places. And it was from one of those remote locations that he had sent little Jimmy a certain picture postcard . . .

"Corey, I've got some interesting news for you," Nicklin called out, his heart pounding as he rose to his feet. "I know where there's a spaceship – a spaceship you can have for next to nothing!"

CHAPTER 11

"All right, Jim – why all the secrecy?" Montane said. "I don't like the idea of keeping all the others in the dark, not at this sad stage of our enterprise."

The door of his camper was closed, the toffee-shaded lamp was creating a mellow glow, and the tea requisites were laid out on the ready-made table formed by Milly Montane's coffin. The two men were sitting on the side bench, their knees almost touching, and Nicklin – his tiredness having completely vanished – was luxuriating in the atmosphere of seclusion and comparative comfort.

"We have to talk about my fee," he said, "and I felt it would be better if we did that in private."

"Fee? You expect a fee?"

Nicklin smiled. "Of course! Nothing in this life comes free, Corey – you should have learned that by this time."

Montane studied his face. "Do you want your money back?"

"Possibly. I'm not sure yet. I might be prepared to go on treating it as an investment in Montane Enterprises Inc."

"You seem to be enjoying yourself," Montane said, pouring out two cups of tea.

"I'm having the time of my life," Nicklin assured him.

"I'm glad *somebody's* having a good time. Very well, Jim – tell me what you want. Let's hear it."

Nicklin sipped from his cup before speaking, deliberately prolonging the moment. "Leaving the question of my money to one side for the present, I want a new job. No more driving in the middle of the night, no more clearing of thistles. I think the title of Executive Vice-President might suit me."

"A grand title wouldn't have any meaning around here," Montane said with a thin smile.

"It would for *me*. And in keeping with my new status I would expect my stipend to be increased. In fact, I expect unlimited drawing facilities – although naturally I wouldn't abuse the privilege. My needs are modest."

"Go on," Montane said, still with his bitter smile.

"And I want a camper all to myself." Nicklin made a show of delicately inhaling the aromatic vapour from his tea. "When I say I want it all to myself, I'm referring to the living space. There would, of course, be drivers provided for my exclusive use. And when we get to our permanent headquarters I want really good hotel accommodation."

"I'm beginning to enjoy myself too – just taking in your performance," Montane said. "You still haven't told me where this mythical spaceship is."

"I'm coming to that," Nicklin replied, his pulse increasing in speed and power. "There's just one more thing."

"And that is . . . ?"

"Danea Farthing," Nicklin said casually. "I want Danea Farthing."

Montane's smile vanished and he abruptly set his cup down, slopping tea into the saucer. "Get out of here, Jim – and never come back. Go on! Get out right now!"

Nicklin settled himself more comfortably on the bench. "A *spaceship*, Corey. A guaranteed way of getting out of Orbitsville before the trap closes. An open ticket to New Eden. God has entrusted you with the task of leading His children to safety, and He has given you licence to employ any means within your power. You explained all that stuff to me not so long ago, sitting right here on this bench, the day you were telling me how I had been well and truly shafted. Surely you can't have forgotten so soon?"

"You are the filthiest . . . " Montane closed his eyes, his face the colour of tallow. "Danea Farthing is a human being."

"I should hope so," Nicklin said with a grin. "There's nothing kinky about me."

"Spare me your diseased humour. I repeat, Danea is a human being."

"She was for sale then," Nicklin said in a voice from which all traces of humour had fled. "So she ought to be for sale now. Have a quiet word with her, there's a good chap."

Still with his eyes shut, Montane clenched his hands and sat without speaking for ten or more seconds, then – unexpectedly – he relaxed and raised his eyelids. His gaze was mild and unperturbed once more.

"I was praying," he explained. "I was communing with the Lord."

"Did He commune back at you?"

"He reminded me that I have only your word for it about this ship. It may no longer exist, for all I know, or it may *never* have existed. He counselled me to stay my anger."

Nicklin nodded thoughtfully. "Verily, He hath counselled you well. Hey, that sort of lingo must be catching!"

"So how about it, Jim?" Montane replied, no longer allowing himself to be baited.

"How about my fee?"

"I think I have ceased to believe that you can deliver a ship, but I confess to being curious about whatever kind of story you have dreamed up." Montane was now speaking in his customary rectorial manner, apparently satisfied that he had gained the advantage in what had become a verbal duel. "Therefore, I have few misgivings in agreeing to your terms."

"Wise man," Nicklin said.

"I'm expecting this to be good, Jim." Montane's expression was calm as he retrieved his cup and removed some drips from the bottom of it with his fingers. "So go ahead and astonish me – where *is* this spaceship that can be obtained for next to nothing?"

Nettled by Montane's change of attitude, Nicklin ignored an inner voice which warned him that he might be rushing ahead too fast. "It's buried near a small town within a few thousand kilometres of Beachhead."

"Buried!" Montane guffawed in disbelief. "Are you trying to tell me that somebody hauled an interstellar ship thousands of kilometres into the hinterland . . . and then *buried* it?"

"Well, he didn't dig a hole in the ground and drop it in there. He covered it with tonnes of earth and rocks."

"Why?"

"It was intended to be a memorial," Nicklin said, wondering how he had got into a defensive posture. "Something like a mausoleum. As I remember it, there was a rich man with a young wife who wanted to be a space flier. He bought her a ship of her very own and she promptly got herself killed in it in some kind of freak accident. So he paid to have the ship transported to his home estate and he made it into a tomb for her. He decided that it didn't look right, however, and I can't say I blame him – a space-going ship *would* look a bit odd sitting in anybody's back yard. Luckily, his hobby was gardening, so he had the ship landscaped – I suppose that's the best way to put it – and, as far as I know, he pottered around it quite happily for the rest of his natural.

"A touching little story, don't you think?"

"Obviously you think it's very funny."

Montane's gaze flickered towards his wife's coffin as he spoke, and Nicklin experienced a pang of happiness as the significance of the involuntary glance dawned on him. He had been slightly worried about how Montane might react to the bizarre tale of a millionaire's folly, but he had completely overlooked the parallel in the two men's lives. Blind chance, otherwise known as the Gaseous Vertebrate, had rendered Montane soft, receptive and vulnerable. *Bless you, Corey*, he thought, *I had forgotten that anybody who lugs his old lady around in a tin box would be inclined to sympathise with the notion of a metal Taj Mahal.*

"I don't think it's the slightest bit funny," he said in overly solemn tones. "It's just that I tend to hide my emotions under a veneer of flippancy." He was rewarded by a momentary flash of loathing in Montane's eyes, a signal that the preacher's defences had again been penetrated.

"What is this man's name?" Montane said.

"I can't remember."

"Where is the spaceship?"

"I can't quite remember that, either," Nicklin replied. "All I can say right now is that it's near a town in the P1 region."

Montane sniffed. "You can't remember much, can you? How did you get this story into your head in the first place?"

"When I was a kid I had a great-uncle, name of Reynard Nicklin, who travelled a lot because he was a surveyor or a cartographer or something like that. He sent me a holocard of the tomb once, and promised to take me there some day. Very pretty and colourful it was – an ornamental garden completely covering this little hill – but I guess I would have forgotten all about it if it hadn't been for the weird background note. That must have made quite an impression on me, because I've had spooky subterranean rumblings about it all day. And tonight at the meeting . . . suddenly . . . there it was!"

"Just a minute," Montane said, frowning, "you got the holocard when you were a *child?* This story about creating a mausoleum . . . How long ago did it all happen?"

Nicklin shrugged. "Fifty, sixty years ago . . . perhaps even a hundred . . . Who knows?"

"You've been wasting my time!" Montane exhaled forcibly, showing exasperation, and his voice hardened. "I sat here and endured your blasphemies and obscenities, and your sheer – "

"Take it easy," Nicklin cut in. "What's the matter?"

"Rust! That's what's the matter – there'll be nothing left of your damned ship by this time."

Nicklin smiled his happy hayseed smile, keeping his mouth in its cheerful U-shape until Montane took heed of his expression and gave him a questioning look.

"They were still constructing spaceships out of the old electronsated alloys in those days," Nicklin said soothingly. "That was before the Earth–Orbitsville trade petered out and the shipyards had to cut back on costs. No, Corey, there won't be much rust or any other kind of corrosion for you to worry your head about. At least, not in the pressure hull, the internal structure and the major components. There might be some problems with all the minor bits and pieces, but even there . . .

"I mean, if *you* decided to use a spaceship as a ready-made casket you'd make certain the whole thing was properly sealed up, wouldn't you? You'd hardly want your nearest and dearest to get mildew. And you definitely wouldn't want bugs crawling up her."

Montane set his cup back in the saucer again, this time with exaggerated care, and when he spoke each word was the splintering of a human bone. "I never thought I'd hear myself say this to any man, but if you speak like that about my wife – *ever again* – I'll kill you, Jim. I swear I'll kill you."

"I'm shocked at you," Nicklin said comfortably. "That was a terrible thing to say to a fellow human being."

"I wouldn't have said it to a human being."

"I'm immune to insults now, Corey. I'm immune to everything."

"Then you must be very unhappy."

"On the contrary," Nicklin said, maintaining his smile. "I've found the secret of complete happiness. Do you want to know what it is? I'll tell you anyway. At all times you keep just one thought uppermost in your mind – that everybody is a piece of shit."

"Does that include yourself?"

"*Especially* yourself, old son – that's the whole point! It would ruin the Big Joke if you didn't include yourself."

Montane shook his head, the movements slow, tired, barely perceptible. "Let's get back to the buried spaceship – where is it?"

"That's something else I can't remember, but I've an idea the letter A crops up two or three times in the name of the town," Nicklin said, wondering if he should compel the preacher to put details of their new arrangement on to tape or paper. "I might be able to find it by going through a P1 gazetteer, but even without the name we have enough information."

"That's what I was thinking," Montane said, giving him a sly glance. "I could find it by myself now."

"Yes, but Renard's people could get there faster – if I tipped them off."

"The ship may not even be available," Montane countered. "There may be descendants who treat it like a shrine."

"The facts we have suggest that the lady died, as they used to say, without issue."

"There could be other relatives. Perhaps they unearthed the ship years ago and sold it for scrap."

"I've already thought of that." Nicklin concealed the lie as expertly as he could. *Christ*, he thought, *the old boy has a point there – I should have kept my mouth shut until I'd done some detective work on my own.* "But the scrap value would hardly cover the excavation and haulage costs."

"And there's always the possibility that your memory has tricked you over the location," Montane said, now apparently enjoying himself. "It's going to be ages before interportal flights are commercially available again – so if it turns out that the town *isn't* in the P1 region I don't see how we can get to it."

"This conversation is starting to lose all its sparkle – and I'm starving." In spite of himself, Nicklin was impressed by the other man's mental resilience, and he was fast becoming angry with himself for having played all his trump cards so early on in the game. The really smart thing to do would have been to take his time, to consolidate his ground step by step. He should have verified the existence and availability of the ship, then he should have found a way to acquire ownership, by bringing in a third party if necessary. Then, and *only* then – when he was in a safe position to dictate all the terms – would it have been safe to talk business with Montane.

So what had gone wrong with his sense of judgement? Nicklin writhed inwardly as he answered his own question. It had been the Danea effect again. The fevered visions of inflicting revenge on her, the lurid and penis-stirring images of debauching the Bitch in Black, had robbed him of all caution and common sense. In short, he had behaved like a mindless creature with a whiff of pheromones in its nostrils, and the full price of his stupidity remained to be discovered.

"If you're really hungry I could have Carlos bring a tray in here," Montane said.

A pleasingly tasteless line sprang into Nicklin's mind at the idea of eating off Milly Montane's coffin . . . *My wife says the dinner's on her* . . . but Montane was touchy about dead wife jokes and had sounded genuinely dangerous over the last one. The objective was to earn his undying hatred, not to be killed by him.

"No need to put old Carlos to all that trouble," Nicklin said. "I daresay I can wait a while longer."

"Very well, but if all this works out – and you do take up your 'executive' position – you may have to get used to grabbing food while you have the chance."

"So you're not going to renege on our deal."

"I'm a man of my word, Jim, and the truth is that you're likely to be of more value to the cause now than you were when you joined us. That's what I call irony." Montane stood up and went forward to the shelf which supported his video set. "I'm going to see if I can call up a good PI gazetteer on this thing and then we'll find out if it jogs your memory. There's no point in wasting any more time."

"I agree," Nicklin said, then became concerned about giving the impression of turning soft and compliant again. "But the job was only part of my professional fee. Remember?"

Montane spoke abstractedly, concentrating his attention on the video's command panel. "If you're talking about Danea, *you* have to remember something. I told you the first day we met that Danea

Farthing is a private individual – any personal relationship she may have had with you has nothing to do with me or this mission."

He's sticking it to me, Nicklin thought in dismay. *He is really sticking it to me! This is what I get for letting my dick rule my head. A crazy old coot, who thinks he's Moses MkII and has conversations with his wife's corpse, is running rings around me!*

"Correct me if I misheard you," he said bitterly, "but I thought you said something about being a man of your word."

"My vows to God take precedence over everything else."

"How convenient!"

"You must try to be consistent, Jim." Montane was still stooped over the video set, apparently finding complexity in its simplified controls, but his words were very much to the point. "A few minutes ago you were happy with the idea that God had given me licence to procure women. If that were the case, He would positively *encourage* me to commit a minor sin like lying now and again – as long as it served His cause."

Thing's can't go on like this, Nicklin told himself, his fingernails biting deeply into the heels of his hands. *There are going to be big changes around here.*

He had no idea of how accurate his prediction would prove to be . . .

PART TWO: THE HAMMER FALLS

CHAPTER 12

The rifle had roughly the same lines as an old-fashioned sporting weapon, but for the most part its appearance was an exercise in cosmetics and nostalgia. Its stock looked like polished wood and was designed to fit snugly into the user's shoulder, although firing produced no recoil; it was operated by a conventionally styled trigger, although a simple button might have been more appropriate for the unleashing of bolts of ultralaser energy. It had an effective range of three kilometres in dry, clear weather; and a computerised smartscope guaranteed impressive accuracy, even in the hands of a total novice.

A perfect killing machine, beautiful in its own way, the rifle looked incongruous among the frayed umbrellas in the antique hall-stand. Nicklin gazed thoughtfully at it for a few seconds, knowing he was supposed to take it outside with him, then he shook his head. On several previous occasions he had slung the weapon on his shoulder when going out to the hill, and each time had felt like an overgrown child playing frontiersmen or soldiers. He took his old sun-hat from a peg on the hall-stand, squared it on his head and – leaving the double doors wide open – went out of the huge house.

The Fugaccia mansion had become a ready-made headquarters for the mission, though not through Montane's free choice. Ves Fugaccia's heirs lived a hundred kilometres to the east, in a well-developed part of the region, and had never taken any interest in the unmanageable property perched right on the edge of civilisation. They had, however, a good nose for business, and on sensing the obsessive nature of Montane's interest they had flatly refused his offer to buy the buried ship and take it off their hands. That would have been a betrayal of their grandfather's trust, they had said. Good Roman Catholics could never acquiesce in the desecration of a loved one's tomb, they had said. But, somehow, their group conscience had allowed them to contemplate selling the Altamura estate in its entirety; and – when their lawyers had thrice succeeded in jacking up the price – their religious and family scruples had vanished altogether.

Directly above Nicklin the sun had just emerged from a nightband, and the day was still cool in spite of being intensely bright. Before him was what had once been the garden fronting the Fugaccia mansion. Now it was a daunting tangle of overgrown shrubs, many of which had been smothered by riotous wild plants, vines and native grasses. In some places the vegetation rose into mounds whose general shape only hinted at what lay beneath – here a summerhouse or an arch, there a fountain or a belvedere. At one point the head of a classical marble statue of a woman raised itself above the leafy ferment, the blank orbs of the eyes contemplating the chaos of greenery in apparent sorrow.

Beyond the ruins of the garden was a small, rounded, man-made hill. It was vividly outlined against a scenic backdrop in which grasslands, lakes and enigmatic forests sifted and tapered through each other, creating horizontal designs which grew slimmer and slimmer until, misted by distance, they merged into ranges of remote grey-blue mountains. Striking though the general panorama was, Nicklin had eyes only for the small hill in the foreground – because the ship was cocooned inside it.

He had just finished breakfast, but he knew, despite the earliness of the hour, that Montane and big Gerl Kingsley were somewhere on the hill, already hard at work with picks and spades. Power tools had been purchased, and at that very moment were on their way from Beachhead with the main body of the caravan, but Montane was unable to hold himself in check. Ownership of the Fugaccia estate had passed into his hands four days earlier, and since then the monkey had been on his back. He *had* to see the ship for himself. Not until he had actually touched its metal skin would he be able to relax in the knowledge that the greatest hurdle of all was safely behind him.

Picking his way along the path that had been hewn through the wilderness, Nicklin smiled as he recalled Montane's antics of the recent past. The preacher had actually broken down and wept on hearing that the ship was an unmodified Type 83.

"Why!" he had said to Nicklin, blinking at him through lenses of tears. "You want to know *why*! Because, you smirking great idiot, it's one of the Explorer class!"

It had taken a few seconds for the significance of the statement to penetrate Nicklin's mind. To him the flight to New Eden was a preposterous fantasy, one which had no hope of being realised, and he had given no thought to the practicalities involved. Had he considered the matter he would have seen at once that, while the crossing of hundreds of light years of interstellar void could be accomplished routinely, dropping down through the final hundred kilometres to achieve landfall gave rise to unusual problems.

The great majority of spaceships constructed in the previous two centuries were designed to ply between Earth and Orbitsville – from the parking orbits of the former to the docking cradles of the latter – and therefore had no provision for transferring personnel to and from the surface of an unprepared world.

Montane had always anticipated the difficulty and expense of equipping his starship with a pinnace, and now – suddenly and unexpectedly – the problem had ceased to exist. "It's an omen, Jim," he had said. "This is the Lord's way of telling me not to despair, that He is still tending His flock."

The sheer irrationality of that proposition had dissuaded Nicklin from trying to argue. The Lord, it seemed, had not tended very hard in the case of Apryl Fugaccia. A penniless hairdresser of Scandinavian stock, she had professionally met the elderly billionaire, Ves Fugaccia, in a Beachhead salon. He had been captivated by the newly minted gold of her Nordic good looks, and she had been equally drawn by the prospect of wealth and limitless opportunities for travel and adventure. She must have counted herself among the luckiest people in the universe when, on their first wedding anniversary, Fugaccia had granted her dearest wish by presenting her with a starship of her very own. Only a comparative handful of exploration craft had been built – the Orbitsville syndrome had seen to that – and the enormous expense involved had been yet another proof of her husband's boundless love. So infatuated had Apryl been with the notion of becoming a planetary first-footer that she had sneaked on board her new toy while it was land-docked at Portal 9, and had donned her HESS (Hostile Environment Survival Suit) without first mastering the intricacies of its breathing-gas regulatory system. Her body had been found in the left-hand seat of the pinnace's cockpit.

How Montane could construe such a pathetic sequence of events as evidence of the existence of a caring Almighty was a source of puzzlement to Nicklin. To him it was a prank worthy of that greatest of all tricksters, the Gaseous Vertebrate, but he had refrained from making any comment, and had continued quite happily with his duties as second-in-command of the mission. For the present those duties consisted of little more than living with Montane and Kingsley in the decaying Fugaccia mansion and waiting for the rest of the team to arrive.

In particular, he was waiting for the arrival of Danea Farthing. He had devised a new plan for dealing with her, one which would take time to put into effect, but which had the merit of promising to make her humiliation – when it finally came – all the more complete.

The thought enlivened his stride as he reached the base of the hill and began to climb. Clearing a way through the vegetation had been easier here because the hill was plentifully endowed with stone steps and paths, exactly as in his dream. He wound his way to the crest on meticulously fitted hexagonal paving and found Montane and Kingsley standing in a broad but shallow excavation which was the result of their combined labours.

Its floor resembled streaky brown glass copiously studded with nodules of grey and white, reminding Nicklin of a gigantic slab of nut candy. The discovery of the fused-earth and rock carapace below the topsoil had bothered Montane at first, because it delayed his progress, but he had been consoled by the thought of the excellent protection it afforded the ship. Seventy years would have been a long time for any metal artefact – even one constructed from electron-sated alloys – to resist the chemical ravages of damp earth.

"Good morning, navvies," Nicklin called out. "How are the calluses today?"

Montane looked up from the drawing he was studying and responded to the greeting in amicable tones. He had been in Nicklin's company almost continuously for three months, while they were finding Ves Fugaccia's heirs and negotiating the purchase of the property, and understood that the best way to preserve their enmity was to masquerade as friends. Kingsley, the huge ex-farmer, who had no time for such strategies, confined himself to giving Nicklin a barely audible grunt.

"You're an engineer," Montane said, beckoning to Nicklin. "Take a look at this drawing and tell me what you think."

"I used to fix egg-beaters," Nicklin replied. "Spaceships are a bit out of my line."

"Take a look at the drawing!"

Nicklin shrugged and did as ordered. The photocopy paper was old and creased, but the original drawing had been even older – a fact which was obvious from the numerous wrinkles and smudges which had been reproduced along with the linework and text. It had been issued by the Nissan-Vickers company of Birkenhead, England, and showed the three principal elevations of a spaceship. The ship had the classical Starflight configuration – three equal cylinders joined together in parallel, with one projecting forward by almost half its length – but it was distinguishable from a standard vessel because of the pinnace. Needle-nosed and stream-lined, shaped by a different set of operational requirements, the pinnace was slung in its flying attitude beneath the central main cylinder.

The title box of the layout established it as the general arrangement of the Explorer-class vessel *Liscard*, but it had been used as the basis for a later and entirely different kind of drawing. Superimposed on the flawless computer graphics of the original were hand-drawn outlines, obviously the work of a landscaping contractor, depicting the rounded earthwork which now covered the starship. Clustered about each of the elevations were thumbnail sketches giving details of path and wall construction, and there were notes about the plants to be sown in various areas.

"Apparently Fugaccia wasn't much of a one for keeping records," Montane said. "This was the only drawing available, and I was lucky to get it."

"You should have it framed."

Montane indicated a pencil mark he had made on the side view of the hill, directly above the nose of the ship. "I'd say this is where we are – what do you say?"

"You might be right, but until we get some fairly acc –" Nicklin paused and looked again at the drawing. "Corey, this thing doesn't even tell you which way is north!"

"So?"

"So we might be standing above the arse end of the ship."

"Oh!" Montane looked abashed for a moment, then his face brightened. "All the more reason to shift dirt, my boy – get yourself a spade and start digging."

With the arrival of machine tools imminent it was pointless to squander muscle power, Nicklin knew, but arguing with Montane in his present state of mind would have been even more futile. Besides, the formerly slight bulge above his belt had become quite noticeable during three months of inactivity, and a spell of hard work would do him no harm at all. He looked about him, wondering if he could find a legitimate task which would be less of a bore than digging, then seized a pick and began to demolish a low stone wall.

The invasive vegetation had been unable to find many good footholds here, and he was able to work without too much hindrance from vines. There was a kind of black satisfaction in obliterating another man's patient craftsmanship, in being an instrument of disorder, and he found it easy to lose himself in the repetitive physical effort. And as he worked he was very much aware of being in a borderland.

Four kilometres to the east was the town of Altamura, its buildings visible as a sparse scatter of confetti in the green immensity that was Orbitsville. It had been founded more than a hundred years earlier by a batch of settlers from southern Italy – a hard-working people who had fully expected their new home to become a prosperous regional centre as the tide of immigration rolled on past it. But actuality and the dream had not coincided; the successive waves of settlers had never materialised. In fact, the well-delineated edge of civilisation had receded slightly, leaving Altamura in a no man's land between the known and the unknown.

There had been no particular reason for men and women to turn back from the area. It had simply happened that way. The tracts of land to the west of Altamura – which Nicklin could survey each time he raised his head – were every bit as rich and inviting as any other part of the Big O, but the mathematics of chaos had dictated that the outward surge of humanity would falter and lose impetus just there.

"There are too many places to go, and not enough folks to go to them," the Fugaccias' local agent had said philosophically, giving his summation in a strong Italian accent. "That's why the town has been slowly dying ever since it was born – a pure demographic fluke."

A talkative man, one who obviously relished storytelling, he had gone on to paint a hectically coloured picture of life in that part of the frontier.

"Mind you, that doesn't mean there's *nobody* west of the Irsina river. Some pretty weird characters have headed out that way from time to time. Some of them were pure misfits – sort of hermits by trade, if you know what I mean – but quite a few had the police on their tails when they went.

"They're still out there. Maybe some have banded together, maybe some are raising their own broods in their own way. Sometimes you see smoke in the distance . . . sometimes you find a cow or a sheep with its hind legs missing . . . sometimes you find a man or a woman, or even a child – unfortunates that have had very bad things done to them . . .

"That's why people around here carry weapons when they go far out of town – and I advise you to do the same."

Recalling the agent's words, Nicklin found it difficult to reconcile them with the prehistoric peacefulness of high summer which lay over the surrounding land. Intellect told him that Orbitsville *had* to have a darker aspect, that where all men were free to live as they pleased some would choose paths whose very existence was denied by anyone who wanted to go on treasuring his night's sleep.

On the positive side, however, was the fact that he had lived for more than thirty years without once encountering the really bad stuff, the moral equivalent of anti-matter. Oh yes, people were shit – that much he had proved – but in general they stopped short of stuff like torture, murder and cannibalism. There was no reason to suppose that the sprinkling of heliumheads, eccentrics and down-right crazies who undoubtedly formed part of the population of the Altamura area were any worse than their equivalents in Orangefield county.

Having attuned himself once more to the bright sanity of the morning, Nicklin worked steadily until he had dismantled about ten metres of wall, then he began levering up the paving slabs of the adjoining path. The work was arduous but satisfying in its own way, and he was surprised to note that two hours had passed when Montane called a break for refreshments.

Nicklin would have walked back down to the house to eat, but Kingsley opened a coolbag and produced bulbs of iced tea, sandwiches and a selection of fruit. Glad to have been spared the journey, Nicklin seated himself on a pile of rubble and joined in the simple meal. The cold tea, which had never been one of his favourite drinks, tasted better than he would have believed possible.

"I think I could take to this life of simple toil," he said, after slaking his thirst.

"I'm pleased to hear it." Montane, now in the role of jovial foreman, nudged Kingsley with his elbow. "You stayed in bed so long we were beginning to think you had died."

Kingsley guffawed, spilling particles of bread from the corners of his mouth.

"I was monitoring the news for you, Corey. I know how you like to be kept informed of all the . . . " Nicklin paused as he suddenly remembered an item which had come in that morning on the audio line from Altamura, one he knew would be of genuine interest to the preacher. "There's been a new development about the green lines."

Montane eyed him intently. "Yes?"

"It's connected with the fields. You know, the vertical force fields above the lines?"

"Yes, yes – go on, Jim."

"Well, it turns out they aren't as inert as they seemed," Nicklin said. "Apparently they weaken the molecular lattice in any piece of material they pass through. It happens very gradually, but some buildings in . . . in Lomza, P83, I think it is . . . are starting to split in half. The buildings straddle one of the lines, and it's gradually chopping them in half – roof beams, walls, floors, foundations, *everything*. It's acting as if it was a very weak valency cutter."

"My enemy never rests." Montane went on chewing a piece of banapple, but he was doing it mechanically now, no longer tasting the fruit. Completing the purchase of the ship had relieved him of a burden of anxiety, and he had since been enjoying a relaxed but active life in the open air. He had actually grown younger in appearance during the unplanned break, but within the last few seconds the weight of the years had come down on him again, hard.

Good job I didn't remember the news about the lines earlier, Nicklin congratulated himself. *This way the old boy's digestive juices have been stopped in their tracks. Or should I say tracts?*

"Aw, come on, Corey," he said, "you can't put everything down to Old Nick. Wouldn't it be more like his style to chop buildings up *suddenly* and let them crash down on people?"

Montane gave him a sombre stare. "I don't know what's in the Devil's mind – he's playing a very subtle game – but I *do* know that when it's over none of us will be laughing. And that goes for you, too."

"I wouldn't dream of laughing," Nicklin said, belying his words with a faint smile.

"You'd better not," Kingsley warned, jabbing in Nicklin's direction with a forefinger which resembled a gnarled billet of wood. "You start laughing at Corey – I'll break bits off your skeleton."

"Go on with your lunch, Gerl." Montane soothed the giant by patting him on the knee, and a certain dryness in his voice showed that he was recovering his equilibrium. "I'll give you the nod when I want bits broken off Jim's skeleton."

End of conversation, Nicklin thought, again obliged to acknowledge the older man's mental wiriness. To show that he regarded Montane's tactic as unsporting, he shifted position until he was sitting with his back to the others, facing down the western slope of the hill. There was no wall or fence to mark the limit of the Fugaccia estate – the foot of the hill shelved into scrub which was punctuated with anvil trees, and beyond that Orbitsville went on for ever.

Allowing his thoughts to return to Danea Farthing and his plans for her, Nicklin wondered how long it would be before the rest of the mission arrived. He and Montane had flown out from Beachhead to New Taranto, whose airport was the nearest to Altamura, and the whole journey had taken only a day. Gerl Kingsley had set off at the same time in Montane's camper and had completed the trip in five days, but to do so he must have driven like a maniac and almost without sleep. Nicklin had derived quite a bit of amusement from trying to decide whether the big man's haste had been inspired by loyalty to his boss, or by a disinclination to spend many nights alone with Milly Montane and her metal coffin. (*Your wife's a nice woman, boss – but she's permanently canned.*)

All the other vehicles had remained at the base camp in Beachhead until four days ago, when Montane had wired the news that all was well. They would be proceeding at the speed of the slowest member, with proper rest halts, and it was hard to predict their time of arrival.

Deciding not to squander his mental energy on the matter, Nicklin was gazing around him in boredom when he saw something faintly peculiar happen.

A few paces down the slope from him was a group of yellow flowers, much resembling tulips, and while he was looking directly at them the head of one of the flowers detached itself from its stalk and dropped to the ground.

With little else to occupy his mind, he wondered idly if such events were commonplace in the botanical world. Orbitsville had many varieties of insects, some with bizarre feeding habits, but surely any bug intent on devouring a plant would tackle it from the bottom. Could there be a type which had a taste for petals only, and which first dragged them back to the nest?

As he was tiring of the speculation there occurred a second strange event – a humming, rushing sound close to his left ear, a brief and fluttery agitation of the air. He told himself that it must have been a hornet, but there had been a disturbing hint of *power* to the sound, and in that instant a preposterous idea was born in his mind.

"Corey," he said quietly, "this may sound like one of my jokes – but I think we're being shot at."

"Shot at!" Kingsley tilted his head back and roared with laughter. The fact that his mouth was wide open possibly saved his life, for the bullet which might have shattered his skull passed cleanly through both his cheeks. He clapped a hand to the bloody, star-shaped exit wound and pitched sideways to the ground.

Nicklin gaped at him, thunderstruck, then realised he was still sitting upright. He hastily bellied down behind the heaps of rubble, losing his sun-hat in the process, fear masked by self-loathing – he had been imbecilic enough to risk death rather than make a chump of himself by needlessly diving for cover. He looked towards Montane, who had also dropped to the ground, and found the preacher staring at him in wide-eyed accusation. Nicklin understood the terror-logic perfectly – he was the one who had talked of shooting, therefore he had caused it to happen.

What next? What the holy fuck do we do next? The questions were a flurry of drum-beats in his mind. *I know! Kingsley will take command of the situation and save us all! Good old Gerl is big and tough and he has farmed wild country all his life and he's probably been shot at hundreds of times and he probably thinks no more of a little bullet wound than he does of a mosquito . . .*

The thought foundered as Nicklin belatedly became aware of Kingsley's condition. The big man was lying on his side and blood was literally pumping out of his mouth. His tongue was protruding and, although it was swathed in gouting crimson, Nicklin could see enough to tell him that it had been ploughed almost in half. He could also see that good old Gerl was not going to take command of any situation, and his feeling of helplessness increased.

"The rifle," Montane whispered. "Where's the rifle?"

"It's back in the house."

"You should have brought it." Montane's face was stern. "You were told to carry it everywhere."

Absurdly, Nicklin's fear was displaced by indignation. "*You* came out first! You and your pal should have – "

His words were lost in the sound of a new bullet strike. This time the slug, having glanced off a nearby rock, howled like a demented being as it flailed the warm air. Nicklin, who had never been close to a ricochet before, was appalled by its sheer ferocity.

"Go and get the rifle," Montane commanded, breaking the ensuing silence.

"But you can't stay up here," Nicklin said preparing to crawl away.

"I'll bring Gerl as fast as I – " Montane made an angrily impatient gesture. "For God's sake, man, *get the rifle!*"

Nicklin nodded and slithered down on to the bared expanse of fused earth. At the far side of it he rose to his feet and ran down the only clear path, bounding recklessly where there were flights of steps. In seconds he had reached level ground and was sprinting towards the colonnaded façade of the house.

Can this really be happening to me? he wondered, his mind distancing itself from bodily turmoil. *Who's out there doing the shooting? Does somebody really want to kill us, or is it just a hunting trip gone wrong, a few drunks taking potshots at anything that moves for the pure bloody hell of it?*

The thought reminded Nicklin that there had been no audible reports from the unseen weaponry. It meant that whoever was out there was using tail-burning ammunition – in effect, miniature rocket projectiles which in spite of dubious accuracy were favoured by some hunters because there was no muzzle blast to frighten off their prey.

Nicklin's mind seized on the new thought, somehow managing to find a glimmer of reassurance in it. The worst of the trouble might already be over if a couple of liquored-up hunters were responsible. Having had their bit of fun, they could easily have developed cold feet and retreated into the bush. The idea took on a life of its own, isolating Nicklin from normal time, expanding its solitary theme into a monotonous fugue. Oh yes, things were bad. There was no denying that things were bad – especially after what had happened to poor Gerl – but they weren't all *that* bad. After all, nobody had been killed. Gerl's face was in a hell of a mess, one had to admit that, but nobody had actually been *killed* . . .

A subjective aeon had passed by the time Nicklin lunged up the broad steps of the house, through the open doors and into the shade of the entrance hall. *I probably won't even have to use this*, he chanted to himself as he snatched the rifle out of the antique oak stand. Even in that moment of extremity the machine-lover in him appreciated the weapon's lightness.

He ran back outside to the sunshine, shaded his eyes and scanned the hillside, fully expecting to see Montane and Kingsley working their way down the slope. There was no sign of them, no movement anywhere. The scene had a slumbrous Sunday afternoon look about it, a Monet landscape quality which Nicklin found quite astonishing. Forcing his mind to deal with real time again, he was even more astonished to realise that only forty or fifty seconds could have passed since he began his dash from the hilltop.

That was a very brief period indeed, no time at all, for somebody who had to tend a wounded man, or for hunters moving tentatively under cover. He started running once more, seeming to swoop above the ground like a low-flying bird. The wilderness of the garden flicked past him, the contrived slope of the hill sank behind him – then he was back on the rubbled centre stage of the drama. Montane was kneeling beside Kingsley, helping him to wad a handkerchief into his mouth, but otherwise nothing had changed during Nicklin's absence. He bent as low as he could, scurried forward and threw himself into a prone position close to Montane.

"Well?" he breathed. "Well?"

"It's still going on."

"You're sure?"

"I saw dust." Montane gave Nicklin an expectant look, a look which ended his naïve hopes of remaining little more than an observer.

"In that case . . . " He slid the rifle to the top of the low bank of earth and pebbles, then slowly raised his head behind the weapon, wondering how much he would know about the event if his brain were to be pulped by a miniature rocket. His life continued. The land lay silent beneath the high sun, a pulsing blaze of tall grass, brushwood and flat-topped trees, betraying no enemy presence.

He moved his head slightly, bringing his eyes into the focus zone of the rifle's smartscope, and at once the scene changed. There was no magnified but curtailed image, as would have been produced by a traditional lens system. Instead, as the scope analysed and edited a superhuman range of frequencies, projecting the result directly on to his retinas, Nicklin saw a glare-free representation of all that lay before him. In that strange, colour-adjusted universe – seen through bright blue cross-hairs – leafy matter was almost transparent. And clearly visible among gauzy stands of ghost-grass were two human figures, glowing with a neon pinkness. They were down on their stomachs, wriggling towards the hill with a snaky lateral motion, their breath feathering up like smoke signals. Not far behind them was a tree whose thick trunk, opaque to the smartscope, seemed to be emitting little smoke signals of its own.

The machine-lover, the game-player in Nicklin took immediate control of his mind and body. He moved the intersection of the cross-hairs on to the nearer of the crawling figures and squeezed the trigger. A breath of heat touched his forehead and the figure abruptly lost its human outlines, becoming a shapeless smear which was further blurred by swirls of luminous pink vapour. A second later, its arrival delayed by the intervening two hundred metres, came a dull, soggy *thud-thud*.

The knowledge that he had heard a man's internal organs and torso exploding would have appalled Nicklin had he been in a normal state of mind, but the game was *on* – and the cross-hairs were already centring themselves on the second figure. He squeezed the trigger again, and this time – amid the blotch of destruction – he actually glimpsed the target's ribcage snapping wide open like some spring-loaded mechanical device.

"Do you think you hit anything?" Montane had appeared at Nicklin's side, and his eyes – inefficient biological organs – were blindly scanning the innocent, sun-drenched scene.

"Oh, yes," Nicklin assured him. "I hit something."

Montane gave him a worried glance. "Maybe we should go down there and – "

"Wait!" Nicklin, still under the spell of the smartscope, had transferred all his attention to the vicinity of the tree. Flickers of pink brilliance informed him that the person who had been standing behind the trunk was now running away and attempting to keep the tree in between him and the dealer of death. But almost at once he was forced to detour around a shrub and, long hair streaming, came fully into Nicklin's inhuman view. The cross-hairs quartered his back on the instant and Nicklin's trigger finger made the appropriate response. The fleeing figure disintegrated, shedding an arm which spun off to one side like a broken propeller.

An unexpected blow on his shoulder startled Nicklin, recalling him to the real world.

"Why did you do that?" Montane's face was distorted, accusing. "There was no need for that."

"Why did I – !" Nicklin pointed at Gerl Kingsley, who had risen to his knees and was fingering a pronged whitish object which was emerging from the bloody hole in his cheek. "Ask *him* if there was any need for it!"

"For God's sake, the man was running *away!*"

"Yeah, to fetch the rest of his clan! What the fuck's the matter with you, Corey? Are you tired of living? Is it all getting too much for you?" The physical after-effects of Nicklin's sprint down the hill and back, seemingly held in abeyance to make him a steady gun platform, suddenly began to manifest themselves. His breathing became harsh and rapid, and a salty froth thickened in his mouth.

"You don't know *what* the man was going to do," Montane said, shaking his head.

"Perhaps he remembered he'd left the bath water running," Nicklin suggested, putting on his smile. *Did I kill three men? Did I really and truly vaporise three men?*

"You can joke? How can you joke?"

"It's easy," Nicklin said, determined to brook no more questions – from without or within. "All you have to do is remember that everybody is a piece of shit."

"We have to get Gerl to a doctor," Montane said, after a pause.

He turned away, but before doing so he gave Nicklin a prolonged look. His eyes betrayed no hatred, which was something Nicklin had expected and could have savoured. Instead, they showed simple contempt.

CHAPTER 13

The coming of autumn had brought many changes, not least in the appearance of the hill itself. Once a perfect ovoid, it had been deprived of its entire upper half, like a gargantuan boiled egg which somebody had chosen to cut open from the side. The lower half was hidden beneath slopes of scree made up of masonry, rubble, clay and jagged fragments of the fused-earth shell. Projecting from the shambles was the entire main cylinder of the *Liscard*, complete with the toy-like pinnace slung under the nose section. The hull of the mother ship, copiously stained with ochreous mineral deposits, was obscured in places by scaffolding, plastic weather screens and banks of ladders.

Digging through to the ship had taken much longer than Montane or anybody else connected with the project had originally anticipated. On breaking through the outer shell they had quickly penetrated about a metre of compacted fill – only to encounter a second shell, also of vitrified earth. Montane had curbed his natural impatience with the consoling thought that his ship had been superbly protected during its seventy years of incarceration, but even he had been taken aback by the discovery of a *third* carapace.

It appeared that the disconsolate Ves Fugaccia had been determined to make his young bride's tomb as inviolable as that of an ancient Egyptian princess. The third shell had proved to be the innermost – with nothing inside it but clean sand – but even then there were further obstacles to entering the ship. All three doors on the upper surface of the cylinder were found to have been welded along the whole length of the seams. Unwilling to have them mutilated by cutting gear, Montane had waited until the side doors of the cylinder were uncovered – and those, too, had been welded.

As Nicklin climbed towards the ship, in the pale lemon sunlight of autumn, he could see that one of the side doors was finally being breached. A valency cutter would have been too fierce and indiscriminate in its action, therefore old-fashioned oxy-acetylene was being employed in the hope of persuading the weld metal to come away without excessive damage to the adjacent structure. Showers of yellow sparks were occasionally visible through the screen of men and women who had stopped work to watch the operation.

The size of the group of spectators was a reminder to Nicklin of another change that had come about, one that he had never envisaged. Soon after the upper section of the *Liscard* had been uncovered, journalists had taken an interest in the proceedings and had begun visiting the site by light aircraft and helicopter. The resultant publicity had attracted quite a few enquiries from people who, swayed by Montane's message, either wanted to work with him or to reserve places for themselves and their families on the flight to New Eden. A fair proportion of them had been prepared, as Nicklin had done, to liquidate all their assets to buy into the project.

One of the earliest had been Scott Hepworth, a physicist from the Garamond Institute, who had arrived at the site one morning on foot, having walked all the way out from Altamura. Montane and Nicklin had been sitting on the front steps of the mansion arguing about the purchase of laundry equipment, when the plump man in his sixties – red-faced and sweating – had approached them . . .

"Mr Montane?" the stranger said. "My name is Scott Hepworth, I'm a top-class physicist, and I want to work for you."

"Everybody calls me Corey," Montane replied, with the wry smile – now familiar to Nicklin – which established him as the humblest of democrats. "And this is Jim Nicklin. Would you like to sit with us for a while?"

"Thank you." Hepworth nodded to Nicklin as he seated himself, took out a handkerchief and began to wipe his neck. "I think I'm a bit too old for hiking around in this heat."

Montane looked sympathetic. "Would you like some tea?"

"Tea!" A look of distaste appeared on Hepworth's roundly

padded face. "The kind of thirst I have can only be quenched with gin and tonic. Any lesser brew would be an insult to the taste buds which have served me loyally for more years than I care to remember. I don't suppose you – "

"I don't believe in strong liquor," Montane said.

Nicklin, who had been prepared to dislike the newcomer, largely because of his overbearing approach, decided not to be too hasty. Many another man – the former Jim Nicklin included – when courting a prospective employer would have pretended to love tea, but Hepworth had come straight out and said he was a boozer. Terrible interview technique, but it indicated that he was his own man.

Discreetly studying Hepworth, Nicklin was interested to note that he did not look anything like a senior scientist at a university which was famed for conservatism and stuffiness. His light-weight suit was cheap and ill-fitting. It was not a case of it being "well-worn but of good cut" – the hackneyed old novelistic phrase which showed that a character had the right sort of background but had "fallen into straitened circumstances". This suit had started out shoddy, and had not improved with time. It was complemented by a rumpled shirt and comprehensively scuffed sandals.

Scott Hepworth was something of an oddball, Nicklin decided, and as such ought to be encouraged. "I've got some gin in my room," he said, rising to his feet. "Ice and a slice of lime?"

"All the trimmings, my boy," Hepworth said, looking deeply grateful.

Rewarded by a disapproving glance from Montane, Nicklin hurried to his room to prepare the drink. He was not particularly fond of gin, having bought it because it was easier to transport from town than beer, but he mixed himself a large one as well, knowing that it would further annoy Montane. He returned to the front steps in time to hear Montane ask the visitor why he had quit the Garamond.

"It wasn't through choice," Hepworth replied easily. "I got *thrown* out." As if there might be some doubt about his meaning, he added, "I was forcibly ejected. Given the boot."

Now positively warming to the man, Nicklin winked as he handed him a dewed glass. Hepworth took it eagerly, but, instead of drinking immediately, held it under his nose and breathed deeply of the aroma.

"May I ask why the university saw fit to dispense with your services?" Montane said, the stilted wording and coolness of their delivery showing that he was far from being impressed by Hepworth.

"I had an argument – some might call it a stand-up fight – with the head of my department." Hepworth smiled into his drink as though enjoying pleasant memories. "He's been trying to show me the door for quite a long time, and I finally gave him a good excuse."

"What was the argument about?"

"I stumbled on some evidence that Orbitsville has jumped into a different universe, but Professor Phair disagreed with my interpretation."

"A different *universe!*" Montane stiffened visibly. "Is this something new? We've already been told that the whole globe has moved."

"Yes, but not so *far.*" Hepworth took an appreciative sip of his gin before going on. "I'm not talking about some kind of warp-transfer into a distant part of the familiar old continuum. I'm saying we jumped into an entirely different continuum – an anti-matter universe where time is reversed."

"But – " Montane glanced helplessly at Nicklin.

"It's a beautiful idea," Nicklin said, vaguely aware of once having discussed a similar notion with Zindee White, "but what about these starships they're starting to use on interportal runs? Shouldn't the ions they scoop up just blow them apart?"

Hepworth shook his head. "I see you've already done some thinking on this, but in your scenario the ships wouldn't be able to operate at all. If they were familiar hadronic-matter starships which had been popped into an anti-matter universe, their scoop fields would *repel* the surrounding anti-matter particles. What I'm saying is that our beloved Orbitsville and everything on it – present company included – has been flipped over in the process of being translated into a different universe. We have also been hurled about forty billion years backwards in time, but leave that aside for the moment. My main point is that *we* are composed of anti-matter now; our *ships* are composed of anti-matter now – so everything works exactly as before."

"In that case," Nicklin said, fighting off bemusement, "there wouldn't be any way to detect the change."

"That's what I would probably have said – before last week." Hepworth drank again, more deeply this time. "For the last three years, on and off, I've been trying to design an ultra-sensitive flow meter for use in liquid oxygen. It had to have a self-contained source of electrons, so I decided to use radioactive cobalt. There were all kinds of design complications, which I won't go into because they're so boring, but cobalt 60 was great for the job, because the nuclei spray more electrons out of their south poles than from their north poles.

"Normally they cancel each other out, but if you cool the stuff right down you can use magnetism to align a lot of the atoms – and you get a blob of metal which shoots more electrons out of one end than out of the other."

Hepworth paused, eyes alert and twinkling, to scan his listeners' faces. "Does any of this ring a bell? A school bell, perhaps."

Nicklin, anxious to make Montane feel dim by comparison, ransacked his memory. "Wasn't there a famous experiment with cobalt 60 . . . back on Earth . . . three or four hundred years ago?"

"There was indeed!" Hepworth said. "The one which proved that the universe is not symmetrical! Perhaps that gives you an inkling of how I felt last week when I hauled my flow meter out of a locker, where it had languished for the best part of a year, and discovered that my little electron beam was going the wrong way!"

Nicklin's mind balked at the implications of what he had just been told. "Perhaps you set the equipment up wrong."

"That's what Professor Phair tried to put across on me." Hepworth gave a reminiscent little smile. "Just before I punched him in the throat."

Montane made a faint sound of disapproval.

"I don't get this," Nicklin said. "Surely, if *everything* in the universe was reversed, including time, all processes and relationships would be unaltered, and you wouldn't be able to detect the change. If your electron beam was pointing at the lab door before the Big Jump, it would still be pointing at the lab door *after* the jump."

Hepworth's smile did not fade. "You're forgetting that parity is not conserved in the weak nuclear force."

"Am I?"

"Yes. Have you a nuclear physics degree?"

"All I've got is a degree of discomfort," Nicklin said. "From sitting on these steps."

"Enough said, I think."

Left with an uncomfortable feeling that he had failed to assimilate a vital point, Nicklin stared at Hepworth's chubby countenance. His thoughts became unfocused as he noticed that Hepworth had an enormous blackhead at the side of his nose. Located just where nose merged into cheek, the blackhead had a faint bluish umbra and was so big that it presented a visible disc. *How can he go around with a thing like that on his face?* Nicklin wondered, his mind surrendering to irrelevancy. *Why doesn't he squeeze it out, for Christ's sake?*

"Something still troubling you, Jim?" Hepworth enquired mildly.

"The time aspect has me stumped," Nicklin said, choosing not to make any offensive personal comment. He no longer had scruples about such things, especially since the day he had exploded three human beings in less than ten seconds, but he was loath to alienate someone who could turn out to be an interesting companion. Good conversationalists were a rare breed among the mission's workers, and the few who had something worthwhile to say had no wish to say it to him.

"Time is one of the great imponderables," Hepworth stated in the grand tones of an unemployed and unemployable actor. He drained his glass, then allowed his gaze to rest for a brief moment on Nicklin's untouched drink. Nicklin, who had almost forgotten the pleasures of rapport, at once handed him the glass.

"Imponderable is the right word," he said. "Where did you get the forty billion years from?"

"I can assure you that I didn't pluck them out of a hat." Hepworth, having got his throat warmed up for action, swallowed half his second drink in a single gulp. "Richard Gott's historic theory proposed that the Big Bang created *two* universes – the one we all used to inhabit, which went forwards in time; and the one we're in now, which is going backwards in time. The Region One universe, as Gott dubbed it, was about twenty billion years old; this one, Region Two, appears to be about the same age – so it's reasonable to assume that we have jumped back some forty billion years.

"The symmetry in that proposal also has a certain appeal to – "

"This is all very interesting," Montane cut in, the dryness in his voice showing that he had become bored, "but I'm afraid the work here calls for practical skills rather than . . . May I ask, by the way, if you're a believer? Do you accept my message that Orbitsville is a trap which the Devil has set for God's children?"

Hepworth snorted. "No more than I believe in that other great trinity – Goldilocks, Cinderella and Little Red Riding Hood."

Well said, Scott, Nicklin thought regretfully, *but your job interview technique grows worse.*

"In that case, I don't think we should take up any more of each other's time," Montane said. "Unless there are other considerations – "

"Considerations?"

"Corey wants to know if you have any money," Nicklin said helpfully.

"Not a penny!" Hepworth seemed as proud of being broke as he had of being fired from his job. "Not a red cent, not a brass farthing, not a sou!" He gave Nicklin a puzzled glance. "Do I *look* as if I've got money?"

Montane placed his hands on his knees with an air of finality and rose to his feet. "I'm sorry you've had a wasted journey, Scott."

Hepworth showed no inclination to move. "I used to design ramjet engines – the same kind that you have on that starship over there – and I can repair and maintain them. I can also, if called upon, serve as a pilot."

Looking ahead as he went up the slope, Nicklin could see Hepworth among the crowd waiting for their first glimpse of the *Liscard*'s interior. The physicist had used most of his last stipend to buy a duvet coat, a garment which made him easily recognisable at a distance because of its violent shade of lime green. Montane, Kingsley and Affleck were there too, plus a number of people whose names Nicklin had yet to learn, but the one person he really wanted to see was missing.

Danea Farthing's absence was a direct consequence of the improvement in the mission's fortunes. First there had been the publicity. Not only did it come free, but the news agencies and television companies were prepared to pay substantial sums for interviews and pictorial rights.

The global exposure had brought in some moral and financial backing – then the enigmatic green lines had entered the headlines again, this time with the discovery that they were visible on the *outside* of the Orbitsville shell. Interest in and support for Montane's cause had promptly increased.

Nicklin was not sure why the reports had caused such a widespread *frisson* of public unease. It might have been due to the fact that a green luminosity had swept the exterior of Orbitsville shortly prior to the so-called Big Jump. Or, more likely, it had been because the force field associated with the lines was known to weaken any material it passed through. If it could slice a building into pieces, the thinking was, perhaps it was doing the same thing to Orbitsville itself.

It mattered not that ylem, the shell material, had for two centuries resisted technology's fiercest efforts even to scratch it. There was a human personality type, exemplified by Montane himself, which had always been susceptible to paranoia and pessimism, to which every unusual event was an omen. They were the kind of people who saw portents of doom in an increase in the bug population, in a portrait falling off the living-room wall, in the creepy twilight which can herald a bad storm.

They were a minority, and only a tiny fraction of that minority were sufficiently motivated to take action, but in comparison to the mission's previous scale of operations they made up an avalanche. Quite suddenly, Montane had been inundated with money and new obligations. He had found it necessary to open an office in Beachhead to deal with the flow of enquiries about the New Eden flight, and to handle legal work in connection with donations and bequests.

And, to Nicklin's annoyance, he had given Danea a special job – a roving assignment in which she made discreet checks on applicants and their families. Nicklin could not guess how someone was assessed as the potential founder of a new race, and even if such vetting were possible he very much doubted that Danea was the right person to do it. She had a gift for weighing strangers up at a glance – he could testify to that from bitter experience – but working out their Adam-and-Eve quotient . . . ?

His principal source of discontent, though he could not voice it, was that his revised scheme for revenging himself on Danea was being impeded. He had been too direct, too brutal in his previous approach; now he wanted to go softly. If he could win her over by being Mr Nice Guy, by courting her with contrition, humour, consideration and gentleness he would do so. It could even go as far as marriage. And only then – when she was totally unprepared, when their relationship was a mirror image of the one they had started out with – would he let her see what it was like to be *destroyed* by the one person you had been unwary enough to love.

The new plan was superior to the old, it had a gratifying flavour of genuine evil to it, but it was nearly impossible to implement unless the victim was constantly at hand.

Nicklin tried to dismiss Danea from his mind as he reached the level at which the undisturbed surface gave way to mud, rubble and slippery duckboards. From that viewpoint the ship, fully a hundred metres in length, resembled a geological feature, something which had been in the earth for ever. It was impossible to imagine the vast outcrop of metal inching along highways on multi-wheel trailers, let alone ghosting through space at more than the speed of light.

He walked along the planks beside which the top of the left-engine cylinder was emerging through the protective sand. As he neared the group surrounding the cutter only one person, Gerl Kingsley, acknowledged his arrival. Kingsley had never doubted that Nicklin had done the right thing in killing the fleeing attacker, and had been overtly friendly ever since. He still had great difficulty in speaking, however, and his sociability was largely restricted to winks and salutes, plus occasional whispers of, "Sewage farm, eh, Jim!"

The cryptic greeting was a reference to the comment Nicklin once made when a woman, smarting because he had bested her in an argument, asked if he felt no remorse over having killed three fellow humans. *Not the slightest – all I did was send three pieces of shit to the great sewage farm in the sky.* He had been pleased by how quickly the remark had echoed through the mission's personnel. It had earned him renewed dislike from practically everybody except Christine McGivern, on whom it appeared to have acted as an aphrodisiac, stimulating her natural inventiveness when they were together in bed.

The incident now seemed unreal to Nicklin, especially as Petruzzicho, the local sheriff, had not even bothered to come out of town to view the bodies. "It sounds to me like you ran up against the Lucci brothers, and nobody around here is going to grieve much over those characters," he had said. "I'll make you a deal, Jim – you bury the evidence and I'll consider the case closed."

Nicklin had done as requested, and that part of the incident had *not* paled in his memory. During the bleak hour it had taken him to bury the remains he had retched so violently and frequently that towards the end he had been bringing up fresh blood. He had chosen to remain silent concerning the bout of squeamishness, feeling that it would not have squared too well with his public image.

On reaching the edge of the group he saw that the woman operating the cutter had almost completed the circuit of the door seam. Skilfully holding the gas nozzle at an acute angle to the line of work, she was melting the weld material and blowing it away in coruscating showers, with minimal damage to the ship's hull. When the last molten blob was gone she stepped back, her torch popping loudly as it was turned off, and Montane took her place.

He had his familiar brown greatcoat buttoned well up to the throat, and appeared quite untroubled by the coldness of the air, in spite of having stood by for a long time. It was obvious to Nicklin that he was trying to look calm, but his mouth kept twitching with repressed jubilation as, amid the congratulations of the onlookers, he grasped the recessed door handle in a gloved hand and pushed it down. The lever did not move. He leaned his weight on it, pushing and tugging, but in spite of all his efforts the door remained firmly in place.

Aw, how could you do *such a thing, O Gaseous Vertebrate?* Nicklin thought, grinning. *You've gone and screwed up Corey's big moment!*

Making no effort to conceal his amusement, he waited near the scene for twenty minutes during which obstinate fragments of metal were coaxed out of the door's seam and quantities of penetroil were pressure-sprayed into its mechanisms. Finally, under the combined efforts of three men, the door was pulled open to reveal a rectangular airlock.

Nicklin, without being obvious about it, had worked his way into the front line of spectators. He was ready to surge forward with them, but held back when he saw that only a slim gangplank led to the inner door, which was already slightly ajar. Two metres below it was a "floor", one which was oddly adorned with printed notices, communication sets and instrument panels, which showed that it laid equal claim to being a "wall". He was reminded that spaceships were designed to manufacture their own gravity by means of acceleration and deceleration. The *Liscard*'s diaphragm decks were now perpendicular to the ground, and the narrow walkway – which facilitated reaching its interior – was there only because the ship had been land-docked at the time of Apryl Fugaccia's death.

Having appraised the situation, Montane turned to face the group and raised his arms. "My friends, we have waited a long time for this moment – for years in quite a few cases – and I want to thank you for all the hard work you have done on behalf of the mission. God has begun to reward you for all those efforts. At last we are about to enter the Ark he has seen fit to provide for us – but there is one thing I would ask you to remember.

"This ship is more than the instrument of our salvation. It is also a *tomb*, and while inside it we must conduct ourselves accordingly – as we would while treading any plot of consecrated ground." Montane paused and gave his audience a sombre stare.

"Our first duty is a harrowing one. We must remove the mortal remains of Apryl Fugaccia from the ship, and transfer them to the last resting place with all due respect and . . ."

Consecrated ground, mortal remains, last resting place. Nicklin, bored with the rhetoric, occupied his thoughts by trying to compose an aphorism. *The art of religious oratory is stringing the maximum number of clichés together with the minimum of . . . let's see . . . fresh verbiage in between? No, the last bit is too stilted, not pithy enough. Virgin grammar? That's even worse. Now I know how Oscar Wilde must have felt when . . .* Nicklin abandoned the composition, becoming apprehensive as he realised that Montane's eyes were drilling into his.

"Naturally, as God's appointed leader of the mission, I am taking it upon myself to move the body, but I will need the assistance of one other person," Montane said, his gaze still fixed on Nicklin's face. "Let's go, Jim."

He switched on a portable light and immediately started across the gangplank. Nicklin swore inwardly, acknowledging that the preacher had scored another point in their private duel. The very last thing he wanted to do was manhandle a seventy-year-old corpse, or even go *near* a seventy-year-old-corpse, but there was no way in which Killer Nicklin could evade the task with half the mission watching. He was, after all, the man of ice.

"I hope this won't take long," he said, shouldering forward through the spectators. "I'm dying for something to eat."

As he followed Montane out of the sunlight and into the shaded interior of the ship he was surprised to find that the air smelled of something like dead leaves. The earthy aroma, which perhaps also hinted of mushrooms, was not what he would have expected in a triple-sealed tomb. He forgot about it as Jock Craig, the electrician, who was carying an armful of lights, crowded into him from the rear. Petra Davies, similarly burdened, was following close behind.

The group moved slowly forward through the ship, with the electricians extending the area of illumination by attaching the miniature suns to every convenient surface. Nicklin's first impressions of a starship's interior were distorted by his being at a right angle to the normal lines of every open space. The webwork of shipfitters' scaffolding and staging, looking as though it had been left in place during a temporary halt in the work, further complicated the alien environment.

Being in the lead, Montane must have found the going even more difficult, but Nicklin had trouble in pacing him as they went through deck after deck. He caught up at a place where the catwalk passed over a circular hatch whose location established that it led down to the pinnace. The two men lowered themselves on to the surrounding wall, which gravity now designated as a floor. Taking care not to tread on the indicator panels and controls, they swung the hatch up to reveal a short dark well. Light spilling into it showed that another circular door at the bottom was already open, a silent invitation to enter the pinnace . . .

Ves Fugaccia's money-wise heirs had been delighted at the chance to unload the Altamura estate, but some remnant of propriety had led them to put in a stipulation. The small family burial plot at the rear of the house was to remain in their name, and the body of Apryl Fugaccia was to be interred in it with all due respect. Although Corey Montane hardly qualified as a priest in their eyes, they had agreed to have him conduct the ceremony. The concession had gratified Montane, in spite of Nicklin's suggestion that things would have been otherwise had the tragic young bride become a convert to the true faith of old Rome.

He would have further demonstrated his scepticism by not attending the burial ceremony – had it not been for an unexpected internal event. The sight of Apryl Fugaccia's small figure in the left-hand seat of the pinnace's cockpit, still clad in her custom-made vacuum suit, had inspired him with the sudden and unmanning idea that disturbing her was an act of genuine crassness.

All dressed up and nowhere to go, he had thought, but no amount of smart braintalk could allay his feeling that the Gaseous Vertebrate had played enough pranks on her, that one more was one too many. Since before he was born, through all the time he could remember, she had been sitting there in the silent blackness . . . flying her expensive toy spaceship into the Dawn of Nothing . . . and, by rights, the pointless, aimless, beautiful flight should have gone on for ever. She should *not* have been grounded by a manic preacher who had been led to her by his capering, morally clubfooted assistant.

So Nicklin had attended the burial ceremony, while the cold airs had drifted in from Orbitsville's endless savannahs, and afterwards he had drunk gin with Scott Hepworth until his ability to taste it had failed.

CHAPTER 14

It had taken almost a year for the starship to complete the journey from Altamura to Beachhead City, and at some stage in that painful, frustrating trek Nicklin had fallen in love with the huge and unprepossessing vessel.

Standing at the front window of the mission's Beachhead office, he had an excellent view of the *Tara* – as it had been renamed by Montane – and could see nothing in its appearance to explain his emotional involvement. The three-cylinder layout had been introduced more than two centuries earlier by the historic Starflight corporation, and had survived because of its efficiency, but even the most romantic of enthusiasts had to concede that it was ugly. Snow was caking on the *Tara*'s upper surfaces, swirling around the scaffolding and gathering in soiled drifts beneath the drive cylinders, giving it the forlorn appearance of an abandoned civil engineering project. The pinnace, which might have added a touch of aerodynamic glamour to the ponderous structure, had been unslung from beneath the nose section and transported separately.

More than ever, to Nicklin's eyes, the ship looked quite incapable of flight, but he felt for it the special passion that some men and women can develop for a machine which was designed for a difficult task and has the potential to carry it out superbly.

The love affair had begun inauspiciously.

When the excavators bared the twin drive cylinders, upon which the ship had rested during its long incarceration, they discovered that Ves Fugaccia had made a mistake of the kind to which obsessive monument builders had been prone throughout history. In his determination to make his wife's tomb impregnable he had swathed it with layer after massive layer of defences – and the combined weight of them had split the ferro-concrete foundation upon which the great edifice was constructed. In addition, somebody had forgotten to seal off the ventilators, purging ducts and drain tubes which had been opened for the ship's overhaul in land-dock.

The apertures were comparatively tiny, almost invisible in the expanses of impermeable pressure hull, but they had been like six-lane highways for the myriads of fungal, crawling and slithering life-forms which existed in Orbitsville's fertile soil.

When Montane's workers opened the doors leading from the central cylinder into the engine cylinders they entered a dank and unwholesome netherworld. It was a jungle of tendrils and threads emanating from huge, pallid, fronded growths – some of them oozing in decay – among which there lived vast populations of things which moved on many legs or no legs at all. For seventy years they had fought among themselves for control of that dark microcosm, squirming armies of them disputing the principality of a fuse box or the kingdom of a transformer housing. They were united, however, in their dislike for the giant invaders from the world of light, and they demonstrated the fact with every means at their disposal.

It took many days for the humans to reclaim and fumigate the drive cylinders, and much longer for the fetid smell – a hint of which Nicklin had picked up when he first entered the ship – to be totally eliminated. And, inevitably, the machinery and equipment in the cylinders had suffered during the alien occupation. Some of the damage had been caused by dampness, but anything soft – insulation, seal materials, vibration mounts and the like – had disappeared into a multitude of tiny digestive systems.

Corey Montane had been appalled by visions of the consequent delay and expense; but the machine-lover in Nicklin had commiserated with the ship itself. *I'll make you well again*, he had promised it, conceiving an alluring plan to comprehend every scientific and engineering principle, to master every system, to learn every part number, and use the knowledge to restore the patient, uncomplaining entity that was the ship to a state of good health.

It was a grandiose project, one which very few would have undertaken, but it had kept him sane during the heartbreaking year on the road. He had built up a library of manufacturers' manuals in book, disk and tape form, and had eased the frustration of each new delay in the journey by telephoning orders for components which could be installed on the move. He had been aided in diverse ways by Scott Hepworth, who had imparted relevant knowledge in exchange for gin, and by Gerl Kingsley, who had thrown his muscular power into physically demanding tasks that a man could not accomplish on his own.

Now that the *Tara* was safely docked on the rim of Portal One the main restoration work was beginning. Nicklin and Hepworth had made a joint decision that every aspect of it could be handled by existing mission personnel, working under their guidance. Montane had been happy to accept that arrangement because it was likely to be the most economical. Moving the ship to Beachhead – an undertaking which had involved building temporary bridges in some places – had cost a fortune, and his financial resources were not unlimited.

The *Tara* was classed as an exploration vessel, and therefore had not been designed to carry large numbers of passengers, but it had the same major dimensions as all other ships of the 5M general type. The ubiquitous 5M label showed that the *Tara*'s three cylinders had an external radius of five metres – and therefore would accept a vast range of standardised off-the-shelf components, including diaphragm decks. At present it had only eight such decks – the minimum legal requirement for stiffening the central cylinder – but the plan was to fit many more at a spacing of two metres, thus making twenty-five available for passenger accommodation.

On that basis, it seemed that the maximum complement for the New Eden flight would be in the region of "two hundred souls", as Montane had put it. Nicklin – for whom it was all a kind of a game, an academic exercise – had suggested that, for straightforward biological considerations, all but a few of the souls should be housed in the bodies of nubile women. Montane had given him the expected lecture on the need to preserve moral standards, making it clear that he wanted to sign up only young married couples with a proven record of church-going.

He had reverted to being secretive about his corporate finances, but Nicklin had picked up enough clues to let him know that the preconditions imposed by Montane were limiting the mission's revenue. There were quite a few eccentric individuals around who were prepared to hand over large sums to secure places on the much-publicised expedition, but only a small minority of them fully matched Montane's stringent requirements.

The argument had reminded Nicklin of a basic fact which at times could slip his memory – that Corey Montane was an irrational being. He was not a religious maniac in the usual sense of the term; he was a certifiably insane person whose delusions simply happened to have a religious theme. His Ordinary Joe dress and general demeanour made it possible to forget about the coffin-cum-teatable, about the consultations with the corpse that lay within, about the deeply seated megalomania, about the lunatic goal towards which his entire life was directed.

It was difficult to imagine anything more ludicrous than the latest revelation – that Montane seemed to visualise the first landing on an unknown planet as something akin to an exclusive Youth For Christ adventure holiday, with air-beds and leaflets on how to erect the perimeter fence.

It was easy to ridicule the preacher and his crazy ideas, but crazy ideas sometimes had a way of translating themselves into reality. The massive, ungainly structure beyond the office window was proof of that. As he watched the snow sifting down over the mountainous triple hull, Nicklin experienced a strange, cool moment of unease. It was preposterous, he knew, but was a day going to come – was it *really* going to come? – when that grimy feature of the landscape would slide down into the portal and, like a seal entering water, be transformed by its new environment into a creature of confidence and surging power? Was it really going to bore through the blackness towards dim and irrelevant points of light? And might people die as a result? He was committed to restoring the *Tara* to its former magnificence, but purely as a *machine* – a fascinating toy – and ideally it would then be placed on static display, in a drowsy museum of technology, so that visitors could wonder at the polish and perfection of every component. It was oddly disconcerting to think that the results of his hobbyist enthusiasm and toil might end up in a decaying orbit around some remote planet, or – just as likely – drifting into infinity.

I'll tell you something for nothing, O Gaseous Vertebrate, he thought. *If she ever does head off into the wild black yonder, yours truly*

152

will be at home in his favourite armchair, feet up and glass in hand, watching the big event on television . . .

"When is this man going to get here?" Hepworth demanded, coming to stand at the window.

"You should ask Corey that." Nicklin glanced sideways, and as always his eyes triangulated of their own accord on the enormous blackhead at the side of Hepworth's nose.

"I wouldn't like to interrupt him, just to ask what's the hold-up with our distinguished visitor."

"The weather is probably delaying him a little," Montane said unconcernedly, without looking up from his desk. "Try to be a little more patient."

"Yes, and try not to fidget as much – you're like a pair of infants," added Ropp Voorsanger, Montane's accountant and legal adviser, from his position at the next desk. Voorsanger was a narrow-headed, narrow-faced man who was about thirty and looked twenty years older. He was also a lay preacher, which probably had something to do with his recruitment to the mission, but he was less tolerant and more severe than Montane in his manner. He had no time at all for either Nicklin or Hepworth.

"I do beg your pardon," Hepworth said to Voorsanger, his plump features showing indignation, "but there is work waiting for me in the ship. *Real* work! Not the sort of unproductive crap that you occupy your time with."

Nicklin suppressed a smile, knowing that the real work Hepworth had in mind was his hourly tot of gin. His original hope that the untidy and verbose physicist would make a good colleague had been realised. In spite of the heavy drinking, Hepworth never became muzzy or unwilling to pull his weight, and Nicklin made a point of backing him in every dispute.

"That's right, Corey," he said. "Scott and I have things to do, and – "

"And I'm tired of sending out search parties for you," Montane cut in. "No, I want the both of you here when Renard arrives. I want you to hear what he has to say, so just try to relax." He raised his head and looked significantly at Hepworth. "Why don't you have a cup of tea?"

Nicklin would have been interested in Hepworth's reply, but at that moment he saw a coloured blur moving behind the translucent

153

screen which separated Montane's office from the next. It meant that Danea Farthing had returned from one of the field trips which took her all over the PI area, and which kept her away from Beachhead for weeks at a time. Trying not to be obtrusive, he walked quickly to the connecting door and slid it open.

"Well?" Danea paused in the act of taking off her snow-dappled cape. She was wearing a belted suit of cobalt blue shot silk which clung expensively to her slim-hipped figure. Her heavy-lidded eyes regarded him with minimal interest, as though he were a piece of furniture.

"Very well, thanks." he said. "And you?"

"I didn't mean that – what do you want?"

"Who says I have to want anything?" *I want you, you cold bitch, because you're the best-looking woman in the universe – and you* owe *me!* "I just thought I'd say hello, and welcome you back to the office."

"Very kind of you." Danea stood quite still, making no move to hang up her cape, obviously waiting for him to leave.

"Have you come straight from the airport?"

"Yes."

"Long flight?"

"Yes."

"How about relaxing with a couple of drinks and a good lunch?"

"I've already arranged to do that, with a friend," Danea said, still not moving. "He's calling for me at noon."

"That's nice." Montane composed a rueful smile. "I just thought I'd ask."

Danea made no response, so he nodded to her and backed out of the small office, sliding the door shut between them. As soon as he was screened from her sight he allowed his sad little smile to develop into the full happy hayseed grin. A casual observer would probably have said that he had been well and truly frozen out, but he had picked up two signs of what he regarded as encouragement. During the exchange Danea had stood with the cape held to her throat, unconsciously – and revealingly – shielding her body from him. That was a Freudian give-away if ever he had seen one. Also, there had been no need, no need at all, for her to disclose that her lunch appointment was with another man. *You're getting there, Jim lad,*

Nicklin told himself with calm satisfaction. *It's taking a hell of a long time – but you'll get to her one fine day – and when you do . . .*

"That didn't last long," Hepworth said cheerfully when Nicklin rejoined him at the window. "Take the advice of an old hand at this kind of thing and give up gracefully – it's obvious the woman wants nothing to do with you."

"You don't understand," Nicklin replied, not pleased by the comment. *How could anybody with a blackhead the size of a dinner plate claim to be an expert on women?*

"Did you ask her out to lunch?"

"Yes."

"And?"

"She already has a date. With a man."

Hepworth nodded. "Probably Rowan Meeks. She met him through the books."

Nicklin would have preferred not to talk about Danea, but the cryptic reference had aroused his curiosity. "What books?"

"The talking variety. Danea spends a lot of her spare time putting books on tape for blind people. Apparently she has a very good voice for that sort of thing." Hepworth paused and gave Nicklin a quizzical look. "Didn't you know?"

"How would I know?"

"There you have it!" Hepworth said triumphantly. "You'll never get anywhere with a woman unless you're interested in her as a complete human being. The trouble with you, Jim, is that you're interested in only one thing – and it shows."

I wasn't always like that, and where did it . . . ? Nicklin interrupted the thought, angry at being required to defend himself. *If this keeps up there's going to be talk about the care and feeding of blackheads.*

"I had an idea that blind people used reading machines," he said, offering a conversational lure which was likely to inspire one of Hepworth's impromptu lecturettes.

"Voice synthesisers are still no good for literary readings, and, the way things have turned out, it looks as if they never will be," Hepworth said, happily seizing on the topic. "It's the old Orbitsville syndrome again. It's more than three hundred years since the first synthesisers were tried out, and you'd think they should have been perfected in all that time. But . . . *but* . . .

where's the motive? The great machine of science and technology has slipped a few cogs and will go on slipping cogs because we allow it to do so.

"Why? Because, on a crowded, polluted and thoroughly kneed-in-the-groin Earth, science and technology promised that one day everything would be put to rights, that one day there would be a perfect world for everybody to enjoy. That's what attracted the funding, that's where the motivation came from. But now the promise has been forgotten – both by the promisers and the promis*ees*. We've *got* our perfect world. We've got millions of them, in fact.

"Orbitsville handed them to us on the proverbial plate, so scientific and technological progress has pretty well come to a halt. Research is only carried out by 'eggheads' who have a personal interest in it, and, even when they do come up with something that has a lot of practical potential, it can't be developed because the kind of concentrated industrial base they need simply isn't there.

"There are quite a few people," Hepworth added portentously, "who would argue that Orbitsville hasn't done the human race any favours."

"You're beginning to sound like you-know-who," Nicklin said, nodding towards Montane, who was still busy at his desk.

"You-know-who is doing some of the right things for all the wrong reasons."

Nicklin was surprised. "You mean *you* want to get away from Orbitsville before the Devil presses the button?"

"No, I just want to get away from Orbitsville," Hepworth said placidly. "I want to see what an anti-matter planet looks like. Nobody but Corey has any intention of going to one, so I'm going to go with him."

"But . . . " Nicklin shook his head in disbelief. "You're saying that if the *Tara* actually manages to take off you'll be on board?"

"Jim, why do you think I joined this preposterous outfit? It wasn't for the miserable stipend that Corey doles out to us, I can assure you. That barely covers my tonic water, let alone the necessary. The only reason I'm here is that, as a paid-up member of the mission, I'm guaranteed a place on the ship when the big day comes."

A pained expression appeared on Hepworth's face. "I wish I hadn't mentioned drink. My thirst pangs were quite bearable until I mentioned the stuff."

"Too bad," Nicklin said abstractedly, still assimilating the news that Hepworth actually planned to journey off into nothingness on the *Tara*. He had tacitly assumed that, like him, the physicist was only hitching a ride on the Nowhere Express, standing on the footplate and preparing to jump clear in his own good time. Also, the subject of the anti-matter universe had cropped up again. To Nicklin, all the talk of Region One and Region Two universes, and of reversed time and electron-spraying isotopes, was merely a game of words – but it was transpiring that, to Hepworth, all these things were as real as his next glass of gin or the whistle trees which on a windy day mourned the passing of summer.

Not for the first time, Nicklin found himself wondering about the ingredient which perhaps had been left out of his mental make-up. For him reality had always comprised those things which directly affected his daily life and immediate well-being. Everything else was relegated to quasi-reality or total abstraction; thus he had always felt himself to be at a comfortable remove from those strange individuals who could dedicate their lives to shining principles or die for great causes. Life was complicated enough and tricky enough as it was. On a lesser scale, it had always been a matter for self-congratulation that he was immune to mysticism and superstition and religion. Scott Hepworth shared the same materialistic outlook, and yet here he was, ready to gamble his life on a desperate plunge into black emptiness, merely because he was curious about the electrical charge of sub-atomic particles. As a motive for risking death, there was not much to choose between it and Montane's bizarre fantasising.

"Explain just one thing to me, Scott," he said. "What difference does it make to *anybody* if it turns out that –"

He broke off as the outer door of the office slid open to admit a man and a woman. Nicklin at once recognised Rick Renard, whose ostentatious style of dress made him a focal point for the drab room, but although the woman's face seemed familiar there was a delay before he remembered having seen her on television. It had been in the Whites' living room, all that time ago, on the day Orbitsville was supposed to have made its Big Jump. That had also been the day Corey Montane and his entourage had come to town and Nicklin's private world had made a Big Jump of its own. In his mind he could hear Zindee White's voice: *Her name is Silvia London.*

"I've always wanted to be in London," he said under his breath, his eyes taking in the woman's full-bosomed figure, the voluptuous lines of which alerted his sexual instincts in spite of being modestly swathed in a charcoal grey coatdress. His amatory bouts with Christine McGivern were becoming too perfunctory and he had a hankering for something fresh.

Hepworth leaned closer to him. "What was that?"

"I think our presence is required, don't you?" Nicklin moved towards Montane and Voorsanger to become part of the little group which welcomed the visitors. Renard introduced the woman as his wife, a fact which in Nicklin's eyes added a certain spice to her appeal.

"I'm sorry we're late," Renard went on when the formalities had been completed, smiling in the oddly challenging manner which Nicklin had noticed before, even via television, and which rendered the apology meaningless.

Montane nodded. "The weather . . . "

"No, the snow didn't hold me back at all, but when I got here I couldn't resist having a stroll around the outside of your ship," Renard said. "It doesn't look much, does it?"

"It looks good to me," Nicklin said quickly.

Renard smiled directly at him. "I doubt if you're qualified to adjudicate."

"Adjudication runs in my family," Nicklin replied. "Why, I learned to adjudicate at my mother's knee." *And I adjudicate that you need a good kick up the balls, you arrogant bastard.* He smiled in return as he projected the thought with all the vehemence he could muster, but the only outcome of the telepathic attempt was a flicker of satisfaction in Renard's blue eyes.

"Why don't we sit down and talk in comfort?" Montane cut in. He gestured towards the cheap table, used mainly for in-office meals, which was the only piece of furniture at all suitable for a conference.

"Why not?" The amusement in Renard's eyes grew more evident as the chair he had selected emitted a metallic protest when he sat down.

For one instant Nicklin wished that Montane had not been so miserly over renting office space and equipment. Then it came to him that he was being lured into a personality duel. Renard was a man for whom every meeting had to be a skirmish, and every relationship a contest. *I'm not playing that game*, he thought, his antagonism towards Renard fading. He glanced at Renard's wife and caught a hint of what seemed to be resignation and embarrassment in her expression. *She doesn't think much of it as a spectator sport, either – perhaps she's in the market for a little diversion.* He moved quickly to ensure getting a seat next to Silvia at the table.

"I have another appointment this morning, so let's get on with what we have to do," Renard said to Montane. "I'm ready to give you four million monits for the ship as she sits. Your team can walk out and mine will walk in, and you won't even have to turn off the lights."

"Rick, I have already told you that the *Tara* isn't for sale," Montane replied. He was impressively cool, Nicklin thought, for someone who was refusing to become a millionaire.

"If you're planning to hold on, waiting for the price to go up, you're making a mistake." Renard was equally emotionless. "An interstellar ramjet isn't really suitable for interportal work, so the offer is a generous one."

"Perhaps, but I'm not interested."

"It won't be all that long before the first of the new short-range jobs start coming off the line – and when that happens the value of your old tub will drop."

Montane sighed. "I hate to appear discourteous, Rick, but you're not the only person whose diary is full – so let's not waste each other's time. The *Tara* is not for sale. All right?"

"I can only offer you the jam – I can't force you to eat it." Unperturbed, Renard leaned back in his seat, drawing more creaks from it.

"Now that we've got my dietary preferences out of the way," Montane said drily, "what was the other proposal you had in mind?"

"How many target stars have you selected?"

"Eight within a thousand light years."

"Good prospects?"

"I'm assured that they are very good." Montane glanced expectantly at Scott Hepworth.

"Omnirad analyses from the Garamond Institute show that three of them have an eighty per cent probability of yielding an Earth-type planet," Hepworth said in his grandest tones.

Renard raised his eyebrows, looking unexpectedly boyish in his surprise. "That's better than you would have got back home, isn't it?"

Nicklin, who had been taking heady draughts of Silvia's perfume, renewed his interest in the conversation as he realised that "back home" meant a different universe. The use of the phrase showed that Renard, hard-headed and materialistic as they come, had accepted the Big Jump hypothesis. Furthermore, he evidently saw the ethereal never-never land of the astrophysicists and cosmologists as a place where it was possible to turn a profit.

"It's a *lot* better," Hepworth said. "Worlds for the picking, you might say."

Renard addressed Montane again. "We can still do a deal. Let me put two or three scientific people on the ship, plus a spare flight crew to bring it back when you have finished with it – and you can still have the four million."

Corey, this is the proverbial offer you can't refuse, Nicklin thought, and almost winced as he saw Montane's patient smile of rejection.

"My conscience wouldn't allow me to go along with that," Montane said. "It would mean denying places to some of my own people. You must realise that I'm answerable to God in this matter."

"All right, I tell you what we'll do," Renard said. "When the ship gets back here I'll lease it out to you for a second round trip. That way you'll be saving *two* lots of souls."

Montane's smile became more patient, more condescending. "The *Tara* will make one flight, and only one flight. There will be no time for another. No second chance."

"Who told you that?"

"God."

"*God?*" The sheer incredulity in Renard's voice betrayed the first tiny crack in his composure.

Nicklin turned away in amusement – Renard probably ate hard-nosed business tycoons for breakfast, but he had never dealt with a deranged preacher whose chief adviser was a dead woman in a box. He discovered that Renard's wife was looking directly at him.

"Could I trouble someone for a hot drink?" she whispered. "Coffee?"

"I could whip up some tea," he replied, also whispering, pleased by the unexpected opportunity to separate her from the others.

"Tea would be fine."

"I'll join you in a cup." He flicked a glance towards Montane and Renard as he left his seat. "This could go on a long time."

"I was beginning to get that impression." She stood up and walked with him to the cupboard at the far end of the office where the meagre refreshment supply was kept. *This is good*, Nicklin told himself. *Things are going well, but Scott was right in what he said. The trick is not to be too direct. Show an interest in the woman as a rounded human being (and this one certainly qualifies on that score). Ask her about her beliefs and hobbies and dreams, and all that stuff . . .*

As he was spooning tea out of Montane's antique caddy he tilted his head, frowned a little and said, "I think I've seen you on television. Was your name London?"

"It still is," Silvia replied. "I kept my previous name when I married Rick."

"I *thought* I was right."

"Perhaps you picked up some of the transmissions from Portal 36 on the day when . . . when everything changed." Something seemed to happen in Silvia's brown eyes as she spoke. It was a swift and fleeting change, the wind brushing the surface of a deep lake, but it was enough to persuade Nicklin that the events at Portal 36 should be left alone.

"Perhaps," he said, "but I'm thinking more of . . . Was it called the Anima Mundi Foundation?"

"Yes!" Silvia's face was animated, suddenly made younger. "Are you interested in Karal London's work?"

Nicklin spurred his memory and it did not fail him. "On the survival of the personality after physical death? Fascinating subject."

"It's the most important subject of all. Have you attended any of the Foundation's seminars or seen any of the publications?"

"No – I've been out in the sticks for the last year or so, and I didn't have much chance to . . ."

Silvia touched his arm. "But you're familiar with the basics of mindon science?"

"I never quite got to grips with it," Nicklin said cautiously as he set out two cups.

"But it's all so beautifully simple!" Silvia continued, still keeping her voice low, but speaking with a fervent rapidity. "The mindon is a class of particle which was postulated a long time ago, but its existence wasn't finally proved until last year. Thanks to Karal's work we now know that mind is a universal property of matter, and that even elementary particles are endowed with it to some degree . . ."

Nicklin went on preparing the tea, nodding occasionally and awaiting his chance to divert Silvia on to more personal matters. Having led off with claims he had trouble accepting, she progressed – in tones of utter conviction – to something called "mental space" in which there existed mindon duplicates of human brains.

He found himself growing bemused under the bombardment of mystical ideas expressed in the jargon of nuclear physics, and still the right conversational opening failed to arrive. *What in hell is going wrong with everybody today?* he wondered as he filled the two cups. *Am I the only person in the whole world who is still anchored in reality?*

". . . shows that a personality is a structure of mental entities, existing in mental space, and therefore it survives destruction of the brain even though it required the brain's complex physical organisation in order to develop." Silvia eyed him intently. "You can see that, can't you?"

Nicklin moved her cup a centimetre closer to her. "Do you take milk?"

She ignored the tea, her gaze hunting across his face. "I really would like to hear what you think."

"I think the whole concept is very impressive," he said. His original dreams of hotel bedroom afternoons with Silvia were fading by the minute, and a disagreement at this stage could put paid to them altogether.

"Impressive." Silvia nodded to show her awareness of the word's ambivalence. "All right – what bothers you most?"

Amazed by how far the conversation had deviated from the one he had visualised, Nicklin said, "I guess it was all that stuff about how a personality is created. If, as you say, all matter has a mindon component – and all that's needed for a personality to be conjured into existence is physical complexity – then you don't need to bring in any biological – "

"Jim!" Corey Montane's intrusive voice was thorned with impatience. "Bring your tea to the table, will you?"

Nicklin put on a rueful expression. "I have to slide over there and do some work – but I'd like to go on with this."

"I'd like that, too," Silvia said. "We can talk some more after the meeting."

He smiled, keeping his eyes on hers. "That's not what I meant."

Her expression remained unchanged for a moment, and he realised she had plunged so deeply into her special realm of metaphysics that she was having genuine difficulty in getting back to the mundane world. But when it came her reaction was unequivocal.

"You said you had to *slide* back to your work – so why don't you do that?" She turned away from him to pick up her teacup.

Nicklin was unwilling to be dismissed so easily. "I was only checking. No harm in checking."

"Do people like you never get bored with themselves?"

"I could ask you the same question," he said pleasantly as he moved away to rejoin the group at the table. He found that events had moved quickly during his absence. Renard had apparently shelved the idea of acquiring the *Tara*, and had assumed the role of broker for every type of component.

"I understand from Corey," he said, "that you're in the market for a couple of dozen 5M decks."

"That's about right." Nicklin was careful not to show any enthusiasm. "We're thinking of putting in perhaps another twenty-five."

"I've got them."

"What price?"

"Oh . . . " Renard closed his eyes for a second, pretending to make a calculation. "Let's say thirty-thousand. Monits, that is – not orbs."

Nicklin ignored the implication that he was a country boy and unaccustomed to global currency. The price was much less than he had expected from a business shark like Renard, and he began to look around for a catch.

"What condition are they in?"

"Unused," Renard said comfortably. "They're pretty old, of course, but unused. Most of them are still in the plastic skins."

Nicklin saw Montane and Voorsanger exchange congratulatory glances, and his conviction that something was wrong with Renard's offer grew stronger. He went over the figures again in his mind, and suddenly he understood the cat-and-mouse game that Renard was playing. *The bastard!* he thought with reluctant admiration. *He's even more of a shit than I gave him credit for!*

"Well, Rick," Montane said, "on that basis I believe we can go ahead and – "

"Before you go too far," Nicklin cut in, "ask Mr Renard if thirty-thousand is the *unit* price."

Montane frowned at him, then gaped at Renard. "But that would make it . . . three-quarters of a million for twenty-five old decks!"

"We're in what's commonly referred to as a sellers' market," Renard said, his lips twitching in amusement.

Nicklin smiled to let Renard see that he too had enjoyed the bit of fun. "All the same, Rick," he said, "don't you think it's going just a teensy-weensy bit far to try selling old decks for three times the price of new ones?"

"Their value has escalated. Most of the new decks disappeared when the exterior stockyards vanished, and my associates have bought up any that were left sitting around the land-docks."

"In that case I'll use older ones,"Montane said doggedly, staring down at his desk.

"We've got most of those, too." Renard slowly shook his head, as though in commiseration. "Interportal trade *must* be restored as quickly as possible, you see, for the good of society. We have to get those ships out there as soon as we can, even if it means taking short-cuts in the manufacture."

"In *that* case," Montane said, rising to his feet, "I'll use the old decks you rejected or missed. I'll dig them out of the ground in scrapyards, if necessary, and I'll glue them together with spit." His voice had developed a kind of magisterial power. "No human agency will stand in the way of the *Tara* being completed – and I promise you that in the name of God."

"You'll need all the help He can give you to get flight certification," Renard murmured.

Montane stared at him in loathing. "Why don't you – ? Why don't you – ?"

"Allow me," Nicklin came in, turning to give Renard a contented smile. "Corey is a man of the cloth and that makes it difficult for him to express certain sentiments – but it's my guess that he wants you to fuck off."

The mocking gleam in Renard's eyes abruptly faded and he turned back to Montane. "You should choose your colleagues with a bit more discretion."

"My colleague's language has grown increasingly vile ever since I met him," Montane said. "It's something I usually deplore – but not on this occasion."

"I've wasted too much time here as it is," Renard said, getting up from his seat. He beckoned to Silvia, who had already set her teacup down, and they walked in silence to the exit.

Nicklin continued gazing wistfully after Silvia until the door had slid shut behind her. "It's the wife I always feel sorry for."

"I noticed you feeling sorry for her," Hepworth said in jovial reproof. "You were trying it on, weren't you?"

"That woman deserves something better out of life than Rick Renard."

Hepworth chuckled. "And obviously you didn't measure up."

"Do we have to put up with this kind of talk?" Voorsanger said to Montane, his elongated face registering disgust. "It seems to me that things have taken a bad enough turn without our having to listen to smut."

"Ropp is quite right." Montane directed a sombre stare at Nicklin and Hepworth.

"I thought we dealt with Mr Renard rather well," Nicklin said. "You in particular, chief. I was quite proud of you at the end." He was still speaking in a flippant manner, and it was only after the words were out that he realised he actually meant them. Montane, crazy or not, had stood up for his principles and beliefs against a rich and powerful opponent.

"The fact is," Montane replied quietly, "that completing the *Tara* is going to take a lot longer than we expected – and I have a feeling there may not be enough time."

CHAPTER 15

Obtaining a new job had proved much easier than Nicklin had expected.

Yip & Wrigley was a new company which had been formed to enter the booming market in medium-sized interportal freighters, and – unusually – had decided to locate its manufacturing facility in Beachhead. Traditionally, Orbitsville had relied on Earth for spaceship production. It had only a few yards with manufacturing capability, and they were sited in Dalton, the great industrial conurbation at P12. Beachhead had always been a spaceport, with limited repair and maintenance facilities, and as a consequence had no pool of the kind of expertise Yip & Wrigley needed.

Tommy Yip, the company's president, had at first been concerned over Nicklin's lack of formal engineering qualifications, and then – as a fellow machine-lover – had been impressed by his practical skills and computer-like ability to carry hundreds of component specifications in his memory. As a consequence, Nicklin had been offered a senior position in engineering management – title and responsibilities yet to be defined – and was expected to take it up as soon as he had disengaged from Corey Montane.

He had mixed feelings as he entered the portal complex on foot and saw the massive triple hull of the *Tara*. It was a fresh, breezy morning in early spring and the ship's skin, now immaculate, was gleaming with the coppery lustre which was peculiar to electronsated metals. The rakish, crimson-and-white shape of the pinnace was in place underneath the nose section, and the *Tara* gave the impression of being ready to go among the stars.

It was difficult for Nicklin to accept that more than two years had passed since the ship, moribund and begrimed, had been hauled into place at the rim of the portal. He had laboured unceasingly during that time, refusing even the shortest vacations, surrendering much that made up normal existence to his private obsession. In many respects he had been like a general waging a bitter campaign against enemies who continually changed their positions and tactics.

Major structural elements – such as diaphragm decks and bulkheads – had been only part of his remit. There had been the thousands of minor components, ranging from stair treads and handrails to storage racks; and the multitudinous systems relating to everything from ventilation to waste disposal. A starship was a machine for keeping hundreds of human beings alive in a hostile environment, and the complexities of that machine were almost endless.

At every stage of procuration the work had been hampered by the unseen forces of Renard's consortium. At the blackest times Nicklin had felt a paranoid certainty that Renard was personally and vindictively blocking his progress, but on the whole he had accepted that the *Tara* was an incidental casualty of the consortium's activities. The real opponent was the immutable law of supply and demand, with some backing from an ancient foe which had been known to engineers since the dawn of technology, and which they had dubbed Murphy's Law.

Nicklin had often been obliged to accept parts intended for a slightly different mark of vessel, and which should have been very easily adapted. But in many cases, as though malign and leering gremlins were responsible, the chance shaping of a flange or the placing of a single stud had been all that was required to trigger vast series of time-consuming modifications. The mission's little army of workers had at times been required to operate a three-shift system, and under Nicklin's close supervision had developed an impressive range of manual skills.

Scott Hepworth had faced parallel difficulties with the *Tara's* drive machinery, on occasion having to employ specialists from outside, but in the end – after more than two years of dedicated effort – the work had been completed.

The bird is ready to fly, Nicklin thought as he walked in the prism of shade cast by his sun-hat. *The only trouble is that nobody is going to open the cage.*

Reaching the main ramp leading up to the ship's passenger cylinder, he paused as he saw Lan Huertas descending to ground level. Huertas, the mission's solitary black man, had been the first person to speak to Nicklin on the fateful day of his induction in Orangefield. He was also the one, making no bones about his personal dislike, who now spoke to him least.

"Good morning, my old buddy, my old chum!" Nicklin spoke cheerfully, following his policy of irritating Huertas with a show of effusive friendliness. "How are you this morning?"

"Okay," Huertas muttered, attempting to slide past.

"I'm really glad to hear that," Nicklin said. "Tell me, my old cobber, is Corey in the ship?"

"Hotel."

"I'm indebted to you." Nicklin gave Huertas a comradely punch on the shoulder and turned away in the direction of the Firstfooter Hotel. The Firstfooter, having depended almost entirely on spaceport traffic, had been in serious financial trouble since the Big Jump, and its management had been happy to give special concessions on the small amount of business Montane brought its way. It accommodated a few families of his pilgrims, mostly from outlying parts of the P1 region, who had come to Beachhead without waiting to be given a departure date.

Nicklin had seen them wandering around Garamond Park in a group, the children delighting in the unprecedented holiday, the parents instinctively banding together to fend off their sense of belonging nowhere. He saw them as pathetic figures who had renounced their stake in one world and would remain in a limbo of irrelevance until they reached another. He felt no concern for the adults, on the grounds that anybody who was so crazy as to give everything away because of a religious fad deserved little sympathy. *You never should beggar yourself unless it's for a really important and sensible reason – such as a snake-hipped woman telling you you're a good lay.* But it was taking the joke a bit far, even for the Great Prankster himself, when the lives of small children were so profoundly distorted.

Nicklin sometimes wondered if Montane was totally immune to experiencing doubt on that issue. Hurling them off into the void towards some putative speck of dirt brought quite a new meaning to the phrase "suffer the little children". Their best hope for the future lay in the fact that the *Tara* had so little chance of ever setting out for New Eden – the Certification Wars, as Nicklin thought of them, were seeing to that.

Warned of the difficulties of getting operational clearance, Montane had carried out an astute move in making all his disciples into shareholders in a registered company. Legally they were now part-owners of the *Tara*, which meant that it had become a private rather than a public transport and therefore was subject to less rigorous controls. Such niceties seemed to be cutting little ice with the Space Transport Department inspectors, however.

Nicklin had seen Metagov officials arrive and depart in droves, most with the fixed prim expressions of bureaucrats who regarded the resurrected ship as a threat to their entire mode of existence. Their philosophy, as he had explained it to an uncomprehending Montane and Voorsanger, was that a bolt hole which had been drilled *in situ* by one worker was not as good as a bolt hole drilled by another worker in a properly licensed factory.

There were two ways out of the impasse, he had added. One was to resort to extensive bribery, at the highest and lowest levels; the other was to burn through the STD locks on the *Tara*'s slideway and drop the ship through the aperture in the dead of night. Montane had treated both suggestions as bad jokes, and apparently was waiting for a divine intervention to enable him to set sail with his band of pilgrim fathers and pilgrim mothers-to-be.

This is definitely the right time to go, Nicklin thought as he walked away from the ship. *I've done all that I set out to do – with the notable exception of Danea – and I'm ready for what the Gaseous Vertebrate has to offer next.*

He came out of the port authority land through a deserted cargo entrance and crossed Lindstrom Boulevard. The crystal pyramid of the Firstfooter was on his right, its sloping aspects mirroring the pale blue archways of the Orbitsville sky. He had just turned in the direction of the hotel when he saw a tall young woman walking towards him. She was wearing a lime sun-hat and matching shorts-and-halter outfit which complemented her blonde hair and tanned skin. The overall effect was of confident, graceful good looks, but what drew Nicklin's attention was that she was smiling directly at him. There was also something about her which struck a mnemonic chord in his mind, and for a moment he wondered if she could be one of the many young prostitutes he had dallied with in the past two years.

"Jim!" she called out. "I was just coming to find you!"

He stared at her perfect, small-chinned face as she drew close and it was the look of recognition in her eyes which completed his own memories. "Zindee! Zindee White!"

She came to him with open arms and clung to him as they kissed. Even in the midst of his pleasurable surprise, he was aware of the pressure of her compact breasts and that she was kissing him full on the mouth, expertly and generously. *This is good*, he thought, *as good as I've ever known it to be . . .*

"Let me look at you," he said as they ended the embrace. "Why, the last time I saw you you were a little girl!"

He had often heard adults use exactly the same words when confronted by a young person who had been transformed in a few years, but he was quite unable to improve on the formula. Biological magic had been at work on Zindee, and he could only stand in awe of the outcome. She was still the child he had known, but that component of her was overwhelmed by the sheer physical presence of a beautiful woman.

"I can't believe this," he said. "What age are you now?"

"Seventeen."

He shook his head. "I can't believe this! Zindee White!"

"You never wrote to me" she said reproachfully.

"I know, and I'm sorry. I didn't forget about you, but things have been happening." ·

"I heard about them. In any case, I couldn't have forgotten about you." She gave him an oddly shy smile and fingered a small bronze disk which was on a chain at her throat. He had taken it to be a medallion, but on closer inspection saw that it was an ancient coin.

"What are you *doing* in this part of the world?" he said.

"Family visit to the big smoke." She took her hand away from the coin for an instant looking saddened, and it occurred to him that either of her parents might have come to Beachhead to attend one of the large medical institutes.

"How are Cham and Nora these days?" he said.

"They're fine. We checked in at the Firstfooter about an hour ago, and the information centre flashed me where to find you." She looked beyond him towards the port area. "I was hoping to get there before you left."

"In other words, you only want me for my spaceship."

Zindee half-closed her eyes. "I wouldn't say that – but I've never even *seen* one before."

"Come on!"

They crossed the boulevard to the port authority gatehouse, where at Nicklin's request a uniformed guard issued Zindee with a visitor's pass in the form of a circular silver badge. As they walked arm-in-arm towards the ship, their sun-hats rubbing edges, Zindee explained that she was planning to take a general sciences course at the Denise Serra Memorial in East Beachhead, perhaps as a prelude to majoring in entomology. Her parents had come with her to combine a preliminary look at the college with a vacation.

"That's great news," Nicklin said. "If you're going to be living in Beachhead for two or three years we'll be able to see each other regularly."

Zindee's step faltered. "But . . . Aren't you going away?"

Her meaning eluded him for a moment, then he gave a surprised laugh. "Christ, no! Nothing, but *nothing*, would induce me to risk my valuable little ass on a trip to nowhere – especially with that bunch of heliumheads."

"I hadn't realised," Zindee said. "I thought you and – "

"Danea? The Bitch in Black? That never came to anything – not that it *was* anything to start off with."

"You sound bitter, Jim."

"Why should I be bitter? She got me out of Orangefield, and that was the best thing that ever happened to me. I'm a new man now, Zindee, my girl."

"I see."

Zindee began to bring him up to date on events and local characters in Orangefield, but in the main her words were passing him by. The distraction was the nearness of her lithe young body, the erotic effect of which was enhanced by memories of the special relationship which had long existed between them. Making love to Zindee would be quite unlike the casual coupling with strangers, the sexual diet to which he had never become fully accustomed. It would be warm, profoundly exciting and – above all – fulfilling. It was precisely what he *needed* at this turning point in his life, and it was a fabulous piece of good fortune that she had materialised out of the past at the perfect moment. Truly, the Gaseous Vertebrate was in a good mood.

"So that's what a starship looks like," Zindee breathed. "It's beautiful!"

"It's not bad," Nicklin agreed, running his gaze over the lustrous hull of the *Tara*, which was coming into view from behind a docks office building. "You should have seen the mess it was in a couple of years ago."

"And there's the portal itself! I can't wait to have my first look at the stars."

"They're nothing to get worked up about," he said. "Would you like to have a look around inside the ship?"

"Can I?" Zindee hugged his arm excitedly.

"You bet!" Again feeling the pressure of her breasts, he wondered if she knew what she was doing, then decided she knew exactly the effect the intimate contact would have. Everything about her told him she was sexually active, and now it was up to him to get things moving. He was twice her age, which might create a problem with the straight-laced Cham and Nora, but there were ways around such difficulties – especially for an old and trusted friend of the family. The idea that he might be able to lie down with the golden child-woman later that same day caused a slow blood-pounding throughout his body.

But don't rush your fences, he told himself. *It all has to happen naturally. Slowly, naturally and inevitably . . .*

"Can we go in right now?" Zindee said.

"Any time you . . . " Nicklin paused as he noticed a car with STD markings waiting near the foot of the main ramp. Scott Hepworth was standing beside it, talking to three men who looked like Metagov officials. The agitated movements of Hepworth's arms made it apparent that he was involved in some kind of argument. He turned abruptly and strode up the ramp, followed by the officials, and the four men disappeared into the dark rectangle of the main hatch.

"We'd better wait here for a few minutes," Nicklin said. "It's going to be a bit crowded inside for a while."

"Even in such a big ship?"

"Now that the fitting-out is finished there's only one gangplank

172

to get around on. Besides, there's likely to be a lot of vile language floating about – not the sort of thing for an innocent maiden's ears."

Zindee stepped back from Nicklin and tilted her sun-hat, giving him a breathtaking smile. "Who says I'm innocent? Or even a maiden?"

Tonight, he vowed, resisting the urge to kiss her again. *It has to be tonight.*

"Zindee," he said, "I doubt if even a sophisticate like you is ready for Scott Hepworth."

"Why not?"

"He drinks too much, he eats too much, he's a slob, he tells lies, he wastes all his money, he has a filthy mind – in short, he has all the qualities I expect of a friend."

Zindee laughed. "What else do you like about him?"

Encouraged by her response, and knowing he had sufficient Hepworth anecdotes to pass a full hour if necessary, Nicklin described how and why the physicist had been thrown out of the Garamond Institute. "Any idiot can see the world in a grain of sand," he concluded, "but only Scott Hepworth could see another universe in a lump of metal."

Unexpectedly, Zindee looked thoughtful. "Is he supposed to be your scientific adviser?"

"We don't go in for formal titles, but . . . yes. Sort of. He's mainly concerned with the engines."

A scornful expression appeared on Zindee's face, making her look like the child Nicklin remembered. "I hope he knows more about engines than he does about physics."

"What do you mean?"

"Jim, even *I* know that the cobalt 60 experiment wouldn't show that Orbitsville had become part of an anti-matter time-reversed universe. Have you never heard of the CPT rule?"

Nicklin blinked. "Should I have?"

"Perhaps not," Zindee said, "but it states that where *everything* is reversed there's no way to detect the change. It also states that your friend made a balls of setting up his equipment."

"But he swears he had it right," Nicklin said. "According to Scott he came up with definite proof of the Big Jump."

"That's ox droppings, Jim."

He smiled on hearing one of Zindee's pet phrases and was reminded of her precocious ability to get things right. "Do *you* think all this stuff about a big jump is nonsense?"

"I don't know if it's nonsense or not. All I'm saying is that no amount of fiddling around with cobalt 60 or any other isotope will produce any evidence, one way or the other."

Nicklin considered the notion that the restoration work on the *Tara's* drive units had been governed by a man who was capable of making basic errors. Or, what was worse, the type of man who refused to acknowledge a mistake once it had been made. It was probably just as well for all concerned that the Metagov inspectorate was proving so stubborn over issuing any spaceworthiness documents for the ship.

"It's all academic, anyway – the *Tara* isn't going anywhere, in spite of all the news stories," he said, shrugging. "Do you want to walk to the front end and have a better look at the pinnace?"

"Yes, please." As they went closer to the black lake of the portal the morning breeze whipped Zindee's flimsy clothing against her body, making her look like a tawny creature from a sexist advertisement. Nicklin became aware that all the men within visual range were staring at her. *You can't have any, folks*, he gloated. *It's all mine!*

"It must be wonderful to fly in something like that," she said, holding her sun-hat in place as she gazed up at the sleek aerodynamic form of the pinnace. Suspended in its flying attitude beneath the *Tara's* nose section, the little ship was quite close to the rim of the portal and the imagination could see it straining to glide forward and swoop down into its natural environment.

"The pinnace is worth a fortune by itself these days," Nicklin said. "If Corey ever gets enough sense to sell up and forget about his loony mission he'll be a rich man."

"You don't think much of him?"

"He's a bollock-brain." Nicklin amplified his statement by telling how Montane took his wife's body everywhere he went and had been overheard conversing with the corpse.

Zindee looked incredulous. "Have you been sniffing something, Jim?"

"It's the truth! The late Mrs Montane is locked up inside there at this very minute," Nicklin said, pointing at Montane's camper which was parked close to the ship. "Corey sleeps in there at night instead of bunking down in the hotel with the rest of us. And he uses the coffin as a tea table."

Zindee narrowed her eyes at him. "This is one of your stories – right?"

"Wrong! I quit trying to jolly people along years ago. I give them the facts dead straight, and if they don't like what they hear that's their problem, not mine."

"How's your popularity rating?"

"Everybody around here adores me," Nicklin said. "Specially this character." He nodded towards the lumbering figure of Gerl Kingsley, who was approaching from the direction of the First-footer, probably on one of the obscure errands he was always running for Montane. "Mind you, I did save his life."

Kingsley slowed down as he came near and gave Nicklin the terrible lopsided grin which was a legacy from the day a bullet had passed through his head. His eyes were firmly fixed on Zindee the whole time he was passing.

"I think he likes you as well," Nicklin commented. "And I can't say I blame him." He tried to slip his arm around Zindee's waist, but she moved out of his reach.

"How did you save his life?" she said.

"Marksmanship." He related the episode that had taken place in the quietness of the Altamura countryside one morning, in what now seemed a distant summer. The events had rarely surfaced in his mind during the intervening years, and as he spoke he could almost believe they were part of someone else's life. By the time he had finished describing the grim aftermath – his disposal of the remains – the narrative, even to him, had something of the quality of a fevered dream.

"In case you're thinking that was another Nicklin special," he added, "I can assure you it all happened."

"I believe you," Zindee said. Her eyes were scrutinising his face and her expression was oddly intent, like that of a person searching for a valuable which had been lost or stolen.

Suddenly uncomfortable, he gestured towards the ship. "I wish Hepworth would get his backside out of there."

"I don't *need* to go inside."

"The old sod is bound to come out soon."

"Perhaps I'll walk over to the edge of the portal and . . . "

Zindee let the sentence go as her attention was drawn to a car which was drifting to a halt close by. It was a convertible with the top folded back. In it could be seen Danea Farthing with a man and woman and two children, obviously new arrivals being given their first look at the ship.

"Zindee's expression changed. "Isn't that . . . ?"

"That's Danea, all right," Nicklin said. "Lock up the silver."

"I didn't realise she had so much *style*." Zindee's voice was appreciative as she took in Danea's tight-belted peacock blue silks and stetson-like sun-hat. She impulsively raised her hand and waved as Danea glanced in her direction. Nicklin, remembering the natural antagonism that Zindee had displayed towards the older woman on their first meeting, was surprised by the action.

"She has a style all of her own," he agreed, giving the words a private bitter connotation, as Danea said something to her charges and came towards Zindee. His reaction to the sight of the sleepy-lidded eyes, bruised-looking mouth and hipless easy-striding figure was the same as ever – a blend of hatred and unadulterated, knee-weakening desire. For three years she had eluded, fended off and frustrated him, displaying an adamantine side to her character which no amount of guile could undermine, and which – though it tortured him to admit it – had brought her total victory in their running battle.

"Hello," Danea said, her gaze solely on Zindee. "Suddenly I'm persuaded that all little girls should be fed on a diet of ice cream sundaes."

Zindee smiled. "You've got a good memory."

"For faces – I'm not so good on names."

"This is Zindee," Nicklin said, putting an arm around Zindee's shoulders in a proprietary manner which Danea would not be able to miss. "Zindee White."

"It's good to see you again, Zindee," Danea said. "You're not joining the ship, are you?"

"No."

"I thought not. We have one family of Whites, but they don't have any connections with Orangefield."

"I'm here on holiday with my parents," Zindee said.

"I wish you *were* joining us." Danea gave her a look of rueful warmth. "Time is running out for Orbitsville, you know. Corey

Montane has told us that many times, and we all know in our hearts that he is right."

Nicklin squeezed Zindee's shoulder. "Corey Montane is the man who thinks he's married to a sardine."

"I have to go now," Danea said, still without looking in Nicklin's direction. "I wish you well, Zindee."

"What did you think of that performance?" Nicklin murmured in Zindee's ear as he watched Danea walk back to the group by her car. "That woman is, without doubt, the silliest and most –" He broke off, shocked, as Zindee pushed him away from her with surprising force.

"Keep off me," she snapped, her eyes flaring with white coronas of anger. "You're not making me part of your pathetic little game."

"*Zindee!*" He took a step towards her, but was halted by the look of contempt which was distorting and ageing her features. "Look, there's been a misunderstanding somewhere. Let's go back to my hotel room and –"

"Goodbye, Jim!" Zindee snatched the bronze coin from her throat, snapping its chain. "And here's something to remember me by!" She threw the coin to the ground at his feet, turned on her heel and walked quickly away.

"But –" Stupefied, he looked down at the coin and a dam seemed to burst in his memory. *I gave her that – on the day I left Orangefield.*

He picked the coin up, with the intention of running in pursuit of Zindee, and had taken a single step forward when silently – and with the abruptness of a door being slammed – the entire world turned black.

Nicklin gave an involuntary cry of fear as for one pounding moment he thought he had been struck blind. The blackness seemed so absolute – there were no street lights, no office lights, no vehicle lights, no floodlights surrounding the ship – that it *had* to come from within, and he was being punished for his transgressions. Then his eyes began to adjust to the darkness, and slowly, like a design emerging on a photographic plate, the delicate ribbed pattern of the night sky unfurled itself above him, spanning the horizons.

Nicklin looked up towards the zenith and saw that the sun was hidden behind one of the opaque bands whose progression across the heavens created day and night on Orbitsville.

177

His fear returned with renewed force as he realised that somehow – and for the first time in humanity's experience – Orbitsville had leaped from the brilliance of morning into the blackness of midnight.

CHAPTER 16

"You can see for yourselves that the trap is closing." Corey Montane's face was grey and haggard as he addressed the group of about twenty workers who had assembled in the mission's third-floor office. To Nicklin he seemed dejected and slightly irresolute, just when he needed to rally and inspire his followers.

"You don't need me to tell you that the Devil is rubbing his hands tonight," Montane went on. "We must get away from this cursed place very soon, my friends – otherwise it will be too late."

Nicklin listened to the message, and for the first time since he had known Montane, felt no urge to scoff. The glowing display of the office holoclock, apparently floating in the air near a wall, showed 12.06 – but the windows were jet black. In place of the usual midday panorama of sunlit buildings and distant hills there were the stacked, serried and scattered lights of Beachhead City at night.

Nicklin's body clock was telling him that something had gone terribly wrong with the natural order of things, but even more disturbing was the feeling that vast *super*natural forces were at work. A mystical and superstitious element of his character – one he would have sworn did not exist – had been alerted, and it was whispering things he had no wish to hear. He had often tried to visualise the helplessness and despair experienced by someone caught in an earthquake. What must it be like, he had wondered, knowing there is no place to run to when the very ground has become your deadly enemy? Now he no longer had to imagine that sense of bleak futility. *Where is there to hide when a great hand parts the curving blue canopy of the sky, displacing night and day, and its owner casts a baleful eye on all that lies below?*

"How soon can we go, Corey?" a man called out. Nicklin

glanced round and saw that the speaker was the electrician, Jock Craig.

"It has to be as soon as possible," Montane replied. "I'm going to the Space Transport Department when – " He broke off, looking surprised, as his words were lost in a rebellious outcry from at least half of his audience.

"Nobody cares about certificates at a time like this," Craig shouted, abandoning the slightly obsequious tone with which he usually addressed the preacher. "We should cut the locks and go right now!"

His words produced a widespread murmur of approval. Montane quelled the sound by the familiar trick of raising both his hands and making a damping movement. The gesture was not as effective as usual, however, and the ensuing silence was less than complete.

"Do I hear you properly, Jock?" Montane said. "Are you proposing that we should leave most of our brethren behind? Don't forget how many of them are still waiting at home all over P1." He pointed at the communication panels, where columns of winking orange lights showed that dozens of callers were waiting to be answered. "What do we say to *them*? Do we tell them to go to the Devil?"

"It's better for some to be saved than none at all," Craig insisted, looking about him for support.

"I think we're all jumping the gun a little," Scott Hepworth cut in, booming, projecting his voice as though addressing a much larger audience. "We've seen one minor disturbance of the solar cage, and apart from that nothing has changed. Some kind of self-regulating mechanism could have been activated up there, something which routinely balances forces and adjusts the shadow pattern now and then. Don't forget we've been on Orbitsville for only two centuries, and that's no time at all in astronomical terms."

Hepworth's admonitory gaze swept around the assembly. "My advice is that we shouldn't panic."

There speaks the voice of cool reason, Nicklin thought. *Trouble is that nobody believes a word of it – and that includes me.*

"Scott is absolutely right," Montane said loudly, doing his utmost to reassert his authority. "We will begin calling in every one of our families, starting this very minute, but in the meantime I want . . ."

His voice faltered – hushed by a silent burst of light – as the daytime world in all its brilliance sprang into view beyond the office windows.

It materialised instantaneously, looking normal and serene and eternal, as though nothing out of the ordinary had ever taken place. Nicklin saw birds wheeling in the sunlit air, and flags stirring gently on the masts above the main passenger terminal. The scene remained pulsing on the eye for several seconds – during which time the people in the room exchanged stricken, speculative glances with their neighbours – then it vanished into blackness again amidst a chorus of terrified shouts and screams.

Nicklin was one of those who gave an involuntary cry because, on the instant of the new advent of night, he felt the entire floor of the office drop away beneath his feet. He *knew* at once that the building was collapsing, and that he was about to plunge down into its ruins. Then his eyes confirmed the curious fact that the office, and everything in it, was still firmly in place. Ashen-faced men and women were clutching at the furniture for support, but – astonishingly – the building showed itself to be perfectly intact and undamaged. A moment later the floor resumed its pressure on the soles of his feet.

The sensations normally associated with space flight were alien to Nicklin; he had never even ventured on funfair parabola rides – but his mind was quick to concoct an explanation for what had happened.

"There has been a temporary loss of gravity," Hepworth shouted above the hubbub, confirming the worst suspicions of all those present. "That's all it was – a temporary loss of gravity . . . nothing to become too alarmed about."

Nicklin gaped at the physicist's untidy figure, wondering if he had any idea how ridiculous he looked and sounded while trying to pass off the loss of gravity as though it had been a minor occurrence like an interruption to the local electricity supply. Nothing like this had ever happened on Orbitsville before. Even the sudden switching of day into night, terrifying though it had been, had not created the same degree of visceral fear, because light was only light after all, and everybody knew how simple it was to flick it on and off. But gravity was *different*! You did not fuck around with gravity. Nobody had ever succeeded in tampering with it or modifying it in any way. When gravity vanished every man, woman and child immediately became a learned professor of physics with a deep understanding of the fundamental forces of nature, knowing that where something so basic to existence could go wrong existence itself was in the balance.

As though the Gaseous Vertebrate wanted to endorse and applaud Nicklin's thought processes, the sunlit world outside the office blazed into being once more, but only for the time it took Nicklin to snatch a breath, then there was night again. The effect was so similar to lightning, or perhaps a thermonuclear flash, that he winced in dread of the appalling detonation which had to follow. Instead there was a profound silence in which came a series of shorter appearances – day, night, day, night, day, night – a calendar month compressed into a dozen stroboscopic seconds. Once or twice during the staccato sequence gravity slackened its bonds, but not so completely as before – then it was all over. Peaceful night reigned outside. The ceiling lights reasserted themselves, shining calmly over the humdrum microcosm of the office and its cheap furniture and all the frightened people who had expected to die.

"My God," a woman said quietly, "this is the end of the world!"

It would be more correct to say that Orbitsville has become unstable, Nicklin mused. *Of course, it comes to the same thing in the end . . .*

Hepworth pounded a table with his fist. "Does anybody know where Megan Fleischer is?"

The mention of the pilot's name was all the catalyst that was needed to convert apprehension into action. Not much was said, there were few outward signs of mortal fear, but everybody began to move, to busy themselves, and Nicklin knew they shared the same objectives – to warn their relatives and friends, to gather up vital belongings, to get on board the ship as quickly as possible. He knew exactly what was going on inside their heads because, suddenly, he was one of them.

Orbitsville was home for countless millions of humans and for two hundred years it had been a good home. Its mountains and prairies and oceans appeared to have the permanence of old Earth, but there were few of its inhabitants who had not, at one time or another, felt a pang of uneasiness over the fact that the Big O was a bubble. It was the most insubstantial object imaginable – a film of enigmatic material with a circumference of almost a billion kilometres and a thickness of only eight centimetres.

Nicklin's life had been one of blissful unconcern about such matters. He had insulated himself from them, or had dismissed them along with other concepts he found difficulty in handling. Nevertheless, a simple distaste for the idea of living on the inner surface of a bubble was part of his primal subconscious. It was out in the open now. The time bomb had detonated, and he had entered a new mental state in which his actions were governed by the compulsion to get away from Orbitsville before the unimaginable happened.

In that land-locked, self-oriented condition his perceptions of what was going on around him became patchy and flawed, magnifying some events and diminishing others.

At one stage he was very much aware of Montane hovering on the fringes of the action, virtually ignored by most of his subordinates. Montane looked like a man on the verge of collapse. He gave the impression of being bewildered, of not quite believing the evidence of his senses. It occurred to Nicklin that he might never have accepted in his innermost self that this day would really arrive. Given the choice, he might have gone on and on until he died, making endless preparations to lead the escape from Orbitsville, delaying the actual event for increasingly trivial reasons.

In another disconnected fragment of time Nicklin found that he was standing at the telephone in a smaller office, with no clear idea of why he was there. He stared at the instrument for a few seconds, waiting for his hold on reality to improve, then told it to connect him to the Whites' room in the Firstfooter Hotel. Almost at once Cham White's red-gold head appeared at the set's projection focus. He was wearing the unnaturally polite smile of a man who has just been sentenced to death.

"Jim!" he said. "Jim Nicklin! What's happening, Jim?"

Nicklin shook his head impatiently "There's no time to talk about it. Do you want to get out?"

"Out?"

"Out of Orbitsville. On the ship. Do you want to go?"

At that moment sunlight washed through the room in which Nicklin was standing, showing that the banded pattern of the sky had shifted again. Cham's image, transmitted through a kilometre of cable, brightened simultaneously.

"I'm afraid, Jim," he said, his squirrel-brown eyes wide with shock.

"We're all afraid, for Christ's sake," Nicklin snapped, losing his temper. "That's why I'm asking you if you want to take off out of here. How about it?"

"Nora and I thought about it more than once. We used to look out for you on television, and I guess that put the idea into our heads, but we never took it seriously enough. We never dreamed it would come to this. We have no tickets or whatever we would need for – "

"The ship will be travelling half-empty," Nicklin cut in, amazed at Cham's Montane-like ability to waste time on senseless trivia. "Is Zindee with you?"

Cham glanced to his left. "She's in the bedroom with her mother."

"Get them both down to the ship," Nicklin said urgently. "I'm talking to you as a friend, Cham. Get them down to the ship – and do it right now. I'll wait for you at the foot of the main ramp. Have you got that?"

Cham nodded unhappily. "What should we pack?"

"*Pack*! If you wait around to pack anything you'll end up fucking well dead!" Nicklin shook his fist in Cham's face and his knuckles went into the image, causing it to swirl like coloured smoke. "Get to the ship right now – and don't let anybody stop you!"

He turned away from the telephone as the last sentence he had blurted out sank into his own consciousness. Other people would want to scramble on board the *Tara* in this extreme hour; people who had no connection with the mission; people for whom the enterprise had been nothing more than an extended piece of silly-season journalism – until the Big O's Day of Judgement had arrived.

Half the population of Beachhead will want to ride, Nicklin told himself. *And they won't take no for an answer . . .*

★

184

In another fragment of time's mosaic he found himself in the ill-ventilated room, across the corridor from the main office, where miscellaneous effects belonging to mission personnel were stored.

Opening his own locker with a thumbprint, he took out the radiation rifle, which had been a useless encumbrance since that far-off morning in Altamura. When the Fugaccia mansion was being vacated he had taken the weapon for no reason other than a feeling that such a dangerous artefact ought not to be left lying around, perhaps for inquisitive children to find. Now it no longer seemed an encumbrance. It looked functional and deadly – qualities which were entirely appropriate to the situation.

He checked the rifle's power indicators, slung it on his shoulder and hurried out of the room.

When Nicklin emerged from the office building with the rest of the mission's staff it was into daylight conditions. The sun had been shining without interruption for more than ten minutes, and the fact that to him it seemed quite a long time was an indication of how much his confidence in the natural order had deteriorated. He moved out from under the building's broad eaves, looked up at the sky and felt a pang of sick dismay.

All his life the alternating bands of azure and lighter shades of blue – representing day and night regions on the opposite side of Orbitsville – had possessed a geometric regularity and perfection. Now they were wildly distorted, and – the feature which brought a clamminess to Nicklin's brow – were visibly in motion. For the most part the movement was a slow writhing, but there were several small areas where the stripes narrowed into lines and ran together in seething agitation. Those patches were forming at random in parts of the sky, boiling and shimmering for a brief period before smoothing out and dissolving.

Looking up at them, Nicklin guessed that a similar convergence had caused the frenzied alternation of light and darkness in the Beachhead region. The shadow play also told him the solar cage was convulsing like an invisible heart in its death spasms. *The end of the world is nigh.*

Quelling a forceful upheaval in his stomach, he looked towards the ship and saw that about thirty people, many of them spaceport workers, had already clustered around the main ramp. They were not attempting to pass Kingsley and Winnick, who were blocking access to the ramp, but the tension in the air suggested it would not take much to start them surging forward. Glancing in the opposite direction, Nicklin saw that the main gates had been closed. A crowd was forming outside. Some of its members were pressing against the bars and arguing with the uniformed guards, who were nervously pacing within. The sections of Lindstrom Boulevard visible between buildings were thronged with cars.

Corey Montane, looking more assured now that the big decision had been forced upon him, ran towards his camper, accompanied by Nibs Affleck and Lan Huertas. A larger group went towards the ramp, headed by the spindle-legged figure of Voorsanger who, incongruously, was carrying a computer under one arm. Four men, Jock Craig among them, were running to the kiosk which housed the slideway controls. The mountainous bulk of the *Tara*, reflecting the sun in a coppery glare, provided a towering backdrop to the scene of complex activity.

Nicklin remained where he was, feeling isolated from all that was happening around him, then became aware of shouting from the crowd at the main gate. He looked in that direction and at once saw Danea Farthing ushering men, women and children through the adjoining personnel entrance. Some uniformed guards had moved outside and were clearing a small space by pushing back intruders, but they were in obvious danger of being overwhelmed. As Nicklin watched, a burly man penetrated the line by sheer force. He darted through the entrance and collided with two guards who had just emerged from the gatehouse. They grappled with him and the three began a lurching struggle which drew alarmed cries from women nearby.

Knots of migrants, some of them carrying suitcases, had already separated from the confusion and were hastening towards the ship. The adults' faces were distraught, but quite a few of the children with them – secure in their innocence – merely looked excited, with eyes for nothing but the gleaming contours of the *Tara*.

Nicklin ran past them, belatedly remembering that Cham and Nora White had no security passes and therefore would be denied entrance. By the time he reached the gate the struggle between the two spaceport guards and their captive was ending. They had glued the burly man's wrists together behind him with restraint patches and were bundling him into the gatehouse.

One of them, a fair-skinned heavyweight, frowned at Nicklin. "You shouldn't be carrying that weapon, mister."

Nicklin glanced at the sky. "Do you want to run me in?"

"Take your people away, and do it fast" the guard said. "We just got word that a mob of two or three thousand have come out of town through Garamond Park. They're tearing holes in our north fence right now and they'll be on top of you real soon."

"Thanks," Nicklin said.

"Don't thank me – I don't want to be in the middle of a war, that's all."

"Wise man." Nicklin ran to Danea and grabbed her arm. "I want to take Zindee and her parents. They'll need badges."

She gave him a thoughtful stare, took three gold disks from her pocket and handed them over. "There isn't much time – Megan is already on the ship."

Nicklin had to think for a moment before remembering that Megan was the pilot. "What about the paying customers?" he said, controlling a new surge of panic. "Many to come?"

Danea glanced at her watch, which was in counting mode. "Four that I know of. They should be here at any sec – " She looked out through the bars of the main gate at the surging crowd. "I see them!"

Nicklin went out through the personnel gate and saw that the hard-pressed guards were already bringing a young man and woman, each carrying a child, into the cleared space. Raising himself on his toes, he scanned the crowd and felt a pang of relief as he picked out Cham White's coppery hair and anxious face amid the leaven of heads.

"Only three more to come," he told the nearest guard.

"Friggin' good job," the sweating man grunted. "We're goin' to go under in a minute."

Nicklin threw his weight against the wall of bodies. For an instant he was surprised at how readily they parted for him, then he realised that the eyes of those in the forefront were on the rifle. He managed to grasp Cham's outstretched hand and drag him out of the throng. Nora White and Zindee followed close behind, literally ejected by the human pressure from behind, though not without some resentful pushing and clawing from the individuals they left in their wake. They were wearing identical one-piece green daysuits, and both looked pale and bewildered. Nora's gaze never left Nicklin's face, as though it had become a source of wonder to her, but Zindee kept her eyes averted.

"Through there," Nicklin said, urging Cham and the two women towards the narrow gate.

"Not so fast!" The speaker was a guard with sergeant's chevrons on his sleeve. "Nobody goes in without a pass."

"It's taken care of." Nicklin handed each of the Whites a gold badge and bundled them into the gateway. The action had a galvanic effect on the crowd. Until that moment some vestige of regard for rules had held them in check, but the sight of three of their number being so arbitrarily favoured drove them forward in resentment. The guards were slammed back against the bars and there was a flurry of vicious in-fighting while they got themselves inside to safety and bolted the personnel gate.

"What are you waiting for?" The sergeant was wiping blood from his mouth as he shouted at Nicklin and Danea. "Get out of here!"

Nicklin ran with the others in the direction of the *Tara*. The adults were shepherding the children who were too big to be carried. As they neared the ship Nicklin saw that Montane and Kingsley were carrying the pewter oblong of Milly Montane's coffin up the ramp. Emigrants were clustered at the foot of the long incline while others crowded up it behind the two slow-moving men. Other men, Scott Hepworth among them, were running towards the slideway control kiosk.

Nicklin barely had time to realise that the kiosk was the centre of some kind of disturbance when, without warning, his surroundings were plunged into blackness. There followed another frenzied sequence of alternations between sunlight and darkness. The changes were occurring two or three times a second, turning the entire scene into a vast stage with characters frozen in place by lightning flashes. Cries of alarm were heard as gravity underwent sickening fluctuations, creating the impression that the ground itself was rising and falling.

The stroboscopic nightmare went on for a subjective eternity – perhaps ten seconds – and then, as before, the sanity of continuous sunlight flooded back into the world.

The late arrivers, freed from paralysis, resumed the rush towards the ship, stumbling in their renewed anxiety. One man threw away a suitcase, gathered up his son and ran ahead with him. Danea and Zindee were together, urging children forward, but Nora White kept staring at Nicklin, as though somehow he were the author of all her troubles and the only one she could look to to put everything right. A strong wind was springing up, probably in response to the contortions of the solar cage, and dust began streaming across the dry concrete.

Nicklin looked in the direction of the kiosk and saw that a confrontation seemed to be taking place between some of the mission's workers and a man in the grey uniform of a port official. The man was framed in the doorway of the glazed booth, angrily brandishing his arms. Deducing what the argument was about, Nicklin broke away from his group and ran to the kiosk.

Hepworth turned to him as he arrived. "This character – he calls himself the slidemaster, would you believe? – is refusing to run the ship out."

"Drag him out of there and we'll do it ourselves."

"He has a gun and he says he's prepared to use it, and I think he's the sort of schmuck that would do just that." Hepworth's plump face was purple with rage and frustration. "Besides, the controls have a coded lock."

"What about the locks on the slideway itself?"

"We burned them off."

"Right!" Nicklin said, unslinging his rifle.

The half-dozen mission workers hastily moved out of the way, creating an avenue between Nicklin and the port official. He was a long-faced man in his fifties, with cropped grey hair and a small geometrically exact moustache. His posture was severely upright and square-shouldered, and his uniform meticulously correct in every detail – except for the gun belt, which looked as though it had come from a militaria supplier. Nicklin guessed that it had been languishing in a drawer somewhere, held in reserve in the hope that an appropriate day of crisis would eventually arrive. *Just my luck*, he thought. *A would-be Roman centurion staving off the collapse of civilisation with a book of regulations* . . .

"There's no time to play games," he said. "You're going to start the slide rolling – and you're going to do it right now."

The official looked him up and down, contemptuously, before shaking his head. "Nothing will move around here without the proper authorisation."

"I've *got* the proper authorisation." Nicklin made a show of activating the rifle. "It's pointing at your navel."

"That curious object!" The official placed a hand on the butt of his old-style revolver and smiled to show that he knew something about weaponry. "It isn't even a good replica."

"You're right." Nicklin elevated the rifle slightly and squeezed the trigger. A blue-white ray stabbed through the roof of the kiosk, explosively vaporising part of the gutter, eaves and plastic rafters, sending a swirl of sparks and smoke down the wind. Even Nicklin, who had good reason to appreciate the power of the weapon, was taken aback by the extent of the damage.

"It's a fucking awful replica," he said to the uniformed man, who had cringed back from the flash. "Now, about the slideway . . ."

"I don't think you'd be stupid enough to use that thing on me." The man straightened up and squared his shoulders as he spoke, but there was a trace of uncertainty in his voice.

Nicklin moved one step closer and gave him the full happy hayseed grin, while his eyes promised murder. "I've killed other men with this, and I'm fully prepared to blow you into two separate pieces – a top half and a bottom half."

For a moment there was no sound but that of the wind, then there came distant shouting from the north side of the dock complex. Nicklin glanced towards it, in the direction of the park boundary, and saw moving flecks of colour which signalled the advance of the expected mob. He swung his gaze back to the official and immediately sensed that something had changed in him.

"I try to do what they pay me for, but there's nothing in my contract about getting myself killed," the man said with a shrug. "No hard feelings, eh?"

Nicklin blinked at him, giving away nothing. "No feelings of any kind. Are you going to roll the ship and stay alive?"

"I'm going to roll the ship. As soon as you get your party on board, away she goes!"

Hepworth moved close to Nicklin and laid a hand on his shoulder. "Jim, you can see what he's up to. As soon as we go on board and seal the ship he's going to run for cover and leave us high and dry. Even if we open the doors again it'll be too late to – "

"I *know* what he's up to," Nicklin snapped, keeping the rifle steady on the man in the kiosk. "We're all going on board now. I'll be walking backwards, so keep a clear space behind me – especially on the ramp. Okay?"

"Okay, Jim." Hepworth moved away towards the ship and the rest of the mission workers backed off with him.

"All right, here's what we're going to do," Nicklin said to the watchful official. "I could easily pick you off at three kilometres with this imitation replica, so there's no chance of me missing you inside two or three hundred metres. I'm going on board the ship now, but I'll have the gun on you every step of the way. Even if you throw yourself down on the floor I'll destroy your little hut and everything in it, including you. Is that clear?"

"I won't do anything stupid." The man glanced towards the north where, at the end of a long row of sheds, it was now possible to discern individual running figures. "How will – ?"

"As soon as I get to the top of the ramp you start the slide moving. Don't wait for the door to close. As soon as you see me up there – roll the ship."

The man almost smiled. "That could be dangerous."

"For *you*," Nicklin countered. "That's when you'll be in the biggest danger. You might get the idea that I'll be too busy with the door locks to keep the cross-hairs on you – but I promise you I won't. The door will stay open until I feel the ship's nose going down, so – whatever you do – *keep the machinery running*."

"I'll be as nervous as hell by then," Nicklin added, beginning to back away, "but the gun will still be on you, and you'd better pray there aren't any power failures. If the slide sticks for even half a second I won't be able to stop my finger from twitching."

"Nothing will go wrong if I can help it," the man said, turning to his control panel.

Keeping the rifle aimed, not daring to glance behind him, Nicklin moved towards the ramp as quickly as he could. He had spent more time than he liked in talking to the slidemaster, but it had been necessary for the man to be very clear about what was expected of him. His peripheral vision told Nicklin that he was being watched by a number of port workers. They had formed an intermittent ring at a discreet distance, nobody caring to move forward in case the crazy man should be tempted to unleash another bolt of lightning.

The expanse of concrete between the kiosk and the *Tara* had become a sunlit arena, with wind-borne scraps of litter tumbling in the dust. Nicklin had full control of the situation because each person there was thinking as an individual, and had an individual's fear of being annihilated. But hundreds of new participants were racing towards the scene, and the formless sound which heralded their arrival told him they were thinking as a mob – and a mob knows itself to be collectively immortal. Were a few of its sub-units to blunder up the steps of the slideway control kiosk the *Tara* would never be able to take flight . . .

"The ramp is two steps behind you," Hepworth said.

"Got it." Nicklin moved on to the slope, thankful for its smooth anti-slip surface, and backed up it. As he gained height he got a more comprehensive view of his surroundings. The entire space-port area seemed to be awash in a riptide of humanity. He reached the entrance to the ship and, keeping the blue cross-hairs centred on the slidemaster, carefully stepped backwards to stand on the interior gangplank.

The *Tara* began to move immediately, and the platform at the head of the ramp slipped away to his right.

"The door hydraulics are on full pressure, Jim." Hepworth was hunkered down by the control panel. "Give the word when you want to close up."

"We have to wait till the ship actually dips its nose," Nicklin replied, while one part of his mind shrieked in disbelief at what was happening. "Our friend in the glass box knuckled under too easily. He isn't finished with us yet."

"But it takes time for the door to close. If we drop through the diaphragm field while it's still open – "

"Don't touch that button till I tell you!" Nicklin made his voice hard, concealing the agonies of suspense and apprehension inspired in him by the ship's almost imperceptible progress towards the rim of the aperture. The leaders of the crowd advancing from the park reached the dockside while he was speaking. Some of them came sprinting towards the ship, punching the air in their frustration, but others were surging around the kiosk.

Don't go up the steps, Nicklin prayed, his brow prickling with cold sweat. *Please don't force me to kill you.*

Far below him the slideway was squealing as its rollers pulverised a two-year accumulation of debris, material which would have been swept out before a routine launch. New fears invaded his mind. What if the debris contained a piece of scrap metal large enough to jam the slide? What if some of the protesters below had got the same idea and were already hurling scaffold tubes into the exposed mechanisms?

He ceased breathing as a pool of blackness began spreading in the lower half of his field of vision. That meant he was now moving out over the portal and, as the door was close to centre of the ship, the whole ponderous structure should be on the point of tilting downwards. His heartbeats became internal hammer blows as the scene projected by the rifle's smartscope began a slow rotation.

"I'm closing her up, Jim," Hepworth said.

"No!" *That's what the centurion is waiting for.* "Leave the door alone!"

"We can't wait!"

The sunlit universe outside tilted further. Nicklin braced himself against the door coaming, keeping his aim. There came a loud whining sound from nearby hydraulic pumps and the door began to swing shut.

"Sorry, Jim – it had to be done."

This is when it happens, Nicklin thought, keeping his eye on the slidemaster through the narowing aperture. The door was closing quickly, aided by the angle of tilt, shutting off Nicklin's view of the world. He saw the man make a sudden movement and in the next instant the grinding squeal of the slideway stopped.

"You bastard," Nicklin breathed, his finger tightening on the rifle's trigger. Little more than a second remained in which to fire, but that was plenty of time for the act of retribution, for the games player to make his final score. He sent the necessary neural command – the execution order – to his finger, but there was no response. The slim rectangle of brilliance shrank into a line and vanished. The door bedded into the hull with a *clunk* and automatic bolts ran their radial courses into the surrounding structure.

What happened to me? Nicklin thought in wonderment. *The centurion was a dead man – but I gave him back his life!*

A moment later he had to let go of the rifle and grab hold of a stanchion to avoid sliding off the gangplanks, then it came to him that the ship was still rotating. And almost at once the balm of weightlessness flooded through his body.

The *Tara* had taken flight.

CHAPTER 17

Nicklin remained clinging to the gangplank railing while he adjusted to the idea that he – *Jim Nicklin!* – had become a space traveller. There was no physical evidence of what was happening to the ship, but in his mind's eye he could see the *Tara* – having wallowed down through the Beachhead portal – drifting out and away from the Orbitsville shell with what little momentum it had. It was quite likely that the ship was slowly tumbling, presenting its pilot with control problems and delaying the moment when the drivers could be switched on.

The only way of getting hard information was from the astrogation screens, and as soon as the thought came to mind Nicklin felt a compulsion to go to the control deck without delay. A spectacular event was taking place, and here in the midship airlock he was blind to it. He looked about him, preparing for the small adventure of flying to the inner door, and encountered Hepworth's scandalised gaze.

"He stopped the rollers!" Hepworth said hoarsely. "The swine nearly stopped us getting away, Jim. If the ship had settled backwards we'd have been stuck there for ever."

But that was in our previous existence, Nicklin thought, wondering how Hepworth could still concern himself with the matter. "He was sticking to his post."

"*You* should have stuck him to his post. You should have melted the bastard, Jim."

"It's all over. Do you want to go up front and find out what's happening?"

Without waiting for a reply, Nicklin slung the rifle on his shoulder and launched himself towards the airlock's inner door, feeling rather like a swimmer entrusting himself to invisible waters. He caught a handrail at the door's edge and, gratified at how natural the movement felt, swung himself around it and on to the broad ladder which ran the length of the passenger cylinder.

It was only then that he became fully aware of the state of near-bedlam which existed throughout the serried decks. The gang-planks, which ran parallel to the ladder, had been crowded with people when the *Tara* made its ungainly dive into space. Now, suddenly disoriented and deprived of weight, they were in frantic pursuit of safer resting places. Some were clinging to the ladder, while others – with much shouting and waving of limbs – ventured towards targets between decks. Children seemed to be crying on every level, and the confusion was made greater by items of baggage and personal effects which drifted randomly in the cramped and cluttered perspectives of the companionway.

Nicklin went towards the prow of the ship with effortless speed, his progress aided by the fact that the engineered environment, so bewildering to others, was totally familiar to him. He knew every cleat, gusset plate and fastener so well that he could have located himself simply by remembering the irregularities in certain welds. He had negotiated his way past six decks when he became aware of a faint gravitational drag and realised that the ship's ion drive had been activated. Almost at once there was a decrease in the ambient noise level as the *Tara's* passengers found a degree of reassurance in the behaviour of everything around them.

The upper decks were quieter, the living space having been allocated to mission workers, many of whom had been left behind in Beachhead. On nearing 3 Deck, two below the control room, Nicklin heard Montane's voice just above. He stepped off the ladder beside the circular hatch which led to the pinnace. That level was partly taken up by stores associated with the pinnace, and therefore had only two accommodation suites – one for Montane, the other for Voorsanger.

Montane and Nibs Affleck were standing at Voorsanger's door, steadying themselves in the weak gravity by gripping the frame. From inside the room there came a dry choking sound. Nicklin's first thought was that Voorsanger was being sick, then he realised the man was sobbing. The notion of the arid and stiff-necked accountant giving vent to tears was almost as strange to Nicklin as any event of the past hour.

"What's the matter?" he said to Montane.

Ignoring the question, Montane turned on him with a look of outrage. "Is this your doing? The launch! Was it you?"

"I didn't have much choice."

"Choice! Who are you to talk about choice?" Montane's lips were quivering with anger. "Have you any idea what you've *done?* Dozens of families were left behind! Ropp's wife has been left behind!"

"That's too bad," Nicklin said, "but there was absolutely nothing I – "

"We can't go on with this," Montane cut in. "We have to go back."

"*Back!* We can't go back, Corey – we almost had the ship taken off us as it was."

"Jim is right," Scott Hepworth said, coming into view on the ladder.

"*You!*" Montane pointed at him with a trembling finger. "You're as bad as he is – you're both in this together."

"You've got to calm down, Corey," Nicklin said. "If we go back now and cradle the ship we'll lose it for sure. The mob – "

"The Lord will confound my enemies." Montane threw himself at the ladder and went up it towards the control deck with surprising agility. Affleck, who seemed to have taken on the role of Montane's protector, gave the others a reproachful look and followed close behind him.

"We'd better go after them," Nicklin said to Hepworth.

"You can't use the rifle. It would probably vent the pressure hull."

"I've no intention of using it," Nicklin said, impatient with Hepworth's new preoccupation with death-dealing. "Besides, this is Corey's show. If he wants to take the ship back nobody has any right to stop him – and I suppose we *might* be able to keep everything under control back there for a few hours."

Hepworth sniffed. "You don't believe that any more than I do."

"That's why we've got to talk some sense into the man." Nicklin got back on to the ladder and went up it at speed, doing most of the work with his hands. When he reached the control deck Montane was already standing beside Megan Fleischer, who was in the centre seat of the five which faced the master view screen. It was being fed by an aft-facing camera and the display on it had the effect of distracting Nicklin from his immediate purpose.

At the bottom edge were two copper-glowing segments, equally spaced, which represented the *Tara's* drive cylinders as seen from a point at the rear of the passenger cylinder. They failed to hold the eye because most of the screen was taken up by the huge, sky-blue circle, with the Orbitsville sun close to its centre, which was the image of the Beachhead portal. Ribbons of a lighter blue, shifting like moiré patterns, formed a background for streamers of milky cloud and the condensation trail of a lonely aircraft. The rest of the screen, dramatising a simple geometric design, was filled by the utter blackness of the Orbitsville shell.

It's really happening, Nicklin thought, eyes and mind brimming. *I'm in a spaceship – and it's leaving the world behind . . .*

". . . hope you realise that it's impossible for any ship to disengage itself from a docking cradle," Fleischer was saying. "If we go back we won't be able to get away again unless somebody in the Port Authority gives permission." She was about fifty and, like many of Montane's appointees, strictly religious. Her neat, regular features were unadorned by cosmetics and, although she was not required to be in uniform, she favoured dark grey suits which were almost military in style. She had abundant chestnut hair, long and flowing, which to Nicklin's eye contrasted oddly with the general severity of her appearance.

"They can't withhold permission," Montane said. "Not now. There have been too many signs."

"Corey, you didn't see what it was like just before we got out," Nicklin said. "The whole place was – "

"I didn't ask for your opinion, Nicklin." Montane's voice was hard and his gaze openly hostile.

"I'm giving it to you just the same," Nicklin replied, noting that Montane had, for the first time, addressed him by his surname. "It would be madness to go back."

"What are you *doing* here, anyway? What happened to the great disbeliever? Why aren't you back in Beachhead, scoffing and sneering, and telling everybody who'll listen to you that Orbitsville will go on for ever?"

"I . . . " Nicklin looked away, vanquished by the preacher's logic and contempt.

"Jim is right in what he says," Hepworth put in. "If we go back we'll lose the ship."

Montane dismissed him with a gesture and spoke directly to the pilot. "I've given you your orders – take the ship back to the portal and put it into dock."

For a moment Fleischer looked as though she was about to protest, then she nodded and turned her attention to the control console before her. She touched several command pads in rapid succession. Hepworth took a step towards her, but his way was immediately blocked by Affleck, whose ravaged face was stiff with the promise of violence.

Bemused, filled with conflicting emotions, Nicklin studied the brilliant blue disk of the portal. He guessed the *Tara* was some five kilometres out from the surface of Orbitsville. At that range the port's docking cradles, massively clamped to the rim of the aperture, were visible as a cluster of tiny irregularities in an otherwise perfect circle. He tried to visualise the scenes that would occur in the dock area when it was discovered that the ship was returning, but his imagination balked. Human behaviour was unpredictable at the best of times, and when thousands of people were driven by primaeval terror . . .

But whatever happens, he told himself, *I've done with killing.*

Almost of its own accord his right hand dropped to the stock of the rifle and ejected the weapon's power pack. He was slipping the massy little cylinder into his pocket when he became aware of a fundamental change taking place in the geometries of the view screen. The change was so radical, so contrary to all his expectations, that he had to stare at the image for several seconds before accepting its message.

The searingly bright blue disk of the portal was shrinking.

His first thought was that Fleischer had defied Montane by directing maximum power into the ion tubes, dramatically speeding up the ship's flight *away* from Orbitsville. Then came the realisation that he was dealing in physical impossibilities – no star drive yet devised could produce the kind of acceleration which would be compatible with what he was seeing. He could feel no gravitational increase at all, and yet the image of the portal was visibly contracting. The only possible explanation was that the view screen was depicting a real event.

The portal itself was becoming smaller.

All activity in the control room ceased. The power to move or speak, or even to think, was removed from the five watchers as the portal dwindled. In the span of less than a minute the huge circle shrank to the apparent size of an azure planet, a moon, a bright star.

It glimmered briefly, amid a haze of after-images, and then it was gone.

The Orbitsville trap had been sprung.

PART THREE: THE SCHEME SHATTERS

CHAPTER 18

"Looks like we got out of there just in time."

The speaker was Nibs Affleck, who normally maintained a deferent silence in the presence of senior personnel, and the sheer banality of his remark served to free the others from their mental and physical paralysis.

"God, God, God," Montane whispered, sinking to his knees, hands steepled beneath his chin. "Do not abandon your children in their hour of need."

"We should try the radio," Hepworth said to Fleischer, his voice surprisingly firm and clear.

She twisted in her seat to look up at him. "Why?"

"I want to know about the other portals. Perhaps what happened at P1 is an isolated phenomenon. We should try to get in touch."

The pilot managed to smile. "Something tells me that would be a waste of time. Especially mine."

"I could do it for you," Hepworth said. He glanced down at the adjacent seat and Nicklin realised that – even in this hour of astonishment, when reality itself seemed to be in a state of flux – he was observing shipboard protocol.

"Be my guest," Fleischer said, turning back to her own area of the console.

As Hepworth sank into the high-backed seat, his movement slowed by the minimal gravity, Nicklin returned his attention to the master screen. It was now uniformly black, the *Tara*'s drive cylinders having become invisible when the rays from the Orbitsville sun were shut off. Several auxiliary screens, fed by cameras aimed ahead of the ship and to the side, were showing patterns of stars – but looking aft there appeared to be a universe without light. Nicklin knew the emptiness was illusory, that Orbitsville's vast non-reflective shell occupied half of the normal sphere of vision, but the sense of being a castaway in a totally sterile cosmos persisted.

Mentally, he was similarly adrift. How was he to come to terms with the simple fact that Corey Montane had been right all along? Orbitsville was *not* eternal and changeless. He had always intuited that it was a product of nature, an object which had somehow evolved to the nth state of matter at which it could never be understood by the human mind. Now he was face-to-face with the concept of Orbitsville as an *artefact*, and that led to the great questions about who had built it and their purpose in doing so.

His rejection of a religious scenario was instinctive, intellectual and complete – but what was left?

As his mind rebounded from what it could not encompass he found himself turning to the more immediate question of what would happen next. Was it possible that, as Montane believed, the forces involved in Orbitsville's transformation were hostile to life? Not solely to humanity – that notion was paranoic to far beyond the point of absurdity – but to every form of animate matter. Could the central sun be extinguished, thus purging the globe of biological contamination? Could the Big O contract like a collapsing star and eventually disappear? Or could it explosively fly apart?

The apocalyptic vision of Orbitsville's shell yielding to mechanical stresses led Nicklin, by association, to remember the green lines which had appeared in many places three years earlier. The force field connected with them was known to weaken the cohesion of steel and concrete – was it therefore having the same effect on the shell material? There had been reports that the glowing lines were also visible on the outside of Orbitsville, which suggested that their influence was indeed able to penetrate ylem.

Reluctant to regard the idea as anything but purest fantasy, Nicklin nevertheless scanned the dark screen more closely in search of radiant green threads. None was visible, but he realised at once that, as the lines had been hundreds of kilometres apart, the camera facing directly astern covered too little of Orbitsville's surface. He tried the lateral images, but in them the angle of sight was too acute to be of any value.

"Nothing on the radio," Hepworth announced, getting out of his chair. "I had to check, but my guess is that Orbitsville has sealed itself up all over. Tighter than the proverbial duck's ass."

"I wouldn't have put it quite like that," Fleischer said, "but I'm in agreement."

"That means we drop any proposal to go back." Hepworth turned to Nicklin. "What do you say, Jim?"

"It seems to me we have no option but to go on with the flight, but – " Nicklin glanced down at Montane, who was still on his knees and praying silently with his eyes closed.

"But what?"

"We're talking like a management committee, but things were never set up that way. Corey is the man in charge."

"Jim! What's the matter with you?" Hepworth's plump face showed exasperation. "Just *look* at him! The man obviously isn't capable of commanding a rowboat, let alone a – " He broke off and made a placating gesture as Nibs Affleck took a threatening step towards him.

"All I can say, Monsignor Nicklin," Hepworth added in a low voice, moving closer to Nicklin, "Is that I never noticed you deferring much to Pope Corey in the past."

"I know, I know." The emotional conflict Nicklin was experiencing made speech difficult. "But he laid it on the line a minute ago. I shouldn't even . . . I mean, if it hadn't been for Corey I would still be . . ."

"It's all right, Jim." Montane had risen to his feet, his face set and unnaturally white. "There's no need for an argument here. A lot of people have been left behind, but that's my fault. I was warned some time ago that direct action was called for, and . . . well . . . I did nothing about it. One day I will have to answer to God for that, and I only hope I can face Him when my time comes."

"In the mean time," Hepworth said impatiently, "we press on to Prospect One. Is that what you're saying?"

Montane shrugged, something Nicklin had never seen him do before. "That's what I'm saying."

Hepworth, looking triumphant, nodded to the pilot. "There you are, captain – do you want to spread your wings?"

For a moment Nicklin thought that Hepworth was trying to sound poetic, then realised he had referred to the electromagnetic scoop fields which had to be deployed on each side of the *Tara* to gather reaction mass. On diagrams their curved shape looked like huge wings, causing interstellar ramjets to be popularly known as butterfly ships.

"We don't need to worry about traffic controllers, and we don't need to worry about traffic," Fleischer said, turning back to the console.

Nicklin watched in fascination as she moved her hands over the sloping surface, causing lanes, highways, townships of coloured lights to spring into existence. This was the first step in taking the ship out of Einstein's domain and into that realm of strangeness where Arthurian physics held sway. Nicklin knew, and only dimly understood, that in order for the ship to travel at multiples of the speed of light it would temporarily cease to exist as far as observers in the normal continuum were concerned.

The massive vessel and everything in it, including his own body, would be transformed into a cloud of particles with more affinity to tachyons than to normal matter. The mode of travel – which had once been described as "crooked accountancy applied to mass-energy transformations" – was magical in its effect. But before it could be brought into play the ship would have to reach a very high normal-space velocity, and there was nothing at all magical about how that velocity was achieved.

It was a product of greasy-overall engineering, spanner-and-screwdriver technology, involving a host of control systems – mechanical, electrical, hydraulic – among which a twentieth-century artificer would have felt reasonably at home. To begin the voyage proper, Megan Fleischer was activating the thermonuclear reactor and feeding power to the flux pumps, thereby unfurling the *Tara's* intangible wings. At the ship's present negligible rate of movement the scoops could do little more than complement the ion drive, but they would become increasingly effective as the speed built up.

"Here we go," Fleischer said after a few seconds, touching the master control pads.

Nicklin felt a slight but immediate increase in weight and was gripped by a numbing sense of wonder as he realised that the great metallic entity, upon which he had lavished three years of devotion, had ceased being an inert object and was stirring fully into life.

Fleischer switched camera channels and the star fields ahead of the ship blossomed in the main view screen. Perhaps a hundred major stars shone with a diamond-pure lustre against a dusting of fainter specks, creating a three-dimensional matrix which seemed to draw Nicklin's consciousness into it. *I must have been blind*, he thought as his gaze roved through the alien constellations. *How did I fail to understand that we were all born for this?*

"Not very good," Fleischer said in a matter-of-fact tone. "Not very good, at all."

Hepworth was beside her on the instant, scanning the console. "What do you mean?"

"It wasn't what I would call a clean start-up. The intake fields seemed a bit slow in establishing themselves."

"It happens in a hundredth of a second." Hepworth sounded relieved and irritated at the same time. "You can't judge it by sight."

"I've been a pilot for more than twenty years, and I *can* judge it by sight," Fleischer snapped. "Besides, that wasn't the only thing I didn't like – the left field wasn't a good shape when it opened up."

"What was wrong with it?"

"It looked a bit . . . flat."

Hepworth examined the glowing butterfly that was the intake field distribution diagram. "It looks fine to me."

"It looks all right now," Fleischer said stubbornly, "but I'm telling you it started off flat."

"It might have met a bit of resistance – God knows what sort of stuff is spewing out of Orbitsville." Hepworth patted the pilot's luxuriantly covered head. "I think you can safely leave the vacuum physics to me."

She twisted away from him. "Keep your hands to yourself, Mister Hepworth, or I'll bar you from this deck."

"Touchy, touch-*eee*!" Hepworth said jovially. He turned to look at Nicklin, enlisting support, his eyes rounded in a what-do-you-think-of-that? expression.

Nicklin gazed back at him unsympathetically, unable to think of anything but Zindee White's scathing comments on Hepworth's qualifications as a physicist. The little that Nicklin had seen of Megan Fleischer had persuaded him that she was a top-class professional pilot, a woman who knew exactly what she was talking about. It was quite possible that a fleeting irregularity in a scoop field was an insignificant event, just as Hepworth had said, but did he know as much about starship drives as he claimed? Montane, desperate for low-cost help, had taken him pretty much on trust . . .

"Something on your mind, Jim?" Hepworth's joviality had evaporated, and there was now something watchful and unpleasant in his expression.

Nicklin recalled the way in which Hepworth would become caustic and angry, and even threaten violence, when challenged on any technical or scientific point. It had happened on many occasions in the past three years, but this would be a particularly inconvenient time for a fresh performance.

"I've got plenty on my mind," he said, glancing at the view screens. "All this is a bit daunting."

Hepworth shook his head impatiently, refusing to be put off. "You're looking at me like I was something you'd just found in your soup – perhaps you think I don't know what I'm talking about."

"You must be nearly as jumpy as I am, Scott," Nicklin soothed. "You *know* I think you're the greatest living expert on everything."

"Don't patronise me, you country – " Hepworth broke off, staring in surprise at the companionway.

A bearded young man in the blue uniform of a spaceport guard had appeared on the ladder. He stared for a moment at the group by the console, raised one hand in a kind of apologetic greeting, then slowly sank from view again.

"This place is getting like a train station," Fleischer said irritably. "I can't have people wandering in here any time they feel like it."

"Quite right!" Montane, perhaps comforted by being given a minor administrative problem, appeared quite composed as he turned to Affleck. "I want you and Gerl to spell each other on the deck below this one. Nobody is to pass you – except those that are here now – unless I give you the word."

"Right, Corey." Affleck, looking gratified, immediately hurried to the ladder.

Montane directed a thin smile at Nicklin. "Jim, as you've decided to grace us with your company on this flight, I expect you to earn your rations. You can start right now by going through all the decks and finding out just how many outsiders have jumped on board. Make a list of their names and bring it to me and I'll decide what rooms we can put them in."

"Okay, Corey," Nicklin said, slightly surprised at how glad he was to see the improvement in the other man's state of mind.

"And tell them I'll want to speak to them in my room, individually, as soon as I have the time."

"Yessir, yessir!" Putting the uneasy confrontation with Hepworth to the back of his mind, Nicklin glanced once more at the main screen – wondering if Prospect One was even visible at that early stage of the flight – then made his way to the lower regions of the ship.

The hot shower felt even more luxurious than he had been anticipating.

He had slept for almost seven hours, disturbed only by occasional dreams of falling, and had risen from his bed feeling both hungry and filthy. The thought of breakfast was alluring, but he had decided it would be more enjoyable were he in a reasonably hygienic condition when he sat down to eat. He had descended through many levels to 24 Deck, where the laundry and shower rooms had been situated because of the ease of supplying hot water from the adjoining engine cylinders. He had washed his underpants and socks and had put them in one of the driers before going into a shower cubicle.

Now there was a blessed period in which he had nothing to do but let the needle sprays cleanse his body. Clothes were going to be quite a problem he realised as he relaxed in the tingling warmth, especially if the voyage were to last for months. Many of those on board the *Tara* had nothing other than what they had been wearing when the panic had gripped Beachhead City. The families who had managed to bring suitcases had thus become instant aristocrats, distinguished from their fellows by a wealth of fresh underwear.

Nicklin smiled as he tried to visualise how Montane would handle the situation. In an ideal Christian society the rich should share their goodies with the poor without even waiting to be asked, but the cynic in Nicklin suspected that things might not work out that way.

Luckily, Montane had been spared similar problems with the ultimate commodity, the one which *really* would have separated the haves from the have-nots. Imperishable food stores had been going on board for weeks, and any shortfall due to the hasty departure was more than compensated for by the *Tara* carrying only half the projected number of passengers.

Paid-up emigrants accounted for sixty-nine of the complement, and another twenty-six mission personnel had been able to join the ship in the dreadful last hour – the remainder being on home leave or simply out on casual errands. Nicklin's census had revealed, in addition to the Whites, the presence of three space-port guards, plus a group of seven men and women who had happened to be working in the dock area at the crucial time.

The total came to 108, which meant that the *Tara* could, if necessary, extend the New Eden quest for as long as two years. Nicklin refused to think what would happen at the end of that time if no suitable world had been found. In the past he had felt some concern about the ultimate fate of the pilgrims, especially the children, but had avoided becoming too pessimistic. No matter how distant the ship might be when the decision to abandon the mission was taken it would always be possible to return to the starting place. The strange mathematics of supraluctic flight meant that all destinations in the universe were roughly equidistant and equally accessible – but there would be no point in the travellers returning home when all doors were barred against them.

A new and disturbing thought occurred to Nicklin as he absorbed the abundant warmth of the shower. It would be a grim irony, one of the Gaseous Vertebrate's finest pranks, if the disturbances in Orbitsville had been transient phenomena – incidental effects which had manifested themselves while the portals were preparing to close. If that were the case, daily life in places like Orangefield would already be returning to drowsy normality. The *Orangefield Recorder* would be preparing waggish editorials about the curious goings-on in the Big Smoke, couples would be strolling in Coach-and-Four Lane and there would be business as usual in the Victoria Hotel and Mr Chickley's orange-lit ice-cream parlour. And in a few years' time the very existence of portals would be a fading memory – and nobody would know about the ghost ship drifting in the void which began a short distance beneath their feet, beyond Orbitsville's impenetrable shell.

The unwelcome vision had the effect of suddenly making Nicklin feel trapped and claustrophobic. He stepped out of the cubicle and began towelling himself dry. The only other person in the washroom was Lan Huertas, who – as usual – refrained from speaking to him. Nicklin dressed in silence, ran a depilator over his chin and left the room.

A short distance up the ladder he began to wonder if the going was easier than it should have been. When he had gone to bed, at the beginning of the arbitrary "night" period, the ship's acceleration had been about .5G. Now it was, perhaps, slightly less, although it was difficult for a novice in such matters to say for sure whether his weight was a half or a third or a quarter of normal. Was this an indication that a genuine fault existed in the intake field generators? Or was it simply that the ship had entered a region in which the harvest of interstellar particles was poor?

The aroma of coffee drifting down from the canteen – or refectory, as Montane styled it – distracted him from the questions. He felt a pang of guilt-tinged pleasure as he recalled that the atrocious cook, Carlos Kempson, had been one of those left behind in Beachhead. One of the new pilgrims, a professional chef, had volunteered to run the canteen, thus making the prospect of a long voyage somewhat brighter.

The levels that Nicklin passed were quiet for the most part, the passengers having been requested to remain in their quarters until 09.00 hours, ship time. A few children were at play in the landing areas common to each deck's four suites, but they were unnaturally subdued. Resilient as the very young always were, they had not had time to adjust to the austere environment of plasboard partitions and arctic lighting.

On 10 Deck, three levels below the canteen, he heard a familiar voice and looked around to see Zindee White standing at the open door of a suite. She was talking to a teenage girl, presumably from adjacent quarters. Nicklin raised his hand in greeting, but before he could say anything Zindee had retreated out of his sight. The teenager gave him a quizzical look as he ascended through the deck above.

On reaching the canteen he saw half a dozen mission personnel – Danea Farthing and Gerl Kingsley among them – seated at one of the narrow tables. Kingsley produced one of his grotesque smiles on seeing Nicklin, but the others studiously ignored his arrival. The reception was of a kind to which he had become accustomed, and from which he usually derived perverse satisfaction. Normally he would have elbowed his way into the group and proceeded to dominate the conversation, but on this occasion the force of silent rejection was overwhelming.

He obtained a bulb of coffee from the dispenser and sat down alone. *Something is happening*, he thought as he sipped the hot liquid, *and it started yesterday morning when Zindee ran away from me.*

Like a drunk trying to reconstruct the events of the previous night's binge, he played the meeting with Zindee on the screen of memory, step by step and in considered slow motion. There was a stranger there . . . a stranger who looked and spoke like Jim Nicklin . . . a stranger who *was* Jim Nicklin as far as the rest of the world was concerned . . .

Isolated, mesmerised, appalled, Nicklin watched the intruder – the usurper of his body – go about his business, which was the pretence of being alive while in reality the essential spark of humanity had been quenched. Observing the encounter was a difficult and painful thing to do, because he had to accept that he and the stranger were as one, and that there could be no apportionment of responsibility or shame.

I was a dead man! I was a walking corpse . . . and Zindee came out of times that were lost . . . reminding me of the good that was lost . . . and how did I repay her?

Nicklin felt the hot pulsing of blood in his face as he watched the simulacrum act on his behalf and heard it speak the lines he had devised for it. The coffee bulb grew cold in his hand. An indeterminate time later he became aware that Danea – her eyes dark and thoughtful – was watching him from the other table. He averted his gaze, smiled the self-deprecating smile of one who wants people to believe he has just remembered an appointment, and left the canteen.

On the cramped landing he hesitated for a moment, with no particular objective in mind, then went up towards the control room. When he reached 3 Deck, easily distinguishable because of the pinnace tunnel, the red telltales on the locks told him that the doors to Montane's and Voorsanger's suites were bolted shut. Both men were probably still asleep – one in the company of his dead wife; the other deprived of the company of his living wife. *Neat touch, O Gaseous Vertebrate!*

On 2 Deck, which housed the pilot's private quarters, he found Nibs Affleck dutifully guarding the topmost section of the ladder. Affleck gave him a barely perceptible nod as he climbed past. Emerging in the control room he saw that two of the five seats were occupied by Hepworth and Fleischer. The main screen was again being fed by an aft-facing camera, but the view was no longer one of unrelieved darkness.

The ship had been under continuous acceleration for more than fifteen hours, allowing the camera to take in a large area of Orbitsville's shell – and the captured image had been transformed. Luminous green lines filled the entire screen in a pattern of complex curvatures which resembled interlocking flowers. The effect was that of a vast array of brilliantly glowing neon tubes laid out to the design of an artist working on a macroscopic scale. In the auxiliary screens the shining filigree spread away in every direction until, condensed by perspective, the lines merged to form horizons of cold green radiance.

"Quite a sight, eh Jim?" Hepworth turned in his seat to look up at Nicklin. He looked exhausted, as though he had not been to bed, but his face showed none of the animosity which had been there the night before.

"I've never seen anything like it," Nicklin said, grateful that the benign streak in the other man's nature had never allowed him to nurse a grudge. It was of some comfort to know that not quite everybody had been alienated by his malaise of the past three years.

"Yes, the old lady's putting on quite a show for us." Hepworth took a silver flask from his side pocket and offered it to Nicklin. "Drink?"

Nicklin glanced at Megan Fleischer and saw that she was in a deep sleep, although still sitting upright. "No, thanks."

"This is an unrepeatable offer, Jim – I haven't even got a bottle tucked away in my room. When this is finished we're on a strict diet of cocoa and carrot juice and similarly disgusting brews." A look of intense revulsion appeared on Hepworth's well-padded face. "Christ! I might even have to drink some of Corey's God-awful fucking *tea*!"

Nicklin chuckled and reached for the proffered flask. A drink of neat, warm gin was the last thing he wanted at that moment, but it represented friendship and that was something for which he had developed a craving. In the boozers' ethic the sharing of the last available drink was a symbol as potent as a wedding ring.

Here's to solidarity, he thought as he swallowed the flat and tepid spirit. *For years there were just the two of us. Two disbelievers, two disciples of the Gaseous Vertebrate – the Lord of Chance – surrounded by an army of bible-thumpers. But we got the ship ready. Between us we got the ship ready . . .*

"Have a seat," Hepworth said. "Her ladyship is in no condition to object."

"Okay." Nicklin handed the flask back as he sat down, his gaze returning to the fantastic glaring traceries of the main screen. "What do you think happened back there?"

Hepworth took a swig of gin. "Who knows? And, if you ask me, it isn't finished yet. I have this feeling in my water, Jim. It's totally unscientific, I know, but I have this feeling in my water that the show has only just started."

"I know what you mean." Nicklin was unable to take his eyes away from the screen. "Those lines must be really bright for us to see them at this range. I mean . . . how far are we away from Orbitsville?"

"Just over two miks. We passed the two-million mark a little while ago."

"I never thought this kind of thing would happen to me," Nicklin said. "James Nicklin – space traveller!"

Hoping he had achieved a natural-sounding change of subject, he tried to work out why the figure Hepworth quoted had drawn a cold feather along his spine. Fifteen hours at say 5G would be . . . His skill with mental calculation seemed to desert him as he realised that by this time the ship should have been on full gravity, its drive becoming more efficient as the build-up in speed allowed the intake fields to gather increasing amounts of reaction mass. The current acceleration felt more like a third or a quarter of the optimum, and there might have been fluctuations while he was asleep, causing the dreams of falling . . .

"Don't overload that walnut you use instead of a brain." Hepworth spoke in friendly tones and returned the flask to

Nicklin, good evidence of his not being antagonised. "Under normal conditions we'd have been a *lot* farther out by this time."

"I . . . ah . . . didn't want to open my big mouth too soon."

"I know – you were being tactful." Hepworth gave him a quizzical look. "I never noticed *you* trying to be diplomatic before. What's the matter, Jim – are you sick?"

Nicklin tried to smile. "I have my off days. What were you saying about the engines?"

"About the engines? Nothing! Not a word! Not a peep, not a cheep! The engines are fine."

"But you said – "

"I said that *under normal conditions* the ship would be travelling a lot faster."

"So what's wrong?"

"Space itself is wrong," Hepworth said peacefully. "You must remember that we're in an anti-matter universe now, Jim. Some things are different here. It's too soon for me to say exactly what the differences are – it could be something to do with the density or distribution of interstellar dust, or it might be something more basic than that.

"If some nuclear interactions are different – as with cobalt 60 – then some of the ship's performance parameters might also be different. For instance, our intake fields might be slightly porous to anti-matter ions. I tell you, Jim – whole new areas for research are opening up all around us."

Nicklin took another drink of luke-warm gin.

I'm going to put all my trust in this man, he thought, repressing a grimace as the alcohol burned in his throat. *I'm going to accept everything he says. I'm going to have total faith in him because nobody – not even the Great Prankster – would cast a hundred souls adrift in a ship that can't fly.*

Again, there were dreams of falling.

In one of them the ship was in orbit around a green planet. The planet had no cloud markings, no oceans, no polar caps. It was a sphere of unrelieved colour – pantomime scenery green, children's paintbox green, remembered holiday green – too rich for normal vegetation. Megan Fleischer had come to Nicklin and confessed that she was unable to fly the pinnace. He had taken over for her, and now he was in the pilot's seat as the little craft plunged – buffeted by turbulent atmosphere – towards the virescent bauble. He glanced down at the controls and terror gripped him as he realised they were a meaningless array of levers and dials. He knew nothing about flying, nothing at all! What madness had made him think he could pilot any kind of spacecraft or aircraft? The poisonous green surface was rushing upwards, expanding, spinning in the windshield. He could see now that it was a swamp – heaving, bubbling, gloating. The pinnace was hurtling into it at many times the speed of sound.

And there was nothing he could do but wait to die . . .

On the following morning, the second day of the flight, Nicklin decided that the only way to survive a prolonged journey was by making himself genuinely useful. The simple disciplines of hard work had sustained him for the year in which the *Tara* had been dragged, inch by inch, from Altamura to Beachhead City, and the experience had taught him a valuable lesson.

"You can trust work," he announced to the emptiness of his room as he got out of bed and began to dress. "Work isn't fickle. Work never lets you down."

There was, he knew, a ready-made outlet for his particular abilities and knowledge. Jock Craig, the electrician, had a good record as a general handyman and had been promoted – in the vague way that Montane handled such things – to the post of "maintenance supervisor". The job would have required Craig to mend anything from a lighting switch to a ventilation fan, but he had been among those who failed to board the ship in time for the escape from Orbitsville.

Nothing had broken down at this early stage of the voyage, as far as Nicklin was aware, but there was one major item of housekeeping which cried out for his attention. The gangway which passed through every deck had been vital for mobility while the ship was lying on its side in dock. Now it was an encumbrance which hindered access to the single longitudinal ladder which ran the length of the ship – and it was time for it to go.

Within an hour Nicklin had eaten a solitary breakfast, sought out Montane and appointed himself maintenance supervisor in Craig's place.

The gangway was made of pressed metal in some places, and in others of simple wooden planks which still bore dusty footprints. Nicklin started at the upper end of the ship, removing sections, cutting them into convenient lengths and storing them in an empty room on 5 Deck. As he cleared each deck he checked that its sliding anti-fire hatch could be moved freely. The work was aided by the low gravity, but hampered by the number of people moving between levels. Having spent one ship day adjusting to their surroundings and getting used to the idea of being in space, the emigrants were beginning to establish the life patterns which might have to serve them for many months.

Looking along the ladder was, for Nicklin, like taking a core sample of the activities on the seriate decks. In the dwindling companionways he could see knots of men and women in conversation, while others progressed between the two public levels of the canteen and washrooms. Children were visible almost everywhere, establishing their hold on new territories or being harried by adults. At one stage there was a bible class going on below Nicklin, a committee meeting of some kind on his level and what seemed like a choir practice several floors above him.

Inconvenient though the continual traffic on the ladder was, he derived comfort from the abundant evidence that the human spirit was irrepressible. Many of the emigrants spoke to him in a friendly manner, some – having tapped into an information grapevine – expressing gratitude for the part he had played in getting the ship off the slideway. These men and women were obviously more in touch with the realities of their situation than his anti-religious prejudice had allowed him to expect, and the idea that they might form a viable colony on a new world gradually began to seem less preposterous.

Twice during the morning's work he saw Zindee White coming towards him. Unable to meet her eyes, he moved as far off the ladder as possible and kept his back turned while she was passing. On the first occasion he allowed himself to hope that she would speak and show some sign of forgiveness, but no contact was made. *That's that*, he told himself grimly. *To use one of Corey's best clichés – I'm reaping what I sowed.*

There was little to tax his mind in the dismantling of the gangway, but he gave the task full concentration, using the physical labour to ease the pressures of self-reproach and recrimination. Having shut everything but bolts, clamps and lashing ropes from his personal universe, he felt a dull sense of surprise when – some time later – he became aware of Nibs Affleck beckoning to him from higher up the ladder.

Making sure he was leaving nothing in a dangerous condition, he followed Affleck towards the control deck, trying to guess why he had been summoned. He knew that Megan Fleischer was deeply unhappy about the weak acceleration, and that she had been engaged in bitter arguments with Hepworth, but he had no responsibilites in that area. Perhaps Montane, increasingly concerned with the trivia of shipboard routine, wanted to discuss illumination levels or the canteen rota. Or, could it be . . . could it possibly be . . . ?

Orbitsville!

Nicklin's premonition gave way to numb certainty as he entered the control room.

In spite of some magnification the main screen now depicted a much greater area of the Orbitsville shell, with the result that the pattern of green lines appeared to have become more intricate. There were hundreds of regularly spaced foci, generating sprays of interlocking curves, resembling flower petals, which confused and dazzled the eye. The vast design had not only increased greatly in brightness, but was now pulsing at a rate of about once a second. Each peak of brilliance washed through the control room, garishly outlining the high-backed seats and their occupants – Montane, Voorsanger, Fleischer and Hepworth.

"You're entitled to see this, Jim," Hepworth said without turning his head. "Something is going to happen."

Nicklin moved to stand behind Hepworth. "When did the pulsing start?"

"A couple of minutes ago – and it's speeding up."

Frozen, entranced, Nicklin stared at the living image as the tempo of light beats increased. It became an eye-stabbing frenzy, the intervals between the peaks lessening, shrinking to zero. And then the screen steadied at an intolerable level of brightness.

A second went by; two seconds; three seconds . . .

Scott was right, Nicklin thought, sick with apprehension, half-blinded by the glare. *Something is going to happen.*

. . . four seconds; five seconds . . .

The incredible filigree of green fire ceased to exist – and in its place there was a new pattern.

Blue-white crescents suddenly filled the entire screen. Row upon row, line upon line, layer upon layer. The largest were in the centre of the field of view, and outwards from them, graduating downwards in size to star-like points, there ran countless curving meridians of dwindling beads. The farther they were from the centre of the screen the fuller were the crescents. In their entirety they formed concentric gauzy spheres, depth leading to depth, at the centre of which was a small yellow sun.

Nicklin's gaze fixed on one of the largest of the side-lit globes, but long before he had brought it into perfect focus – identifying the blue and green variegations as oceans and continents – an inner voice had told him he was looking at a new-born planet.

Orbitsville – equal in area to millions of Earths – had *become* millions of Earths.

CHAPTER 19

The utter silence in the control room lasted for minutes, during which the image on the screen continued to evolve.

Unable to take his gaze off the spectacle, Nicklin groped his way around the empty seat beside Hepworth and sat down. As his eyes gradually recovered from the punishing overload of green light he began to take in more and more details of the fantastic scene and to interpret some of its elements.

He saw that the sun was not enclosed by the blackness of space. The multiple layers of planets in the foreground had prevented him from realising that the sun was at the centre of a pale blue disk. The circle of blue exhibited shifting moiré patterns of a paler shade, and – in spite of the alien nature of the visual setting – it looked achingly familiar.

"That's the sky," he breathed. "I mean . . . We're looking at the inside of Orbitsville."

"You're right." Hepworth sounded calm and emotionless, the scientist in him having displaced the merely human observer. "Feast your eyes on it while you can, my boy. You have slightly less than eighteen minutes – then it will disappear for ever."

"Eighteen minutes?" The precision of the term added to Nicklin's sense of awe. "How do you know that?"

"Well, it seems that the Orbitsville shell has been converted into smaller spheres, each about the size of a small planet." Hepworth glanced along the row of seats. "Are we in agreement on that one? Nobody wants to claim it's all an optical illusion?"

Fleischer nodded. Montane and Voorsanger, gaping at the screen, appeared not to have heard.

"I think we can assume that the conversion was universal and simultaneous," Hepworth went on, seizing the best opportunity he would ever have to deliver one of his impromptu lectures. "That *feels* right to me, if nothing else. The entire shell broke up all at once, and was converted into smaller spheres all at once – but we can't see it that way because Orbitsville was eighteen light minutes in diameter. For us, the conversion will appear to be progressive . . ."

Nicklin lost the sound of the physicist's voice as soon as he had, belatedly, worked out for himself what was happening. He watched in fascination as the blue disk expanded in the view screen, its edge appearing to dissolve and vaporise into a mist of planets. The disk, with its crazed pattern of day and night bands, was the sunlit interior of Orbitsville – but he knew that it no longer existed, that he was seeing it by virtue of light which had started on its journey while he was still in a lower part of the *Tara*, working on the gangway.

For the first time in his life, he began to get some inkling of Orbitsville's true size. The vast sphere had already met its enigmatic end, but by virtue of sheer immensity it was clinging to an illusory existence, reluctantly yielding up its substance at the speed of light.

To suffer a C-change, Nicklin marvelled, *into something rich and strange* . . .

The circle of striated blue expanded off the edges of the screen. Fleischer touched a camera control, dropping the magnification to zero, and the field of view was increased by a factor of ten. The circle continued its growth, spewing millions of new worlds in a silver fog at its rim, but the pace of enlargement slowed with the light front reaching the widest aspect of the shell. It was still racing across Orbitsville's doomed, dreaming landscapes – annihilating them at a rate of 300,000 kilometres a second – but, as the direction was nearly parallel to the watchers' line of sight, lateral change was temporarily minimised.

There was a period of near-stasis which lasted for more than a minute, then the azure circle began to shrink.

The contraction was barely perceptible at first, but in accordance with the laws of spherical geometry there was an acceleration – and an acceleration of acceleration. The blue circle dwindled fiercely, boiling itself away in a steam of planetary creation. In a final silent implosion it vanished behind the stellar corona.

The sun remained – unaffected and unchallenged – at the centre of a spherical cloud of new-born worlds.

Nicklin was frozen in his seat, breathing at only the shallowest level, staring at the incredibly beautiful display on the main screen. His mind was scoured out. He felt cold, chastened and uniquely privileged – as though the whole of Creation had been reprised especially for his benefit. He felt that he ought to speak – but what was there to say?

"My eyesight isn't what it used to be," Hepworth came in, "but those *are* planets, aren't they?"

Nicklin nodded, forcing his larynx into action. "They look like planets to me."

Montane emitted a hoarse sobbing sound. "They are *not* planets! It's all part of the Devil's trickery! It's an illusion."

"I thought we dealt with that notion at the start," Hepworth said, with a patience which conveyed impatience. "What we have just witnessed was the creation of millions of planets out of the material of the Orbitsville shell. The big question now, or one of the big questions, is – is everybody still alive on them?"

"Everybody has to be dead," Montane announced. "Everybody is – *dead*!"

Nicklin, who had thought his capacity for wonder exhausted, was freshly awed by Hepworth's imaginative power. "How? How could anybody possibly be alive after all that?"

"How me no hows," Hepworth replied. "I don't think we'll ever understand *how* it was done. But – and don't ask me to explain this either – to me it seems that the whole exercise would have been pointless unless life was preserved. Don't you see that?"

"I want to see that. I want to see that very much."

"How much magnification can you give it?" Hepworth said to Megan Fleischer. "A hundred?"

She nodded, fingers moving on a panel in the armrest of her seat. A tiny red circle appeared near the centre of the screen. It adjusted position slightly to enclose one of the glowing specks, then it began to expand, magnifying the contained area, progressively obliterating the rest of the screen. The object it enclosed was quickly revealed to be a black disk surrounded by a thin circle of brilliance.

"That one is too nearly in line with the sun," Hepworth said. "We're looking at its night side, but the halo demonstrates an important point – it has an atmosphere. It proves, to me anyway, that whoever dissolved Orbitsville had our best interests at heart."

"You're a fool," Montane whispered. "The Devil is our enemy."

"Go out to one side a bit," Hepworth said to the pilot.

The red circle immediately collapsed to its former size, moved to the left and centred itself on another mote of light. The process of magnification began again, and this time the target expanded to become a bright crescent which was – unmistakably – dappled with green and blue beneath the white curlicues of weather systems.

"There you are," Hepworth said triumphantly. "A prime piece of Orbitsville real estate, parcelled up a different way."

Nicklin's mind made a dizzy leap. "Will we be able to see cities?"

"Possibly, but the trick would be to find them." Hepworth made a sweeping gesture which took in the jewel-dusted margins of the screen outside the crimson circle. "What was the surface area of Orbitsville compared to, say, Earth? Wasn't it something like 650 million times bigger? If nothing has gone to waste, that means we have about 650 million new planets out there – and our little handful of cities would be fairly insignificant."

"I'll start a radio scan," Fleischer said. "It's a bit soon to expect –"

"Stop this!" Montane shouted, lurching to his feet, face contorted into a pale mask. "I'll listen to no more of this . . . blasphemous *mouthing*!"

"We're talking science now, Corey," Hepworth said calmly, kindly and with more than a hint of condescension. "Sooner or later you'll have to start dealing in the facts of the situation."

"Facts! I'll give you facts! Those are not real worlds – only God can create real worlds – and there are no cities. Every single soul we left behind has been claimed by the Evil One. They are all *dead*!"

Voorsanger shifted uneasily. "Just a minute, Corey. I'd like to hear what – "

"That man speaks for the Devil," Montane cut in, voice rising in pitch. "I'm warning you, Ropp, if you listen to him you will put your own immortal soul at risk."

"But if there's a chance that my wife is still alive!" Voorsanger paused, looking oddly shamefaced but stubborn, and when he spoke again he avoided Montane's gaze. "If there is any chance at all that Greta is still alive . . . and that all the others might still be alive . . . is it not our duty to turn back and try to find them?"

"But you *saw* what happened out there!" Montane's voice was cracking, becoming an articulated shriek. "How can you even – ?"

He stopped speaking, mouth and eyes widening in shock. He clapped his right hand to his chest and at the same time pressed the left to his back in a sudden twisting movement, almost as if he had been transfixed by an invisible blade. His tongue flickered for a moment, snake-like, depositing saliva on each side of his chin. Affleck, who had been standing by the ladder, darted to Montane's side and lowered him into his seat.

"See what you done!" Affleck growled, switching a baleful stare between Voorsanger and Hepworth. "If Corey dies . . . "

"I'm not going to die, Nibs – it's all right." Montane took several deep breaths and, unexpectedly, produced a weak smile. "There's nothing for you to be alarmed about."

"Corey, you ought to lie down."

Montane squeezed Affleck's arm. "Just let me sit here, my good friend. I'm going to be fine, you'll see."

Affleck nodded uncertainly and backed away to his post by the ladder.

"I must apologise for my little display," Montane said, addressing the others, and now, in contrast to his previous hysteria, sounding gentle and reasonable. "I accused Scott of blasphemy, but *I* was the real blasphemer. I presumed to make myself the channel for God's divine wrath, and He sent me a little reminder that pride is a mortal sin."

The clichés are just the same, Nicklin thought in dismay, his mind diverted from external wonders, *but this has to be a different man.*

"Doctor Harding is with us," Voorsanger said. "I think I should ask him to come up here and – "

"Thank you, Ropp, but I assure you I am in no need of medical attention." Montane's eyes were bright and humorous as he looked at Hepworth. "Go on with what you were saying, Scott. I want to hear the scientist's view of the Devil's handiwork."

"It was all a bit speculative," Hepworth said, obviously in some doubt about the effects his words might have on Montane's state of mind.

"Don't be so modest! You were doing a wonderful job – laying down scientific laws that both Our Lord and the Devil have to obey. Go on with it, Scott – I really am interested." Montane, becoming aware of the saliva on his chin, drew the back of his sleeve across it, momentarily dragging his mouth out of shape.

The action was so atypical of the normally fastidious preacher that Nicklin felt a twinge of unease. *Corey, are you in there?* he thought. *Or have we a stranger in our midst?*

"All right, let's try to be as rational and unemotional as we possibly can," Hepworth said in a subdued voice which hinted that he too could be concerned about Montane's mental well-being. "Corey believes that Orbitsville was dissolved by the . . . um . . . Devil for the sole purpose of wiping out humanity, and I'm going to refer to that as the Malign Hypothesis. I disagree with him, so I'm going to champion the opposite point of view – the *Benign* Hypothesis.

"I have little doubt that the spheres we can see on our screens – all 650 million of them – are not 'real' planets in the normal astronomical sense. I would say that they are hollow shells, just as Orbitsville was a hollow shell; and I would say that their gravity is generated by the shell material, just as Orbitsville's gravity was generated."

"You're assuming that they have gravity in the first place," Montane cut in.

Hepworth nodded soberly. "That's right, Corey – I'm making that assumption."

"Just checking, just being *scientific*." Montane gave the others a conspiratorial grin which made Nicklin want to cringe away from him.

"To proceed," Hepworth said, "the Benign Hypothesis actually requires us to regard those artificial planets as being as durable as the 'real' variety, perhaps more so. We should also think of them as being ideal cradles for intelligent life – custom-designed, if you like, for our needs."

Nicklin tried to make the imaginative leap, and failed. "You're getting away from me, Scott," he said. "How . . . *how* can you possibly justify that?"

"It's implicit in the theory, Jim. It's implicit in the fact that the conditions in Orbitsville itself were so *exactly* what were needed for the human race to thrive and flourish. How often have we heard

Corey advance the same argument, that it was no coincidence that Orbitsville drew us into it – like wasps being lured into a jar of honey?"

"You can't fall back on – " Nicklin glanced at Montane's avid, watchful face. "Are we talking science or religion?"

"Science, Jim. Science! Though I don't mind telling you I would love it if some kind of devil or demon or imp or fucking familiar were to materialise in here at this very moment." Hepworth palmed his brow. "I'd be more than happy – believe this – I'd be more than happy to sell my immortal soul for a bottle of gin. Or even a glass!"

"What about this hypothesis?" Nicklin said, beginning to feel impatient.

"As I said, there is every evidence of design. Look at the green lines. They weakened building materials, remember. I would say that was a warning for us to keep off them – because they were dangerous boundaries." Hepworth glanced at the awesome image on the main screen. "I wouldn't mind betting that all *that* was achieved without the loss of one human life. I know how preposterous that sounds, but for beings who have total control of every geometry, every dimension – possibly including time – it could be done."

Montane snickered. "When does the Good Fairy appear?"

Hepworth inclined his head thoughtfully, half-smiling. "That's as good a name as any for the entity who is in control out there. It fits in well with the name of the hypothesis. I like it, Corey – Good Fairy! Yes, I like it."

"You could abbreviate that a bit," Nicklin said, feeling slightly awkward, like a reticent person who has been forced into a public debate. He and the others had just witnessed the most stupendous event imaginable, and it seemed inappropriate for them to be engaging in a quiet philosophical discussion so soon afterwards.

"You mean God?" Hepworth blinked his disagreement. "It's hardly His style is it?"

"All right, can you tell us who the Good Fairy is, and what she's up to?"

"The Good Fairy is the entity who designed and constructed Orbitsville in the first place. She must be as far ahead of us in evolutionary terms as we are ahead of amoebae."

"*I* could have said something like that," Nicklin protested. "Scott, I hate to say this – but your theory doesn't seem to take us very far."

"Mr Hepworth, could I ask you about the benign part of it," Voorsanger said, his narrow face pale and intent. "What makes you think that my . . . that everybody we left behind is still alive?"

"Occam's razor. You don't do all *that* . . . you don't go to all the trouble of creating two-thirds of a billion new homes for privileged customers and then allow the customers to die. It simply wouldn't be logical."

"Logical! Oh dear, oh dear! *Logical*!" Montane leaned far back in his seat and smiled at the ceiling.

Nicklin noticed, with a return of his uneasiness, that the smile seemed to be off centre. An obscure heavy-dictionary term flickered in his mind – *plaice-mouthed* – together with a horror vision of Montane's facial tissues having turned into an inelastic dough, allowing his mouth to be permanently dragged out of place when he wiped it. *Are we all going mad? Has the encounter with the Good Fairy been too much for us?*

"I want to believe you, Mr Hepworth," Voorsanger said, his eyes fixed on Hepworth's face, pleading. "Do you think we could find the right . . . planet?"

"I don't see why not." Hepworth's grandiloquent manner was returning. "If Orbitsville's equatorial material has remained at an equivalent position in the world cloud – and it seems only logical that it should – then – "

"For Christ's sake, Scott," Nicklin cut in, raising his voice. "Don't get carried away! I can hear the wheels going round in your head. You're adding bits and pieces to your so-called theory as you go along."

Hepworth wheeled on him and Nicklin saw in his eyes the beginnings of the sudden rage that so often transformed him when his scientific authority was challenged. There was a moment of silent antagonism, then Hepworth's plump face relaxed. He stood up and slowly walked around the control console, taking up a position beside the main screen, like a teacher with a blackboard. The screen was still largely occupied by the image of the single planet.

Hepworth gave Megan Fleischer a perfunctory smile. "Would you please revert to the general view?"

The pilot's hand moved slightly and the planet vanished. The cloud of worlds again dominated the screen, enclosing the sun in a gauzily bejewelled sphere of impossible beauty.

"In your slightly rusticated and untutored way, you were actually making a valid philosophical point," Hepworth said in mild tones, looking directly at Nicklin. "There is a classic test which can be applied to any good scientific theory. You make a prediction based on that theory, and if the prediction comes true the theory is strengthened.

"Would you be more kindly disposed towards my brain-child if we went through that process? If I were to make a prediction, here and now, and if – as some of us might put it – the prophecy were to be fulfilled? Would that bring a smile back to that cherubic countenance of yours?"

"*Don't make a banquet of it*, Nicklin thought irritably, refusing even to nod.

"Very well," Hepworth went on, an actor enjoying the centre of the stage. "I will now stick my neck out and predict that these worlds . . . which have just been created by the Good Fairy . . . all 650 million of them . . . will soon disappear from our sight."

Fleischer sat up straighter. "How can you say a thing like that?"

The question reverberated in Nicklin's mind as he stared at Hepworth's jowled and silver-stubbled face. The physicist looked more disreputable than ever in his smudged and shoddy clothing. This was the scientist manqué, the man who had allowed gin to leach his brain to the extent that he could flunk on high-school basics, but whose imaginative power seemed to encompass galaxies, universes, infinities.

I'm listening to you, Scott, he thought, all animosity and scepticism gone. *Say what you have to say – and I'll believe you.*

"It's all built in to the Benign Hypothesis," Hepworth said, indicating the world cloud. "I don't need to tell anybody that these planets are not in orbit around the sun. If the cloud is in rotation, as Orbitsville was, planets in the equatorial band *might* be in orbit – but I don't think they are. The entire system is impossible in terms of our celestial mechanics. It should fly apart, but it won't, and that is because some force is keeping those planets in place – just as another unknown force kept Orbitsville stable."

Fleischer raised one hand a little, like a student in class. "It seems to me that you're advancing reasons for the planets *not* to disappear."

"Yes and no. I'm saying that they *could* remain exactly where they are – if the Good Fairy wanted things to be that way. *But* – and this is the nub of everything – what would have been the point in dissolving Orbitsville in the first place?" Hepworth spread his hands and looked at each of his listeners in turn.

"Essentially, very little has changed out there. Instead of one huge Orbitsville there are 650 million little ones – turned inside out, of course – but if things stay as they are life will quickly return to normal. The cries of wonder and alarm from ordinary people will soon die down, because that's the way ordinary people *are*. There will be a few adjustments to make, of course, and the *annus mirabilis* will excite historians, philosophers and scientific researchers for many centuries to come – but, in *essence*, everything will be pretty much the same as before."

Hepworth paused, apparently distracted from his grand theme by the discovery that his shirt had crept up over his bulging stomach. He spent a few seconds stuffing it back into his pants before fixing his audience with a sombre gaze.

"So, I put it to you," he said, "what would be the point in leaving all those brand-new planets where they are?"

"Perhaps there isn't any point," Nicklin said. "Perhaps that's just the way it's going to be."

"That's another line of thought – call it the Null Hypothesis – but I don't like it. I don't believe that the Good Fairy squanders her time and energy."

Nicklin found himself floundering in the onrush of new concepts. "All right – where will the planets go? And *why* will they go?"

"That isn't part of the bet," Hepworth said simply. "I can't explain the wheres and whys – all I'm saying is that the planets *will* be relocated. They may disappear suddenly, all at once; or the process may be a gradual one. For all we know it has already started – "

"It shouldn't be too hard to find out, provided our old planet-search programme can handle that many points," Fleischer said, beginning to address her main computer. "What we might be able to do is monitor say a one per cent sample, and then . . . " Her voice faded into an abstracted murmur as she became involved in the mathematics of the self-imposed problem.

Voorsanger glanced apprehensively at Montane before fixing his gaze on Hepworth. "All this is enough to start me questioning the whole purpose of this flight."

Hepworth nodded. "Are you saying we should go back?"

"I suppose . . . " Voorsanger glanced again at Montane and his face suddenly hardened. "Yes, that's what I'm saying."

"How about you, Jim?"

"How would I know?" Nicklin said, unable to suppress the feeling that it was monstrously unfair to ask him for a judgement on such a vast issue and with so little hard evidence available. "Besides, we're talking like a management committee again."

"All right, we'll ask the boss." Hepworth looked at Montane. "How about it, Corey?"

"You fools!" Still grinning, Montane continued to stare at the ceiling. "You poor *fools*!"

"I don't think Corey is quite ready to give us a considered opinion." Hepworth gave Affleck a meaningful look. "Nibs, why don't you see if you can find Doctor Harding and bring him up here? I think it would be for the best . . . "

Affleck shuffled his feet, looking tortured, then stepped on to the ladder and sank out of view.

Hepworth returned his attention to Nicklin. "How about it, Jim?"

"How about you?" Nicklin said, putting off any kind of decision. "What do you say?"

Hepworth gave him a strange little smile. "It's a tough one – especially without suitable lubrication. There's so much to find out about this universe. I'd like to go on, and at the same time I'd like to go back."

"That's a *lot* of help," Nicklin said. "It seems to me that as you started the – "

"Gentlemen!" Megan Fleischer cut in. "Allow me to make up your minds for you – we have to turn back."

"At least there's no equivocation there," Hepworth said coldly. "Would you mind telling us how you arrived at such a firm conclusion?"

"I don't mind at all." Fleischer smiled in a way that signalled her dislike for the physicist. "This ship isn't fit to carry out an interstellar flight."

"What?" Hepworth's belligerence was immediate. "What are you talking about, woman?"

"I'm talking about the drive, *man*. We're losing the left intake field."

"Nonsense!"

Hepworth leaned over the control console, staring down at the field distribution display. Nicklin followed his line of sight and saw that the glowing butterfly had become noticeably asymmetric. He watched in chill fascination as, in the space of only a few seconds, the left wing – changing shape all the while – shrank to a writhing speck and finally blinked out of existence. In the same moment he felt a queasy upsurge in his stomach which told him the ship's acceleration had been sharply reduced. There followed a ringing silence which was broken by Fleischer.

"As commander of this vessel," she announced in clear, precise tones, "I have decided to abort the flight."

"You stupid *bitch*!" Hepworth shouted.

He turned and ran to the ladder, reaching it in two grotesque low-gravity bounds, and lowered himself through the deck opening. Several seconds went by before it dawned on Nicklin that Hepworth was on his way to the engine cylinders. Gripped by a sense of unreality, he stood up and looked at the others half-expecting to receive some guidance as to what he should do next. Fleischer and Voorsanger gave him blank stares; Montane continued to grin wetly at the ceiling.

Nicklin loped past them and sprang on to the ladder. He went down it in the normal manner for a short distance, then realised that the quickest way to proceed in the low-gravity conditions was by a controlled fall. He curled his fingers loosely on the stringers, took his feet off the rungs and allowed himself to drop.

The fall was gentle and easily controllable by tightening his grip. Far below him he could hear Hepworth bellowing at people using the ladder to get out of his way. On almost all the decks that Nicklin passed there were children to applaud his unorthodox descent. Some adults eyed him with less enthusiasm, and he knew they were experiencing the qualms that travellers had always felt on noticing a disturbance in shipboard routine. It occurred to him that they would feel considerably worse when they learned what the disturbance was all about. The future of the New Eden express was being threatened from without and within.

He caught up with Hepworth on 14 Deck, the first on which there was access to the engine cylinders. Hepworth had already tapped his authorisation code into the lock and was dragging the shielded door open.

"What do you want?" he demanded, scowling at Nicklin with the face of an enemy.

What's happening to us? Nicklin thought. "Scott, I'm with you. You're not the only one who sweated in here. Remember?"

Hepworth's brow cleared at once. "We've got a minor problem down here, Jim. That Fleischer woman would just *love* it if the whole drive complex packed up, but it isn't going to! I know exactly what's wrong – and I know exactly how to put it right."

"That's good," Nicklin said, unhappily remembering Hepworth's previous assertion that the weak acceleration was the result of unfavourable conditions outside the ship.

"It's the output gate control mechanisms," Hepworth said, stepping over the door's high threshold into the bleakly illuminated environment of the engine cylinders. "They were *never* right! I told Corey that from the start. The contractors who overhauled them were a bunch of know-nothings, but he wouldn't part with the money for a dependable job. Not Corey! And now that the inevitable has happened that bitch up above is trying to shift the blame on to *me*!"

Hepworth was moving towards the left output chamber as he spoke. Nicklin followed close behind, trying to make sense of what he was hearing. He had had little to do with the gates and their associated mechanisms, partly because they had been Hepworth's jealously guarded territory, but also because the gates themselves were blocks of ferro-molybdenum weighing in the region of 600 tonnes each. In spite of their enormous mass they had to be moved quickly, with three degrees of freedom, to direct the magnetic flux of the *Tara's* intake fields.

The support frames, controls, gears and resonance motors were heavy power engineering, and outside the scope of Nicklin's fields of expertise. He had always worked alone and had taken no interest in anything he was unable to lift without help. But in spite of his limited knowledge, as he trailed behind Hepworth through the inhuman environment of the engine cylinder, he found himself again experiencing doubts about the man's qualifications and practical experience.

What he had seen portrayed on the ship's control console had looked, to him, like a straightforward collapse of the left intake field. At a guess he would have said that a flux pump had developed one of the dozen or so faults to which such complex machines were prone. But he was relegated, condemned, to the role of bystander because of his cursed lack of relevant training. *Could* the field have withered in a way that, to the experienced eye, told of a failure in gate mechanisms?

Hepworth reached the massive bulkhead of the field emission chamber and, breathing heavily, began tapping the access code into the lock.

"Scott, what are you doing?" Nicklin grabbed Hepworth's upper arm. "You can't just walk in *there*!"

Hepworth angrily shook his arm free. "I know what I'm doing. The whole complex has shut down automatically."

"But you don't know what the residual level of motor activity is! There could be . . . I mean . . . "

Nicklin strove for the right form of warning, the formula with which to penetrate the shell of Hepworth's irrational fury. He knew a lot about magnetic pulse motors, and on a small scale had seen the havoc they could wreak when suddenly frustrated in their normal activities. For as long as five minutes after a serious breakdown they could emit bursts of gyromagnetic energy which, flitting through the vicinity like poltergeists, could invade metal objects and invest them with a pseudo-life of their own. He had seen cables writhing like snakes, and pliers leaping from work-benches with enough force to shatter windows. In those cases the kinetic force had been released by broken motors no larger than his fist – and the motors in the field emission chamber were the size of beer kegs.

"There's nothing wrong with the motors," Hepworth snapped. "The trouble is in the gate control rods, and I know exactly where."

"But at least look at the monitors and . . . " Nicklin gestured at the panel beside the door and his voice faded as he saw that all its dials and counters were inert.

"Somebody put the wrong fuses in that thing," Hepworth said defiantly. "It's a redundant piece of junk anyway."

"But you told Corey . . . you told us all that the work on your side of things was finished weeks ago! What else have you declared redundant around here?"

"All essential systems are functional."

Nicklin stared into the physicist's eyes and saw something there which terrified him. "Fleischer was right about you, wasn't she? You're not up to the job!"

The punch Hepworth threw was both clumsy and slow, but when Nicklin tried to avoid it his feet, lacking purchase in the low gravity, skidded out from under him. Hepworth's fist hit him squarely in the stomach as he went down. He landed on his back and slid into a tool rack. Mentally rather than physically shocked, he gripped the rack and drew himself to his feet as Hepworth was disappearing from his view in the emission chamber.

"Scott, I'm sorry," he called out. "Please don't go – "

His voice was lost amid a series of violent reports from within the chamber. Metal was striking on metal with a ferocity which punished Nicklin's ears and numbed his brain. The clamour went on for perhaps ten seconds, and somewhere in the heart of it he heard a different kind of sound. It was a softer impact, less strident than the others and with several elements – a crushing, a pulping, a gasp. The mechanical bedlam reached an awesome climax and then, quite abruptly, slackened off. In the ringing aftermath Nicklin could hear a single piece of metal bouncing, come to rest, vibrating – then there was total silence.

He remained where he was, petrified, staring at the baffle screen which prevented him from seeing far into the emission chamber. Gyromagnetic demons had been unleashed behind that screen, he knew, and he was not venturing into their lair until it was safe to do so. *Five minutes*, he thought. *I'll give it a full five minutes from now – just to be safe . . .*

He began counting the time on his wristwatch.

Don't get me wrong on this thing. I'm not actually saying that old Scott is dead. No, sir! He isn't making any noises – I'll grant you that – but that doesn't mean he's been defunctified, not by a long chalk. He could be cowering inside a locker, wondering what the hell happened. Perhaps he has filled those awful fucking baggy pants of his and is too ashamed to come out into the open. What a bloody scream that would be!

Almost two minutes had passed when there came a single loud *clank* from behind the screen.

"Scott?" Nicklin whispered. "Is that you, Scott?"

As if answering the query, the wrenches and screwdrivers in his pockets stirred into life, twisting and squirming like trapped animals. He gave a quavering moan as the rack upon which he was leaning shuddered and briefly became a discordant carillon, every tool on it clattering its individual note. But the agitation soon passed. His new fear evaporated as he realised that the gyromagnetic demons had, in their death throes, given birth to and sent forth a horde of mischievous kinetic imps.

Another nice touch, O Gaseous Vertebrate! You really had me going there for a moment. But there's just one minor point – does this mean that Scott is really dead? Extincticated? Exanimated? Kaputorised?

Two minutes further on Nicklin heard a faint sound to his right. He looked in that direction and saw a young man in the uniform of a spaceport guard. It was the same young man – obviously a restless and inquisitive type – who had earlier intruded on the control deck. He studied Nicklin's face for a long moment and then, without uttering a word, placed a finger vertically against his lips and retreated out of sight.

When five minutes had gone Nicklin advanced slowly to the door of the emission chamber. From the narrow space between the bulkhead and the baffle screen he could see part of a surreal world of grey metal masses, grey cabinets and twisted control rods, the whole accented with streaks of red here, and spots of red there.

When he moved to the end of the screen and looked around it the first thing he noticed, lying almost at his feet, was Hepworth's head. It had been untidily severed, *very* untidily severed, and the face was turned up to his.

Nicklin felt his own face become an equally contorted death mask, and his mind immediately ricocheted into the safe universe of the absurd and the irrelevant. *Look at the blackhead at the side of his nose. Just look at the frigger! Maybe I should squeeze it out before anybody else sees him like this . . . do him a last favour . . . mark of respect . . .*

235

Part of Nicklin's mind which still dealt in logic told him there should be a body close by. On the perimeter of his vision there was something which just might have qualified as a body, but he was unable to direct his gaze on to it. Groaning with each breath, he backed out of the emission chamber and went to the nearest commset. He spoke the pilot's number and her face immediately appeared on the screen.

"This is Jim Nicklin," he said.

"I can see that," Fleischer replied drily. "Well?"

"Is Doctor Harding up there?"

"Yes, he's looking at Corey. Why?"

"Scott is dead. Somebody has to . . . gather him up – and I can't do it." Nicklin took a deep, steadying breath. "Ask Doctor Harding if he would come down to 14 Deck right away. Tell him his professional services are required."

In times of crisis – Nicklin had discovered – small, familiar comforts assume an inestimable degree of importance. There was no potable alcohol in the ship's medical supplies, thanks to Montane's prohibition, but it had turned out that Jon Harding had a bottle of brandy in his personal kit. Harding was not the *Tara*'s official medic – he was a paid-up pilgrim, accompanied by his wife and two children – who happened to be a general practitioner, and was standing in for the appointee, who had been a casualty of the sudden departure from Beachhead. He had prescribed and dispensed a large measure of brandy for Nicklin's condition of shock. Nicklin had almost wept with gratitude on being handed the well-filled bulb, and now he treasured it more than an orb of gold.

It was "night" time and, although the clamour of the previous hours had subsided, the ensuing silence was far from being restful. Too much had happened in too short a time. The passengers had been alarmed and confused by the news of Orbitsville's transformation – as was evidenced by the crowds which had formed around the television monitors on several decks. And then, in close succession, had come the cut in acceleration, Hepworth's sensational death, and the announcement that the *Tara* was turning back.

Voorsanger and Fleischer had gone on the general audio system to say that the ship was returning to investigate the world cloud at close range – which was a diplomatic understatement rather than an outright lie. They had emphasised that the return was a minor event and should be viewed in the context of what was scheduled to be a months-long voyage, but too many doubts and fears had been aroused in the passengers' collective consciousness. Danea Farthing, and a few others of the mission's long-term staff who were fully acquainted with the situation, had spent hours in counselling anxious parents – with only qualified success.

Nicklin could sense the icy apprehension which was abroad in the ship's lower decks. The chill of it was deep within him, and slow to disperse. He had never really enjoyed brandy in the past, but as he sat with Voorsanger and Fleischer in the control room each sip he took yielded nostalgic pleasure beyond description. He could imagine himself, were the right circumstances ever to return, devoting the rest of his life to the worship of the fiery spirit. That possibility, however, had begun to seem more remote than the stars.

Harding had done heroic work in removing Hepworth's remains from the emission chamber without help. The *Tara*, as a ship of the Explorer class, was capable of being flown by one person if necessary. Its designers had done their best to anticipate every adverse situation a small crew might have to face, but they had overlooked the possibility that, occasionally, the crew might become even smaller. There was no suitable storage space for dead bodies. The oversight had created problems for Harding, and he had solved them by sealing Hepworth's corpse in wrappings of plastic and transferring it to a free corner of the ship's deep freeze facility, thus enabling Nicklin to enter the emission chamber and prepare a damage report.

Nicklin had found that one of the gate positioning rods had failed, just as Hepworth had diagnosed. The broken rod had jumped its bearings, displaced other rods and damaged two servomotors – something Hepworth had *not* thought of and which had cost him his life. But the root cause of the trouble had been more fundamental.

The sequence of disaster had been triggered by flux pump coils burning out. Automatic cut-outs had been slow coming into action – another fault – with the result that for a split-second the left intake field had been wildly misshapen. And it had been the system's attempt at correcting the field distortion that had made impossible demands on the output gate controls.

Enter Nicklin and the doomed Hepworth from stage left . . .

Nicklin squirmed in his seat as he wondered how badly the drive complex in the right-hand cylinder might be affected by the gangrene of Hepworth's incompetence.

The ship as a whole was in good condition. The thermonuclear power unit could be trusted, because it was self-contained and designed to run for centuries. Much the same could be said for the short-range ion drivers, and Nicklin also had faith in anything for which he had been responsible. So there would be no structural failures and the *Tara's* passengers were assured of regenerated oxygen, ventilation, light, heat and water.

All of which meant that, should the ship fail to reach a safe haven, they would be reasonably comfortable while they starved to death.

Their lives depended on the trouble-free functioning of everything in the right-hand drive cylinder. And Nicklin could visualise the ghost of Hepworth down there at that very minute – bragging, boozing, issuing worthless guarantees, threatening violence to anyone who questioned his ability . . .

"I've just come from Corey's room," Voorsanger said. "He is still asleep and Jon says he'll probably stay that way for the next six or seven hours. I think that could be something of a blessing for all of us, don't you?"

"It's probably a blessing for him," Fleischer replied in a tired voice. "I don't see what difference it makes to the rest of us."

"Well . . . He's less likely to . . . ah . . . object too strenuously to our going back if he finds we're already well on the way."

"He can object all he wants," Fleischer said firmly. "I'm the commander of this vessel. *I* made the decision to return, and nothing will make me alter it."

Good for you! Nicklin thought, sympathising in full with the pilot. She was becoming increasingly terse and irritable, and he could see why. She was a professional who had somehow allowed the religious side of her nature to blind her to the fact that she was joining a company of fools. It had become apparent to Fleischer that her faith in Corey Montane was going to cost her plenty, possibly her life, and she felt deeply embittered as a result.

There's a good chance of the Gaseous Vertebrate gaining another convert here, Nicklin thought, allowing a few drops of brandy to float on to his tongue. *We'll just have to see how it goes.*

"The Lord will decide everything in the end," Voorsanger said, reproving the pilot for her lack of humility. "Anyway, it makes *me* feel better to know that we're on our way back."

"I'll probably feel the same way – when we actually *begin* travelling back."

"But you turned the ship ages ago!" Voorsanger pointed at the sun and its fantastic retinue of planets on the main screen. "That's a forward view, isn't it? It says so underneath. Nought degrees! That means the camera is looking dead ahead, doesn't it?"

Nicklin smiled to himself as he took another minuscule sip of brandy, conserving the precious supply. Voorsanger was undoubtedly a good man with financial facts and figures, but it was obvious that he had not thought much about balancing the books in which the *Tara*'s energy transactions were logged.

"Yes, I turned the ship around," Fleischer said with some show of impatience, "but we had been accelerating for roughly thirty hours at that point and were travelling away from the sun at more than 320 kilometres a second. The ship is now pointing its nose at the sun, and it thinks it's moving in that direction – but it's actually flying *backwards*.

"We're trying to discard speed, but with only half of the original thrust available it will take us about sixty hours just to come to a halt and we'll have covered more than fifty million kilometres. *Then* we can start heading back to the edge of the world cloud, but the return leg is going to take even longer than the outward one."

"I see," Voorsanger said gloomily. "I thought we'd be able to start the search quite soon . . . in a couple of days . . . "

Fleischer shook her head. "Eight days minimum. That's assuming nothing else goes wrong – and around here that's a pretty big assumption."

"I think we all realise that." Voorsanger gave Nicklin a disapproving glance. "I warned Corey about giving responsible posts to inebriates."

"You shouldn't speak ill of the dead," Nicklin said in a pious voice.

"When I said inebriates I was including you, though I must

admit your friend was worse. I never met him when he didn't reek of alcohol – it's no wonder he wasn't fit for his job."

"The booze had nothing to do with it," Nicklin countered. "Scott could make even *better* cock-ups when he was cold sober – he had a natural flair for it."

Lovely epitaph, he added mentally, wondering when the emotional trauma associated with Hepworth's death was going to catch up on him. They had spent too many lonely bull sessions together, holed up on rainy nights in odd corners of the gutted ship, for him not to have pain in reserve. It was banked away for him, accruing interest. Before long he would become a pain millionaire.

"Always the jokes," Voorsanger said. "But they don't alter the fact that Hepworth has endangered the lives of a hundred men, women and children."

"Scott was a good man," Nicklin replied, provoked into a declaration he knew to be totally out of context and, in most people's eyes, indefensible.

"Scott was a male chauvinist dinosaur," Megan Fleischer came in, her voice so matter-of-fact that Nicklin, even in his weariness and mild intoxication, knew it had to herald something important.

"But I'll say this much for him," she went on, fingers at work on the computer panel. "He was absolutely right about those planets disappearing – the world cloud has started to thin out."

"There you are!" Nicklin was about to comment on the power of Hepworth's imagination when an unwanted new thought crept into his mind. "If Scott was right the cloud will disappear altogether."

"That's possible. It may even be probable."

"Can you say how long that would take?"

"Not really," Fleischer said, very much the cool professional. "I don't know how representative my sample is, and I have a feeling the computer is a little confused by points moving in behind other points, thus apparently reducing the real number. I'll have to refine things a bit more for it."

"Let's put it this way," Nicklin said, wondering if the pilot had chosen to tantalise him, "will it take longer than eight days?"

"The computer is saying thirty to forty days, so we ought to be all right." Fleischer's face was unreadable beneath its crown of luxuriant hair. "Though I have no idea what the margin of error is –

and I am, of course, assuming that the planets are disappearing at a constant rate."

Thank you ever so bloody much for that last bit, Nicklin thought, fixing his gaze on the main screen. The gauzy sphere of the world cloud now had a new fascination for him, quite apart from its breathtaking beauty. He raised the drinks container to his lips and, no longer in the mood to conserve its comforts, jetted warm brandy into his throat until the bulb was empty.

A fresh element of uncertainty had been introduced to a situation which already had too many life-threatening variables. He stared at the world cloud, trying to force his perceptions into a radical new mode which would enable him to detect the Good Fairy at work – dispatching planet after planet after planet into the unknown.

All thought of sleep had deserted him, but in a short time his eyes and mind tired of the impossible task he had set for himself. It was warm and quiet in the control room, and it was possible to forget that he was inside a pneumatic bomb, hurtling through the interstellar void under doubtful control. His seat was unexpectedly comfortable, the brandy was exercising its benign influence, and he could have been in another time and place. This could have been Orangefield – drowsing in ageless security – preserved in the amber of distant summer afternoons . . .

He was awakened by a startled cry from Megan Fleischer.

He jerked upright, fully expecting to see that the gauze of the world cloud had dissolved into patches and threads, but the image on the main screen was exactly as before. To his left Voorsanger was struggling out of sleep, and Fleischer was knuckling her eyes while staring intently at pulsing lozenges on the console.

"There's somebody in the pinnace!" She clapped a hand to her forehead, no longer the imperturbable commander. "It's going! It's *going!*"

Nicklin twisted his way out of his seat and made a low-gravity swoop towards the ladder. He went down it at speed, but before he reached 2 Deck he saw that the floor plate had been slid into place, barring access to the deck below. He dropped to his knees, gripping the ladder with one hand and tugging at the plate with the other. There were no locks on the plate, but it moved only a centimetre or two and then stuck. He knew at once that it had been tied in place from underneath.

"Nibs!" he shouted. "Are you down there, Nibs? What the hell do you think you're doing?"

As if in answer to his questions a multiple tremor ran through both ladder and deck.

"The pinnace has gone." Fleischer's face had appeared above him in the control-room hatchway. "There was nothing I could do about it."

Nicklin pounded on the floor plate. "Nibs, if you don't move this plate out of the way I'll come down there and kill you." He thought for a moment about the contradictory nature of the threat and decided on a change of tack. "Mr Voorsanger wants to go down there. This is serious, Nibs."

A moment later he heard some fumbling from below. He was able to push the plate aside and saw Affleck standing at the open door to Montane's suite. The fire plate on 3 Deck had also been drawn over and lashed in place, sealing the level off from the lower regions of the ship. The rectangular shape of Milly Montane's coffin was projecting a short distance through the doorway, and the lid was missing.

Oh Christ, no! Nicklin thought as he lowered himself on to 3 Deck, with Fleischer and Voorsanger following from above. Nicklin halted and looked down into the coffin. It was empty, just as he had known it would be. The white satin lining was nested in the shape of a human being, and the depression was ringed with stains, like a contour map, the colours ranging from pale yellow to black. A sweet, sickly and faintly spicy smell – the pot-pourri of corruption – hung in the air.

"What's going on here?" Megan Fleischer demanded, pushing against Nicklin from behind.

He moved aside and gave her an unobstructed view of the coffin. She looked at it, turned back – face quite impassive – and pushed her way between Nicklin and Voorsanger to reach the ladder. She clung to it and began a harsh dry retching, measured and painful, regular as breathing.

She didn't know about the extra passenger, Nicklin realised. *Welcome on board the good ship* Lollipop, *captain.*

"None of you got no idea how it was with Corey and me," Affleck said defiantly, his nose purple against the unnatural pallor of the rest of his face. "I *had* to do what he told me to do. I owe my life to Corey."

"Not any more," Nicklin replied. The torrent of events in the past minute had numbed his mind – and the nearness of the obscenely yawning coffin was not helping matters – but it was dawning on him that none of the mishaps so far encountered by the New Eden pilgrims was in a class with the latest grim development.

Without the pinnace to ferry them to a safe landfall, the hundred-plus men, women and children on board the *Tara* were condemned to remain in space for the rest of their lives.

"If you ask me," he said to Affleck, still speaking like an automaton, "you and Corey can call it quits."

CHAPTER 20

Montane knew that he had to act quickly in the first few seconds after separation.

The passenger cylinder of the *Tara* was visible above him, its coppery curvatures glowing in the weak light of the Orbitsville sun. The mother ship was in retardation, which meant – thanks to the arithmetic of relative velocities – that it was trying to *overtake* the pinnace. There was a real danger of the little ship colliding with the front end of the giant's engine cylinders and then tumbling back along the sides to be engulfed in the invisible but lethal exhaust flare.

It was many years since Montane had done any kind of flying, but he had retained the instincts of a pilot. He slammed the throttle to the FULL POWER position and at the same time pushed the single control column forward.

The nose of the passenger cylinder immediately slid backwards and out of sight, while at the same time the view ahead of him underwent a dizzy change. The sun swam upwards and passed out of his field of view, and the vast cloud of pseudo-planets which surrounded it partook of the same motion. For a giddy moment the jewelled curtain streamed vertically, then it too was gone, and the blackness of space filled the cockpit's forward transparency.

Montane brought the control column back to the neutral position to prevent the pinnace continuing on a circular path which would have taken it through the *Tara's* exhaust. The star fields ahead of him obediently settled into place, steady and serene, and he knew that he was once again flying away from the deadly web which the Devil had spun around the sun.

God in his infinite mercy had laid the universe and all its riches out before him – and each one of the brilliant points ahead of his speeding craft held infinite promise for the future.

Montane began to laugh, and as he laughed the nightmare years were erased from his memory. He was a young man – what could have made him think otherwise? – and the optimism and potency of youth suffused every part of his body.

And the Lord had appointed him to the most glorious and fulfilling task imaginable.

"It won't always be easy for us," he said to his young bride. "We may have to face great hardships when we reach the New Eden, but we will overcome them as long as we preserve our faith in Him and our love for each other."

"I know that, my darling," Milly replied, smiling at him from the cockpit's left-hand seat.

The pearl silk bridal gown emphasised her slimness and utter femininity, but he knew she also had an inner strength which would enable her to overcome any adversity the years might bring. The gladness he felt at simply being near her was almost unbearable.

"I don't think I've ever seen you looking so lovely," he said, briefly touching her wrist.

She made no reply, but her smile grew wider.

CHAPTER 21

The idea that he had just been sentenced to death was strangely easy for Nicklin to accept.

He felt neither fear nor anger – just a kind of sad resignation, which might have been the result of emotional overload. A more likely explanation, he decided as he stood with the others on the landing of 3 Deck, was that he had known in his heart for some time that this moment was inevitable. It had been rolling towards him, down a narrow alleyway of time, ever since that sunny afternoon in Altamura when he had first met Scott Hepworth. It had been accelerating all along, gaining momentum from each unexpected new event – within the ship or in the cosmos beyond – and now its force was irresistible.

I'm turning into a fatalist, he thought. *And just in time, too!*

"Might as well get this thing out of the way," he said, putting his foot against the end of Milly Montane's coffin. He thrust hard, propelling the coffin into the suite, then he closed the door. "Might as well keep the place tidy."

"Corey must have gone mad," Voorsanger whispered.

"Nobody is going to argue with you on that one. I'd say that Corey parted company with us a long time ago."

"But where does he think he's going?"

"He's going where the rest of us are going, but he'll get there sooner," Nicklin said. "There's no food or water on the pinnace – and not much oxygen."

"Would somebody kindly . . . explain to me what's been going on here?" Fleischer was gulping as she spoke, fighting to control her stomach, and her forehead was dewed with sweat.

"Corey's wife died a long time ago, but he wouldn't allow her to be buried on Orbitsville." Nicklin, who had had years to get used to the bizarre story, was unable to imagine how it must sound to Fleischer, hearing it for the first time in such extreme circumstances. "I . . . ah . . . don't think he could stand the idea of taking her back to . . . "

"You're insane," the pilot whispered, her eyes wide with incredulity. "You're all insane!"

Don't look at me, lady, Nicklin thought, then it came to him that he had little grounds for indignation. "Maybe you're right," he said. "That would account for a lot."

"If only I'd known what I was letting myself in for," Fleischer said, dabbing her brow.

"Perhaps Corey will come back." Voorsanger's gaze travelled around the other faces, and his eyes seemed to plead with them. "The children . . . "

I wish you hadn't said that, Nicklin thought, his awareness suddenly expanding beyond his own concerns and prospects. There were many children among the pilgrims who had believed that Corey Montane was going to save their mortal bodies and immortal souls. The adults had made a serious blunder and would have to pay the forfeit, but the little ones – the innocents who had been given no say in the matter – were going to exit from their short lives in suffering and bewilderment.

There ought to be a law, Nicklin thought. *Somebody should have made a law against this kind of thing. A long time ago.*

The pain within him intensified as he faced the fact that Zindee White was also on board. She and her parents had placed *their* faith in another false prophet, and as a consequence . . .

His recriminations were interrupted by the faint sound of a male voice filtering through the hatchway above.

"The radio!" Megan Fleischer, who had been clinging to the ladder, took proper hold of it and rapidly climbed out of Nicklin's sight.

"That's Corey," Voorsanger said, his voice quavering with vindication and relief. "I *knew* he wouldn't desert us. I'm going to speak to him." He went to the ladder and drew himself up it close on the pilot's heels.

Nicklin edged past Affleck, who seemed dazed and quite unaware of the new development, and followed Voorsanger to the control room. By the time he stepped off the ladder Fleischer was in the central chair and busy with the communications panel. The voice on the radio grew louder and clearer.

"I repeat, this is spaceport control at Silver Plains, P202," it said. "We are picking up your autoscan transmission on the general band. Is there anybody there? Please respond immediately if you are receiving this signal. I repeat, this is the spaceport control centre at Silver Plains, P202."

"This is W–602874 answering your call, Silver Plains," Fleischer said, her voice harshened by the long bout of retching. "Are you receiving me?"

There was a delay of several seconds before the voice on the radio was heard again. "This is spaceport control at Silver Plains. We are picking up your autoscan transmission on the . . . " It went on to repeat the earlier message, almost word for word.

"They didn't hear you," Voorsanger said nervously.

"Give them time," Fleischer glanced at the communications panel. "They're calling at a range of roughly thirty-five million kilometres. Our radio signal is taking a couple of minutes to get there. And we'll have to wait as long again for a reply."

"At least there's somebody there to hear us," Nicklin said, still trying to grasp the full significance of what had happened. "This means that Scott was right. His Benign Hypothesis is working out better than he'll ever know."

"It may also be more benign that he'll ever know." The pilot smiled at Nicklin for the first time in their acquaintanceship. "If all the old spaceport facilities are still in existence – and that call suggests that they are – we ought to be able to get another pinnace. Perhaps several."

"That does sound . . . benign." Nicklin returned Fleischer's smile, tentatively, almost afraid to accept the priceless gift she was offering. "Did you say several?"

"There were four different types that I know of in the Hilversum Space Technology Centre at Portal 16."

"Operational?"

"I flew two of them last year," Fleischer said. "When I was adding the Explorer class to my general licence."

"So . . . "

"So, the new plan is to locate Hilversum among that lot." Fleischer, in a gesture oddly reminiscent of Hepworth, waved an arm at the image of the world cloud on the main screen. "It should be easy enough to do, as soon as they pick themselves up off the floor and get back on the air the way the people at Silver Plains have done.

"We then go into orbit around the Hilversum world; they shuttle us down to the ground; and what happens after that is up to the Lord."

"We can only beg for His guidance and protection," Voorsanger came in, his voice newly charged with religious fervour. "Now that Corey is no longer with us I think it falls on me to organise general prayers for our deliverance."

Nicklin opened his mouth to comment on Orbitsville's sudden change of status – from Devil's snare to safe harbour – then decided it would be the cheapest kind of sarcasm. The very word had once meant tearing at flesh, and he had gorged himself to the full in the past three years. Besides, he had run as fast as anybody when the portents had come and the end of the world had seemed at hand.

"I think you should wait for some hard information before you say anything down below," Fleischer said, after a pause.

"Of course, but are we going to have a four-minute delay every time we speak to someone back there?"

"No. When we finally reach standstill and are starting on the way back the delay will have gone up to about seven minutes."

"Isn't there something else you can do?" Voorsanger made a show of looking at his wristwatch. "How did we talk to Earth in the old days?"

Fleischer shook her head. "This ship has no tachyonic equipment."

"What?" Voorsanger turned to Nicklin with a look of reproach on his compressed features.

"You were the financial expert who decided it was too expensive," Nicklin said, amazed at how quickly Voorsanger, once he had persuaded himself that death was no longer imminent, had reverted to the role of tetchy business expert for whom a wasted second was a wasted fortune. "Besides, the *Tara* wasn't supposed to need anything like tachyonics – the plan was to get out of Orbitsville and keep on going."

"The plan was also to have a ship that was *capable* of – "

Voorsanger broke off as the radio speakers gave a preliminary click.

"This is Silver Plains," the same male voice said. "We are receiving you, W–602874. Can you confirm that you are the Explorer-class vessel *Tara*? We have you listed as land-docked at Pı for overhaul and modifications. Over."

"*Tara* confirmed," Fleischer said at once. "We got out of Pı just before . . . things started to happen. One of our drive units has failed and we are currently retarding in preparation for return to any available port. We have also lost our auxiliary craft. Repeat, we have lost our auxiliary craft. Can you arrange for the retrieval of approximately one hundred passengers from parking orbit? Over."

"That's the big question," Nicklin said as Fleischer relaxed back into her chair. "Is Silver Plains likely to have anything which could help?"

"We can only hope and pray. We don't even know what happened when the portals closed up, do we? If it was a simple iris-type process you would expect that any ships which were in exterior docking cradles would have been shut out of Orbitsville. Then when Orbitsville dissolved and – how do you put it? – all the geometries were reversed, all those ships would have wound up *inside* their respective new planets. Is that how it seems to you?"

"I hadn't even thought about that part of it," Nicklin replied. "I wonder if everybody got out of them."

"There was enough time – for ships that were actually in the cradles." The pilot, rapidly regaining her professional composure, sounded almost casual. "But there must have been a few ships in transit between portals at the time. I'd like to know what happened to them. Even if they were somehow, by some kind of miracle, injected into orbit around new planets – how will the people on board get down to the surface?

"Ships with a surface-to-space capability are rare birds – as we very well know – and those that may still be available will only be on planets which happen to have spaceports. Even on the equatorial band that could be as few as one in a hundred." Fleischer's voice became abstracted, fading almost to inaudibility as she developed the line of thought.

"I wonder how far Hepworth's Good Fairy is prepared to go to preserve human lives. I mean, how good is she at detail planning?"

Another good question, Nicklin thought, realising that even the qualified optimism he had begun to feel over the fate of the *Tara* had been ill-considered and premature. Fleischer had said that there were four pinnaces at P16, but there was a strong probability that all four had been in exterior cradles when the portal closed. In that case it was possible, as she had suggested, that they were now inside Hilversum's brand-new custom-built world.

It all came down to the fact – an echo of Montane's oft-repeated warning – that everything had been made too easy for the inhabitants of Orbitsville. The great shell had been rotating at a rate which meant that the portals in the equatorial band had a velocity exactly equal to that of a ship which was in orbit around the sun. That had made embarking and disembarking through a portal extremely simple. It had also made it pointless for an ordinary commercial spacecraft to carry the equivalent of an ocean liner's lifeboat.

Lifeboat, Nicklin mused. *LIFEboat. The character who thought up that name knew exactly what he* . . .

He lost track of the thought as the radio speakers gave their preliminary click well in advance of the four-minute interval which had been anticipated.

"This is spaceport control at Hilversum, formerly Portal 16," a male voice said tentatively. "We are receiving an autoscan transmission. Please identify yourself. Over."

"He sounds more scared than we are." Fleischer gave the others a wry smile which warmed Nicklin towards her. "I wonder who he thinks is calling."

"Answer the man," Voorsanger said impatiently.

"This is spacecraft W–602874 answering your call, Hilversum. Are you receiving me? Over." Fleischer glanced at the communications panel then settled back in her chair. "That's the call I was hoping for. We'll soon know how we stand."

Voorsanger moved into the chair beside her. "How long will it take?"

"Hilversum is farther away along the equator. The range is nearly seventy-five miks this time, so the round-trip delay will be over eight minutes."

"That's too long," Voorsanger said in sepulchral tones. "We should have been tachyonic."

"I can wait eight minutes. Every reply we get increases our chances of getting out of this alive – and I'm hoping to raise a hundred spaceports in the next few hours. If two of them are functioning there's no reason every port there is shouldn't come on the air."

As he listened to the pilot Nicklin felt a growing respect for her tough-minded style of thinking. Whereas he was allowing himself to swing between optimism and despair, she appeared to be holding steady, concentrating her experience, talent and mental energies on maximising their chances of survival. There had been 207 portals on Orbitsville's equator, virtually all of them developed as spaceports, and they represented a vast reserve of hardware and manpower which could be tapped to bring the *Tara* in from the cold.

The big battalions are on our side, he thought. *Now, if only I could forget about* . . . He tried to fend off a secondary thought, but it was coming with too much speed, too much power. *If only I could forget about the time limit. The world cloud is thinning out – just the way Blackhead Hepworth said it would. The new planets are going somewhere, and – according to the Benign Hypothesis – it's somewhere good. And if we don't get ourselves bedded down on one of them pretty damn quick it's going to be lonely out here* . . .

He tried not to think about the prospects for all those on board the *Tara* if the ship were to be left in orbit around a barren sun. The food would last two years, but would anybody in his right mind want to hang on right to the end, in a drifting tomb in which the dead were beginning to outnumber the living? And in which the taboos against cannibalism were outmoded? It would be better to steer the ship into the sun long before that unimaginable degree of horror was attained, but even that would result in protracted and agonising deaths for the little ones. The best plan might be to override all the safety mechanisms and vent the ship, thus ensuring that suffering was kept to a minimum.

Nicklin, suddenly beset by feelings of suffocation, pulled air deeply into his lungs and wrenched his thoughts on to a different course. He was grateful to discover that Voorsanger had asked Fleischer about the procedures for putting the ship into parking orbit about a planet and transferring its company to the surface. The subject was life-oriented, and he poured his consciousness into it, managing to lose track of the minutes until – with heart-stopping abruptness – the speakers again emitted their now-familiar preliminary click.

"This is space traffic control at Amsterdam, formerly based on P3," a woman's voice said. "We are receiving your autoscan signal on the general band. Please identify yourself. Over."

"Things are looking up," Fleischer said calmly.

She was reaching towards the communications panel when the speakers were activated yet again. This time the call was from Peking P205. Nicklin listened in a kind of pleasurable bemusement as Fleischer dealt with the two new contacts. The family of communities on Orbitsville's equator had survived the dissolution, and were reaching out across space to gather in their prodigals and strays. The only appropriate response was to acknowledge hope – anything else would be a betrayal of the human spirit.

Within moments of Fleischer having sent identification messages there came a second response from Hilversum.

"Hilversum calling in answer to your query, *Tara*," the man's voice said, "we have two Type–11 pinnaces in land dock. Both have transfer facilities compatible with the Explorer class, and both can be operational within three or four days. We foresee no difficulty in evacuating one hundred personnel, so set your mind at rest on that score. We will get you out of there, and that is a promise, but before I end this transmission I have another message for you."

There was a brief pause – during which Nicklin, Fleischer and Voorsanger exchanged looks of surmise – then a different male voice was heard.

"*Tara*, this is Cavan Gomery. I'm head of the astronomical section here at STC. I want to back up everything my colleague has just said – all you have to do is get into orbit and we'll take care of the rest. In the mean time, I'm asking for your assistance with another problem.

"You don't need to be told that something very big has happened to Orbitsville, but you may not know that the residual planets are reducing in number. We don't even know how to *begin* explaining this, but we need as much data as we can get to help us put a handle on the problem – and you are in a unique position in that respect.

"Can you send us a wide-angle, general view of the residual sphere? We need a good picture from you, and we need it for as long as possible to help us make the best computer predictions about the rate of disappearance.

"I will stand by for your answer. Over."

For the remainder of the "night" period Nicklin watched and listened as Fleischer dealt with an increasing volume of radio traffic – each new contact adding to the proof of Hepworth's Benign Hypothesis.

Eventually calls were coming in from spaceports which identified themselves with P numbers in the region of 100. Those calls, originating on the far side of the world cloud, were subject to a forty-minute delay in responses – a chastening reminder of the scale upon which Orbitsville had been built. As the electronic babel built up to a level where Fleischer had to institute computer procedures to impose order, it came to Nicklin that what he was hearing represented only a tiny fraction of the newly created worlds which filled the main screen.

Radio communications had never been possible within the Orbitsville shell, and therefore only those planets which happened to have former spaceports had a voice in the new congress. A far greater number had library access to the relevant technology, and Nicklin had no doubt they were hastily building the equipment which would allow them to speak to their neighbours in the close-packed sky. He also had no doubt that they would be seeking some kind of reassurance.

That was the common factor in all communications being received by the *Tara*. The radio messages, beneath the terseness and jargon, gave a composite picture of a civilisation which had been jarred out of its age-old complacency. Nicklin had been so preoccupied with his own traumatic experiences that he had spared no thought for the vast majority of humanity who had been going about their humdrum daily lives when the transformation had come. But the voices on the control-room radio gave him an inkling of what it had been like to live through the ultimate bad dream.

There had been the distortions of the sky patterns, the terrifying fluctuations of gravity, the sudden alternations between day and night, culminating in stroboscopic frenzies which stopped the heart and suspended reason.

Then had come the . . . *snap*.

For some it had been followed by a new kind of daytime, with once-familiar landscapes rearranged and the sun wildly displaced from its normal position at the zenith. For others there had come a new kind of night, with the glowing archways of the heavens replaced by millions of blue brilliants, shimmering in every design the eye wished to impose on them. And for those on the extreme edge of the world cloud there had been the first experience of night as their forebears on Earth had known it – a direct look into the spangled blackness of interstellar space.

As well as responding to the *Tara*'s distress, those on the spaceport worlds were communicating with each other, symbolically huddling together in the face of the unknown, seeking answers to questions which could not even have been formulated a day earlier. What had happened? Why had it happened? What was going to happen next? Were the new planets being relocated by some kind of dimensional sorcery, or were they simply ceasing to exist? Were *all* the planets going to disappear, or would the thinning-out process eventually stop and leave a handful of worlds in stable orbits?

For those on board the *Tara*, there was a set of questions in a special category of urgency: how rapidly was the world cloud dispersing? Were the disappearances evenly diffused through the cloud, or were there zonal effects which had not yet been detected? Was the dispersal taking place at a uniform rate, or was it accelerating?

In short – what were the chances of the ship reaching the safety of Hilversum before that planet blinked out of existence?

Try as he might, in spite of all his resolves to think positively and hopefully, Nicklin was unable to keep that particular question from dominating his mind.

Effectively, he lived on the control deck, leaving it as infrequently and for as short a time as possible.

On the second night of retardation, when all the lower decks were dim and quiet, he went down to the canteen to have a coffee, and was surprised to find Danea Farthing sitting at a table in the otherwise empty room. He knew she had been working flat out all day, relaying explanatory messages from Fleischer to worried families, trying to convey to them something of the pilot's stoic optimism.

It was a task Nicklin did not envy. Little had actually been put into words, as far as he knew, but a number of the pilgrims bitterly regretted ever having heard of Corey Montane, and their feelings of resentment and betrayal were close to the surface. In particular, Nicklin dreaded having to face the Whites – but for his intervention in their lives they would still be in Beachhead City, which now seemed a haven of security.

On entering the canteen he drew a bulb of hot coffee from the dispenser. His first instinct was to leave with it in silence, but he became aware that Danea was watching him with the enigmatic and moody-eyed intentness he had noticed earlier. He decided, with some misgivings, to risk her resumption of full hostilities.

"On your own, I see," he said, taking a seat nearby. "I suppose you miss Christine." The words were out before he could do anything about it, and he was immediately appalled by his ineptitude. He had begun with a banality, and had swiftly progressed to tactlessness.

"I think you have more reason to miss her than I have," Danea said mildly.

Nicklin lowered his gaze and stared at the coffee bulb as his cheeks began to tingle with embarrassment. Why had he not left the canteen while the going was good? To stand up and depart now would be the action of a complete bumpkin, and yet to remain would only increase his discomfiture.

"What's happening up above?" Danea's voice was neutral. "Any new developments?"

"The planets are all developing polar caps," Nicklin said, grateful for the new conversational opportunity. "You know – caps of frost or snow at their north and south poles. It makes them look like all those old pictures of Earth."

"That's interesting, but it isn't what I meant."

"We still don't know how fast they're disappearing. But some pretty good telescopes and computers are working on it."

256

Nicklin sipped his drink. "I think we'll get an answer soon."

"That's good." Danea smiled in a way that revealed utter weariness and her heavy-lidded eyes locked with his. "Are you sorry you left Orangefield?"

What sort of a question is that? Nicklin thought, floundering. *That question could mean anything!*

"Danea, I – " He was reaching out to touch her hand when there came the sound of someone on the ladder.

"I'm glad somebody else can't sleep – do you mind if I join the party?" The speaker was the blond, bearded young man in spaceport uniform, the same man that Nicklin had encountered before and who seemed to spend most of his time wandering around the ship. Without waiting for a reply he took a drinks bulb from the dispenser and sat down beside Danea.

"Jim, have you met Per Bosshardt?" she said.

"Hi, Jim!" Bosshardt smiled broadly. "We keep seeing each other around – at odd times."

Nicklin nodded. "Yes, we do."

"I've got fifty-two pals with me to liven up the party," Bosshardt said, producing a deck of cards from his breast pocket. "How about a game?"

"I'm sorry," Nicklin said, rising to his feet. "I have to get back to the control room now."

"Too bad." Bosshardt gave him a genial wave. "See you around, Jim!"

Nicklin glanced back into the canteen as he was stepping on to the ladder. Bosshardt was already dealing cards which, because of the minimal gravity, were skittering all over the table. Danea was laughing delightedly as she trapped some of the fleeting rectangles with her forearms.

"Are you sorry you left Orangefield?" Nicklin muttered to himself as he climbed through the higher levels of the ship. "What kind of a question is that?"

As the night wore on it occurred to Nicklin that he would probably feel better were he to sleep in his bunk instead of dozing in the seat beside Megan Fleischer. The circumstances of his existence were unnatural enough without his failing to take proper rest – but he had a compulsion to remain close to the main screen at all times.

The image of the world cloud, beautiful in its symmetry, was his past, present and future. It gave the impression of being serene and eternal, but that was only because of the limitations of human perception. The Good Fairy was at work in the cloud, deciding the fate of entire planetary populations at the rate of perhaps hundreds in every passing second, and Nicklin felt that if he stared hard enough and long enough he might find evidence of her design.

Billions of human beings on those newly created and ephemeral worlds were deeply apprehensive about the future. The prospect of being magicked out of the normal continuum – perhaps of ceasing to exist at all – was a terrifying one; but it was a sad commentary on the plight of those on board the *Tara* that they were praying to be part of that final disposition. A plunge into the unknowable was infinitely preferable to the alternative facing those who had been lured into joining the New Eden express.

Adding to Nicklin's sense of helplessness was the fact that, in spite of all appearances, the ship was actually flying backwards. It was aimed at the world cloud, its drive unit was thrusting it in the direction of the world cloud, but such was the speed previously attained that – two drawn-out days after entering retardation – the *Tara* was still receding from its goal.

"There's no point in fuming about it," Fleischer had told him. "Personally, I thank God for every hour that the drive keeps on functioning."

I suppose that's one way to cheer yourself up, Nicklin had thought, tiredly wondering if he would be able to recognise the moment at which the ship eventually came to a standstill and began the return flight proper. It was decelerating continuously, which was why he had a certain amount of weight, but there had to come the instant of turnaround, during which the ship – by definition – would not be moving at all. If it was not moving at all, neither accelerating nor decelerating, it would have to cease generating gravity even though the drive had not been shut down.

But that doesn't sound right. I must be too dog-tired to think properly. I'll just have to go over it again . . .

He struggled out of sleep to the uneasy awareness that something had altered in the ambience of the control deck.

It took him a few bleary seconds to identify the change – the level of noise from the communications system had fallen. His uneasiness increased as he realised that the sounds of radio traffic had been diminishing for some time. Ever since Fleischer had been forced to computerise and regulate the flood of incoming calls, the speakers had been emitting a near-continuous series of code signals between actual messages. Now, however, they were quite silent.

Nicklin sat up straighter and glanced across the other chairs. Voorsanger was absent, but Fleischer was frozen in an attitude of utter concentration, staring at the image of the world cloud. Nicklin's heart lurched as he noted the pilot's expression.

"What's happening?" he cried. "Is there – "

She silenced him by raising one hand while she addressed the communications panel with the other.

". . . is definite," a man's voice was saying. "We've got it! The residual sphere is being stripped from the outside. There are five skim-off bands – call them whatever you like – two in the northern hemisphere, two in the southern, and one very close to the equator. All the bands are widening rapidly, God help us! There is no way of predicting how long it will be before this station is . . . "

The silence in the control room became total.

Nicklin focused his gaze on the world cloud, and – now that he knew exactly where to look – he could see evidence of the Good Fairy's handiwork. There was a subtle, twinkling agitation along the equator. But in essence it was the opposite of twinkling. It was a disturbance in a motionless pattern caused by the progressive disappearance of tiny light sources.

The world cloud was visibly being unwound . . . like a vast ball of wool . . . into nothingness.

"They've gone," Fleischer said in the voice of a timid child. "The spaceports have all gone."

"We don't need spaceports," Nicklin shouted, refusing to play the game of logic. "We can keep on going! We can go into orbit around *any* fucking planet!"

"What good would that do? If we can never land?"

"It would be better than being left out . . . *here*!"

"Perhaps you're right." Fleischer nodded as she considered the proposition, and then – incredibly – her face lit up with perverse triumph as she saw how to refute it.

"The trouble is, Mr Nicklin, that we can't *reach* any – as you put it – fucking planet. Things have changed for the worse out there. The disappearances speeded up while you were asleep . . . and they're still speeding up . . . and within a matter of hours there'll be no planets left – fucking or otherwise!"

CHAPTER 22

There was a peculiar *rightness* about what he was doing now, Nicklin decided.

For a period of some twelve hours he had sat in the control room, mesmerised, watching the world cloud disappear at an ever-increasing rate. In the beginning the process had been almost imperceptible, then a darkening sparsity had become noticeable in five widening strips. The effect had added to the awful beauty of the spectacle, giving the cloud the semblance of a pointillist painting of one gigantic banded planet. After that the dissolution had become all too apparent, as swath after swath thinned out into a blackness through which remote stars were beginning to show. At some point in the progression the *Tara* had finally discarded its outward velocity and begun the painfully slow return, but nobody in the control room had noticed its change of status. It had been impossible for the watchers to do anything but *watch*. Even their ability to think seemed to have been suspended as the discrete entity which had once been Orbitsville was reduced to filmy wisps, to fast-fading strands of gossamer, and finally to nothing. Nothing at all. The 650-million new-born worlds had been dematerialised, and only a small sun remained, the lone source of light and heat in a region of emptiness which extended for many light years all around.

What comes next? Nicklin had thought numbly. *Where do we go from here?*

What had come next, within a matter of seconds, was an intercom message for Nicklin from a woman who had been bathing her children in the communal washrooms on 24 Deck. She was angry because the water temperature in the showers had become erratic, and she wanted the fault corrected without delay. She also wanted to know why Nicklin spent all his time lounging around on the control deck instead of attending to his duties.

The reminder that life would make its quotidian demands until the very end had come as a blessing to Nicklin. He had left the seclusion of the control room immediately, and now – a man with an important mission – he was working his way down through the most populated levels of the ship. Because the *Tara* was carrying only half of its projected complement, the passengers had largely been free to decide where they would be accommodated, and the majority – obeying their instincts – had chosen the forward section, as far as possible from the engine cylinders.

By the time he reached 14 Deck, the first to give access to the engine cylinders, the sounds of human activity were fading above him. He continued his downward drift, fingers barely touching the stringers of the ladder, and was passing 17 Deck when, almost of their own accord, his hands clamped on the dural bars, bringing him to an abrupt halt. There followed a moment of total confusion, then he realised what had caused the autonomous reaction.

A short distance to his right, in the curving primary wall of the passenger cylinder, there was a door leading into the adjacent engine cylinder.

To someone not so well acquainted with the metallic bones and guts and nerves of the *Tara* the sight of that door would have had little or no significance, but for Nicklin it came as a psychic hammer blow – because he knew there was no engine access door on 17 Deck.

He froze in place on the ladder, looking around him. The rest of the small landing was exactly as it should have been. Behind him there were two doors leading into passenger suites, and stencilled signs clearly proclaimed that he was on what he *knew* to be 17 Deck. He had no need of the signs to tell him where he was – the surrounding rivet and weld patterns would have been enough – but he was confronted by an engine access door where no engine access door had any right to exist.

The door was real. He could see scratches on the green paint. He could see smudges on the nine white tablets of the lock's keyboard. The door was *real*!

"This is a dream," he said aloud, relieved at having explained the inexplicable. "This is one of those cognisant dreams, and to prove it – "

He punched the edge of the deck beside him with careless force and gasped as pain swept back through his nervous system from the point of impact. He looked at his knuckles and saw that patches of skin had been curled back. Tiny lentils of blood were appearing on the subcutaneous tissue.

There was no doubt that he was wide-awake – and the engine access door was still in place.

My memory for numbers has gone haywire, he extemporised as he stepped off the ladder and went to the door. *A little molecule of the grey stuff has flipped or sprung a leak or whatever it is they do when they're starting to wear out. You always* could *reach the engines from 17 Deck. The fact that I don't remember it that way is neither here nor there, and to prove it . . .*

He tapped the admittance number into the lock – 8949823 – and smiled as he heard the lock solenoid operating. *Still got a few numbers left!* He slowly pushed the door open and found himself looking into an enclosed space not much larger than a telephone kiosk. The arrangement was wrong, absolutely and totally wrong for the *Tara*, but he was now committed to proving to himself that wrong was right, and he stepped over the high threshold with a certain amount of brashness.

As the door sighed shut behind him he saw another door in the left-hand wall, and beside it was a small niche of the type which normally held fire-fighting equipment. In the niche was a body-curved flask of silver, upon which somebody had enamelled the words: DRINK ME. The lettering was excessively ornate and Nicklin grinned as he recognised Scott Hepworth's handiwork.

So you forgot about one of your stashes, you boozy old sod!

Still amused, he picked the flask up. It felt warm, and when he shook it he heard and felt the sloshing of a small amount of liquid. On impulse he removed the cap and took a drink of what proved to be tepid gin.

A real Hepworth special, that was. He loved his geneva with fresh tonic and all the trimmings, but when necessary he would take it any way it came. As some playwright or other put it – when the mood was on him he would drink it out of a sore. I bet old Scott would be turning in his plastic wrapper if he knew he had missed this last drop.

There's just one thing I don't understand, though.
How come the gin is still warm?

Moving like a man in a dream, filled with premonitions that he was doing the wrong thing, Nicklin opened the inner door. Beyond it was a dimly lit space which seemed too large to be contained within the five-metre radius of the engine cylinder. Nicklin went in, allowing the door to close behind him. Above the door was a single bulkhead light casting a wan glow over a semicircle of empty deck. That was wrong, too, because most of the space within the cylinder should have been taken up by massive engine components. He tried to see beyond the vague boundary of illumination, but the outer darkness was impenetrable. An air current tugged momentarily at his hair and clothing, and it seemed sweet and pure, as though he were standing at the edge of a midnight plain.

After a few seconds a figure appeared in the darkness, coming towards him, and he groaned aloud – cowering back with knuckles pressed to his mouth – as he saw that it was Scott Hepworth.

"Good man, you found my medicine!" Hepworth said, taking the flask from Nicklin's inert fingers. "Where did I leave it?"

Nicklin groaned again as Hepworth raised the flask to his lips and took a drink. His neck seemed intact beneath his rumpled collar, but as he swallowed a clear fluid welled out through the front of his shirt.

"Go away," Nicklin mumbled through his knuckles. "You're dead!"

"Don't be so plebeian in your thinking, my boy," Hepworth said jovially. "Do I *look* dead?"

Nicklin studied the apparition before him and saw that it was perfect in every detail, from the smudged shoddiness of the clothing to the blue-rimmed blackhead at the side of the nose. "Get away from me, Scott," he pleaded. "I can't look at you."

"Very well – but I must say I'm deeply disappointed in you, Jim." Hepworth began to back off into the darkness. "I could have helped you with what's coming next. There are others waiting to meet you, and I could have helped you deal with them . . . "

As the Hepworth thing faded out of sight Nicklin grabbed the door handle and twisted hard. It refused to turn, just as he had expected, and now two other figures were approaching. One was Corey Montane – grinning a wet, lop-sided grin – and the other was a pretty young woman who looked quite wholesome and normal, except that the handle of a kitchen knife was protruding from her chest. The knife was moving in tune with her heart beats.

"Milly and I are happy now, Jim," Montane said, slipping his arm around the woman's waist. "And I want you to know that you can be happy, too. All you have to do is – "

"You're dead too!" Nicklin shouted. "Don't come near me! You're dead, and you're trying to make me think that *I'm* dead as well, but I'm still alive and this is only a dream!"

Montane and his wife exchanged concerned glances, all the while moving closer to him. "I hate to see you like this, Jim," Montane said. "And it's all so unnecessary. All you have to do is listen to – "

"*Fuck off!*" Nicklin screamed, covering his eyes.

He remained that way for as long as he dared, afraid that the two dreadful beings were stealthily closing in, bringing their sympathetic faces closer to his. But when he lowered his hands Montane and his wife had gone. The surrounding darkness was intact again, except that he could now see farther into it and his former impression of standing on a vast plain was reinforced. In the spurious, half-perceived distance there was the hint of an enormous presence, black curvatures imposed on blackness. Could it be a hill, a mountain of obsidian, repelling the light of unseen stars?

What have I done to deserve this? Nicklin asked himself, making another futile attempt to open the bulkhead door.

"I'll tell you what you've done," a familiar and yet unidentifiable voice said from just beyond the pool of tallowy light. "You have filled your head with negative thoughts and false concepts, little Jimmy Nicklin – and now you must suffer as a result."

"Who are you?" Nicklin quavered, sickened by a new premonition. "And why do you call me Jimmy? Nobody has called me Jimmy since – "

"Since you were a little boy, isn't that right?" The towering shape of Nicklin's great-uncle Reynard advanced into the cone of dismal light.

Nicklin cringed as he saw that this was not the figure of the scarcely-remembered *real* Uncle Reynard. This was the fearsome Uncle Reynard of the dream. This was the terrifying shape that his mother had insisted on treating as a perfectly acceptable human being in spite of the fact that it was over two metres tall, had spiky red-brown fur, feral yellow eyes, and a long snout surmounted by a Disney-animal nose which resembled a shiny black olive. And, as had happened before, recognition robbed the animated image of its oppressive power.

"You can't frighten me," Nicklin challenged.

"And why should anybody be frightened of a fine, handsome fellow like me?" the fox said, preening in his nineteenth-century wing collar and patched frock coat. "I fully understand why you wanted nothing to do with those other characters – especially the woman! Did you see the *knife*? – Ugh!" A look of revulsion passed over the fox's stylised features. "Between ourselves, Jimmy, you did the right thing in getting rid of that lot."

"I'm getting rid of you as well," Nicklin said. "You don't exist!"

"What a peculiar thing to say!" The fox cast a worried glance over his shoulder, then gave a laugh which exposed all his pointed teeth. "You wouldn't be able to talk to me if I didn't exist. It stands to reason, doesn't it? You see, this is mental space – and mental entities are just as real here as physical entities. You remember what you were told about mental space, don't you?"

Nicklin shook his head. "I wouldn't allow you to exist in *any* kind of space."

"Don't do this to me, Jimmy." Uncle Reynard glanced back into the darkness again, spraying cartoon-style droplets of sweat into the air from his forehead. "I can help you with what's coming next. You've got to have your interview with Gee-Vee, and I can – "

"Go away!"

The fox took a step backwards, his entire body beginning to ripple, and suddenly he was a thin, balding, unhappy looking man of about forty. Nicklin felt a stirring of old memories. The creature before him purported to be his real Uncle Reynard.

"You can frig off too," Nicklin said.

"Don't do this to me, Jimmy," the creature pleaded. "All right, perhaps I *was* a bit too friendly with your mother after your old man died. Maybe you felt sort of betrayed – and I can't say as I

266

blame you – but that's all in the past. You're a grown man now, Jimmy, and you must know how it is when a healthy young woman is – "

"Go away!"

"Let me explain something very important to you, Jimmy," the creature said in an urgent whisper. "You think this is all a dream – but it *isn't*! You're in mental space now, Jimmy. You must remember what you were told that day in the Beachhead office by Silvia London. You remember her, don't you? The one with the big knockers? Well, everything she said was absolutely true!"

Nicklin frowned. "That would mean you have an independent existence of your own, and that I can't harm you."

"Yes, but I'm not a true mindon entity." The creature shot a quick look behind itself, in the direction of the mountainous presence which might or might not exist in the blackness, and its disconsolate expression turned into one of purest misery. "Your real Uncle Reynard is somewhere else in this continuum. The only reason I exist at all is that I'm a projection of part of your childhood personality, and if you start interfering with things – "

"You mean – if I grow up."

"You grew up years ago, Jimmy." The creature produced a shifty, ingratiating smile. "You grew up great! The way you exploded those three ape men in Altamura was a treat to watch. Specially the third one, when he thought he was getting away. And then there's the Farthing bitch. I'll tell you something for nothing, Jimmy – she's sorry she ever got on the wrong side of you. If you went to her right now you could – "

"*Go!*" Nicklin commanded, his entire consciousness given over to hatred. "*Cease to exist!*"

The creature gave a snarl of fury. Its face began to flow . . . extruding a bestial snout, teeth becoming fangs . . . but before the metamorphosis could be completed the entire apparition shimmered out of existence.

Nicklin was left alone, but not alone. Beyond the cone of sickly light, far out across the half-perceived plain, an enormous shape was moving. In the absence of spatial referents it could indeed have been as large as a mountain, but it also – was this possible? – might have had a human configuration. What was the name of that statue? The one of the man sitting with his fist pressed against his forehead?

Jim Nicklin, the entity said, its voice a silent thunder between Nicklin's temples, *the time has come for us to speak to each other.*

"I don't want to," Nicklin quavered, amazed by his ability to emit any kind of sound. "I don't want anything to do with you."

That is not true. You know you could not have gone on for much longer as you were.

Nicklin pressed his back against the metal doorframe – his sole remaining contact with the universe of rationality. "Who are you?"

Come on now, Jim! You know perfectly well who I am.

"How . . . how could I?"

Because you have communed with me many times throughout your adult life.

"Communed? I've never been a believer. The only deity I ever acknowledged was . . . the Gaseous Vertebrate!"

Well done, Jim.

"But that's impossible! You're just a sort of a private joke. I mean, I invented you!"

No, Jim – I invented you.

Somehow Nicklin managed to resuscitate the argumentative side of his character. "I'm sorry, but I can't go along with that," he said. "It doesn't even make dream-sense to me."

You always have to make things difficult. I simply wanted to personalise myself for your benefit. Your conception of the Gaseous Vertebrate . . . the Supreme Prankster . . . is as near as you have come to visualising a higher order of being.

"I meant him as an analogue of blind chance."

Yes, but you personalised him.

"Nevertheless, it's wrong to think of you as the Gaseous Vertebrate?"

It doesn't have to be wrong.

"Are you claiming to be God?"

I am not claiming to be God – but you may think of me that way, if you please.

"This could go on and on. I prefer Gaseous Vertebrate."

So, after much circumlocution, you are back where you started – I am the Gaseous Vertebrate.

"Are you also the Good Fairy? Did you create the artefact I knew as Orbitsville?"

At last you have asked a sensible question, one to which I can give a sensible answer. No, I did not create Orbitsville.

"Have you any objections to telling me who did?"

I have no objections at all, Jim. I am willing to provide all the knowledge you are capable of assimilating. Your mind is part of my mind at this unique moment in cosmic history. The only limits to the amount of knowledge you may gain are the limits of your own mentality.

"Did you say my mind is part of your mind?"

Let's have no rhetorical questions, Jim. You know what I said.

"But it's important to me. There are little questions as well as big questions. For instance, I would like to know why I am not afraid. I have wandered into a surrealist nightmare, and I have witnessed horrors – "

The horrors were of your own devising.

"All right, but I'm alone in what might easily be a Dali landscape with what might easily be a black statue the size of a mountain . . . and yet I am not afraid. Why is that?"

You are in mental space now. You exist as a mindon entity – and, as such, you are immune to all the fears which trouble a carnate being.

"I see. So that's why I can hold a conversation with a sentient black skyscraper."

There is no conversation. For the moment your mind has been encompassed by and united with my mind. You must take what you can, and make of it what you will.

"Very well then – who built Orbitsville?"

Orbitsville was devised and constructed by beings who are more highly evolved than humans. In their one direct encounter with humans they chose to call themselves Ultans. That is as good a name as any.

"Why did the Ultans construct Orbitsville?"

They did so in an attempt to alter the fate of the entire cosmos. A few of your fellow human beings have already discovered that mind is a component of matter. And it is not a minor component. In some regards it is even more significant than gravity, because its attractive force is sufficient to close the universe. Gravitation alone could not do that.

"I remember that woman . . . Rick Renard's wife . . . trying to tell me something like this."

Yes, but she was more concerned with an incidental effect – the continuance of personality after physical death. The true importance of the class of particles known as mindons lies in their cohesive power. Without the mindon/graviton component an expanding universe would continue to expand for ever. One of your fellow humans, with quite a poetical turn of mind, has stated that it is the thinker in the quietness of his study who draws the remotest galaxies back from the shores of night.

"I don't see what this has to do with Orbitsville."

The history of the cosmos could be described as a series of Big Bangs and Big Squeezes, to use the inelegant phraseology of which your scientists are so fond. At the instant of each Big Bang two universes are created – one composed of normal matter and going forward in time; the other composed of anti-matter and going backwards in time. Both universes expand to their limits, then the contraction begins, and eventually, when time has run its circular course, they are reunited and the stage is set for a new Big Bang. You will, of course, appreciate that terms such as matter and anti-matter are completely subjective.

"I'm not stupid."

There are some complications – such as tachyon and anti-tachyon universes – which I do not intend to trouble you with at this juncture.

"Very kind," Nicklin said. "Go on."

At the instant of the last Big Bang – which I believe to have been the eighteenth in the Grand Sequence – two symmetrical universes were created, as had always happened before. But their evolution did not follow the established pattern. A great asymmetry developed because – for reasons which have not made themselves apparent – intelligent life failed to evolve anywhere in the Region 2 universe.

Under those circumstances, without mindon cohesion, the Region 2 universe was destined to go on dispersing for ever – and without the contribution of its matter the nature of the next Big Bang will be radically altered. And as a consequence, the cycle of cosmic renewal will be disrupted.

Some Ultans viewed that prospect with disfavour on philosophical grounds – and they took steps to correct the great imbalance.

"They built Orbitsville!"

Yes.

"It was a mind collector! And that explains the Big Jump – Orbitsville *was* relocated in the anti-matter universe! When the Ultans were ready they simply moved it!"

The situation was more complex than that, because other Ultans – also motivated by philosophical considerations – opposed any meddling with the course of nature. But, basically, you are correct.

"And was that all it took to change the future of an entire universe? I'm not used to thinking on this kind of scale, but the effect of one sphere seems – to say the least of it – disproportionate."

More than one sphere was constructed, Jim. To be sure of capturing a viable stock the Ultans placed similar instruments in every galaxy of the Region 1 universe. Each galaxy, depending on its size, was given anywhere from eight to forty of the spheres, all of them in localities favourable to the development of intelligent life. Your race's discovery of the one you refer to as Orbitsville was not entirely fortuitous.

"But there are at least a hundred billion galaxies!" Even in his discorporate form Nicklin was humbled by the sudden insight into the extent of the Ultans' efforts to influence the shape of the space-time continuum itself. "And if you multiply that number – "

Do not concern yourself with the mathematics – suffice it to say that the Ultans pursued their misguided ambition on such a large scale that my brothers and I were obliged to move against them.

"But is it not too late? I saw Orbitsville being dissolved into millions of planets, and I saw them all disappear. If they have been dispersed all over the galaxy . . . "

I intervened. The new planets have indeed been dispersed – but it was done under my direction. They have been seeded into the Region 1 galaxy from which Orbitsville came.

A new question was beginning to form somewhere in the depths of Nicklin's mind, but he shied away from it. "They've gone back?"

Yes, Jim. You see, the Ultans were wrong to impose their will, their necessarily limited view, upon the natural ordering of Totality. The imbalance between Regions 1 and 2 in the present cycle heralds great change – that is quite true – but change is the instrument of evolution. Resistance to change is wrong. Totality must be free to evolve.

"Will the Ultans be . . . punished?"

They will be advised and watched, but they will not be harmed. My brothers and I partake of Life, and we serve Life. The Ethic requires us to do everything in our power to ensure that no mind units are lost as a result of our actions.

"Is that why you are here? Is that why you are speaking to me?"

As I said earlier, the dialogue is entirely within your own consciousness. It is part of your private reaction to the fact that your mind is encompassed by mine while I am transferring your ship back to the Region 1 universe. You are interpreting the experience in your own way – for others it will be different.

"Do you mean that for them it's a religious experience? They're seeing what they believe to be God?"

They're seeing what they believe – just as you are seeing what you believe.

The question which had earlier formed itself in a part of Nicklin's consciousness tried to obtrude once more, and once more he was unable to deal with it. "Are we all going to live?"

Yes, Jim – I have plucked your little ship out of the body of my stillborn brother, and I have placed it on the surface of an eminently hospitable world in your home galaxy. You are all going to live.

"Thank you, thank you." Nicklin began to feel an unaccountable sense of urgency. "Is our time together coming to an end?"

There is no time as you understand it in mental space. In one version of reality the transfer has taken a billionth of a billionth of a second; in another version of reality it has taken forty billion years.

"But the dialogue is drawing to a close."

You are reaching your limits.

"There is just one more question. Please! I must know the answer."

Across the midnight plain the dark presence seemed to stir slightly. *I am listening.*

"Who *are* you?"

But you no longer have any need to ask that question. The half-

272

perceived entity was definitely moving now, growing taller, preparing to depart. *You KNOW who I am, don't you, Jim?*

"Yes," Nicklin murmured, the vessel that was his mind at last filled to brimming. "I know who you are."

CHAPTER 23

The six Curlew aircraft of Woolston Skyways were ranged in line, waiting to carry their separate loads of passengers to the regional centre of Rushport. Curlews had been chosen because of their ability to operate from unprepared grass strips. Each would take a maximum of ten people on the two-hour hop to Rushport, where they would then be put on an airliner for the 8,000-kilometre flight to Beachhead City.

Behind the Curlews were three smaller and faster jets belonging to the news agencies which had been first to get their people to the scene. Looming over the aircraft, making them look like toy miniatures, was the burnished coppery hull of the *Tara*. And beyond the ship was a lake which stretched to the horizon, its waters sewn with diamond-fire by the low morning sun.

No matter how old he lived to be, Nicklin had decided, he would never get used to a sun which traversed the sky. On the previous evening, scant hours after the *Tara's* return, he had watched the first sunset of his life, unable to take his eyes off the searing disk as it slid below the horizon. Like many others of the dazed and bemused pilgrims, he had spent most of the night in the open, staring at new constellations and waiting for the sun to reappear. Even though he had known in advance that it had to show itself on the opposite side of the world, the fact that it actually did so filled him with a profound wondering. The confirmation that he now lived on the *outside* of a sphere had come as a quasi-religious experience for one accustomed to the insularity of Orbitsville. He felt exhilarated, and dangerously exposed to the vastness of the universe, a micro-organism clinging to the surface of a ball that was hurtling through unpredictable space.

And in keeping with the diminutive size of the new world in

comparison to Orbitsville, the pace of human affairs seemed to have speeded up to match the flickering, inertia-less activities of creatures whose cosmos is a drop of water . . .

In one instant the *Tara* had been drifting in deep space; in the next it had been resting on a sunlit, grassy plain.

The ship's clocks showed no lapse of time, but every individual on board – children included – had recollections of a time outside of time. From what Nicklin could gather, the common experience – unlike his own – had been a brief and wordless communion with a benign deity, one who was shrouded in white light, rendered invisible by mingling glories.

They had emerged from it as essentially the same people, with all their previous beliefs confirmed beyond all doubt. The first thing Ropp Voorsanger had done was to lead the entire company out on to the lush grass and conduct a service of thanksgiving. And never in human history could there have been a congregation so united in its unshakeable faith. After all, they had been part of a general and undeniable miracle. They had been lost, and now they were saved, and their salvation had come about through a Divine Intervention. They had been justified, as no others had ever been justified, in sending up their cry of Hallelujah!

Nicklin's experience had been unique, because he had been necessarily transformed. He had come out of it with a *new* set of beliefs which required him to revise his internal model of reality. Thereafter he had to acknowledge the existence of a supreme being. Giving it the name of God, or the Good Fairy, or the Gaseous Vertebrate made no difference to the central, essential fact that he could no longer live his life as a sceptic.

While waiting, alone beneath the stars, he had wondered if the impact on his personality could have been any greater had he been persuaded to accept the existence of the Judaic God – and not of the ultimate, non-mystical Personality.

You KNOW who I am, the Personality had said, and the uncanny thing was that Nicklin had been prepared long in advance for the revelation. He had almost reached the truth that grey wintry morning in the Beachhead office when Silvia London had preached that all matter had a mindon component, and that all that was needed for the development of an immortal personality was the existence of a sufficiently complex physical organisation, such as the human brain.

Nicklin had begun to argue that if physical complexity was all that was needed to conjure a mind into existence there was, in principle, no need to insist on a biological element. It should have been possible for *any* sufficiently complex organisation to develop an intelligent personality. And, taking that argument to its logical conclusion, what better candidate could there be – in the category of complex, multi-component physical structures – than a galaxy?

The concept of an intelligent galaxy was hardly new – scientific visionaries such as Firsoff had advanced it as far back as the middle of the twentieth century.

But to be confronted with the actuality!

Years would pass, Nicklin knew, before he could hope to assimilate the knowledge that he shared the stage of eternity with beings like the Ultans, so advanced and so powerful that they could presume to remodel the entire scheme of creation to their own desires. And that – as far beyond the Ultans as the Ultans were beyond humans – were what he might think of as the Galactians. They were unimaginable, incomprehensible entities, yet so life-oriented that they could concern themselves with the welfare of individual mind units.

Nicklin had to admit the remote possibility that the *Tara* had been positioned where it was because of some vague and tenuous paraphysical decree that matter would be drawn to its own point of origin on the old Orbitsville shell. But his new instincts told him that the Personality – which had referred to an inert Region 2 galaxy as its "stillborn brother" – had made a conscious and personal decision in the matter.

The implication was that *all* mind units were uniquely and individually important. They were *all* immortal, and would *all* partake in a grand scheme of evolution and assimilation which would lead to the ultimate convergence of Life. The further implication, for those receptive to it, was that no life had ever been wasted, and that . . .

"Good morning, Jim!" The speaker was Cham White. He and Nora had climbed the hummock which Nicklin had chosen as a vantage point, and both were breathing heavily from the exertion. "What are you doing up here?"

Nicklin waved a greeting. "It's a good place to think."

"You have more than most of us to think about, haven't you, Jim?" Nora said, a smile appearing on her gold-freckled face. "I seem to remember that you were quite the atheist in the old days."

Nicklin nodded. "As you say, Nora – I have a lot to think about."

"We came up to bid you goodbye for the time being," Cham said. "We're heading back to Beachhead and then Orangefield as soon as possible."

"You don't feel like staying on here and helping Voorsanger to found his new Holy City?"

"It was an inspiring sermon he gave this morning." Cham fingered his grimy trousers with a look of humorous distaste. "But I think I'll wait until the first hotels have been built and the plumbing put in."

"Cham White!" Nora dug him with her elbow. "That's an affront to the Lord."

"These pants are an affront to *everybody* – I can't wait to get changed into something decent."

"I'm off!" Nora shook Nicklin's hand, kissed him lightly on the cheek, and started down the slope.

Cham waited until she was some distance off. "Jim, I don't know what happened between you and Zindee, and I don't want to know," he said quickly. "But I have a feeling she'd like to speak to you before we leave. Will you come down and say goodbye to her?"

Nicklin's heart began to pound. "Of course, Cham."

He walked beside Cham, his eyes scanning the various centres of activity. Lines were forming near each of the Curlews, but quite a few families had elected to remain with the *Tara* for the time being, and children belonging to them were darting excitedly between knots of adults. Journalists were wandering about with cameras, and civic officials from Rushport – including welfare people and a few police – were also going about duties which only they seemed to understand. The fluttery beat of an approaching helicopter added to the impression that the randomly chosen patch of open countryside had become a focus of interest for the rest of the world.

Radio communications had never been possible on the old Orbitsville, but Fleischer had been able to call up the Beachhead spaceport without any difficulty – and it was apparent that what she had said had caused a sensation, even on a world whose inhabitants should have been sated with wonders. It was just as Hepworth had predicted, Nicklin thought. Astronomical marvels were all very well for those who were interested in that kind of thing, but a hundred people magically returning from the dead was genuine, honest-to-God *news*.

He forgot about the overall picture as he picked out the green-clad figure of Zindee standing alone close to an orange-splashed bandanna shrub. Before Nicklin could move to prevent him, Cham veered away from his side – no doubt being tactful – leaving him to approach Zindee on his own. As he drew near she eyed him with a strangely intent speculation which, inexplicably, reminded him of his last meeting with Danea.

"Hello, Zindee," he said awkwardly. "I hear you're going home."

"Yes." Her eyes hunted over his face. "Back to Orangefield, for a while."

"That's good," he said, unable to meet her gaze. "Ah . . . I have to go now, Zindee. Ropp needs me on the ship."

"Why?"

"Why what?"

"Why does Mr Voorsanger need you on the ship?"

"Well, you see . . . " He strove to find a good, plausible reason for leaving. "The ship was never intended to sit on soft ground like this. When it's in the horizontal attitude it's supposed to sit on six special cradles below the major hard points. The way things are now the soft ground is pushing on the skin and distorting the sub-frames, and that could cause pressure leaks and all kinds of – "

He broke off, nonplussed, as Zindee gave a delighted laugh.

"That's a load of male ox," she accused. "You're a liar, Jim Nicklin! That was one of your stories! You made it all up out of your head!"

"Well . . . " He looked into her eyes, judged his worth by what he saw there, and felt something which he could only describe as a return of joy. "Perhaps you're right."

Zindee stopped laughing. "What happened to you, Jim?"

"I . . . " He spread his hands, helplessly. "I lost my way, Zindee. That's about all I can say."

"It's enough." She came close, put her arms around his neck and kissed him. The pressure of her slim body against his was pleasantly asexual, and in her hair he detected the childhood smell of clean perspiration. He hugged her for a long moment, then stepped back, searched in a pocket and brought out the old coin which had once hung around her neck.

"Will you have this back?" he said.

"I was going to ask you for it." As she was accepting the coin the propellers on one of the nearby Curlews began to turn. "It looks like they'll be taking off soon, Jim – you'd better move quickly."

"Move?"

"Yes, *move*! Danea's plane will be going in a couple of minutes. Are you just going to stand there and let her fly off to Beachhead on her own?"

He followed the direction of her gaze and saw Danea in the knot of people waiting by the nearest aircraft. Beside her in the group was the uniformed figure of Per Bosshardt.

"She may not be on her own," Nicklin said, wondering if he had caught Danea looking in his direction.

"Go over there and find out." Zindee's small chin had the determined set he remembered so well from her earliest days. "Jim Nicklin, if you don't *do* something I'll never speak to you again. Get yourself over there!"

"All right, all *right*!" He walked slowly across the intervening grass, blood pounding in his ears, and stopped when he was about ten paces away from the group, unable to think of what he might say. Danea eyed him from under her flat black sombrero, but did not move. Standing close to her, Bosshardt gave him an easy, slightly interrogative smile.

"Danea," Nicklin said desperately, "I need to talk."

He waited, not moving, knowing that everything was in the balance. If Danea invited him to go closer, so that he would have to talk within earshot of the others, there would be no real point in his doing it. In the shade of the sombrero her face was utterly beautiful, and as unreadable as ever. Several seconds dragged by, then she left the line and came towards him.

"What do you want to talk about?" she said, heavy-lidded eyes cool and only slightly inquisitive.

His mind went blank. "What are you going to do in Beachhead?"

"For a while – nothing. I need a holiday."

"We all need a holiday," he said, trying to smile. "We've been through a lot."

"Yes."

"Well . . . Perhaps I'll see you in Beachhead some time."

"Perhaps." Danea glanced back towards the watchful group by the aircraft. "The plane is ready to go."

"Yes." Nicklin took a deep unsteady breath as he realised that no other moment in his life would have the same karma potential as this one. "Don't go on the plane, Danea. Not today."

Her eyes widened. "What are you saying?"

"I'm saying I don't give a damn about the money. I'm saying I'm sorry for all the things I said in the past and for the way I treated you. I'm saying I don't want you to leave. I'm saying I love you, Danea."

"That isn't enough, Jim." Her voice was low, tremulous.

"What else is there?"

"That morning in Orangefield . . . when I went out to your place . . ."

"Yes?"

"Do you believe . . . do you really *believe* that I loved you that day? If you have any doubts, Jim . . . if you have even the slightest lingering trace of a doubt . . . we'll never be any good for each other."

"I believe," he replied fervently, blinking to clear his visiton. "I swear – "

"Don't swear," she murmured, placing one finger vertically against his lips. "You've said it – and that's all I had to hear."

She moved into his arms, and as they embraced he became aware that they were being watched by dozens of people on all sides.

"We're making a spectacle of ourselves," he whispered. "How about going for a walk?"

Later, as they lay together – surrounded by a blaze of bandanna shrubs – they talked about their plans for all the years that lay ahead.

"Even though Corey is dead, the work he started looks like going on and on," Danea said dreamily. "I like the idea of founding a new kind of city here – with the *Tara* as a kind of centre piece – and there'll be so much to do."

"It would make a good memorial." Nicklin cast his mind back over the previous three years. "I used to disagree with just about everything Corey said, but – and this is the weird bit – I see now that he was absolutely right. It was all in the choice of words. He used the vocabulary of religion, and I would have preferred the vocabulary of science, but he *knew* that Orbitsville was a trap . . . a dead end . . ."

"You've changed, Jim." Danea raised herself on one elbow and looked down at him. "On the ship . . . when it happened . . . did you see God? Just like the rest of us?"

Should I tell a lie? Nicklin thought. *If I can accept the idea of an intelligent galaxy – simply because it is a structure of sufficient complexity to exist as a mindon personality, what do I say about the entire universe? Is it not the ultimate structure? Is it not, therefore, the ultimate mindon personality?*

Is it not . . . therefore . . . worthy of the name of God?

"I saw what everybody else saw," he said to his loved one, and he smiled as he spoke. "Would I tell you a lie?"